The Secret Storm

Books by

PEGGY TROTTER

Year of Jubilee
Reviving Jules

~Unchained Souls Series~
The Secret Things
The Secret Storm

The Secret Storm

Unchained Souls Series Book 2

PEGGY TROTTER

RANSOMED-EVER-AFTER BOOKS

First Edition, 2018
ISBN 13: 978-0-692-19883-4
ISBN 10: 0-692-19883-0
Library of Congress Control Number: 2018911643
Printed in the United States of America

All Scripture used in this book are from the Amplified Bible (AMP)
Copyright © 2015 by the Lockman Foundation. Used by permission.
www.Lockman.org.

Cover Illustration © 2018 by Zanne Davis
Edited by Nancy Clark

*To those who harbor
secret anxieties and secret fears.*

The Lord calms and strengthens all.

"He hushed the storm to a gentle whisper,
so that the waves of the sea were still."

Psalm 107:29

Chapter One

Stormi Zobroski ignored her mother's voice at the door and gripped the next stud in her tongue. "Forty-three."

"What are you doing in there? Get out. I need to use the john."

The clank of the metal stud clinked against the side of the glass jar. *Don't dump it.* Smallest vanity ever. And grungiest. Eyebrow studs were history. Nose, top lip, and ear studs gone, too. Bingo. Face cleared.

The door rattled. "You hear me?"

"I need a couple of minutes." She lifted her torn tank and made quick work of removing the three remaining studs beneath her clothing. Several hundred dollars were represented in the mound of metal in the jar.

Finished. Stud naked.

Her lips twitched as she met her own eyes in the chipped mirror. Those green/blue/gray eyes seemed to have such an issue picking one color or another. She'd always despised the color of her eyes. Blue the color of a June sky would have been much better. Or violet, deep iris purple, so captivating. Nope. She had...tealish muck.

Focus on the task.

She fingered the stubble above her ear and stroked the jagged rainbow Mohawk that had become her signature look. Blue, red, yellow. Clown hair. Not washed in six months. At one time, she'd been proud of that.

The dreadlocks resisted the wide-tooth plastic comb like a toddler in a muscle-seized fit. Tears collected in her transfixed eyes as she forced the knots from her hair. Strands stretched and popped, creating a multi-colored ball in the dirty sink.

When the locks freed, she parted and combed it straight down. She grabbed the dye box from the back of the toilet and examined the color. It was as close as she could get to her natural blond.

With the scissors, she lopped off the stringing ends, finishing with hair about three inches long. More needed to come off, but she wanted to hide the shaved sections above her ears. Plus, time was limited. This was a start.

The dye covered all vestiges of her multi-colored mop. She slicked it down. Now, the wait. She hardly recognized the creature in the mirror. Loud banging sounded at the door.

"Get out of there."

Stormi pulled the door open. "Sorry."

Her mother pulled back, eyes running over Stormi's face and hair. "Finally got rid of all that git-up? About time. Get out. I'm about to pee my pants."

Better not to confront. Stormi walked through her mother's bedroom.

"You better not get that stuff all over this bathroom." The door slammed.

"Yes, Mother."

The door whipped open, her mother's features thunderous. "And if you think I'm buying that subservient sass, think again."

Stormi clenched her jaw and kept walking. She gained the living room, turned right, and marched across the dipping floor of the kitchen, through the back porch, and into her small sanctuary. Nothing more than a shed linked to the house as an afterthought. She shut the oversized door.

Why had she come home? She glanced around at two twin beds and the metal rods, hanging from chains, filled with clothes. Nothing was hers anymore. Mother hadn't wasted much time getting rid of her stuff. True, she'd been officially gone seven years, four to college and three on her own earning her doctorate. Still, shouldn't there be something left?

She rubbed her chilled hands together and headed straight for her phone. No message from Alan, and she refused to text him till the cleansing deeds were done. The outside door slammed, and Stormi breathed a sigh of relief. Mom off to another card party.

The car door sounded, and Stormi rose to return to the bathroom to complete her task. Out the kitchen door window, Mother's sky blue car pulled away. The tenseness in her body eased. After a steamy shower, she emerged, rubbed the fog from the mirror with a towel, and looked full on her reflection.

That same old insecure, rebellious teenager stared her straight in the eye. Only older and less rebellious. And wiser. Much wiser. Her fingers probed the pierced knobs, wondering how long before they disappeared. She flipped up the hair and assessed the stubble. Nothing but time could repair that.

She applied a little gel and dried her hair, the hot air burning the bald spots. Well, not necessarily pretty, but better. Back at her phone in her room, she sent Alan a text. ***Well, it's done.***

She played with what was left of her hair, trying to get a good look of herself in the small rectangular mirror of her make-up case. Her phone flashed.

Done what?

She sank onto the bed, typing with her thumbs. **Hair-blond, metal-gone.**

Not what it's about, he returned. Alan, ever the pastor.

4 me it was.

Then-congrats. But study.

Stormi's eyes went to the Bible sitting on the other bed.
Have been. And will. No going back.

She tossed the phone on the pilled brown blanket that served as a bedspread and stepped over to the other bed to grab her Bible. The wind blew through the narrow window sending the navy satin curtain dancing into the air. The one thing she loved about this room. Two windows exactly opposite of each other in the rectangular space. Perfect crosswind.

She settled beneath the window and looked out on the neighbor's big house with its long porch, pew snugged against the wall, inviting one to rest. The window's low position allowed her to set her chin on the wooden sill. Memories rushed in. Not all good. Most not. She reached back and grabbed the phone.

Trust God to lead you.

Stormi smiled at the text screen. Long distance social media conversion. Someday she hoped to meet up with her old high school classmate again. Oh, how she'd tortured him. Meanness, just plain meanness. He, a straight-laced Christian all the way. Never wavered. Now he pastored and she...a new creature.

The Bible flopped open in her lap where the bookmark lay. Second Corinthians chapter five. Her finger whisked down the column to verse seventeen. *Therefore if anyone is in Christ, he is a new creature; the old things passed away; behold, new things have come.*

The breeze wafted in, sending the glossy curtain across her face. She swiped it aside smoothly from her unstudded face. Indeed the old had passed away.

◆ ⋯⋯ ◆

Concrete floor, two parking spaces for cars, a bathroom, a countertop, and a fireplace. What had the previous owner been thinking? The old garage establishment had been transformed into somewhat of a living space. Still, the two large roll-up doors were a little unsightly, not to mention drafty, though that wouldn't matter until winter advanced a bit more.

Yet Stormi counted her blessings that the previous residents had enclosed a toilet, sink and shower, and put in kitchen cabinets as well as a large bar with stools. She had the basics, at least. But better still? Cheap. No more living with Mother and her demands. Her phone buzzed on the countertop to the side of her only door. The back door.

She rolled her eyes when she peered at the number. Speaking o' the devil. Mother. Ignore her again and face greater wrath? No, thank you. Stormi pushed the button.

"Hello."

"You picked a fine time to move out. Leave it to you. Always thinking of yourself."

Stormi wiped imaginary crumbs from the cool countertop. "What's going on, Mom?"

"You. The house is a wreck. I need you here. I can't do this all on my own, you know."

"I cleaned the house before I left."

Her mother breathed an impatient sigh into the phone. "That was two weeks ago."

Stormi rotated the bottom of the phone toward the ceiling and closed her eyes to count to ten. Why couldn't her mother be normal? Like, *How are you?, How's the move going?*, or *I miss you.* Etc. Ridiculous to expect that now. "I told you I was leaving."

"What good does that do me? You owe me. Three weeks of free rent should mean something." Her voice slanted into familiar cutting sarcasm. "Obviously it doesn't."

She could imagine her mother, planning her latest card party or bingo extravaganza, and it was tempting to explain that if she were healthy enough for those events, she could do a little laundry. Stormi bit both lips to keep it from spilling forth. Honor. *Honor.*

"I'm sorry the house is a mess. I can try to find someone to clean it for you. I'm sure it wouldn't cost too much to have someone stop in once a week, and I could help pay for it—"

Swear words met Stormi's ears. "Oh, *you.* You think I want a stranger in here doing what my daughter ought to do? Forget you. I'll call Kim. She's more like my real daughter than you ever were anyway."

The phone slammed in her ear. Stormi gave a great sigh. If she had a dollar for every time her mother's boyfriend's daughter trumped her as a model offspring, she could have paid a maid for her mother for a year. She ran both hands in a routine pattern over her face. Brows, bridge, nose, lip. Then a swipe down both ears. Nodules still very much there. She pushed away the mother-guilt that had started to settle. More of her stuff still waited in the Saturn Ion to grace her new abode.

She ran her hand through the short hair over her ears and mentally calculated it to be slightly less than an inch. Good. Soon she could get a cut and brush away the dull straw hair she'd dyed several weeks back. Everything new. Away with her mother's narcissistic shame. New job, new town, new goals, new life.

At the car she dragged out several more boxes of clothes and knick-knacks she couldn't part with. Back inside she piled them beside her college air sofa and air chair in front of the fireplace. She lifted one side of her mouth. Nice combination. Blow-up furniture and a fireplace. One spark and whoosh.

She set up two TV trays and plunked her laptop on one and pressed the on button. With screwdriver in hand, she re-attached the back to her desk chair and gave a sigh of accomplishment when she slid it under the small table. Almost like home. Actually, better than home.

She turned and surveyed the rest of the thirty-by-thirty enclosure. Lots more space. She could actually park the car inside. Her snort lit up the air. Rich. Her, on a blow-up sofa in front of a roaring fireplace, with her Ion in the background. Could be worse. She could be at Mother's.

Better check on her podcast and finish it. Contemplations about what to do with the rest of her house would wait. Shakespearean Studies would not. Her students would truly have an excuse not to sign in and complete the newest assignment. Besides, how would she pay for her new garage if DeLong University fired her?

She glanced behind her at the far white wall. Appropriate for a background. The box near her feet yielded her books, syllabus, and notes. Time to load up chapter six.

Once she filed her presentation, she fetched her walking shoes from the box near the door. Next, donning her heavy coat and topping her head with a turquoise beanie, she stepped out her back door and circled around the left where her faithful car waited. Drawing in a deep breath of chilled air, she decided to walk.

She hit the sidewalk at full throttle and had to tone down the speed on the downslope towards town. The bay greeted her around the corner, and she slowed to soak in the ambiance of the small fishing village of Stone Haven. Dove Harbor stretched wide with several fishing boats lining the weathered docks. Wooden stairways littered the sheer rock face of the bank.

The first dock, one farthest from the mouth of the bay, drew her attention. Ten men lined a rough-cut table filled with fish and hacked away, flinging bloody parts into the water. They passed the carcass down a line until it was reduced to a headless, gutless piece of meat in the cooler at the end. The smell of rotting fish, even in the cold air, made her turn her face away. Never had been a seafood fan. Yet here she was. Go figure.

Her phone buzzed again. Her sister.

"Yeah?"

"Mom's driving me crazy. You need to get home and find out what's wrong with her. I can't take it anymore."

Stormi pushed the phone underneath her beanie to hear better, although certain she didn't want to. "ShaVonn, I'm eighteen hours away."

Silence. "I thought you lived with Mom?"

"I told you I was moving out."

"Where are you?"

"In Stone Haven." Why did her sister never pay attention to what she told her?

A tisk and a huff of air. "Stone Haven? Why there of all places? Isn't that like in New Hampshire?"

Stormi wiggled her nose which had turned frigid. "We've already discussed this."

"You always leave me with her. She's uber demanding. The constant nagging will kill me. I just know I'll die before she does."

The wind gusted and caught Stormi's breath, and she ducked across the road against a brick building to block it. "I had to start over, you know that. God—"

"Yes, I've got it. God changed your life. Etcetera and so-on. Meanwhile, Mother is pushing me over the edge."

At the corner a door beckoned. She paused in the shelter to finish the conversation. "I'm sorry, ShaVonn. I'll try to help out. You know there's no pleasing her unless you are at her beck and call every moment. She's capable of cleaning her own house and taking care of herself."

ShaVonn went on her usual cruise through hopeless lane, a familiar route of recalling every misstep Mom and Dad made for the last twenty-five years. "I know. Yes, I remember."

"I really want to move to the Bahamas so I never have to see her again. I'm sick of the guilt."

"I'm sorry." Stormi hoped ShaVonn had reached the end of her bitter stream.

"You don't know what it's like to be the eldest."

"True." She gripped the building. Would that be a helpful statement or one to set her off again?

"Well, I'm personally jealous you're a thousand miles away. I'll go over there and appease her. I'll have to apologize for something I didn't do just to make her happy."

Stormi closed her eyes. "Whatever you think is best."

Why? Why go over there? She could feel her insides scream, but she stifled it. ShaVonn usually buried herself by constantly trying to placate their mother which only exacerbated her neediness.

"I gotta go, bye." ShaVonn's clipped tones barely registered before the line went dead.

Stormi dropped her arm to her side, tempted to bang the phone against the brick until nothing but dust lay in her hand. Instead, she turned and pushed through the glass door of Calvert's Grill. Inside was darkened with lights hanging over a U-shaped bar in the middle. Had she missed the tavern sign?

The few hunched patrons at the bar grew still and stared at her. She pulled her mittens off and approached. It smelled of fish and beer. Shocker. But something else drifted in the air.

Chapter Two

Cheeseburgers.

And right now, that bun-encased beef sandwich ranked only nine doors down from Heaven. Stormi bellied up to the bar on the opposite side of the rough-looking characters. A frazzled-haired heavy-set woman approached, mouth drawn in disapproval. "What can I getcha?"

"A cheeseburger?" A jukebox kicked on in the back. The muted country music echoed in low tones to the front. "You do have cheeseburgers, right?"

She pointed to the menu hanging above the other patrons' heads at the bar.

"Oh, good. And a cherry coke? To-go, please."

The woman nodded, her gray pot-scrubber hair frozen in disarray. She sauntered to the back, pulled a raw burger from the fridge, and flipped it on the grill while starting a conversation with the man on a stool near the end of the counter.

She studied the characters opposite. A weathered bleach-blond, toothless beer-belly, handsome jobless Johnny, and a braggart bovine. These characters weren't much different from the last fraternity party she'd attended. Except twenty years older. Stormi dropped her eyes to the yellowed butcher block countertop. Her mother's old game of categorizing people and poking fun at them still followed her. It had served her well even in college.

Now, shame filled her. She'd been transformed. Recognize it for what it was. An outpouring of insecurity. Probably why she had tried so hard for ten years to break the stereotype, defy all categories. The hair, the studs, the partying. Her hand touched the cell phone in her pocket, tempted to text Alan. No. Poor man. No doubt sick of her questions and neediness. Accept people, love people, move on.

"Five thirty-five." Brillo head set the to-go bag on the counter in front of her.

"Right." Stormi scraped a ten-dollar bill out of her pocket and slapped it to the counter.

The woman went to the cash register and murmured something to handsome jobless Johnny. They both laughed. Irritation rose in her, either from being gossiped about, or for her categorizing again.

After the woman had returned her change, Stormi stepped to the heavy door and exited. She strolled across the road, not sure why she'd ordered it to go, only knowing she didn't want to stay in there. Huge waist-high poles looped with ropes protected walkers from the edge of the rocky bank and a bench near the end of the point looked like a good resting spot. What an idiot she was. What sane person picnicked in such freezing temperatures?

The ten men below pumped the bilge pump on the small trawler, several dirty white coolers resting near the wooden steps. They were dressed in canvas bibs, long rubber boots covering their legs. They worked like clockwork, cleaning the nets and scraping out the floor of the boat.

Two boats rested together, and the men often hollered to one another, indicating teamwork. Stormi ignored the icy breeze while comparing the names splayed across the back of the boats as they organized and readied equipment. *Sea Wheat 1* and *Sea Wheat 2*. Father and son? But the men appeared younger, perhaps brothers?

They coupled up on the dock and carried coolers up the long flight of stairs. Laughter accompanied them, but exhaustion lined their faces.

The last man, a huge football-player type, caught her eye and grinned, throwing up a wave. "Hi."

Stormi nodded, shifting her eyes to the landscape. They rattled by, balancing their loads between them. Their voices faded, and she bit into her cheeseburger. Good and greasy. Sipping the cherry coke brought back one or two almost fond childhood memories. The clanging of the coolers against the truck bed caught her attention for a moment. As she finished the burger, the fisherman at the end of the line settled on the bench next to her.

"It's cold but nice, huh?" He leaned over and peered at her with coal black eyes. Dark stubble covered his chin, a black beanie hiding his hair.

She cleared her throat. Football player/superjock. Old habits died hard. "Yes, the view is beautiful."

"Good catch today. You new here?"

She nearly choked on a swig of soft drink at his lack of finesse.

Concern filled his eyes. "You okay?"

Once she managed to clear her throat and wipe the moisture from her eyes, she managed to croak. "Sure."

"I've never seen you here before."

The other men approached, their deep voices intertwined in conversation. One of them slapped the jock's back as he went by. "Let's go, Dummy. Lots of work to do."

Her new friend looked up. "Yeah, sure, Hoge."

The men thundered down the steps in a flurry of canvas and rubber.

"I gotta go. Hope you enjoy your sandwich." He grinned, showing his white teeth, the middle two slightly overlapped, and then he rose and followed the others to the dock below.

Stormi slurped her drink through the straw and blew out vapor puffs of carbon dioxide. Strange. All the men she'd met, all the parties she'd attended, she'd never been hit on quite like that. No clever conversations, no irritating pickup lines? Just as well. She was done with that.

Fresh start. Her loose morals lay in the dust behind her. She stood and stretched. Time to head home and find some wood for that fire. Plus, there were still boxes to sort. Maybe she'd make brownies. If she had a pan.

She struck out on the sloping sidewalk, following Shore Drive up to her house. Tomorrow she'd head over to the university for her meeting with the other professors in her department. First visit to the actual campus. She wanted to make a good impression.

This weekend, she needed to purchase a bed, maybe a few homey touches. A lamp? A painting? Her head swiveled back to the bay. The *Sea Wheat 1* and *Sea Wheat 2* sailed tandem away from the dock. Beautiful. Yes, a sea painting. With a small boat. The large man aboard *2* raised his hand in a wave.

❧ ⸱⸱⸱⸱⸱⸱ ❧

Ake Pearson stared towards the shore. His eyes followed the woman strolling up the strip of sidewalk to the brow of Blackberry Hill. He turned when she disappeared behind the trees, and set his face into the cutting wind drifting in from the Atlantic Ocean.

"Help with the nets."

Hoge's voice held impatience, and he hurried to grab the lead rope, wondering why his brother seemed ill-tempered already as they hadn't reached their coordinates yet.

"You like the look of that woman, Dummy?" Delbert's mousey face grinned, and he jammed his elbow into his ribs.

Ake shrugged. "She's pretty, sure."

Delbert laughed. "Need to take you to the big town. Find you a lady."

"Shut up, Delbert," Hoge growled.

Twins Heff and Neff Goozerburg, nicknamed Double Goose, both gave a burst of laughter, their red furry faces flushed from the elements. "ShutdupDelbertshutupDelbert."

Ake leaned against the railing and ignored the usual banter, turning his head to deflect the wind. Stepping into the wheelhouse threatened to set his brother off, so he declined that small luxury. The 2 steered north once it broke the head waters while 1 headed east. At Hoge's holler they let the net out, their hands flying to keep up with the wench. Ake concentrated, knowing he could lose a finger if he lost his focus.

The flagged location drifted ahead. Ake searched the waters to catch sight of a good school of fish. Hoge returned to the wheelhouse and checked the coming weather. Two trips in one day would hopefully make up for the storm brewing for tomorrow morning. Waves lapped at the sides, and the flock of birds swarming the boat gave searching calls. Ake set his gaze on the horizon which always reminded him to pray for Mom and Pop.

The boat tossed a bit, and he turned his eyes toward the waves coming in. Ake wondered if it would be snow or rain. Heff and Neff sharpened knives behind him and readied the coolers. He checked the cables on the wench and glanced toward Delbert, knowing he hated being out near dark. He and

Hoge both had wives and kids, which added responsibilities and an evening void of their presence. Shore had disappeared, and Ake wished to see its comforting cliffs.

The boat bobbed more as the caps of the waves turned white. The twins released the seiner net and the weights pulled it down while the buoys bobbed to the surface. Hoge navigated the boat to open it up like a waiting fish purse.

"Pull 'er." Hoge yelled the command, and the four of them moved as a tuned machine.

The wench screeched and yanked in the net. Haddock flopped to the bottom of the boat. Ake gripped the rope, mentally counting the pull. Mackerel, herring, a couple of good sized tuna. Still not what they'd hoped. But the cost of their lives made it worthwhile. They cranked for thirty minutes and hustled around the twenty-four footer to flip the catch into the haul buckets. Several crabs came in, enough for them all to take home.

Delbert set up a cutting surface.

"You daft?" Hoge yelled. "With the waves growing, we'll hack our fingers off."

The boat shuddered in the renewed waves, and Delbert dismantled the table while Hoge set the motor for full speed home. The wind and waves increased the knots enough to help them come abreast of Dove Harbor thirty minutes early. *Sea Wheat 2* had already docked and raised the trouble lights for a night cutting.

Distant thunder sounded behind them as Hoge pulled in the dock. Heff and Neff tossed the full baskets to the team already hacking at the weathered wood tables. Delbert secured the vessel, and Ake jumped the bow onto the dock and took his place among the fish cleaners. The sooner they all got to work, the sooner they could all go home. Icy rain began to fall and covered most surfaces before they'd finished.

Near midnight, Ake took a deep breath as he entered his house. The wind had picked up and the lightning lit the darkened pole barn apartment. He headed for the bathroom in the dark, undressed, and took a quick shower then sank into his recliner. There would be plenty of rest time tomorrow. The storm lulled him to sleep.

He woke mid-morning staring at the ceiling. Mom and Pop would be up. He pushed the footrest in and stood to stretch. It didn't take long to dress and head up the sloping meadow to his parents' house. Icy balls pelted his hood as he strode across the clearing. Each step crunched under his feet.

He opened the back door and entered the porch. Mom waved at him from the kitchen window. The stubborn door yielded under his bulk. "Morning."

"Good morning, Aiken." His mom, tall and slender, enveloped him in a hug. "You sleep well?"

"Yep."

"Hoge have you out late?"

"Of course. How's Pop?"

Her weathered face grew wistful, but she gave a smile. "Confused."

Ake's brows drew together as he sat at the familiar round kitchen table. "Bad morning?"

She shrugged, patted her white hair, and poured him a cup of coffee. "He woke up searching for you boys. Couldn't comprehend you were grown up men."

Ake nodded and took a sip of the bitter black coffee. "How'd you convince him?"

"I didn't."

Pop appeared in the doorway, hunched over, hands in his pockets. "Too cold to be playing outside. Tell your brother to get in here."

"Okay, Pop." Ake shot a glance at his mother who ran her left-hand knuckles down her pale wrinkled face like she always did when Pop's mind left reality.

His father shuffled through the kitchen, barely raising his feet from the ground. His button-down beige sweater reminded Ake of Mr. Rogers on the public television channel of his youth.

"You boys don't listen," Pop muttered. He arrived at the pantry door, paused, and then turned to meander back through the kitchen door.

Mom shook her head. "The storm makes him restless. I think somehow, even though he can't remember why he's anxious anymore, on some level he worries about you boys."

"Gonna turn to snow this afternoon, the radio said."

"Uh-huh." She reached out to pat Ake's hand. "You're such a good boy to check on us. You shouldn't have troubled yourself in this mess."

Ake grinned at her. "You and Pop ain't no trouble. Besides, I figure if I stick around, you might feed me."

She laughed and Ake's heart rose. With Pop's old-timer's disease, he searched for ways to lighten her day.

"Well, you got that right." She rose suddenly and wrapped her arms about his neck. "Oh, Aiken, what would I do without you? You've always been the son that melted my heart. Hogan is a good boy, too, now, don't get a big head. But you always understood things that Hoge had no clue about."

Ake patted her arm before she pulled away.

"Hey, woman." Pop's voice rose from the other room, and a sad tension dropped on his mother's face.

She snugged her best grandmother sweatshirt down over her hips. "I'll be back."

Ake tossed the coffee down his gullet and glanced out the window. Due to be the first nasty storm of the season. The strange woman at the dock tugged at his memory. He hoped she was accustomed to the weather, or she'd be in for an adventure.

He crossed his arms and leaned back in the chrome chair. He'd liked her eyes. Couldn't decide why she'd caught his attention. No, he knew. The way she sat, so elegantly. Like a visiting princess.

With a deep breath, he stood and wandered to the sink. He'd do up the morning dishes to save some work for his mother, though the task might take her mind from the dismal thoughts of his father's failing memory. Nevertheless, he'd help her out and then maybe motor by the bay to see the height of the waves.

Chapter Three

Realizing it was probably her dumbest idea for the day, Stormi quickly slipped on her shoes. After zipping her coat and crushing the turquoise beanie on her head, she set off toward town. Ten steps later, she decided boots needed to be added to her list of must-haves. But she stomped through the snowy mess, amazed at how white everything looked. Almost like a blizzard.

She slid but caught herself with an undignified grasp at a nearby electrical pole. That little scare slowed her pace down the hill, and she crossed the pressed down street near the corner of the grill. A loud scraping noise drew her attention. A huge snowplow drove by, spewing dirty snow to the roadside. Thankfully it was on the other side. She slipped into Calvert's Grill, shook off the snow in the breezeway, and then stepped into the main dining area.

The same characters dotted the bar area with a few new faces including her football jock. He grinned and waved at her when she settled in a stool near the end.

Brillo head pushed away from the counter and sauntered to her. "What can I getcha?"

"A cherry coke, please. Large. To go."

She nodded and went straight to the fountain. Stormi rubbed her mittens together to ease the chill to her hands. The big screen T.V. on the left blared the hockey game and most of the patrons reacted to a missed shot with dismay. She glanced toward it. Hockey—complete mystery. A sport where players could beat up one another and get away with it.

The woman brought her drink. Stormi paid for it and made her way to the door. Outside with the snow floating down, she took a sip. Yes. Totally worth it. The door banged behind her and out popped her friendly neighborhood football jock.

"Hi."

"Hello." She checked the road to make her getaway. To her dismay he followed.

"No cheeseburger today?"

She glanced at him. Tall and, even with the thick canvas coat, muscular. She looked away. Not her type anymore. "Nope."

He followed her across the street. "You should try their fish sandwiches. We supply their fish straight from our boats."

She reached the curb on the other side, ready to leave this cowboy behind. "You don't say? Thanks, I'll have to try it sometime."

But he turned with her and sloughed through the snow beside her.

"You live on Shore Drive?"

Venturing into creepy. "Close by."

He shoved his hands in his pockets. "I can give you a ride home. You live in Duckett's old place?"

She stopped. This was just too much. Her chin rose a tad, and she gave him a cool look. "I appreciate the offer, but I'm fine."

A hurt look entered his eyes and, for some reason, she felt a little ashamed. Like kicking a newborn beagle pup.

"Sorry. I guess I got carried away. Just thought I'd save you a trip in the snow."

Her cheeks creased with humor at his face so filled with innocence.

"Hoge always says I knock people over with kindness."

Stormi laughed. Despite her earlier promise to mark this one off her list, he intrigued her. "Who's Hoge?"

The man shrugged and glanced up the road. "My brother."

"Well, kindness never hurt anyone," she assured him. "Although a ride sounds nice, I barely know you."

He grinned and stuck out a big rough paw. "I'm Ake Pearson."

One of her eyebrows climbed. "Nice to meet you."

"Who're you?"

She hesitated and then relented. Becoming part of the landscape meant meeting people here in Stone Haven. "Stormi Zobroski."

His grin widened. "It's storming and that's your name."

"That's right." Her gaze went beyond his wide shoulder to Dove Harbor. The waves were white-capped, and the horizon disappeared into the thickness of the snow. Her head tilted up, watching the flakes plummet. One fell into her eye and she flicked it away. "Does it always snow this much?"

A rumble of deep laughter greeted her. "Yep. Lots of snow here. Lots of storms. You came to the right place."

She studied his features, and he studied her back. "Don't suppose you want that ride now that we know each other."

Wow, he moved fast. Maybe she'd misjudged him. Maybe he bided his time until he moved in for the kill. "I don't think knowing one another's name constitutes a relationship."

His brow furrowed. "Okay. Sorry."

"As much as I'd like to continue this interesting conversation, I need to go. Nice to meet you."

Her sarcasm seemed lost to him, and he gave a big smile and waved. "Sure. Have a great day."

She turned and hurried away. When she flicked a glance behind her, he'd returned across the street and headed back to the grill.

What a strango. She'd pegged him a cocky football jock, but his demeanor seemed devoid of any pretenses. With a shrug she hurried through the thick clusters of snow. Her quiche would be finished any minute. A black truck drove slowly up the incline and honked. She let out a squeal of surprise and nearly stumbled.

As the vehicle passed, she could see her new acquaintance waving at her from the window. Great. The freak was going to follow her home. But he sped up, spitting snow from the back of his deep treaded wheels and turned at the intersection. She gave a sigh of relief. As much as the slippery snow allowed, she quickly picked her way to her back door and slid inside.

The quiche smelled heavenly as she unzipped her coat and shook the snow from her shoulders. She pulled the beanie from her head and fingered her short hair. Once the snow let up, she'd find a good stylist and get a sharp modern cut. Her transformation was almost complete.

She settled at the bar with a plateful of quiche, her cola, and her phone. Her text icon showed a new message. What? The university meeting was still on? Were they kidding? How would she get to the meeting in this storm? She gave an aggravated sigh then glanced at the time. Oh, she needed to leave, like *now*.

She shoveled the egg mixture into her mouth, making a mental note to file the tasty recipe. With a longing glance at the rich brownies, she hurried over to her outfit, pressed and waiting on her inflated armchair. She pulled it on, grabbed her purse and cola, and headed for the car.

The snow still fell in huge fluffs. In Georgia, no one went anywhere when it snowed. These people were crazy. She settled into the car and shut the door, a pile of snow landing on her armrest. The faithful Ion turned over, and she parked her drink into the cup holder and flung her purse to the passenger's seat. She buckled her seatbelt over the quivering in her stomach. Driving in this stuff wasn't on her bucket list.

She eased from the parking space and then crept down the hill. Praise God for front wheel drive. Her lips tightened into concentration and she patted the dashboard. "Come on, baby. You can do it."

She came to a sliding halt at the stop sign, and her heart jerked in fear. Holy Moley. How would she ever make it to Fulbright, some fifteen miles to the south? She gritted her teeth, prayed, and pulled out into the intersection. A vehicle appeared from the right and she screamed, slamming on the brakes. The Ion skittered, refusing to stop, and the truck struck her front fender. Everything spun for a moment and then screeched to a halt.

Her mouth hung open, and she gasped shallow breaths. Her door flew open, and there stood Ake Pearson, a look of concern across his face.

"You okay?"

"I...think I am." She sat frozen for a moment before unbuckling her belt. Her shaking legs swung from the car and she rose. His hands steadied her.

"Are you sure?"

She spun at him. "You didn't stop. And now you've hit me. This is all your fault."

His brows rose and his gaze flicked to the street. "I don't have a stop sign. You do."

"I..." She closed her mouth. Fear and anger mingled inside, and she fought to keep them leashed. "You—"

"I'll call Max so he can fill out a report."

Max? "No. I must get to Fulbright. I don't have time to fill out an accident report. I'll be late."

He nodded. "Well, I'll tell him you can come in and do it later."

"No." She stuck to her guns and continued to blither. "I have to leave, now. Now, I say. This storm will make me late already. I can't be late. I just can't."

She stepped back into her car and turned the key. A horrible whining began, first quickly and then slowly before cycling back. Her fist struck the dashboard and she tried again. More of the same met her ears. It wasn't going to turn over. She stared through the white speckled windshield at the blizzard, and her heart sank. She'd lose her job. The car door opened again.

"I don't think it's going to start."

"You think?" she spat.

He stood there staring, and she pressed her forehead into the steering wheel between her wet mittens to block him out.

"How 'bout I push it to the side and take you to Fulbright?"

It took a moment to register. She turned her head and glared at him. "What?"

"Put it in neutral and I'll push it aside."

She gave an impatient sigh. Who did he think he was? The heavyweight champion of the world? She threw the gearshift to N and leaned back in her seat. He slammed the door closed. Then, to her astonishment, the car began to move.

"Steer to the side." He instructed with a muffled grunt.

She checked the rear window and did what he asked. Several agonizing moments ticked by until her car rested against the curb. The door opened again.

"There ya go. Should be safe for now. Come on."

Her mouth fell open. "I can't just gallivant off with you."

"Gallivant? No, I'm taking you to Fulbright. Isn't that where you said you had to go?"

She fixed her eyes on him. Was he kidding? But his face appeared open and quite serious. Fine. If nothing else, she'd be in the evening news as a missing person. Or a murdered one. She stepped from the car.

"Fine, Ake Pearson. I accept your help. But I have family that will miss me if I don't turn up."

His brows drew together and he shrugged. "Okay."

He hurried to the truck and opened the passenger door with a big smile. She whirled away and stomped over to examine the damage on the front fender. Minor, but still a pain in the hiney. She slipped and skated to Ake's truck where he held the door.

"Thank you." She tried to make her voice show true gratefulness, but she fell a bit short.

She snapped on the seatbelt and looked around the cab of the old Ford truck. At least it was clean, although it did smell a bit like fish.

He jumped into the driver's seat, grinning like a boy on show-and-tell day. "Ready?"

She cut her eyes to the front glass. "Yes."

The truck fired up with a rumble, and he threw it into gear. He fishtailed out into the center of the road, and her fingers gripped the armrest. Even if the accident was her fault, driving like this would soon put them in the ditch. He lowered his hand to the gearshift and downshifted.

"It's starting to get slippery. Better kick in the four-wheel drive."

The truck steadied and clung to the road. She gave a sigh of relief. He pulled out into the highway toward Fulbright. Maybe she wouldn't become a headline.

"So what's in Fulbright?" he questioned, turning his black eyes on hers.

"DeLong University."

"Oh. You go to school there?"

"No. I work there."

Silence stretched, and Stormi watched the snowy landscape pass, wondering how he could see where he was going.

"Doing what?"

"Hmmm? Oh, I teach several English courses online."

"That's cool." He had one hand on the steering wheel and the other on the gearshift. His hands were encased in thick leather work gloves.

She supposed she should carry her side of the conversation for courtesy's sake. "And you fish, correct?"

"Yeah. My brother and I have two boats. Well, he's really in charge. I just help. Hoge's really smart about keeping everything going."

She nodded. "I suppose that would be a big undertaking. I'm sure he appreciates your assistance."

He grinned. "I can tell you're really smart, too. Me, I didn't do so good in school. Hoge would laugh to know I was driving over to the university."

She studied him, but his attention stayed on the road. "Why would he find that funny?"

He gave a short burst of laughter. "I've never been to no college. Couldn't go if I wanted to."

Her face puckered. Was he a dimwit? "Did you graduate high school?"

"Oh, sure. But English was the hardest. I had a special class for it."

This information puzzled Stormi. Special class?

With a quick glance, he finished his thought. "It's why they call me Dummy."

She took in a sharp breath. "You shouldn't let them call you such a name. That's just mean."

He shrugged. "It's true. Can't read. I got a strange way with numbers though, Hoge says. I know the count of each type of fish by the time the last one falls into the boat. My mom says it's a gift."

Outrage lodged in her throat. "Are you telling me your own brother calls you this derogatory name?"

One of his eyes screwed up when he took a glance at her. "Huh? No, he calls me Dummy, not derogawhatever."

"Derogatory. It means a name that's making fun of you, unkind."

"Oh. Gotcha." He shrugged. "Well, folks been calling me that since I was a kid. Guess it stuck."

She tried to calm the boiling anger inside by drawing in a slow breath. "You should tell them to call you by your proper name."

"It's okay. They don't mean nothing by it."

She could see the sign for Fulbright some distance ahead. But he slowed and turned on the next road.

"I don't think you should have turned yet." Perhaps he really shouldn't be driving. If he couldn't read, how did he know what the signs said?

"No. This is a shortcut. And the road's not so curvy. Don't worry. I'll get you there."

She gripped the chevron-patterned fabric of the seat, praying he was right.

Chapter Four

Sure enough, tall brick buildings loomed ahead. Hope rose in Stormi's chest. "Where 'bouts you need to go?" He lowered his head to glance about the campus.

"Um...hold on." She withdrew a piece of paper. "Columbia and Vine."

"All right." He pulled out slowly, and they eased into a parking lot about three blocks further down the road. "I believe this is it."

She blinked at the building. Shiresheck Building/Language Arts. She gathered her purse. "I think you're right. And right on time."

"Glad to be of service." He nodded with a grin.

"Oh."

His brows rose. "Forget something?"

Her mouth hung open. "How will I get home?"

"I'll wait right here for you."

She stared at him. "You can't do that. It's freezing out here."

He crossed his arms over his broad chest. "Much colder out on a boat than here."

Her chin rose. "I can't ask you to do that."

But he shook his head. "You might not ask, but I'll be here."

The snow seemed to be coming down even harder, masking the building's sign. "Perhaps you could wait inside? I'd feel much better if you were indoors. I hate to say that I'm not sure how long this meeting will last."

His glance took in the building. "If that'll make you happy, let's go."

To her surprise, he jumped out and circled the truck to assist her. He may not have graduated at the top of his class, but his manners were impeccable.

"Thank you." Sincerity rang in her tone this time.

"No problem."

Was he joking? She'd been a huge problem. Her heart smote her as she flipped up her hood and scurried through the snow with her dress shoes. Almost instantly she skidded across ice and let out a howl. He gripped her and kept her from landing in the snow piled along the side of the walk.

"Here, let me help you."

Biting her lip at her lack of independence today, she slid her hand into the crook of his elbow. With his help she navigated the slippery walk to the door. He pulled it open and she entered. She paused in the high-ceilinged foyer. A beautiful glass chandelier hung from the center surrounded by a dome of windows. Natural light lit every corner and the marble corridors shone. Hallways separated into three directions.

"I'm supposed to go to the fifth floor," she murmured, checking her paper again.

"There's the elevators." He motioned to the right.

"Oh good." She strode to the gleaming doors and pushed the up button. Her gaze caught on him still standing at the entry door. "What are you doing? Come on."

"I can wait here."

She took a deep breath. "No, I can at least find you a chair."

He shrugged and joined her. Together they stepped into the elevator. She surveyed him as they lifted. Jeans—clean—gray canvas jacket, black beanie, thick stubble hid his chin. Not exactly business casual. Tough noogies. He'd brought her, she wouldn't shed him. He gave a small smile. She smiled back. He may not have been blessed with intellect, but he struck her quite handsome, nonetheless.

The doors slid open and they exited. A woman sat at a high rounded desk in a small foyer.

"May I help you?"

Stormi rubbed the three nubs on the left side of her lip. Would they notice the piercing holes hadn't completely disappeared? No time to be nervous now. She shuffled forward with what she hoped was a professional smile. "Yes. I'm here for the faculty meeting of the English department."

The woman gave a cool smile behind the tiny microphone clipped to her ear. "That is to take place in Conference Hall J. Down this hall, make a left, second door on the right."

"Thank you. Oh. Um, my friend has been gracious enough to drive me here in the storm. Is there a place he may sit and wait?"

She nodded, her eyes doing the once over and returning to hers a little guarded. Then she addressed Ake. "I'll show you the break room. There's coffee and refreshments there."

Stormi gave a nervous smile and waved to Ake who grinned. He disappeared behind the corner, and she felt a bit of a loss. As difficult as it had been to actually get here, his presence had taken her mind from the impending meeting. She nibbled her lip, her stomach dancing in nervousness. Following the woman's directions, Stormi wandered down the hallway and found Conference Hall J.

The room yawned large with rich woodwork. Large paintings of founders lined the walls. Narrow dark wood tables and black chairs stood in rows. The men clad mostly in black suits, and women dressed in dark A-line skirts with jackets, spoke in small huddles in muted syllables. Her eyes went to the modern navy bellbottom pantsuit that had seemed just the right choice at the time.

The stiffness of the people's postures tempted her to run down the hallway to hunt down Ake in the refreshment room. Several sleek expensive briefcases rested beside chairs, and top of the line laptops occupied the strips of narrow tables.

She shuffled forward, feeling quite out of place with her simple tablet. Trying not to call attention to herself, she chose a chair near the outside of the row facing the front platform. She fiddled with her purse to ease the awkward feeling. She glanced longingly toward the door.

This wasn't her. She knew her English, yes, literature, yes. But this pompous meeting of windbags, no. Her fingers probed each piercing nub one by one, and then fluffed her sagging hair. She was categorizing again. Yet if they only knew...

A panel of somber dressed men and women filed up onto the platform. A rush of thankfulness quivered through her. Just get it over with and be on her way. People sat around her, maybe fifty in all. She opened her plain paper app and darted glances around her co-workers. Shrugging off her coat, black tattoo swirls peeked out at the edge of her slinky sleeve. She slumped down and tugged the silky material down.

☙ ⋯⋯ ☙

Ake inserted the coins and chose the button with the almond icon with cappa-something. Cappuccino maybe? With almonds? Or almond milk? He'd never had that before. And this machine? Man, it was the fanciest he'd ever seen. Seven kinds of cappuccino, ten kinds of coffee, five kinds of, what he could only figure as, hot chocolate.

The paper cup dropped down and filled with hot brown liquid ending with a head of foam. He grabbed a spoon and a couple of sugars. He'd heard of cappuccino but had never sampled it himself. Nothing like trying something new on a stormy, cold day.

A grin shot across his face. Stormi. He liked her. Sure, he hated that her car was wrecked, but he'd enjoyed the conversation over. She was one of the few women that would even talk to him.

He sat at a small round table in the empty room, added sugar, and stirred. The woman didn't wear sensible footwear though. Lucky for her, he was here to keep her from ending up in the snow. Shame to mess up that navy pantsuit she'd been wearing, though he wondered how she kept warm in that gauzy get-up. He tipped the chair back and brought the cup to his lips. The chair came down with a crash.

What in thunder was this stuff? Did people actually drink it? He shuddered, stood up and flung the whole cup into the trash. Nasty brew. No more for him. He bellied back up to the offending machine. Plain coffee, black. It didn't always pay to try something new.

He selected the middle button. That should be medium, right? Ake taste-tested it before he returned to his seat. Fine. Drinkable. He added sugar and stirred, his eyes going to the windows on the far wall. Snow fell in heavy sheets. Since his old black truck could take a couple more feet, it didn't worry him. And he had chains in the tool box.

His gaze followed the gray walls of the breakroom. A few empty tables surrounded him. Paper lists crowded a small corkboard near the door. A colorful banner hung on the far wall, stamped with cat feet and an illustration of a growling cougar. So this was college.

Hoge had attended Boston University for a couple of years. Studied business. If it were nothing but numbers, he could probably handle it. But the reading, well, no way. The old shame washed over him. Why had he blurted out to Stormi he couldn't read? It was usually something he kept quite guarded. Not something he wanted advertised. Sometimes it set people talking real slow and loud in his face like he couldn't understand a common sentence.

He shrugged. Nothing he could do to change it. Hadn't hampered him much anyway, for the most part. He did his job, enjoyed the little things in life, and loved his family. God had always assured him those were the most important things.

His eyes blinked. After the late night last night, he could do with a little snooze. He leaned back and folded his hands across his chest. He'd just as well make up a little sleep.

Something shook him, and he inhaled a deep breath before opening his eyes. It was hot in here. He looked up and found Stormi looking at him, humor evident in the twist of her lips.

"Catching a cat nap?"

He chuckled. "I suppose. We were up late cutting fish. Guess I nodded off."

A crease appeared between her brows. "I'm sorry you had to wait."

"I didn't notice." He stood and stretched. "Go like you hoped?"

Her teeth caught her lip, and her fingers clenched the strap of her purse. "Well enough. I'm relieved I won't have to come back until spring."

She turned and peered out the windows before casting a dismayed face at him. "Oh, my. It looks worse than ever."

"My truck will get ya through, no worries."

They padded to the door and down the hall to the elevator. The place smelled like new carpet.

"I hate to say it, since it means my car is wrecked, but I'm kinda glad you're driving."

Laughter erupted from his throat. "Driving in the snow is old hat. Been doing it since I was twelve."

She turned towards him in the elevator, seriousness in her gaze. "Well...thank you for bringing me and waiting for me. I truly appreciate it."

He studied her earnest face and grinned. Yep, she was the prettiest woman he'd ever spoken to, hands down. Rescuing her had been pure pleasure.

☙ ⋯⋯ ❧

Stormi forced the back door of her house closed and stood for a moment. A foot and a half of snow, and it continued to fall with a vengeance. Funny how God had sent her a guardian in a black truck to ensure she got where she needed to go. At the time, the accident hadn't seemed such a blessing, but now? Alan often preached about looking for the blessings, and she had definitely seen that.

She pulled the phone from her purse and texted. ***God sent a guardian today. So thankful for—***

The phone vibrated in her hands. Marla. Great. "Hello?"

A stream of curse words met her ears and then a squeal. "Didn't think you'd pick up. How's it going B?"

Stormi sucked in a lungful of restraint. She and her old best friend hadn't parted on the best of terms. Still, she wouldn't pass up the chance to witness. "Hey, Marla. Everything's fine here."

Her friend cursed again. "Stormi. You sound like a librarian chocked full of stuffy old books with a bun pulling your face tight. You eating prunes and lemon rinds for breakfast, lunch, and dinner?"

Mocking laughter stiffened Stormi's backbone. "No. Quiche, actually."

"Quiche? Artsy. Parisian, even. We could do that, you know. We always talked about backpacking through Europe. The wine, the cheese. The adorable little tables. Al fresco. Oh, and did I mention the wine? And the exotic men? Hmmm. It might get you out of that funk you're in."

She inhaled deeply. "I'm not in a 'funk,' as you so eloquently put it. I'm a Christian now. My priorities have changed."

"You're brainwashed is what you are." She swore. "I know plenty of 'Christians,' and they don't go around changing their whole lives because of God. It's your life, Stormi. You can do what you please. It's not a sin to go to Paris. Besides, everyone thinks you've lost your mind. Just come back home."

The old temptations to do just that rose up, and she closed her eyes. The familiar yet maladjusted life she'd led beckoned. It whispered how much easier going back would be than striving against the grain here in this new place. But then she remembered the emptiness after every party, every man. No, she hardened her resolve. "I'm sorry I'm disappointing everyone. But I had to leave. I'm different now. Not just a little different. Completely transformed. God's Son died for me. I won't take that lightly."

Marla let out a stream of obscenities, and Stormi set her teeth. "You're a freak. I couldn't stand going through life in a boring bubble of churchiness. You'll come crying back to your friends when those straight-lace conservative, closed-minded d-bags reject you. See, if they don't."

The phone went dead in her hands. She plopped on the stool and covered her face. Tears burned her eyes and a sob rose. Nobody in her old world understood, or even tried. She'd been friends with Marla since fifth grade. They'd dyed their hair together, pierced and tattooed together.

In high school they partied with one another, survived broken relationships leaning on each other. They even survived college, their first jobs, and all the drama, the endless drama. They'd been inseparable. Marla knew her better than any other person.

Except now. She swiped away the moisture from her face and glanced down at her phone. Alan. She backspaced the, **so thankful for**, and replaced it with, **could use some prayer though**, and pressed send. Alan would petition the Father for her. Meanwhile she pressed her head to the counter and prayed.

∿ ⋯ ∿

The gorgeous petite stylist eyed her hair with false sense of brightness. "Not to worry. We can fix this in no time."

The beautician picked up the scissors and began to snip. Stormi took a deep breath. She'd waited for months for this day and now it was finally here. A chic new bob was just the thing to get some of her confidence back since her argument with Marla last week.

"This cut will accentuate that great jawline you have."

"Thanks." Stormi studied her reflection in the huge mirror. Did she have a great jawline? Not sure. She only knew she'd never been short for a date, or rather a one-night stand, which was a more accurate description of what transpired.

The woman clipped shorter and shorter, leaving her bangs longer so they fell in a spike beside her left eye. The stylist dried her tresses towards the front of her face, sprayed a tad of hair spray, and she was finished. Stormi sat up.

As the beautician held the mirror, Stormi followed the boy cut from the tiny spikes in front, exposing her whole ear, to the shaved duck tail in back. And the long layered bangs jutted to the left of her eyes giving a dash of modern urban to the style. She turned her head side to side and fluffed it.

"Like it?"

Stormi took a breath. It suited her thin angular face. She smiled. "Yes. I do. I really do. It's perfect."

Chapter Five

Stormi removed her beanie and Ake stared. She caught his gaze and turned with brows raised. "You like my hair?"

He nodded. "You look like a cover of a magazine."

She adjusted herself on the hard, cold bench overlooking Dove Harbor, but Ake couldn't stop staring.

Stormi laughed. "Yes, my inbox is filled with offers from Vogue."

Ake pulled his gaze away with some effort. *Don't stare at folks, Ake,* his mother's age-old admonishment rang in his ears. "You're like Tinkerbell. A pixie princess."

Laughter burst from the lithe woman seated down the bench from him, and he cocked his head, not sure how to interpret her glee.

She sobered. "I'm sorry. I'm not laughing at you, just your vision of me. It's quite a compliment."

Ake cast his gaze to the men below. Hoge would be plenty mad that Ake was spending so much time in conversation with this beauty. Nevertheless, he couldn't draw himself away. He shrugged. "That's okay. People laugh at me all the time."

The woman beside him stilled, holding the lidded cup close to her chin. He set his eyes on the horizon and wondered how his mother fared with his pop.

"Oh, Ake. I'd never laugh *at* you." She edged a little closer. "You are wonderfully refreshing."

He turned his face to hers, not sure how to respond. "Well I better go. We got a long day of fishing ahead. Least the sun's out. Hoge will have my hide if I don't get down there and get the nets ready."

With a deep breath, he stood and ran his hands down his canvas bibs, thankful for the long underwear beneath. She stood too, took the last sip of her drink and tossed the cup into the blue dinged trash barrel behind the bench.

"I hope you catch a netful."

He grinned. "I'm praying for several netfuls."

She stepped forward and startled him by touching his arm. "You're right. Praying. That's exactly what we should do. Thank you for reminding me."

A fairy pixie princess. That's what she was. It brightened his day just to talk to her. "Are you going to be down here every morning?"

Her eyes opened wide. "I don't know. Why?"

He nudged the crunchy snow at his feet. "No reason. See ya."

Through his pursed lips a whistle came forth as he scurried down the rough wooden timbers. Hoge could yell and scream and the warm feeling inside wouldn't budge. He cast his eyes to the horizon and sent up a prayer for his mom and pop. Then tagged one on for Stormi.

❧ ⋯⋯ ❧

Stormi perched back on the bench, intrigued by the men below readying the boat. One in particular kept her attention. Never in all her years of carousing had she come across such an innocent man. Absolutely no mind games. Just simple conversation, real concern. And though he let off like he lacked intelligence, a special kind of wisdom shone from his wide brown eyes. A wisdom which she pondered. He appeared to be a fellow Christian. Was he?

She tugged the beanie back on her head to battle the gust of wind. That would be her next question. Alan prodded her to align with other Christians for the sake of friendship and strength. Counting Ake Pearson as one of these would definitely aid in that accomplishment.

The men loaded on the boats and the engines started up. She shivered, her cheeks numb. Why was she still here? She had a perfectly good home a few blocks to the north. Ake moved to the stern of the boat and looked towards her. His left hand raised in a wave. Had this been what she waited for? With a deep feeling of satisfaction, she waved back and watched their boat drift from the harbor.

Later, when the afternoon sun dipped toward the western tree line, Stormi hurried along the snowy sidewalks. Work had gone so smoothly, she'd nearly forgotten to pick up her car from the shop. She couldn't wait to have her vehicle back. Walking everywhere was great exercise, but with the cutting north wind, she'd just as soon drive. How many blocks had she hiked? Too many to count.

With a thankful sigh, she stepped to the glass door of Ray's Auto Body shop and pulled on the metal handle. She paused inside to wipe her feet on the burgundy mat and absorb the heat. Glass surrounded the waiting room area and only one other person sat in the chairs that rimmed the room on two sides. The air smelled of grease and gasoline, and behind the gray counter hung auto necessities and nonessential necessities.

Her gaze swept the selection hanging from the white peg board. Air fresheners, tire gages, windshield wiper blades, auto emblems, decals—lots of them. Decals of depicting families came in stick, skull, and smiley. Then peace signs, deer antlers, car brand names, and the list went on. On the shelf beneath rested car polish, car wax, tire cleaner, and touch up paint cans.

She stepped to the counter and rang the buzzer near the cash register. To her right, a door with a glass pane revealed a couple of cars on lifts with men working under them, their arms stretched up into the guts of the vehicles. A red mustang and a black something beyond that. Good. Hers didn't appear to be up in the air still. The older man, with whom she'd left it, had assured her it would be finished by late afternoon.

The door swung open, and in stepped a dark-headed man dressed in a navy shirt and black pants. Emblazoned across the left pocket in bright yellow was Ray's Auto Body with a little red car speeding away. Wiping his hands with a grimy, gray rag, he stepped behind the counter. Disappointment rushed to her gut. This was not the same man she'd spoken with a few days ago. This guy was much younger.

"Hello." He smiled with the gleam of perfect teeth. "What can I do for you?"

"Hi, yeah, I actually dealt with Ray a few days ago. He said I could pick up my car today."

His smile widened, and his arms took a wide clasp on the edge of the counter. Humor danced in his clear blue eyes. Her gaze took in the charming dimple that clefted his chin, the lean cheeks, and fit physique which bespoke of one who worked out. Drop-dead gorgeous. Stormi filled her lungs with air and stomped down the urge to flirt.

"That's my father. But since my parents named me Ray, as well, perhaps I can be of assistance?"

Ah. Game on. Yep, could have spotted him way off. She glanced out the window to break eye-contact. "Sorry, of course. I have the tan Saturn Ion."

"Oh, that."

His response drew her attention.

His smile lost some of its intensity, and his face took on empathy. "We're waiting on a part for that. It's not expected to be in until tomorrow. If you leave a number, we'll call you as soon as it's finished."

"Sure." She rattled off her cell phone number and clenched her mittened hands. Great. Another day without transportation.

He wrote down the information and glanced up. "We can rent you a car. And in this instance, I can waive the fee. Let me get you set up."

She studied him as he stooped behind the counter and pulled out some forms. He picked up a pen and lifted his brows. His voice lowered. "I could even throw in dinner if you're up for it."

His smile ignited a warning flame. Uh-huh. She'd been here before. Many times. Flee. *Flee.*

She flashed a brilliant smile and backed away from the counter. "You know what? I'm good. Just call me when it's ready."

His brows descended. "It's no trouble."

She threw a, "That's okay," behind her shoulder as she swung through the door into the frosty air. A long cold walk home. Just what she had planned. She closed her eyes momentarily and lowered her head into the wind. Better to freeze than to revisit wrong choices. Before becoming a Christian, the conversation would have gone quite differently.

"I could even throw in dinner, if you're up for it."

Her eyes would have danced, and she would have tilted her head to the side and thrown out a hip. "Dinner. That's sounds intriguing."

He would have leaned forward and dropped his voice. "Yeah, we've got a great steak place on the edge of town. Maybe we could throw in a movie, too."

She would have giggled and pretended to be coy. Maybe she'd have touched his hand which would have brought up his burning eyes to hers. "Not sure. I'd have to check my schedule."

Then he would've laughed a low sexy laugh. "I haven't even given a date yet."

"Oh." More giggles. "Well, for you, I'll clear out my calendar. Say, Friday?"

The tapping pencil on the filled out form would have been his sign of triumph. "Sure, Friday. Six, okay?"

Then she would have smiled, bit her lip, and muttered a, "Sounds great."

They would have exchanged information for pick-up, gone to a rated R movie, come back to her apartment, and whoaaaa. Same life all over again. A string of unfulfilled nights of random handsome men, cascading her back into an abyss of immorality and dissatisfaction.

What was that verse, what was it? Think, *think*. It had a lot of two's. Her brain scrambled. *Never mind. Just remember the words.* "Flee the evil desires of youth and pursue righteousness..." The rest of the verse disappeared into foggy memory. She repeated it to herself, the cloud of her breath baptizing her in meaning. With a deep sigh she stepped into the road. A loud honk skidded her to a stop, her heart in her throat.

The huge truck's fender rested within inches of her. A door slammed and Ake came bolting around the front. "You okay? Dear God, tell me I didn't hit you."

She huffed a couple of cleansing breaths and laid a hand on her heart. "No, I'm fine. Just freaked out. That's all."

His hands came down on her shoulders, and his black eyes surveyed her. "Are you sure? When you stepped off the curb, I thought I'd killed you."

She gave a nervous laugh. "I guess I wasn't watching where I was going."

His wide face cleared. "Well, the Lord must have been watching out for you, 'cause you stepped right out into traffic."

"I did? Huh."

Ake's arm slid around her shoulders and turned her towards his vehicle. "Here, let's get in the truck and get out of the street."

Numbly she allowed him to steer her towards the passenger seat. She got in and he closed the door. He hurried around the front and jumped into the driver's seat. "Where were you going?"

"What? Oh, just home." She rubbed her hands up and down her arms, glancing around the busy intersection.

"I'll have you there in no time. You might want to put on your seatbelt."

She shook her head to clear it. "Of course."

He pulled out into the plowed street, and she kept her eyes on the mounds of snow on the curbs.

"Stormi?"

She turned to stare at him.

"You really need to watch where you're going."

The concern on his scruffy face lit a smile on her lips. "I think that's what I was doing. Only in my head."

Puzzlement wrinkled his brow. "Come again?"

Issuing a deep breath, she said, "Never mind."

He pulled into her drive and she gave a sigh. Safe at home.

"Well, you're sure you're all right?"

She peered at him in his canvas coat and black beanie, his brow crinkled. "I'm fine, Ake. Thanks for rescuing me—again."

Ake motored up the lane of his folks and veered right down to the drive towards his pole barn apartment. Still couldn't get the worry out of his head from nearly running Stormi over.

"Dear Heavenly Father, thanks for stopping me," he murmured to the interior of the truck as he pulled into his one-car garage. He punched the button that closed the huge door and exited the vehicle. Tools marred the bench to his left around the unfinished copper rose arbor he was making for his mother. Course, it'd been there since late summer.

With a shrug he ignored the mess for another day and grabbed the snow shovel and the rock salt. Mom and Pop's sidewalk still had ice, and he'd thought about it all day. Of course his mother seldom got out unless he or Hoge sat with Pop. Still, not worth taking any chances.

He strode out of the side door, his boots crunching through the foot of snow. The depth helped to propel him up the slope into his parents' backyard. But he kept walking around the side to the front walk. For an hour he chipped and scraped at the walk until the entire span of concrete cleared. Then he liberally sprinkled the area with rock salt.

His stomach rumbled with hunger, so he collected his supplies to head back to the pole barn. The back porch light flipped on as he trudged down the slope, and his mother stuck her head out the door.

"Got chowder."

He paused and turned. His mother spoiled him. "I'll be back."

After returning the shovel and rock salt to the garage, he headed up the incline and then thumped up the wooden stairs he'd cleaned the night before. His mother spooned up the thick white soup into the heavy crock bowl as he shoved the door shut. Clam chowder. His favorite. He slid into his usual chair.

"Is Pop good?"

Mom patted her puffy white hair and took the chair opposite. "Fair to middlin'. And he's sleeping now. How's my sweet boy?"

Ake shrugged. "Fine. Great now with this chowder. I got your walk cleaned."

"I heard ya. Wish you didn't have to babysit us."

He laughed and then bowed his head for a quick prayer of thanksgiving over his meal. "Just taking care of things."

Silence settled between the two of them until he brought up his gaze. "Something wrong?"

Mom ran her left hand knuckles up and down her cheek. "Hoge said you met a woman."

Ake set the spoon in the bowl and leaned back in the chair, crossing his forearms across his chest. "Yeah. Her name's Stormi. She's not from around here. I think the snow throws her for a loop."

His mom dropped her eyes and fiddled with the edge of the light blue placemat. "Your brother seemed concerned."

"Why?"

She shrugged. "We don't want you to get hurt, Ake."

"No worries, Mom. Women never take to me." He stood and placed the bowl in the sink.

She rose and hugged him. "If you're sure..."

"I'll stop by tomorrow and see if you need anything. Love ya, Mom." He stepped to the back door and tugged it open. Women never did notice him, and that was okay. Besides, he didn't want just any woman.

He wanted Stormi.

Chapter Six

Ake stomped to the bottom of the hill and entered his front door. He knocked the snow off of his boots and then lined them up on the rubber mat before padding into his bedroom. In the dark he stripped down and pulled on a pair of baggy shorts and a black t-shirt. Then he meandered to the extra bedroom.

His eyes flicked to the clock as he came through the door. Near nine o'clock. Just enough time to pump some iron, and then he'd finish up his current project. He headed to the treadmill in the corner and punched on his favorite Christian band on the CD player. He finished his run in good time before moving to his weight bench.

Counting methodically as he pumped the fifteen pound weight with his left arm, his thoughts strayed to his mother's last topic of conversation. What had Hoge said to cause her to fret? Sweat dripped down his forehead, and he reached for a towel while focused on finishing the set.

He stood, shook out his shoulders, and reached for one of the water bottles. His fingers worked it from the plastic package of thirty-six. Once he twisted the lid off, he guzzled half the bottle in one swig.

The wind picked up outside as he strolled through the darkened house. Despite the weather, inside it was too quiet. He cleared his throat just to hear a noise. With another swig, he finished the water and tossed the container into the sink. The plastic bottle rattled around in the metal tub, accentuating the stillness. With a shrug he returned to the extra room and went to the desk in the corner.

A red Austrian crystal and pearl necklace lay on the velvet cloth, awaiting a clasp. Then he'd begin the matching bracelet. Then earrings. There'd be no problem finishing it before Mother's Day. The problem came when he faced Hoge's ribbing. He grasped the tiny clear faceted bead and slid it onto the nylon thread. It fell to its place beside the opalescent pearl. Now a pearl, then a clear. It didn't matter. Mom would be thrilled.

He flicked on the small lamp on the desk and hunched forward. A turquoise bead rolled across the black velvet and settled against his hand. Same color as Stormi's beanie. Perhaps when he finished, he'd begin a jewelry set for her. Would that be the color Stormi chose? Maybe he'd ask her.

∽⋯⋯∾

Stormi pressed save on her new podcast and snatched her phone from the counter. Seemed her phone never rested. The flash indicated a new text. Hmm. Alan. She pressed the balloon to access the screen.

You find it?

Leave it to Alan not to forget. She laughed and thumbed the phone with her message. ***No, haven't looked yet.***

She flopped onto the air sofa and blew up her bangs. Man, she was tired.

2 Tim. 2:22, flashed in her message balloon.

Right. With a grunt, she reached and grabbed the Bible from the far side of the couch and flipped through it, settling on the reference he'd given. She preferred the actual book, adding notes and dates. Sure enough. *Run away from youthful lusts—pursue righteousness, faith, love, and peace with those who call on the Lord out of a pure heart.*

Perfect. The exact one. She picked up her phone. ***Bingo. Is there one that tells me whether I have to visit my mom on Thanksgiving?***

She pressed the back of her head against the sagging couch and pushed her feet out farther. The empty fireplace mocked as she shivered. The place was downright frigid. She'd start a fire if she knew how. And if she had wood.

Her phone flashed. ***There is.***

Alan's message caused her to sit up. Was he kidding? ***Seriously?***

"Brrr," she muttered and stood to search for a thick hoodie. After slipping one on, she checked her phone. The words caused her to roll her eyes.

Number 5. Honor your father and mother.

She grabbed a fuzzy turquoise afghan and sat on the far end of the couch. Air swooshed to the other end below her rear while the far end rose off of the floor. Stormi shook her head. At least she had new lamps, a new frame of art, and a new carpet at her feet. Still, the air couch was pushing her last nerve.

She rotated the phone horizontally then tapped the screen, and had to backspace four words. Didn't want to send "That sou D's like a crop.pout." Shocker. Auto-checker? Pshaw. Auto-incorrector.

Instead she sent, ***That sounds like a cop out.***

She flipped her Bible to Exodus twenty and perused the Ten Commandments. Yep, number five. How did he know which one? Oh, and there was more about elongating her days if she chose to honor her parents. She growled.

God's precepts cover a myriad of things. Alan. Being so Alan.

Thanks for ruining my day! She added a smiley face and stood. The phone in her hand began to ring. A quick glance told her it was an unknown, but she thought she might know who was calling.

"Hello?

"Is this Stormi Zobroski?"

"Yes."

"This is Ray's Auto Body. Your car is ready if you'd like to pick it up at your convenience."

Satisfaction washed through her. At last. And it had only taken two extra days. "I'll be right down. Thanks."

She hung up and headed straight for her white puffer coat hanging by the door. Beanie on, coat zipped. She couldn't wait to get her little baby back. The stiff wind reminded her why she hadn't gone to the docks this morning, even though she longed to see Ake. But this couldn't be helped. She had to get her car back.

A few relentless snowflakes fell here and there as she made the corner of Calvert's Grill. She shivered and resisted the urge to barge through and soak up the warmth. Instead she lowered her head and kept walking. Some twenty minutes later, she swung into the shop. This time the place was empty of customers.

She stood a few moments at the door just breathing in warm air. Shaking off the cold, she stomped her new white boots and stepped to the counter. The door to her right swung open before she could even press the buzzer.

"Afternoon." Young Ray sauntered to the counter with a huge smile.

"Hello. I'm here to pick up—"

"The beige Saturn Ion." He held up the keys with one finger through the keyring. "Got it all ready. Even vacuumed the interior, topped off the fluids, and filled her with gas."

She squelched a rude noise burst. And how much would she pay for that? She pulled the keys from his hand.

"On us, of course. For your inconvenience." He stepped to the cash register and punched in the number from the yellow form in his hand. "If you'll sign here, and pay this, it's all yours."

Her purse. She'd walked right out without it. Her mouth dropped open. "I can't believe I've done this, but I forgot to bring my money."

His brows lifted.

She met his questioning eyes. "I...could I just drive it home and pick it up? I promise I'll be right back."

"I suppose I could do that. If the price were right."

Her eyes flared. What was he pulling now? "What do you mean?"

A smile lit his face. "Dinner and a movie? You never answered earlier."

Oh great. Bargain Bob, glad to do anything for you with plenty of invisible strings. She glanced outside. The snow had picked up. "It's not really ethical, is it?"

He laughed. "I suppose not. But, we don't get too many gorgeous women in here, and I can't resist your charms."

Oh, brother. She blinked and set her mouth in a line. Fine. Dinner and movie, period. It would save her a long walk in the snow, and this creep would have to pay for the food and entertainment. Perhaps she'd order filet mignon or lobster.

The smile she pulled was stiff. "I guess it's the least I can do for a favor."

He nodded. "Great. How about Saturday?"

She clamped her hand on the keys and headed for the door. Maybe she'd stand him up. That might be fun. "Sure."

"It's out front to the right on the side of the building—"

The door clipped the rest of his sentence while she hurried to her little car. The vinyl seat greeted her with an icy firmness. But she didn't care as she eased the vehicle from the lot. Being out of the wind was blessed Heaven. It didn't take long to ride across town on Firestones and retrieve her purse.

When she arrived back at the shop, disappointment filled her to see Ray's Auto Body's friendly neighborhood flirt master in charge of the gray counter. She harrumphed as she pulled herself from the car and tramped toward the glass office.

"That didn't take long. You must live nearby."

Smooth as a laxative. "Yes, on Shore Drive."

She pulled her bank card from her purse and handed it to him.

He swiped it and returned it. "So Saturday. Six okay?"

Her mind spun on how she nailed the time in her mythical conversation. "Actually..."

"We can do five, or even seven."

Her chest swelled with an impatient breath. "Fine. Seven."

She left her address with him, all the time wondering why. It wasn't a sin to date the man, but it sure put her on a similar track of where she'd been. It left a sour taste. With a last wave she hurried from the waiting room and got in her car. When she lifted her eyes, he stood at the door. She shoved the keys into the ignition and started the motor, anxious to be away as quick as possible.

What had she done? And why? She hammered the heel of her hand into her forehead. Man, she was thick. How could she have a lower interest in this man? And there were now prerequisites. She rolled her eyes. Snap.

The car slid to a stop in her driveway, and she wasted no time getting inside. It wasn't like she had to marry the guy. A simple date. Then finito, over, see-ya-later, Charlie. Yep. She could handle that. *2 Timothy 2:22.*

She dismissed it from her mind. Instead, she'd find a new recipe and try it out. Definitely more pleasant.

⇜ ⋯⋯ ⇝

"Ma, must we always listen to Christmas music? For Pete's sake, it's Thanksgiving for crying out loud." Hoge's voice rang out over the table.

Pop chimed in. "For Pete's sake."

Ake grinned as he glued his eyes to the sweet potato casserole on his stoneware plate. Wouldn't do for Hoge to see him grinning. Every year was the same.

"Now, Hoge. Don't you get all sideways now. It's the beginning of the holiday season."

"And it's tradition." Mom's sister, Phoebe, tweaked her fork in the air to give her point an extra emphasis.

Mom's brother, Ralph and his wife, Donna, chuckled at the usual turn of conversation. Hoge harrumphed, and Ake let his eyes settle on the Christmas tree straight in his line of sight in the living room from the far end of the table.

"I like it, Grandma." Hoge's youngest at five, Lucy, wreathed in smiles and curling blond hair, stuck up for her grandmother.

Ake's mom laughed and patted the kindergartener's hand. "I knew I could count on you, Lucy. Now, you remember when you're a grown-up lady to have your Christmas music on when you put on your Thanksgiving meal. And always have your tree up."

Lucy's smile widened, and she sought Ake's eyes. He winked.

"Ma, please. Don't force that nonsense on my daughter." Hoge groused.

Mom just laughed, but her face sobered when Pop stood. He didn't move, just stood there. Ake rose as well. "I'll get him, Mom."

"Thank you, Ake."

Linus, Hoge's oldest, took the distraction as an excuse to leave the table and isolate himself in the living room with his phone. Ake tried to catch his eye to give an encouraging grin, but the boy ignored him. Deacon and Crew, Hoge's two middle boys, seemed bent on poking one another hard enough to unseat the other. With a sigh Ake guided Pop to the bathroom down the hall. As he waited outside the door, the conversation floated to his ears.

"...you don't say. Well I'm thrilled. 'Bout time that boy found himself a woman."

Hoge's huff sounded loud even down the hallway. "She isn't the woman for him. She's a citified floozy."

"Hoge." His mother's voice carried censure. "Be kind."

"I am telling it like it is. He's fascinated with her. She's all slicked up with her fancy hairstyle and expensive boots. For all I know, she's some kind of crazy Wiccan."

"What's that?" Phoebe's voice cut into the conversation.

Dad's flush inside the bathroom shut out the answer. The door flew open, and Pop stepped out. He turned and hiked down the hallway toward the dining room as if Ake weren't there. Like the invisible man, Ake followed.

"Are you dating a witch, Ake Pearson?" Phoebe's shocked eyes widened.

Ake settled into his chair and pulled it forward once his father was seated. "Ain't dating no one."

"Well, your brother said she's some kind of wicked woman."

"Wiccan, Phoebe." Mom corrected. She turned sympathetic eyes to his. Poor Mom. Always taking up for him.

Ake shook his head. "Not sure who you're talking about. Could you pass the stuffing?"

"Dummy, you know full well who we're talking about."

"Don't call your brother names." Pop preached with his finger directed at Hoge.

His brother paused only a moment. "Yeah, yeah, okay, Pop. We're talking about that wild woman at the harbor you talk to all the time."

Ake took his time spooning the homemade oyster stuffing onto his plate, feeling the eyes of the ten people at the table. Wishing to stop the silence, he shrugged. "I just talk to her. She's nice."

"I think it's lovely." Hoge's wife, Joni, chimed in, shooting daggers at her husband.

Hoge grumbled and went back to his mashed potatoes. Lucy grinned at him, and Ake's heart lifted. Mother's eyes lingered, studying, and Ake's lightened mood took a dive. She was worried. Phoebe saved the day.

"You remember Fred Havernam from high school, Maude? He was two years below you, four years below me. Done married him a Muzleem. Yep. Right there in front of God and everyone."

Thankful the conversation turned to another subject, Ake glanced out the dining room window. Snowing lightly again. Stormi's grey eyes invaded his thoughts. Much like the sky. He took a deep breath and spooned more stuffing into his mouth. Why they discussed his association with her puzzled him. A woman of her caliber would never be interested in him.

He turned his attention back to the ruckus at the table. Pop had spilled his drink. Mom and Phoebe leaped up to grab towels. Hoge's disgust with the get-together glared from his face. Pop stood and shuffled off into the living room. Even though the holidays still had some of the same elements of the years before, it wasn't quite the same.

Chapter Seven

Stormi eyed the buffet restaurant through the rain-soaked windshield. Was she kidding?

"Park over there. Not here." Her mother's voice soured. "Over there. I knew I should have driven."

Her mother swung from the vehicle, slammed the passenger door, and opened an umbrella.

"Happy Thanksgiving," Stormi muttered to the empty interior of the car. With a sigh she grabbed her purse from the backseat and exited the car. Her mother had already entered the restaurant which had quite a crowd for a national holiday of home cooking. Stormi parked her purse on her head to shield herself from the rain and hurried to the front door.

She was soaked by the time she entered and spotted her mother at the cash register. With an impatient wave, Stormi rushed to catch up.

"You'll have to pay for your own. I don't have much money this week. ShaVonn always tries to make me pay." Mom grabbed a black tray. "Decaf coffee."

Stormi pulled a tray from the stack and collected napkin-covered silverware. She ordered a soft drink and paid for her meal. Mom had already selected a booth in the far room.

"My turn." Mother swished by.

Stormi reached the table, sat, and bowed her head. After she'd thanked God for her food, she prayed for the energy and patience to endure Mother's holiday hysterics. Lucky ShaVonn. Ensconced in her mother-in-law's luxurious home, enjoying a deli-baked turkey and the fixings. Still, when her sister did show up, she would face Mother's ever frothing jealousy that ShaVonn loved her mother-in-law more. That miserable exhibition would take up most of the evening meal from the local fried chicken establishment in town. At least they had good coleslaw.

Her mother returned to the table and Stormi left, feeling guilty for enjoying the separation from her. Nevertheless, when her plate was filled, she meandered back to the table, wondering what avenue her mother would take to berate her on this trip.

"Really, Stormi. Can't you shorten your bangs? They're in your eyes. You should get a sensible cut, like a pageboy, or a shag."

"Shags went out in the nineties."

Her mother drew up her body, and her face contorted into a stiff mask. "They did not. My hairdresser gives shags all the time. Just like Florence Henderson. And she was famous."

Stormi glanced to her mother's hair which was dyed too dark for her age. It brought out the wrinkles on her face and made her appear pale. And considering her ancient stylist, it was no wonder she still gave shags. All of her patrons paid their weekly bills with their Social Security checks.

"I'll check into it, Mother."

"I could ask Maxine to trim it. I bet she could fit you in for a good cut."

A shiver chased its way down Stormi's spine. "I'm leaving tomorrow."

"Yes, and why, I ask you. You just got here."

Stormi wanted to stand and sing in opera, "Because of your lovely ambiance, Mother dear." But she froze into a shadow of herself to keep her sanity. "I know. I'm sorry."

"Well, you should be. I have no idea why you moved so far away. What were you thinking?"

The opera continued in Stormi's mind. *Because I must breathe fresh air untainted by your negativity.* Instead she said, "I know. I'm sorry."

"You are always sorry. But you're never here when I need you."

"Again, sorry."

"Is that all you're eating? You've always been too thin."

Mother proceeded to continue the discussion of how ShaVonn had failed her as a daughter, and how Stormi, although bright, raced down a similar path.

Stormi studied the people around her as her mother continued to point out her various flaws, lauding her cures to fix the entire situation. And the mental opera soon turned quite repetitive into, "Lord, deliver me from this day."

The evening meal with ShaVonn and her family didn't improve the general theme of the Thanksgiving extravaganza. Over a bucket of the colonel's extra crispy, Stormi had to revisit the same opera house, with practically the identical performance as lunch. It turned out to be a short visit, for ShaVonn soon had enough of Mother's thick layer of guilt and packed her two kids and husband up in the car and drove away.

Mother left shortly, leaving Stormi alone in the small dank house. She sighed. It was just as well. In her room she rested on the floor under the same window she'd sought sanctuary as a child. The temperature in the room chilled her as there was no heat source in this section of the dumpy house. Just like old times. Too much freaking like old times.

She rose, dressed for bed, and then snuggled under a mound of blankets on one of the single beds. Another glorious holiday. She squinted her eyes closed and began to pray for everyone on her prayer list, putting her mother at the top. Mother had done the best she could, she supposed, and Stormi was thankful for her raising.

Stormi fingered the still-swollen piercing on the right side of her mouth. It seemed most resistant to healing. A little like her. *Help me heal, Lord. And help me love those who don't know how to love.*

⤬ ⸱⸱⸱⸱⸱ ⤬

Stormi glanced up at Ray over the goblet of water. The restaurant's dim interior failed to hide the burgundy silk tablecloths and the golden silverware. She ran her finger around the golden trim on her salad plate.

"Yeah, once I graduated from the University of Florida, I decided to come back home. You know, take over the family business scenario."

Stormi took a deep breath. Could the night get any longer?

"Had a lot of great times at UF. Wow." He laughed and spun the vodka glass on the dark ring on his gold placemat. "I could have stayed in college forever."

He raised his glass and took a swig. His second drink. And he drove. Nervousness spun in her belly. Everything screamed too familiar. His cocky glances. The bragging. The alcohol. Ray held up his empty decanter and motioned to the white-shirted waiter as he passed.

Stormi stood. "I need to visit the ladies room. Excuse me."

She felt him turn to ogle her from behind, and she let out a groan. The waiter passed her with the clear, one hundred proof vodka bottle, and it was all she could do not to head to the exit. Instead she pushed the heavy cherry door of the ladies lounge open and bellied up to the mirror. Toilets flushed in the room beyond, but here in the small powder room decorated in floral, she stood alone. Thank God.

She set her silver glittered purse on the counter and examined herself in the mirror. Why had she agreed to this date? Had she lost her mind? She settled into the busy floral chair and tucked her legs into the long ruffles at the bottom. She pulled out her phone. Poor Alan. About to get another earful.

Ake Pearson's face skittered across her thoughts. How much more pleasant it would be sitting on a freezing bench exchanging conversation with her dark-eyed friend. She wondered if he even possessed a cell phone. Probably not. A grin tugged at the corner of her mouth. He seemed much too fundamental for that. A man's working man. And there was no denying he worked hard with his big rough hands and muscle-swollen shoulders.

She twisted her lips to the side. Who knew she'd be such a fan of a blue collar bear? Suddenly she wished she could call him. Just to talk. Hear him laugh. No snide comments, no hidden agenda, just pure sweet togetherness. She glanced at her reflection. What a nut. She must be lonely or something to crave such a connection.

Several women walked through the room to exit, and Stormi rose. She fluffed her hair and stared at herself in the mirror. *Don't be an idiot. Go finish this, whatever it was, and go home. And stop thinking about a man who barely graduated from high school.*

She patted her hair then rolled her eyes. Now she felt like a creep. Ake Pearson had proved to be a true friend and she had just slammed him. Thankfully, for once, she hadn't said it aloud. *Sorry, Ake. You're not a dummy. You're unique.* She blinked at herself for several minutes, wishing once again it were Ake at the table instead of Ray. With a sigh she picked up her purse and returned to the land of King Ray.

꒦ ⸱⸱⸱⸱⸱⸱ ꒷

Stormi hurried down the snowy sidewalk. She was late. Ake would already be gone for sure. She skipped the grill for now and headed straight for her usual bench. Excellent. Both *Sea Wheat* boats rested against the dock. The men appeared slower today. Perhaps the harsh drop in temperature had affected their usual enthusiasm. She seated herself on the bench, hoping Ake had not descended into the hull of the boat.

She began to lose hope however, when *Sea Wheat 2* headed out to the bay. Still a couple of canvas-covered men hobbled around the icy dock. One broke away and started up the steps. When he lifted his head, she met familiar eyes.

"Hi."

"Good morning." Her voice carried a little too much enthusiasm.

He perched on the end of the bench and held up a thermos. "I need to get some hot coffee. My coffee maker broke this morning."

"Oh, sorry."

He shrugged. "No big deal. The Grill opens early. I'll be back."

She chewed her chapped lips and then fished around in her pocket for some lip balm. The big man on the dock looked up and scowled. Ake's brother. Stormi wondered if he were irritated at Ake's absence. He turned away, and she shifted her eyes to the still blue water and gray sky. Hard to believe they would go out on such a cold day.

Ake returned and resumed his previous seat, presenting her with a cup. "Cherry coke?"

Pleased he'd remembered, she smiled and accepted the gift. "Oh, you didn't need to do that. But thanks."

He took a swig from his thermos. "Everything okay with you?"

"Sure."

He nodded and glanced down at the dock. "Have a nice Thanksgiving?"

Stormi swallowed. "Not really."

He turned to her. "Oh? Why?'

She shrugged. "Long story."

"Wish I could hear it."

The icy air invaded her neck, and she pulled up the hood. "Why?"

Ake set his eyes on the horizon. "Sometimes it helps to talk it out."

She nodded. "I suppose so. Except in my case."

He set his gaze on her and she felt a tug to continue. "My family put the capital D in dysfunctional."

His brows pulled together.

She waved a hand at him. "Suffice it to say, they have major issues."

"I see."

Two men broke away from the pack on the dock and hurried up the stairs. One big redhead with a huge beard and one dark haired man with thin lips and big gums. As he passed, big gums slapped Ake on the shoulders.

"Never going to happen, Dummy. Give it up."

The other man laughed and muttered something to the other.

Ake dipped his head and then lifted his gaze to the ocean view.

"What was that for?"

Silence met Stormi's ears which struck her as unusual. How she hated that nickname. Ake in his normal habitat just spoke his mind. But something seemed to have stopped it up.

"Ake?"

His eyes fastened on hers. "Nothing. They're just teasing me."

"About?"

He took a deep breath. "They think I want you as my girlfriend."

A laugh burst from her, but his lowered head frightened the mirth away. "I'm sorry. I'm not laughing about that, really, just it sounds like high school."

Ake gave a small smile. "Yeah."

The sadness written on his face sobered her. "Really, Ake. I wasn't laughing at the thought of us being boyfriend and girlfriend."

He nodded. "It's okay. I only had one date my Senior Prom. Hoge found a girl to go with me, but she said it wasn't like that either. She did it as a favor. I understand."

Fury and sorrow fought a battle in Stormi, and she shoved her mittened hands into her pockets. The men returned from the grill with hot drinks, pounding Ake on the shoulder again and laughing. It took a large amount of control not to knock those two down the stairs. When the two men made it to the dock, one of them handed a Styrofoam cup to Ake's brother. More scowls.

What complete blockheads. As if Ake didn't deserve a normal blissful life of marriage and a family. A perfect plan began to formulate in her mind. "You know. We could pretend."

"Huh?"

"We could give them a real show. Shut them up for good."

Ake's eyes crinkled. "I don't follow you."

She scooted closer and shot him a grin. "We could pretend we were together. A couple. Then they wouldn't tease you."

He shook his head with a start of a smile. "I'm not much into pretending."

"It wouldn't be complicated." Brilliance lightened her demeanor. She arched closer and tilted her head coquettishly, the flirt that never failed to provoke a man's attention. "You wouldn't have to say anything about us. You could just shrug it off. Or just smile. What's between a man and a woman is private, after all."

His dark eyes, open and trusting, glued to hers. "I don't know how that would work."

"I do. We could kiss."

Chapter Eight

A ke's mouth fell open. "What?"

She giggled. It was perfect. "Right here, right now."

He swiped the heavy stubble on his chin. "I'm not sure what to say."

"Come closer." She patted the spot next to her. Without a word, he rose and obeyed. He appeared much larger beside her. A man's man. She rested her hand on his arm. "Okay, now, we'll just stay close a minute, make sure they are watching. We'll lean forward intimately, gradually. Like two lovers. And then, we'll kiss."

His gaze went to the dock. His fingers gripped the thermos. "Listen, I'm not too good at the kissing thing."

She laughed. "It'll be just a normal kiss."

A grin tugged at the corner of his mouth. "My normal kiss is a peck to my mom's head. Is that what you're talking about?"

With a giggle she pulled the thermos from his hand and set it on the bench. "No, silly. A real kiss. A man-to-woman kiss."

His face grew serious. "Can't say I'm familiar with that."

"What? You've never kissed a woman?" Was he joking? A smile crept across her face.

"No."

Her grin disappeared. "Never?"

"No."

"Oh. I—" What to say to that? "Do you want to?"

From the way he was examining her lips, she knew she had her answer. "Okay, put your arm over my shoulder here."

She worked his heavy arm around her back. Hey, if this man wanted to know how to give a romantic kiss, he'd come to the right gal. And boy, would she play it up. "Perhaps you could put your other hand here, on my cheek."

"Uh-huh."

"And then we look deep into each other's eyes for a moment and—" Before she could finish her coaching, his lips latched on hers, warming, exploring. It caught her off-guard, but she soon rose to the challenge and pulled him into her embrace, teaching him the fine art of lip-locking. Just for good measure she slipped her hand from her mitten and looped her fingers into the locks of hair at the nape of his neck.

For someone with zero experience, he took to it like a pro. The smell of his clean male skin combined with the firm pressure of his lips mixed up some kind of witches' brew that she drank in like an intoxicating beverage. Sweet passion nudged her as his beard brushed against her skin.

The kiss deepened, and Stormi could sense his urgency. Her own yearnings needed a hose down, as well. They had to come up for air and cool this train off. She wrenched her lips from his. He sat there pressing against her, mouth parted, eyes trained on her face with open desire. She swallowed. Intense longing urged her for an instant replay. Wow. So much for pretense.

"Okay, now we ease apart." She positioned her hands against his chest to get him to move. "A—part."

He edged backwards, his hungry gaze never leaving hers. The air almost pulsated between them.

"And that's how you do it." Stormi licked her lips. Reality check. Just helping the guy out. Yet, somehow she felt like she'd stolen a juice box from a child.

He gave a slight nod.

"See, look. They saw." She jerked her head toward the dock which detached his gaze from her face.

"Uh-huh."

All three men stood staring. Hoge's mouth hung open. Ake, however, didn't seem very thrilled with it. He lowered his head.

"Ake?"

"Yeah?"

A shiver of regret slithered through her body. *Don't get carried away. Keep it in teacher/student mode.* "Let's stand and give one last kiss."

"Huh?"

"Stand. Here's your thermos."

The man stood and worked his way toward the steps. Stormi followed. "Now, true lovers would give a parting kiss."

He paused obediently. She snuggled herself into the cove of his body. All she had to do was put a little frosting on the cake. Nothing wrong with that. "Like this."

Not much conversation proceeded from his mouth, but he nodded, his dark eyes probing her face. His solemnness made her attempt some humor.

She gave a small laugh. "You look as if I'm torturing you. Am I torturing you?"

"No."

"Upsetting you?"

"No."

The canvas of his jacket scraped against her cheek. "Put your arm around me again. That's it. Now we—"

"I think I got it."

His lips covered hers once more. Gently, like a caress. Ake's powerful arms cradled her and bent her body slightly backwards. Yes, he was a quick study. Maybe not as iconic as V-J Day in Times Square, but definitely classy. She let herself relax and sighed, ecstasy radiating through her body. How lovely it would be to complete the rhapsody. Glide along on the pleasure of his maleness, so defined, so—his lips left hers.

"See ya." Ake breathed.

He tromped down the stairs before she could try to decipher the expression on his face. The men leaped aboard the *Sea Wheat 1* and set it into motion. Just as they reached the mouth of the bay, one man came to the stern of the boat and raised his left arm. Ake. Stormi gave a small thoughtful smile as she waved back. She took a deep gulp of icy air. Somehow the whole plan curdled her stomach. She'd relished his kiss, yet had she helped him? Or hurt him?

ꙮ ⋯⋯ ꙮ

Ake stared at the gash in his forearm. He'd been foolish to reach out while the winch sucked in the netting. The metal edge had sliced him open. Hoge was there in a moment with gauze and wrappings, stemming the bleeding.

Hoge flung commands at the men behind him. "Turn the boat back to the harbor, Delbert. Double Goose, bring in the net."

His brother pushed him to the side of the boat, away from the winch.

"We can't go in. We're not done."

"You are." He barked. "What were you thinking, Dummy? You've been doing this since you were in diapers. That broad's got you messed up."

Ake couldn't answer that given there was much truth to it. Hoge wrestled him to the bench.

"Durn it, Dummy, sit down."

"I ain't no kid, Hoge."

His brother slapped a hand to his forehead. "Don't you know you could've yanked your arm plumb off? How long do you think I could keep you alive then, Ake. Huh?"

Ake pressed a hand to the red spot blooming through the bandages. "It's just a cut. Not a big deal."

"Are you joking me? That's going to need a hundred stitches."

Hoge disappeared into the wheelhouse and brought out more bandages. Ake glanced about at the other three men whose usual banter had disappeared. They scurried about, finishing the catch, casting uneasy eyes at the pair of them. What trouble he'd caused. Hoge crouched before him and pressed more gauze squares to the cut.

"I'm sorry, Hoge."

The big man shook his hooded head. "I know."

Then his brother leaped up. "Get this doggone boat turned home. Cut the net if you have to, let's go."

The vessel's engines cut and reversed. The cold air on Ake's numb cheek only served to remind him that he'd failed his brother again. He turned his eyes to the horizon and began to pray.

ꕥ ⋯⋯ ꕥ

Stormi gave a muffled scream. This laptop was junk. Her entire podcast was lost somewhere either in cyberspace or hidden on that stupid hard drive. She stood and shoved the chair. It tumbled to the ground. Grrr. Nothing had gone right today. Ever since she'd given a little kissing conference with

Ake, her entire day had gone from bad to worse. Her burger had no cheese, she'd tripped on the sidewalk and skinned up her knee, and she'd dropped her keys three times at the door. Man, she was afraid to leave the house.

She drifted over to the stool at the kitchen counter and parked herself. Ake. He'd been on her heart all day. Like an ache. A first kiss shouldn't be falsified. She'd taken that from him. What kind of lowlife did that? Only she knew the answer too well. With a groan she planted her head in her arms. It had started out as a game, giving up a pawn to capture the queen. Only, she'd injured the pawn.

She stood and paced. How could she fix this? From her perspective, it was simple. Just fake it, put them off the scent, move on. But from his viewpoint, it was so much more. How had a simple kiss mutated into destroying an innocent man?

At one college frat party, she and Marla had made a pact to French as many guys as they could. A little contest for their warped world. She'd won. A hundred and seventeen, and spent the night with the last one.

She clamped her hands to her head. There were certain things she wanted to forget. That was one of them. Poor Ake. Blessedly innocent. Charmingly eager. The room closed in like claustrophobia. She'd dodge death if she had to, but she had to get out. After pulling on her gear, she set a smart gait towards the corner grill.

Her guilt hammered her. This icy sidewalk was the perfect revenge. She needed to fall all over again. Bang her head. Be knocked unconscious. She deserved it.

Once she reached the bottom of Blackberry Hill, right before she crossed over, she caught sight of the *Sea Wheat 1* docked below. Ake's brother stepped to the top step near her bench. He froze when he saw her.

"You."

She stopped. Great. She wouldn't go down in a horrific anonymous fall. Instead she'd be bludgeoned to death by this brute. Fine. So be it.

"Delbert, take him in your truck. I'll be there in a minute."

Across the street four men walked towards the parking lot. One of them was Ake. They got in a white double cab truck and exited.

She stepped up to the tall man. "Yes?"

He looked nothing like Ake. Not one bit. Brown hair, green eyes, wooly beard embracing what could only be a stubborn chin.

"Leave my brother alone. Got it?"

Her brows rose and she stifled a harrumph. "I'll give the usual he-man woman-hater's reply, just to please you and fit in. *Says who*?"

"Oh, I know about women like you. You take a man, and you stomp him."

This time the snort didn't obey, and it flew right out of Stormi's mouth. "What are you talking about?"

"My brother, dimwit. Stay away from him."

He went to leave, but she grabbed his heavy jacket. "Excuse me, but your brother is old enough to decide for himself who he wants to be around."

The man seemed to grow several inches as he inhaled. "Now, I'm going to tell you this once and once only. My brother isn't like other men. He's...different."

Fury froze her face. "You mean, a *dummy*?"

Answering rage rose in his eyes. "Now, look here—"

She stretched herself to her full height and barely measured up to his chin. But it didn't matter. Her sense of guilt grew her well over six feet. "No. You listen. How dare you call your own brother by such a derogatory name? He's not different. He's a man. And you treat him like a circus freak. What makes you believe that you know what's best for him?"

He stepped away, hatred plain on his face. "All I know is, you kiss him, and now he's in the ER."

Stormi blanched, all bravado gone. For a moment the world spun. "What?"

The man spun and strode to a big red pickup with dually rear tires. Stormi lost no time and sprinted toward him, but he sprang in the driver's seat. She yanked at the locked passenger door and then banged on the window. The look he gave told her he wouldn't be opening it anytime soon. With a grit of her teeth, she took advantage of the truck's pause while Hoge switched the gear into drive. She planted her booted foot on the running board and swung aboard the truck bed.

At the exit of the parking lot, the truck came to a jolting stop. The door opened, and he appeared at the cab's back window.

"Get out."

She shook her head.

"I said, get out of my truck."

With her mittened hands she grabbed the rope in the truck bed and wrapped it around her. "You can throw me out if you want, but I'll find the hospital."

He stood there a moment. Something flickered in his gaze. Without a word he jumped into the truck and off they went. Stormi slammed against the tailgate as the truck's wheels spun and threw stones. She clutched the top, hoping to avoid being flung to the front of the truck when he stopped. No doubt he'd make her pay.

Suddenly the truck slowed and then braked. She closed her eyes and gripped the tailgate. He came around the bed of the truck. Okay, she'd wanted a head injury earlier. Here it came. The tailgate lowered. There he stood, hands on hips.

He closed his eyes. "I shouldn't have done that. It's just..."

She wedged her body up, rubbing a bruise on her knee.

"He's my brother, you know. I've been looking out for him for years." He looked off to the left. Then hung his head, reminding her of Ake.

"I need to see him," she whispered.

He nodded. "Get in the truck."

She shook her head. "You'll leave me."

"No, I won't. I promise."

All fury gone, his earnest face convinced her he told the truth. Without a word she stepped down with his helping hand. He slammed the tailgate shut and thumbed the clicker to unlock the door for her to enter the passenger's seat.

When he slid into the driver's seat, she stilled him with a hand to his arm. "I'm sorry I caused hurt to Ake. He doesn't deserve it."

He clenched his jaw and shoved the vehicle into drive.

Chapter Nine

Ake's pale face and bandaged arm smote Stormi once he came through the emergency door. It was all she could do not to break down and sob like a three-year-old on the first day of preschool. His crooked grin also nearly undid her, but he seemed genuinely glad to see her. Hoge went to the desk to straighten out insurance, and the three stooges left to finish taking care of the boat.

Despite her resolve, tears filled her eyes. "Oh, Ake. I'm so sorry. This is all my fault."

He shook his head. "It's not your fault. I reached out too far. It happens."

She searched her pockets for a tissue but came up empty.

"Here." Ake handed her a red paisley handkerchief.

A handkerchief? Red, just like her grandfather used to carry. Her sniffles doubled in intensity, and she felt his arm wrap around her.

"I'm fine. It's just a few stitches." He held up his bandaged arm.

She nodded at his simple explanation, his offer of comfort. He consoled her. Crazy backwards. "I'm just making this worse."

Laughter came from Ake's deep chest. "You could never do that."

Hoge walked up. "Come on. They've given you some powerful meds. I don't want to have to carry you into that pole barn you call home."

Ake laughed, and the three of them exited through the sliding glass doors. Somehow on the way, Stormi talked her way into riding all the way to Ake's house tucked behind his parents' older home on the edge of town.

Once inside Hoge eyed her. "Listen. I'm only leaving you here because he's about to be toast. And you owe him."

"Hoge." Ake protested.

"Shut up. I'll be waiting in the truck for you." He pointed at Stormi as if committing a sentence of jail time.

She nodded. No time to argue. The door slammed shut and she spun. "Are you really going to be okay?"

"Yeah." He grinned. "I won't be falling asleep anytime too soon either if you want to stay."

"Ake, they gave you painkillers at the ER."

He laughed and pulled his hand from his pocket. "You mean these?"

Her mouth fell open. "Young man, you take those right now."

His grin widened. "I'm twenty-eight. How old are you?"

"Twenty-five."

"I win."

Her brow furrowed and she chewed her lip. "Really, Ake. I think it's best to take them."

He shrugged. "Maybe later."

"How many stitches?"

With a sigh he stretched out on the couch. "Fifty-nine."

"Fifty-nine!"

His head flew back in laughter. "That's nothing. Mom told me I had a hundred and twenty on the backside of my head when I was a kid."

She drew closer and perched on the old wooden rocker. "What happened?"

He took a sip from a water bottle Hoge had left for him. "Don't remember."

"What do you mean you don't remember? How could you forget one hundred and twenty stitches?"

A honk sounded from outside. "Hoge will be back in like a hornet if you don't head out."

She glanced toward the door then around the room. The large room combined well with the open kitchen. Very neat and simple. Perfect for Ake. "Do you need anything?"

"Nope."

"Are you sure?"

His white teeth shone from his wide smile. "I'm a big boy, Stormi."

She swallowed. Yes. There was no doubt of that. Ake was all man. "Okay. Promise you'll take those meds?"

"I will if I need them."

"Please, Ake. Don't make me crazy."

"Fine. I'll take them. See?" He tossed the two pills into his mouth and washed them down with a gulp of water. "Happy?"

"Immensely." Another honk made her stand. "I better go. I've already faced the wrath of the mutant gorilla once today."

Ake's brow drew together.

Whoops. She shouldn't have brought that up. "Anyway, I'll stop by again once you've had some rest."

"Promise?"

"Of course." She pulled the door shut only to come face to face with the overgrown, angry primate, otherwise known as Hoge.

"What took so long?"

She shrugged, slipped by him, and hurried to the truck. He stomped behind her and got in the driver's seat. "Oh, don't think we're done. You're going in that house and explaining this whole thing to my mother."

"What? I don't even know what happened. And I've never even met your mother."

"It doesn't matter." He slung the gearshift into drive, and they flung snow up the grade to the house on the hill. He exited the truck, came around, and yanked her door open.

"Out."

She unfastened her seatbelt and slid to the snow. She'd do it for Ake. Face the wrath of Mom. He clutched her arm as if she would flee and escorted her up the back walk to the wooden steps. Without a knock, he swung in.

"Mother. Visitors."

A tall elderly woman appeared at the door. Great. Ake's mother was old. *Old.* Her face opened in a sweet smile, her green eyes welcoming. A weird sort of twist knotted up Stormi's stomach.

"Hoge. What a treat. I haven't seen you since Thanksgiving. And who's this?"

"It's *her.*"

Something akin to puzzlement skittered across her face. Then she shook her head. "I'm sorry, dear. You'll have to be more specific."

"Ake's witch."

Stormi sucked in air like a gasp.

A sternness crossed the gentle face in front of her. "Hogan Daniel Pearson, what a thing to say."

A shadow fell across the doorway behind her.

"Stop calling your brother names."

Hoge gave an exaggerated sigh. "Yeah, yeah, sorry, Pop. Mom, this is that woman I told you about."

But the sternness never left those green weathered eyes. "We'll not talk any further, Son, until you apologize to this young lady."

"Ma—"

The woman displayed a jaw of iron and crossed her arms across her chest and whispered. "Now, Son."

Hoge gulped a huge breath. "I'm sorry I called you a witch. Can we stop pretending I'm a child now?"

The smile returned to the older woman's face, and she grasped Stormi's hands. "Since he won't grow up enough to give a proper introduction, I'll do it myself. I'm Maude Pearson, Hoge and Ake's mother."

"Nice to meet you. I'm Stormi Zobroski."

"If we're done with the niceties, how about you tell her about Ake's ER visit?"

The woman's face crumpled. "What? Oh, Hoge."

But the big man pointed to Stormi. What a wimp. "It's fine. He cut his arm on the boat, somehow. But he's fine. Nothing to worry about."

"Hoge?"

"On the winch. Because of her, his brain was disengaged."

Stormi could feel the woman trembling. "Stop Hoge. You're scaring your mother."

"Well, tell her why he injured himself." Hoge crossed himself with those thick arms.

The older woman pulled away. "I've got to go to him. Stay with your father."

Hoge moved to stop her. "No, Ma. He's fine."

The woman went to the back door, pulled on her boots, and grabbed an old coat from a hook. "I'll be just a minute."

"Mom. It's slick. You'll fall."

As if Maude Pearson had muted her older son, she wrenched the door open and stepped through.

Hoge tailed his mother, stopped at the door, and then pointed at Stormi. "This is your fault. Durn it. I'm driving her down there. Stay with Pop. Don't let him out and don't let him burn the house down."

The door shut in her face. Sensing a presence behind her, she spun. A hunched elderly gentleman stood there.

"Tell the boys it's too cold to play outside." He stood and stared at her.

Stormi glanced around the kitchen, unsure what to do. "All right."

He seemed to be satisfied with that and turned to disappear down the hall.

No, she'd changed her mind. She deserved more than a simple head injury. Much more. A third-world disease, coma, and jail time. Far, far away from Hoge.

Stormi tapped her tooth with her forefinger. So the laptop cooperated today, but her brain did not. She stomped like a spoiled child and paced away. The last thing she wanted to do was be here. Doing this. Now. She tugged at the long spike of bangs. Navigating toward the lone window, a rush of cold air met her feet. But she ignored it and surveyed the snowy road instead.

If she remembered right, Ake's house was not terribly far. But she should call. And she didn't have his number. She face-palmed herself. It was the same loop she'd been on all morning. Like a bad computer program. She huffed, tramped to her inflated couch, and flopped down. Grabbing her phone she pressed the balloon to send a text.

Blather. Not what she wanted to do, and not with whom she wanted to do it. Alan would have good advice, true, but he couldn't give her updates on Ake. She sent an angry stream of air up and shot her bangs off her forehead. Surely he hadn't gone to work this morning. Or would that angry, immature brother of his force him? Oh, if he had, he was on the right road for a slap down, that was for sure.

She growled and rose. Fine. *Calm down.* She took a deep breath and eyed her boots. *Stop the loop and go.* In ten minutes she'd parked herself in the car and slid around the last curve to what she hoped was Ake's house. Those fear-packed reality shows needed to add navigating icy roads in a small four-cylinder car. Absolutely terrifying.

She slid to a stop against the huge snow bank to the side of Ake's garage. Thankful to have arrived, she eased from the car. Surveying the driveway, she knew she'd never get out of here till spring with her bumper embedded in the huge snow bank. But she was here now. She swung the door shut and hurried to the front door. Not a spot of snow graced the walk, therefore no impending head injury, she hoped.

After knocking for a full five minutes, her heart sank. He was gone. It played out in her head like a bad Shakespearean play. That dirty scoundrel Hoge had dragged poor injured Ake from his sick bed and put him on that dangerous icy boat. All this production needed to increase the drama were rats rife with bubonic plague, biting Ake as he pulled in the tangled net. She twisted her lips to the side. Okay, maybe the adding of the horrible disease went a little over the top. Still, it added a little humor to the dismal situation.

She spun and eyed her car, rubbing her hands up and down her thin leather jacket. Why she'd grabbed her old jacket, perfectly adequate in Georgia, but here, in the stinking Arctic Circle it was—

"Hey. Stormi. Up here."

From the back door of Maude Pearson's house came Ake. Had she ever been this glad to see someone?

"Ake." She jumped and waved. *Thank you, God, he's not on that boat.*

She maneuvered through the hard-crusted snow heaps with care, while he crunched right through. Soon he had his arm looped through hers.

"How's the injury?"

"It's good." He pulled her up the hill.

"It can't be good. They gave you more than fifty stitches."

He shrugged. "Yeah, but some inside, some out. It's not as bad as it sounds."

She realized they approached the house, and Maude Pearson stood at the back door. She waved. Stormi gave a small swipe of her hand. "I can't stay, Ake."

"Come on. She's got oatmeal. Always makes way too much oatmeal. We need someone else to eat it."

"Oatmeal? Bleck. I don't eat oatmeal."

He paused and gave her the once over. "You ever have it?"

Well, that would've required her mother to belly up to the stove in the last twenty-odd years, so no. That glop had never even been in a pot inside her childhood home. "No."

"Trust me. A little cinnamon, a little banana. Delish."

Once up the steps Maude drew her into the house and had a hot bowl of spiced oatmeal set in front of her in no time flat. And it was—edible. The texture could use a change, but watching Ake converse with his mother proved priceless. He'd definitely inherited his mother's positive spirit. Was she for real?

"It's delicious, isn't it?" He grinned.

She nodded.

"Oh, Ake, you do a heart good." The older woman rose with a laugh from the table and patted her son's arm. "I'd better check on your dad."

"What brings ya by?"

"You." She spooned another slimy spoon of oatmeal into her mouth. It did go down warm.

Ake grinned. "I told you I was fine."

"I figured that brother of yours had you out on the boat today."

He chuckled. "Hoge? Pshaw. His bark is worse than his bite."

"Still..." Stormi's belly filled with the warm mixture. "I could probably get used to this slimy goo, but the texture is a little weird."

"Pearson tradition. Mom makes it every morning."

She brought up her eyes. "Seriously?"

He grinned. "Yup. Pop has it every morning."

"That's a lot of oatmeal." She eyed the bandage on his left arm beneath the rolled cuff of his red flannel shirt. "Does it hurt?"

He cocked his head and shrugged. "Eh."

"Clearly, that's a, 'yeah.' Me and my stupid plan."

Ake's dark eyes caught hers. "I wouldn't take it back."

Stormi cleared her throat and abandoned the spoon. She sat back in her chair. "Yeah, but now, your Mom and brother, they all think—"

"Like you said, just shrug."

She assessed him. It was odd to see his thick arms and shoulders without a canvas covering. Somehow he didn't look much smaller. Without the beanie his features appeared even more charming, his hair lifting in slight waves curling here and there. He seemed more relaxed.

The starting beard on his face made Stormi think he hadn't shaved since before the injury. It made his jaw and cheeks look black like his eyes and hair. Ake was one handsome man. He grinned.

She raised a brow and shrugged. Time to change her thought pattern. "I think I'm stuck."

His face clouded. "Huh?

"My car."

He let his head roll back in understanding. "Oh. Yeah, you're not stuck."

She straightened. "I am. I tagged the snow bank."

"I'll get it out."

A burst of laughter popped from her lips. "I want to see that. You, wrestling the car above your head."

He stared at her a long time, and she returned the favor. "I like being around you, Stormi Zobroski."

There it was again. Just honesty. Had she ever known anyone so boldly honest? She smiled. His dark trusting eyes had no secrets. And she had to agree with him. She enjoyed being with him too. So refreshing. Which made faking it that much easier. "You think we just, you know, keep up the pretense? Show those idiot friends of yours they don't know everything?"

"Don't call your brother names," came Pop's voice from the living room.

Stormi burst out laughing. "I guess I've been told."

Ake grinned ear to ear, and she soaked in the pure companionship. Simple stuff. Precious togetherness. A laugh, a joke. Complete acceptance. Without her scraping her nails against the insurmountable wall of conditions and guilt. How she longed to embrace a life where people truly cared. Where things were honest and plain. A place where she'd fit in, acknowledged as a person of great value, no matter what. Gazing in Ake's eyes gave her an inkling that maybe such a life could be real.

❧ ⋯⋯ ❧

Somehow she'd overslept. But her podcast was finished and a relaxing Saturday stretched out before her. The early December wind whipped at Stormi's collar as she stepped into

Calvert's Grill on the corner. Hopefully a cheeseburger would get her back on track today. It had been a lazy morning.

The smell of fish wrapped around her as she bellied up to the worn butcher block counter and put in her order with Madge. She'd even earned a smile from the Brillo-headed woman. But Stormi had to admit, being referred to by name made you feel like you fit in.

Imagining all the stereotypes that had popped into her head when she'd burst through those doors, she racked her brain as to her own moniker. *Naughty girl turned nice*? A chortle almost burst from her. *Born-again bad girl*? Maybe. Anyway, she'd begun to fit into this strange neighborhood, and she welcomed it.

The bell clanged behind her, but she didn't bother to turn. It was probably toothless beer belly, or more accurately, Mitty, whose kids had swindled away most of his money. Poor guy. Several of the usual patrons nodded and waved. A large form settled beside her on the stool.

Madge circled, her gray countenance lightening. "Afternoon, Ake."

Stormi swung her head. Sure enough, Ake sat beside her, grinning. A full beard now bloomed on his jaw, but his furry face still held his genuine frankness.

"Two fried fish sandwiches, Madge, and hot coffee.

The waitress gave a smirk. "Big surprise. You've been ordering that since you were twelve."

She walked away thumping her pen to her order pad.

"Hello." Her greeting earned a hundred watt smile.

"Hi."

Handsome jobless Johnny, which Stormi now knew as Carl, an army vet with an artificial limb, addressed him from the other side of the u-shaped bar. "I saw on social media that your brother got a new couch. Joni seemed pretty happy."

Ake nodded. "Yep. That's what I'm doing now. Getting rid of the old one."

Madge harrumphed. "Tell that old Hoge to pitch it himself."

Ake shook his head. "Naw. I don't mind. Guess I'll take it to the Salvation Army and see if they'll take it."

"Yeah, I ditched my old recliner there," Carl returned.

"Not me," the weathered bleach-blond responded, whom Stormi now knew as Sheena, recovering addict. "I always have a big yard sale every year. Last year I earned seven hundred dollars."

Several let out low whistles and the advantages vs. disadvantages of yard sales continued across the way. Stormi focused her eyes on Ake, who was already assessing her.

"How's the arm?"

"Fine. Stitches are out. Good as new." He pulled his arm out of his thick coat and worked up his shirt sleeve. An angry red gash ran down the underside of his right forearm.

Stormi's stomach clenched. "That looks horrible, Ake. You shouldn't be lifting couches with it still looking raw."

He readjusted the material back over the wound. "The doc cleared me, so I figure I can do most things."

"Hoge with you?"

"Nope."

Madge brought her to-go sack and her Cherry Coke. She took Stormi's money and hiked back to the cash register.

Ake's brows descended. "You're not eating here?"

"I hadn't planned on it."

"Oh."

The sag of his shoulders was comical. She glanced around. How embarrassing would it be to unpack a to-go bag just to eat with Ake? The jukebox kicked on in the rear of the restaurant and the whine of a steel guitar filled the space.

"You could get yours to go, and we could head to my house to eat it." She kept her voice low, hoping to keep Mitty, Carl, Sheena, and Madge from adding their two cents.

His face brightened. "Okay."

Well, this had worked out nicely. She didn't have to trudge up Blackberry Hill against the wind. His sandwiches soon arrived, and they hopped down to head for the exit. Too late the thought came. What did everyone think of them leaving together? Perhaps it would add to the whole "relationship" thing. She couldn't help a glance behind her. Yes, several pairs of eyes were fastened on them. Yard sale conversations just got pitched out the door. She and Ake were sure to be the new topic.

Ake led her to his old black truck with an enormous couch in the bed. She thankfully scurried to the passenger side where he held the door. As he drove, wheels spun in her head. A couch? Hmmm.

Chapter Ten

"So, where are you taking this couch?"

He glanced at her before answering. "I thought I'd take it to the Salvation Army Store over in Fulbright. Why?"

"I...need a couch."

He pulled in her driveway and threw the gear into park. "No problem. I'll carry it in."

Her mouth dropped. "I can't just take your brother's couch."

"Why not?"

She sputtered, clutching her brown bag from the grill. "Well, I should pay for it or send a donation. I don't want to be a charity case. Besides, you shouldn't just lug that in by yourself."

He grinned. "You could help me."

For a moment she just stopped and took in his wholesome face with his cheerful smile and a dash of twinkle in his eye. He was really quite gorgeous with his dark eyes, hair, and beard. She'd pondered why he captivated her so much, and she hadn't settled on the exact reason yet.

She'd dated much more handsome men. Richer, more powerful men. Yet even now as she surveyed him, sipping on her cherry coke, her day had brightened as soon as he'd appeared. No one else had ever done that. She pushed it aside for more study and shot him a mock glare. "Me? I'm going to carry a couch?"

He reached over and squeezed her bicep. "Sure. No problem. The couch is a lightweight." His door protested in squeaky volume as he swung from the vehicle. He reappeared at her door and opened it. "But right now, we eat."

Stormi led Ake to the back and let them both in. Thankfully the place was clean. She dropped her keys and bag on the counter and removed her coat. He did the same. Thankful for the burgundy ribbed turtleneck and undershirt, she rubbed her upper arms in the chilly air.

"What is that?" He pointed to her couch and chair and then edged over to investigate.

"Oh. That's my current furniture."

His faced twisted comically. "They're like...balloons."

She laughed. "Yep. And they fit nicely at the dorm. But I think I've outgrown them."

He stabbed a finger at the vinyl. "This holds you up?"

"For the most part."

He grinned and turned to settle his large form in the center of the couch. Both ends curled up in rejection of all that weight. His laughter burst out. She hurried with her camera phone aloft. "Wait, wait. Don't get up. That's hilarious."

He sat inches from the floor with a huge smile on this face. She clicked several shots, giggling at his predicament.

"All right." He grunted. "Give me a hand."

She set the phone down and returned to pull him out with both hands. He rose on a chuckle. "Sure glad I didn't go to college if that's all they had."

"No, silly. That's just what I had. And it worked okay for me."

Giving the air furniture one last inspection and a shake of his head, Ake drifted over towards the two bays where the old garage doors still hung. "You sure have a lot of cold air coming in here. You need some insulation. With some two-by-fours and drywall, you could re-make this whole wall."

Stormi went to stand near him gawking at the far wall. "I suppose. But I wouldn't know how to do any of that."

"I do."

She patted his arm and turned to head back toward the counter. "You've got enough on your plate, Ake Pearson. Fishing, taking care of your parents, delivering couches."

"It wouldn't take long."

The plates clattered together as she pulled them down from the only overhead cabinet. "I suppose, if one knew how."

He rotated and came to stand beside her. "Well, I do. We could knock out that project in a weekend or two."

She blinked at him. "I couldn't ask you to do that."

"You didn't ask." He grinned and settled on a stool. "I like your place. Nice and open."

"Yeah. It's a caveman's dream, I suppose." She settled her form close to him and unwrapped her sandwich.

"You want me to ask the blessing?"

For a moment she said nothing. Then, dawning washed over her. "Oh, sure. The prayer."

"Father, thank you for this food you've given us, amen." He pushed his wrapper aside and took a bite.

Lovely to have someone to pray beside you. Even such a simple prayer. A pleasant sensation swelled within Stormi's chest.

Ake chewed and swallowed. "Anyway, my mom said this used to be the old garage when she was little. Duckett's Garage. Her dad, my grandpa, used to get his car serviced in here. I guess it went through several owners, and then it went out of business. Finally someone just sided it over and turned it into a house. Never would've guessed that the garage doors were still in here."

"Yeah well, I wished they would have put in a front door. What house doesn't have a front door?"

"We could do that, too."

She took a swig of drink before answering. "What?"

Ake tore into his second sandwich. "We could insulate, drywall, and add a front door."

"No, Ake. Too much work." She rose and tossed the remains of her lunch in the trash.

"It would be a lot warmer. And it would make the house have more value if you decide to sell."

Her face quirked. "Why would I sell?"

"Just in case."

She shrugged. "I don't know."

"Well," he crumbled up the paper and washed the last of his lunch down with coffee, "let's start with the couch and maybe I'll talk you into it."

Ake had been right. She carried her side of the couch without any difficulties. Deflating the blow-up couch was exhilarating. Her new denim-covered couch showed a little wear, but overall looked clean and comfortable. She flopped on it. "Oooh. Snuggly."

He grinned and sat next to her. "Yeah, and look. Both ends stay on the ground."

She laughed.

"I've taken a lot of naps on this couch and can tell ya that it's pretty cozy."

The soft denim nearly matched the jeans she wore, and she pressed herself against the back cushion. Somehow knowing Ake had napped here made her like it even more.

"Now, the wall."

She groaned. "You're not going to leave this alone, are you?"

"Nope."

"Do you really know what you're doing?" She shot him a look.

"I built my own house."

Well, that did carry some weight. "The whole thing?"

"Yep."

She studied his face. "You're an interesting person, Ake."

His face contorted. "What do you mean?"

With a shrug she sat up to face him. "You know. Once you told me you struggled in school. Yet, you know all about fishing and built your own home."

He stared at the empty fireplace. Was he embarrassed? She reached up and turned his face to hers. "That's something to be proud of."

ఌ ⋯⋯ ಌ

Ake stared into her stormy eyes. This was exactly why he couldn't get her out of his mind. Everyone else treated him like—well, a dummy. But she always pointed out how smart he was. And for the life of him, he had no idea how she did that. But he soaked up the admiration in her eyes. "God's given everyone different talents."

Her eyes grew misty, and she dropped her hands. She bounced from the couch and turned around several times. Finally she blurted out. "I'm a Christian."

Fire snapped from her eyes. Passion flared from her hands, those small hands. She seemed to be waiting for something. "Okay."

"Ake!"

His gaze went back to hers. "Yeah?"

"Are you?"

"Of course. Since I was a small kid."

She pulled her hands in and crossed them over her middle, tugging the end of her sleeves over her hands. "Oh. I—just became one. Well, I mean, just a few months back."

He rose and grinned. "That's great. You want to join me for church tomorrow?"

A quirk started at the side of her mouth. "I've been meaning to find a place. So...yeah."

"Cool." He gestured to the far wall. "Now, if we get the supplies, we could start tonight. We've got a long winter coming up."

She walked to him and reached a hand up to tug on his beard. He flicked his brows. "What was that for?"

"I don't know." A full bellied laugh bubbled from her. "I thought I wouldn't like your beard, but it's growing on me. And I suppose the thought of fixing that wall is growing on me, too."

He nodded, supposing that kissing her was out of the question since there was no one here to witness it. But he sure did have a hankering to pull her tight against him. She, grinned at him, hands on hips, chest thrust out, and a swagger to her body framed behind by the window's light. He rubbed his hands together to stop them from reaching out. That's how he'd gotten into trouble before. His first crush sure hadn't welcomed his clumsy attempts.

Somehow, the expression in Stormi's eyes made him think this situation proved to be quite different. But he reined himself in nonetheless, dreading her possible rejection. No, he'd take this camaraderie with her rather than risk everything. Besides, she needed him. The winter would get a lot worse, and she'd be in here freezing. Sure was glad he'd stopped at Calvert's. 'Course, he'd had the notion he might catch her in there.

Her gray eyes were back on him. She sure did study on him a lot, and it put a wondering in him as to what shot through that sweet head of hers. Did she consider him a big dummy? A big strong dummy without a brain? An old movie swept his thoughts. Like a scarecrow with straw for brains, only bigger and denser. Ray Newhouse, star quarterback on his high school football team, had called him a "fencepost." Hadn't been a compliment.

Despite his misgivings, he brushed the bangs from her forehead. She didn't back away. Her hands twined up together under her chin, the edge of her sleeves tugged over her hands, her gaze firmly locked on his. A petite pixie, she fascinated him. He cleared his throat and forced himself to step away and collect his coat. An age-old adage smote him. A gentleman kept his hands to himself.

"Ake?"

Stormi wrung her hands while Ake ordered parts at the hardware store counter. A Ma and Pa place, it was filled with parts with little organization. She wondered briefly if she could afford all the stuff he rattled off. But that wasn't what was on Stormi's mind. The strangest expression had crossed Ake's face before they'd left her house, and she still obsessed over what it could be about. Had he seen? Those horrid tattooed sleeves never seemed to be one hundred percent hidden.

The image of pink cherry blossoms vined around her skin with black, fishnet Victorian lace, interspersed with light blue butterflies filled her mind. Both of her arms were entirely covered, ending in a scalloped edging at the wrists. This often peeked out even from long-sleeved shirts. She'd kept it hidden the last several months. Her hair had been an easy fix. The studs embedded in her face and skin had taken more time to heal, but for the most part—gone. But the double full-out tattooed sleeves were here to stay.

Alan preached to her about the insignificance of the marks, yet she knew they represented the life she'd led before her conversion. It had taken weeks to get both of them applied. Rarely had she been sober when she'd visited Ink, Inc., for her appointments lasted hours. Hours of needle pricks. Hours of pain. Marla had been at her side then, partaking of all the goods of the tattoo parlor's illegal painkillers. The whole foggy memory made her want to retch.

She shot a glance at Ake, but he smiled and led her out of the store. They got in the truck and had the supplies loaded in back. Ake's gaze rested on her several times on the way to her house, but she was busy running her finger from one shoulder to the other, thinking of the lacy tattoos beneath her fingers, wondering if a good man like Ake would be repelled. They stopped briefly at Ake's house for tools and were soon on their way to her place.

They pulled into her driveway, and she forced her mind away from the horrible thoughts converging in her mind. Instead she helped him carry in the new purchases. Ake lugged in stacks of wood as if they were bags of cotton balls. She dreaded pulling her coat off.

Ake wasted no time, and Stormi paced, unsure what to do, so inside herself with worry. She held boards when he asked her to, and he kept up a lively chatter to make the time pass. Soon the entire wall was framed in and only needed insulation.

He slung his hammer back onto his tool belt and unsnapped it. "I don't know about you, but I'm hungry"

Dinner. Oh, poodles and Chihuahuas. Why hadn't she thought of that instead of sulking around most the afternoon?

He tilted his head. "You okay?"

"Yeah. How about pizza?"

"You mean, here?"

She spun to find her phone. "We could order and have it delivered."

"Perfect."

She looked up the number while Ake perched on a stool. When the pizza place answered, she rattled off a quick order and then hung up. She turned and pulled a cold water bottle from the fridge and set it before him.

"Oh, I'm sorry. Did you like that kind of pizza? I didn't even think to ask."

His face slowly split into a grin. "I eat most anything."

"Good." She stared at him and tugged at her sleeve edge.

"What's wrong?"

She shook her head. "Nothing."

Suddenly the ground didn't feel familiar. She'd never been shy by any means, but things seemed to spin from her control. He continued to study her. She looked away.

"Why do you do that?"

"What?" Even to her own ears she sounded defensive.

He pointed to her sleeves where she'd tugged them over her hands.

Yeesh. No way they were going there. "No reason. More water?"

"No. I'm fine," he replied.

She settled on the stool alongside him.

"You want me to go?"

His voice was low, his eyes gentle, and she wanted to cry. "Of course not."

He nodded, but puzzlement stayed crinkled on his face, and the guilt inside Stormi bloomed hot and thick. Maybe Hoge was right. She'd been a player. He—an innocent. She didn't deserve to have him even as a friend. Maybe he did need protection from her. Maybe her moniker was nothing more than *tattooed seducer*. She bit her lip and tried to squelch down the anger that rose with the thought.

A loud knock sounded on the back door. She breathed a sigh of relief, thankful the pizza delivery guy had arrived. But when she opened the door, an angry Hoge stood there.

He gave her a glare and stepped around her.

"I knew I'd find you here. You're supposed to be at our house, remember? Lasagna—ring a bell?"

Ake stood, confusion marring his handsome face. "Is that tonight?"

"Yes, Dummy. I reminded you yesterday."

Ake shuffled. "Sure, sorry. I'll be right over."

Hoge paused at the door to point his finger at her. "You're not doing a lot to make me think you're a good influence."

Stormi resisted biting his condescending digit and dropped her eyes. He strode from the room.

Ake rubbed the back of his neck. "I'm sorry, Stormi. I guess the project sorta threw me off. You're welcome to come with me. Joni makes great lasagna."

Stormi tightened all her muscles to keep the grief inside until she could shepherd Ake out the door. "No, I understand. Go. And I think I'll bow out for church tomorrow. Maybe some other time."

Ake nodded, and tried to smile. "I'm really sorry. Don't mind Hoge. He's just mad at me, not you. See ya."

Once he left, she shut the door and turned off the lights. Tears in the dark didn't seem as real.

Chapter Eleven

Hoge sat like a huge thunderhead on the driver's side truck cushion. His brother had beckoned him into the cab for a private conference once Ake arrived at Hoge's house.

"Don't talk to Stormi that way, Hoge." Ake kept his voice soft and even.

"What?"

"You heard me."

Hoge growled and his voice came like a whiplash. "You mean to sit there and tell me what to do? While you bay after some wild woman? I don't get you."

Ake let the silence stretch, but Hoge was having none of it.

"Why her? Some stranger? You need to find someone who knows about how you were raised, Ake. A person who knows where you came from."

"Like you?"

"Yes. Thunderation. It's going to take a special woman for you."

Special.

Ake's voice became quiet in the cab of the truck, the darkness outside only making it more so. "I know you think I'm retarded, Hoge. That I ain't smart enough to have a normal life like you. I've always been protected by family and friends, and I appreciate that. Everybody thinks they know what's best for me, but I don't get to go home to a warm house filled with my own family, with my own wife. And I want you to think about that, Hoge. Going home, alone, every night. Would you trade for that?"

Steam seemed to evaporate from Hoge's body. "No. You know I wouldn't."

Ake nodded. "Well, I know you don't like Stormi. But I do. And maybe she's just a friend. Probably is, because you always point out, I'm not smart. But I like being around her, and I don't think it's fair for you to say mean things to her because of it."

Hoge let out a big sigh. "I don't want her to hurt you, Ake. She's...worldly."

"I know. But I can't have you saying mean things to her."

In the darkness, the porch light of Hoge's house flicked on. Joni's signal for them to hurry. "All right. I won't. I hope you know what you're doing, Ake."

He shook his head. "I never do. I just let God take care of it."

ᔆ ⸱⸱⸱⸱⸱⸱ ᔆ

Ake sped up the treadmill until he was in full throttle. Sweat poured from his body. The lasagna had been extra good tonight, but Hoge had been in a sulky mood. Joni had ribbed Ake in the kitchen about his "girlfriend" making him lose track of the time and practically missing family dinner night. She urged him to bring her with him on the next dinner night. Well, he would certainly ask. Again.

He powered down the machine until he finished his three mile run at a medium walk to cool off. Good thing he hadn't let it slip that he'd rather eat pizza with Stormi any night of the week than eat Joni's best lasagna. He shook his head. The woman was getting to him. Something had been on her mind today, but she'd shut him out. That didn't sit well.

He finished his weights before taking a quick shower, and then he settled at the bead table. The ruby and crystal necklace and bracelet for his mother hung from a nail on the wall. He should box it up in case she came over for some strange reason. Course with Pop ailing, she wouldn't venture out unless someone stayed at the house.

A new creation of black wire and turquoise beads now covered his work space. He picked up his needle nosed pliers and carefully completed another turn of a spiral black wire and inserted the colored bead at the end. It would be perfect for Stormi. Like rounded lace around her neck with the burst of light blue beads catching the light. He could imagine her in a slinky black dress with the spiraled necklace about her neck. He'd make a bracelet and earrings, of course, though he'd never seen her with earrings. But she sported pierced holes, so he assumed she wore them. Yes, she'd be a vision.

He'd like nothing better than to have her on his arm. Not sure where they'd go in such a get-up. He didn't even own a suit that fit him anymore. Mom usually kept him supplied, but Pop had distracted her from her usual fawning about his clothes. He'd gained some bulk in his shoulders and chest. There was no way the last suit coat would fit now.

His flip phone sounded from his bedroom. He rose to fetch it.

A voicemail from Joni. Naw, really Hoge, worried about him. Had she really asked if he'd made it home? Like he was some lost boy.

He typed back a thumbs up, striving to press the right keys. With a sigh, he cleared the smiley face and got it in correctly. Thank goodness for visual icons and symbols.

So Hoge and Joni were back to checking on him all the time? Was he back in high school? He snapped the phone closed and took a breath, settling himself on the edge of the bed. Sure did appear a good time for praying. He sat in the dark and poured his heart out to his Savior and then lay down and fell into a deep sleep.

Stormi avoided the bench at the dock for a week. Since the weather was positively frigid, she knew she wouldn't be missed. Still, pacing the thirty by thirty foot enclosure nearly drove her insane. Her legs froze mid-stroke. It was official. She had no life.

Her phone buzzed. An unfamiliar number popped up. Important, or no? Always the main question. With a sigh she pressed the green button.

"Hello?"

"Hey, it's Ray."

Ray. Ray? *Ray who?* Realization dawned like a polar plunge. Drop-dead gorgeous, Motor-head Ray who basically blackmailed her into a date. That Ray. She lifted a finger gun to her temple and pulled the thumb trigger. She'd lost Russian roulette of the unknown number.

"Uh, yeah. What's up?"

"Been thinking about you."

Adding double corn-syrup sweetness to the words only made her roll her eyes. Hadn't she already granted him his one mercy date? "That right?"

"I've been wondering what you've been up to?"

Oh, the games people play. Devilish horns pricked at her skull. "Actually, I'm trying to insulate my house."

Silence thundered. *Take that, you nosy mechanic.*

"You personally? You're insulating your house?"

"Sorta. This place is cold."

"Hmmm. You ought to call Harner's Construction. They can throw that up quick."

She flopped on her new couch and thoughts of Ake getting wind of her piecing out his job walloped her. This wasn't fair. He'd started the project, and she was just being a shrew by using it to shut this rake up.

"But, you know. I'm handy around a car. I'm sure I can figure out a little insulation, as long as it's not too major."

She sat up in horror and gave a nervous laugh. "Just kidding. Really. It's all under control."

"Well, hey. I'm here for you. We can do that or club hop. Your choice."

What? When had this become an either–or situation? Cramps shot through her stomach, and she cringed as she spoke. "No, really. I've got a man on it."

A superior laugh. "Then you're free to go out."

"Uh..." *Tell him. Tell him you'd rather strip wallpaper with your teeth from the top rung of a second story ladder. Tell him you'd rather clean an airport floor with a Q-tip balanced in your left ear. Tell him something. Anything.*

"Really, it's not—well, I'm just not the club-hopping girl—"

"Great. Let's do this insulation thing."

Stormi swallowed. In the proverbial corner. "We can go out—"

"All right. Now you are talking. Saturday?"

Amidst the bile gathering at the back of her throat, she listened as he made arrangements for their second date. This couldn't be happening. Why had she been so cavalier? Where had all her familiar finagling gone? He rang off and she buried her head in the couch. She'd lost that nasty edge that had always given her an advantage, but had always left her in the emotional gutter in the end. As a new creature in Christ, she had a new take on life.

Only, she'd not been honest. And now it stabbed her in the back. *Ake*. What would he think? Tears bit her eyes. She knew exactly what he'd think. He'd be crushed. Pressing her head into the crevice of the cushions, she prayed with all her soul for a solution.

❧ ⸱⸱⸱⸱⸱ ❧

Ake wondered how the smell of pine filled the church even though all the greenery was fake. Yet it did. The poinsettia's bright red colors in front of the preacher's podium completed the Christmas colors through the church. It felt odd to sit on the back left side while his parents and Hoge's family sat in their usual spot six rows back from the front on the right. But this is where Stormi had sat when she'd arrived. Like a dummy, he'd failed to offer a ride. No wonder everyone called him that.

Still, he belted out "Amazing Grace" with added force this morning, pleased Stormi stood beside him clutching the hymnal. Her hair had an added whip of spikiness today, giving her an extra bit of sassiness to her look. It made him want to stand and grin at her. Any minute he expected her to reveal her blue translucent fairy wings and soar above his head, stroking the hanging greens.

Instead, her knuckles turned white from the force of the heavy book. He reached over and supported it. She shot him a stiff mouth twitch, which he supposed was a smile. Hard to tell. She sure was strung tight this morning. They sat, and she fidgeted with the long navy skirt and then proceeded to yank at her sleeves. He laced his fingers in his lap to resist the urge to stretch an arm on the pew behind her. As tense as she was, she might just explode.

He trained his gaze on the pastor and tried to ignore the sense of elated pleasure that swelled his shoulders. After all, this was about God, not about the gorgeous woman at his side. Stormi opened her tiny Bible and searched for the passage.

Ake stretched his neck, hoping she wouldn't attempt to share. She didn't and he breathed a sigh of relief.

When the service ended, Ake stood and didn't miss the optic arrows Hoge shot at him. He shrugged and exited the pew to let Stormi out. The woman seemed bound for glory and in a right hurry. He strode behind her. She slipped by the pastor, who hadn't quite set up his usual vigil at the door, and Ake lowered his head to follow. A hand flopped on his shoulder.

"How's it going?" Deacon Frank Harper shot out a wrinkled meaty hand.

Good 'ole Frank. Always had a piece of gum for the kids. Yet right now, Ake wasn't much of a mood to yak at him.

"I'm fine, Frank. Hope you're the same. I gotta scoot now, though. Excuse me."

Once out in the cold, he turned toward the parking lot in time to see Stormi's little Saturn shoot out of the lot. Huh. He shoved his hands into his pockets and set out to his truck. Seemed odd he hadn't seen her in a couple of weeks. He'd have thought if nothing else, she'd have wanted him to complete the insulation project they'd started. Or at least that was the excuse he'd planned on using.

The truck spun out of the lot, and a twinge of guilt settled on his shoulders. He looked into the rear view mirror, hoping Hoge didn't stand on the sidewalk with his hands out. Thankfully, just several members made their way to their cars.

He cut through town and made it to her place in a matter of minutes. Her driveway was empty, but he parked there anyway. After a couple of minutes, her tiny beige car pulled in beside him. He jumped out.

"Hey, you were in a hurry, huh?" He grinned as she swung from the car.

She shrugged. "Not really."

He stepped back to allow her to pass, and she hustled by gripping the strap of her leather purse. A car pulled up behind their two vehicles and she stopped fleeing. If that was what she was doing. Sure did appear that way. Ray Newhouse jogged toward them in a sleek leather jacket.

"Stormi. I was hoping to catch you." Ray slowed and a slow grin crossed his face. "Hello there, Dummy. I haven't seen you in ages. How's it hanging?

Ake's smile faded. "Yeah, fine. It's been awhile."

Ray laughed and swore. "Sure has, you old fencepost. Heck, I haven't planted a football in the back of your head in years."

"You two played football together?" Stormi hovered near the corner of the house as if she might leave them both in the driveway.

"Well, I played. Starting quarterback, I might add. Dummy was my bodyguard on the line. Isn't that right?"

Ake struggled to keep his face expressionless. Ray had taken great pleasure in seeing how many times he could drive the pointed end of the football into the back of the skull. "You might say that."

Stormi stepped closer, an odd look on her face. "Ray, his name is Ake. It irritates me that people keep referring to him as 'Dummy.'"

Ray grinned. "Sorta fits him."

Stormi's facial features flattened. "Did you need something?"

Ake rubbed the thick beard, hoping the conversation didn't return to football.

A smile split Ray's handsome face like a practiced infomercial. "Just thinking about you, babe, and wondering when we could go out again. That bar was rocking last week, right?"

The air seemed to ooze from Ake's lungs, and his gaze darted to Stormi. Her eyes dropped and her face paled.

"Figured we could hit up another place I heard of on the coast before New Year's. Then maybe cruise on over and watch the ball drop. Yeah? Now that's the way to party."

Ake couldn't move. An ache started in his gut and spread throughout his body.

"We'll talk later, Ray. Goodbye." She pivoted and strode around the corner.

"Guess her monthly visitor has stopped by, you know what I mean?" A bark of a laugh escaped Ray. "Tell ya what. I know you're working on a project for her. I'll let you soften her up for me. Let her know I'll be calling later. Later, Dummy."

Laughter followed Ray back to his sports car. The engine revved and the hot import shot away from the curb.

Chapter Twelve

Ake clenched his hand inside his wool coat, unsure of
what to do. Unsure of what to think. He inhaled the cold air
and glanced around the neighborhood. Maybe he should just
leave. His gaze landed on the copse of trees behind Stormi's
house. Several minutes ticked by. He heard the door open. She
peeked around the corner, with no coat. Her teeth worried her
bottom lip and Ake couldn't look away.

"You coming in?" Her voice was soft as down.

He took another breath and let it go slowly. "Not sure."

She took a step closer, yanking the sleeves over her hands.
Her teeth chattered, and her nose tinged to a rosy glow. She
had to be freezing. Yet, he was frozen inside. This is how it
always worked. He wanted the prom queen, and the prom
queen wanted someone else. Everyone always knew the drill
but him. A dummy for sure.

"It's not what you think, Ake."

He reached up and adjusted the black beanie on the back of his head. "You know, I think I better go. Mom's probably got her clam chowder on, and I wouldn't want to miss it."

"Ake."

He walked to the driver's side of the truck. "Ray said he'd call sometime later. Bye."

With little thought of his truck's transmission, he slammed the gearshift into reverse, vaguely aware of Stormi's huddled figure rushing towards him. He jammed his right foot onto the gas pedal and fishtailed it all the way up the hill.

Stormi caught her breath as she watched the old truck scramble up the hill and disappear. Her heart fell to her feet. Never had she seen Ake angry, but something had been there in his eyes. But it looked more like surprised pain. A sob rose and she covered her mouth. She'd betrayed him. She'd clutched that proverbial rug and yanked it from beneath his booted feet.

She hunkered to the sidewalk and bowed her head. How would she ever explain it to him? How would he ever believe her? Tears sprang to her eyes, and she rose and hurried to the door. She slipped inside to the ringing of her phone. With a heavy heart she checked the number and groaned. *Mother.* Could the woman have worse timing?

"Hello?"

"Where have you been? I've been calling all morning."

"Church."

"Church," She spat. "You're brainwashed is what you are. Such nonsense. Wish you'd give your family that much attention."

Sobs worked their way up her throat, and she pushed the phone from her ear to collect herself. "What do you need, Mom?"

"Are you coming for Christmas or not? I'm not cooking a ham, if that's what you're thinking."

Christmas? Was it here already? "That's not till next week."

"Well, little priss, I have to get my plans in early or you don't show up. And I'm giving you my old vacuum cleaner for your Christmas gift. It's not that old."

Stormi shuddered, recalling her mother taking it to her boyfriend's house to vacuum up the flea infestation his hound had caused. "Oh."

"I don't have the money to buy everyone a gift. You coming or not?"

A solo tear crested and leaked down her face. "Can I call you back?"

"We always do Christmas Eve, not Christmas, you should know by now. Unless you're too busy for me."

"Okay. That's fine. Mom, I gotta go. Goodbye." She stabbed the red phone button and sank into the corner of her couch. *Lord, Lord, how did I get here?* She slumped forward, burying her face into a pillow.

"Merry Christmas, Ake." His mother greeted him at the door with a hug. The smell of ham and spices filled the compact kitchen. A chorus of voices from the front room indicated Hoge and his family had gathered there. Then a familiar laugh.

He pushed away his somber mood and gave his mother a smile. "Merry Christmas, Mom. Aunt Phoebe made it?"

Her smile beamed from her face making the wrinkles in her seventy-four-year-old face more evident. "Yes. She made it in just a few minutes ago. And she brought her little dog."

Well, that would add some humor to the day. Hoge would be beside himself. He hated that dog. Ake couldn't resist the knowing look in his mother's eyes, and he gave a short laugh. Then he sobered. "How's Pop?"

Mom's face lost a bit of its shine. "He's good, but he doesn't remember my sister, Phoebe. I think he does recognize it's a holiday, so he hasn't lost everything, yet."

They walked tandem through the wide doorway. Hoge and his wife, Joni, rested on the couch. His brother parked his hand at the edge of the couch to keep the yappy little Chihuahua from jumping on the cushion.

Hoge's eldest son, Linus, at fourteen, had his nose pressed to his smart phone. Crew and Deacon wrestled for the recliner in the corner while Aunt Phoebe lauded the room with her newest aches and pains with excruciating detail. Sweet five-year-old Lucy sat on the floor near the tree, taking in the entire room with huge eyes.

"Course they drained that cyst. It was a bit bloody, but my doctor didn't seem much concerned. They sent it off to the lab, and I'll know the results by next week. Then he checked the boil that had developed right there in the hair follicle on my big toe. That's what I get for shaving it last summer. Plum nasty. There was a bit of yellow pus. He lanced it and had me putting on some of those warm compresses, and I'm on antibiotics for the ten days." She paused to shake her head. "Which will cause me to get the yeast infection. Then round I go again."

Hoge's posture indicated he was less than thrilled by Aunt Phoebe's run down of medical maladies. Or maybe the dog had him on edge.

Phoebe leaned forward and tilted the rocker to allow her to slowly rise. "Well, there's the little man. Ake, you get over here and give your old Auntie a hug."

He stepped forward and enfolded her in a generous hug. She smelled of past-ripe oranges and the pages of an old book. Despite the fact it wasn't an overly pleasant odor, it brought back memories of Christmas pasts when Pop had been healthy and he and Hoge but boys.

"Hello, Aunt Phoebe." He patted her back and tried to release her before she did. Then he maneuvered himself to the couch and settled near Hoge. Joni flicked through a decorating magazine but paused to greet him.

Pop wandered into the room looking confused, and Mom guided him to an extra folding chair near the doorway to the kitchen. Pepe barked at Pop, and Phoebe hushed him.

"Oh, yeesh," Hoge breathed. "Time to eat yet, Mom?"

She leaned against the doorway. "Not quite yet. Soon though. When's your follow-up appointment, Phoebe?"

Hoge gave a low growl and rose to meander down the hallway whether to the bathroom or just to burrow himself into a quiet place. Pepe followed him yipping. Ake stifled a laugh.

Joni stood. "I'm going to rush things along. Excuse me, Ake."

Some thirty minutes later they gathered around the table, hands joined, Hoge asking the blessings on the food. When he finished, Ake settled into his usual holiday chair and smiled. There was no place he'd rather be. He patted Pop's hand and passed him the sweet potatoes. Pop stared at him with vacant eyes, so Ake spooned him a couple smaller pieces and set the bowl in the center of the table.

"Eat, Pop."

The old man obeyed and lifted the fork. Nope, no place he'd rather be, but a few things he'd like to change. Ake's glance fell on his mom. She laughed at something Phoebe said, and a small smile lit his face. At least Mom didn't have to face caring for Pop alone today.

"Here, Pop. Have a little ham."

His father nodded, and he slid a small piece to his plate. Ake's gaze drifted to the windows as the same holiday conversations flowed around him, the ham platter still clutched in his hands. He longed for one more person to pass the ham to. He drew in a deep sigh. But he supposed Ray Newhouse would do that this year. Someone called his name, and he turned back, and yielded the ham.

ShaVonn raised her tea glass and clunked it against her absent mother's. "Merry Narcissistic Christmas!"

Stormi rolled her eyes before catching her niece's trembling lip. "ShaVonn, shhh."

Her sister rose and stomped into the kitchen. "I know, I'm sorry."

"It's okay, Vivie."

The eight-year old blinked her eyes. "Why did Grandma leave?"

Marv, ShaVonn's husband muttered, "Because she's nuts."

Stormi shot him a pointed glance and then turned a sunny smile on her niece. "Hey, why don't you go get that package covered in My Little Kitty paper and unwrap it. The one over by the window. There's one for Liza, too."

Three-year-old Liza clapped her hands and struggled to climb off her booster. Marv rose and hefted her down.

"Are you sure?" Vivie wiped away a tear, but hope filled her eyes. "Can I, Dad?"

"Yep."

The two girls launched into the living area as ShaVonn returned to the table and sank into her chair.

"Every freaking year. Seriously. Mom ruins every holiday. I can't stand it anymore."

Stormi took a deep breath. "I know. The meal was great though, ShaVonn. Thanks for having Christmas at your house."

ShaVonn snorted. "Yeah it was so great, Mother had to have a conniption fit and storm out of the house."

Marv grunted. "That's because she's nuts."

"All right, Marv. We get it. Trust me, we *so* get it." ShaVonn grabbed another pumpkin bar. "Screw the diet. I'm having another one."

The girls' squeals lit the air as the Barbies came to light. Wedding Barbie for Vivie and Butterfly for Liza. Stormi wondered how long Butterfly Barbie had before the toddler chewed her feet off. With a sigh she rose and started collecting the dirty dishes.

"Just leave them."

Same old fight. "No, ShaVonn, I can have them loaded in the dishwasher and everything put up in fifteen minutes. You did most of the cooking. It's only fair."

ShaVonn gave a humorless laugh. "You know what would be fair?"

Grabbing a brush at the sink to scrub off the dishes, Stormi mentally sang what she knew would fly from her sister's mouth next. 'Tis the season for a mom who's normal, fa-la-la-la-la, la-la, la, la. Instead we celebrate ruined holidays, tra-la-la-la-la, la, la, la, laaa.

"A mom who cares about someone besides herself for once. Like her grandkids."

Stormi clenched her teeth. So close. "That would be nice."

The girls came tearing into the kitchen.

"Thanks Aunt Stormi." Vivie slammed into her hip with a huge hug.

Liza giggled and gave a quick hug, too, before both girls ran back to their bedrooms to enjoy their new-found toys.

"Well, Liza will have that doll's clothes ripped off in ten seconds flat." ShaVonn rose and collected a storage container for the left-over mashed potatoes.

A laugh burst from Stormi. "Here I was thinking the feet would take the hit."

Marv rose and waddled into the living room. On went the TV.

"You'll shoot your eye out."

ShaVonn burst out laughing. "Our family should be made into a movie. We could become a classic Christmas Show. At least we'd make some money.

"At this point, I'd take a free shot with a BB gun." Stormi snipped.

ShaVonn laughed. "Hey, we're doing that? Let's fill that puppy with Valuim. Maybe the girls could then have at least one nice memorable Christmas with their Grandmother."

"Good point."

"Do you remember last Christmas?"

Oh, boy, here we go. On to reminiscing over the last twenty years of spoiled Christmases. Stormi prepared a large supply of her uh-huh's and her yeah's while ShaVonn continued, then let her mind wander to Ake. The hurt expression on his face had haunted her the last week. Add to that the unpleasant conversation with Ray Newhouse, where she supposedly 'broke up' with him when they weren't even dating.

"Then there's the whole, guilt trip thing." ShaVonn's voice penetrated Stormi's thoughts. "What is with that? Like it's our fault we were born? You know?"

"Uh-huh."

Stormi sighed. She had to find a way to break the ice between Ake and her. It was just too hard to show up at his house, spouting how it was a misunderstanding and the whole works. Besides, why did she even feel responsible for explaining in the first place? They weren't a real couple. They were just putting on to impress his brother and shipmates.

"And if I have to hear how I should have married Lance Rushton one more time, I'll scream." ShaVonn's tirade continued. "She thinks just because he owns a hotel that I should've put up with his lies for the rest of my life. All she thinks of is money. She is so stinking tight. For goodness sake, her used vacuum is your Christmas present. Unwrapped, filthy, and sitting under my Christmas tree."

"Yeah."

And why did she feel so horrible? If only Ake hadn't been there when that horrid, horrid Ray showed his face. If she could just erase that five minutes and jump back in time, but she couldn't. She slammed the last plate into the dishwasher.

"Easy on the china, there Hammertime. Those aren't Mom's hand-me down cheapies."

"Sorry."

"Anyway, like when I was pregnant with Vivie..."

Marv caught her eye when he approached to hand her an empty glass, and he shook his head while his wife ranted, slinging left overs into plastic storage containers. Stormi gave a tight smile. Bless Marv's heart. He was a saint.

ShaVonn paused a moment and Stormi leaped on the opportunity. "I'm going to go get the girls if we're ready to open gifts."

ShaVonn shrugged. "Huh? Oh, yeah, okay, I guess."

Stormi thankfully disappeared down the hallway.

❧ ⋯⋯ ❧

Mid-January passed before Stormi opened the door to a frosted Ake. Snow cascaded behind him, threatening to stack the thick flakes to record highs. The man in front of her resembled a moving snowman, beard sporting small icicles, his dark eye brows covered with crystals. She yanked him inside the house, ignoring the wet snow that fell from him in hunks, and tugged him to the fireplace. He appeared more canvas-encased monster at this point, looking thicker than ever with layers of outerwear.

"Ake, what are you doing? You're positively freezing."

He huddled by the hearth for a few minutes, and she hurried to heat up some coffee. Her new machine spit out a boiling brew in a matter of minutes. By the time she'd returned, he'd seated himself on the stone hearth.

"What in the world are you doing here? It's white-out conditions out there."

With slow movements, he pulled the thick gloves from his hands and unzipped his thick canvas jacket. She grabbed the heavy wet coat and hung it on the coat tree near the door. When she turned, he had cupped his hands around the steaming coffee cup.

"Nice weather, huh?" A grin creased his wind-burned face.

She shook her head and crossed her arms over her chest. He was plain adorable. Why try to tamp down the return smile or the surge of pleasure that stole through her? "Only you could find this weather pleasant."

He raised a dark brow while pulling at the icicles hanging from his thick beard. "Good coffee."

With an exaggerated sigh, she parked her fists on her hips. "Seriously, Ake. There's not many people who would venture out in such a mess. What are you doing here?"

After a long drink and a java exhale of pleasure, he set the stoneware cup on the hearth and stood. "Couldn't stop thinking of how cold you might be. I never did finish the insulation."

"Oh, that." The enthusiasm of seeing him faded as she remembered their last encounter. She probed his expression, but his dark eyes were on the framed-out wall. Not much showed in his expression. She yanked on her sleeves of her black turtleneck.

"Won't take but a shake to finish it." He strode forward, tool belt already in place.

"No, Ake. Honestly, how could you trudge over here just for that?"

But he'd already grabbed one of the giant rolls of insulation and sliced open the package. She tugged on her pointed bangs and wandered closer. Wasn't it time to explain? Would he just start working as if nothing had wedged between them?

"Ake, about Ray."

"Wha?" He grabbed the ladder and adjusted it in the corner. Then he climbed to the ceiling, dragging the end of the long roll.

She sidestepped the swaying insulation. Was it wise to distract him now? He adjusted the long swath of fiberglass in between two vertical two-by-fours and fired the staple gun into the wood. Stormi flinched. No way. She wandered back to the kitchen area and brewed some hot chocolate for herself.

On the stool at the bar, peeking over the steaming cup, she had to admit the scenery was lovely. Hunky Ake made short work of sealing in the drafty wall with efficient movements. If she didn't know any better, she'd have thought he was a construction worker. His bulky shoulders and burly bearded face made him well suited for a manly magazine cover.

A grin crossed her face, and her brow twitched. She grabbed her phone. If no official photographer appeared in her kitchen, she'd be the first to record the pleasing man muscle for the imaginary issue. She snickered.

He paused at the bottom of the ladder and glanced her way. "You laughing at me?"

His serious face caused her pause. "Of course not. Well, maybe a little."

The expression on his face sucked the air from her lungs, and she sprang from the stool to hurry over to him. "Not like that, Ake."

A shadow passed over his stiff features. "How many ways are there to laugh at someone?"

She reached up and grabbed his biceps. Whoa. Insulation-pumped swell. Firmly, she pulled her mind from the lure of his physicality. "I was thinking how you ought to be on the cover of a magazine. You know, something like, *Construction Times*. Or *Home Improvement Newsletter*."

He raised his brows. "Why?"

She let out a laugh. "Have you looked at you?"

His brows drew together. "What do you mean?"

"Ake! You're gorgeous."

He glanced off at the fireplace and then shrugged. As he scrubbed his beard, he turned sheepish. "I think you're just changing the subject."

A laugh burst from her. "Are you kidding? I've known a lot of men..."

Her voice skidded to an abrupt stop, and somberness plastered her instantly. She stepped back and turned her face against his probing stare.

"Like Ray?"

She clenched her teeth at his intense regard. "No, not like Ray."

He nodded, but his expressive dark eyes clearly confessed his doubt.

"I'm serious, Ake. There's nothing between Ray and me. I went out with him a couple of times just because, well, I got backed into a corner. I actually hated every moment of it, even if you don't believe me."

His cheeks filled with air and then expelled with a whoosh. "Don't reckon it matters. The stuff between us is just pretend, anyway."

Stormi narrowed her eyes and crossed her arms tightly over her chest. That statement jabbed at her sense of decency. He turned, grabbed a piece of insulation, and began to climb. She chewed her lip, disliking where the conversation had ended, but unwilling to start it up again with him dangling from a rickety ladder. Fine. She'd fix some lunch.

The ladder continued to make metallic echoes behind her as she pulled the stew beef from the fridge. Thankful soup had been on her mind when she shopped last, she set the red meat in the frying pan to brown. Then she peeled and cut up the veggies. She grabbed the tomato juice from the cabinet and selected a variety of spices. Soon the room filled with delicious smells.

She grinned as she buzzed around. Perhaps the way to thawing Ake was through his stomach as the old wife's saying went. Either way, maybe it would open him up a bit. He seemed as tight as a clam today. She added refrigerated crescent rolls to the oven as the thick brown soup bubbled.

Ake's boots rang out as he thumped down the aluminum ladder once more, and she meandered to the far wall to meet him as he stepped to the concrete. "Hungry?"

"Sure."

"You got time to take a break?"

He nodded before setting aside his gear. She hurried across the room to pour the fragrant soup into bowls. He came over and settled on one of the stools. She grabbed the butter from the fridge and deposited the rolls in a basket. With a cheesy smile, she set her burden down and leaned forward, her hands planted on the counter.

"What's that?" Ake caressed her wrist right where the black swirls on her skin had peeked below her cuffs.

She jerked her hands away, sending one of the bowls off the end of the counter. The glass shattered, sending hot stew and shards splattering across the floor. Tears rushed to her eyes, and she parked her wrists behind her back.

He stood and rounded the counter, not to pick up the mess, but to stand in front of her. "You okay?"

With a blink she nodded and spun to grab the paper towels. But he was there, taking it from her hands and plopping the roll on the counter. His hands, instead, gripped hers and brought them up, peeling away the sleeve of her shirt. His eyes met hers when she attempted to jerk away, but he held her easily.

"Stormi?"

Her throat convulsed. She couldn't lie to him. She wouldn't. The shame of the marks burned her soul. "I have...tattoos."

Chapter Thirteen

A ke shrugged. "Oh."

Then he snatched up the roll of towels and set about gathering the stew covered glass fragments spread across the floor.

What? That was it? No distaste? No disapproval? No disappointment, lectures, judgements, Bible references—nothing?

"That's it?" Those two words came out a little crass.

He hesitated in mid-swipe and fixed his gaze on hers. "I'm sorry, what?"

She tugged the sleeves over the inked black lace and glared at him. "Aren't you going to reprimand me? Or give me a speech about the evils of tattoos?"

He stood, his dark brows bunched. "Uh...no. Why?"

A few breaths brought her fury into focus. Why *was* she upset? She blinked at him and realized she expected him to treat her like she would've reacted. His composure sent a wave of peace into her heart.

"Well, it says in the Bible not to do it."

"I know."

She squirmed. "Doesn't it repel you?"

"Should it?"

The man was definitely misnomered. He was no dummy. As a matter of fact, Stormi had never faced anyone with such profound wisdom. She probed his features. "I hope not."

A smile crept across his bearded face. "No danger there."

An overwhelming desire to hug him tugged at her, and she resisted the impulse. Had anyone ever fully accepted her like he did? Well, her friend, Alan, had never judged her, but Ake's pure validation of her worth stole her breath. Her throat clogged, and she stopped battling the desire to wrap her arms about him.

With a small cry, she rushed forward and embraced his muscled form.

❧ ⸱⸱⸱⸱⸱⸱ ❧

Ake froze into place. Hard to hug back with his hands filled with sharp pieces of stoneware. He settled his triceps on her shoulders, wishing he could make the most of her pity hug. Much like his prom date, Haven Griffith, whose boyfriend had been too old to attend the school function, for that was all it was. Still, Hoge wasn't even present, nor the twins. It made it seem real.

"You oughta come with me to Hoge's."

She pulled away. "What? Uhhh. No."

Ake moved to toss the rubbish in the trash and returned to the spill, where Stormi now knelt.

He dropped to his knees. "My sister-in-law said I should bring you. It's our weekly family dinner."

She scrubbed at the spatters. "I don't think that would be smart."

He paused. "I suppose not."

In the middle of a wipe, she hesitated and sat back on her haunches to study him. He tried to hide his hurt at her choice of words. "Who will be there?"

"Mom and Pop, Hoge, Joni, and their four kids. The usual bunch."

She continued to eye him so he offered a smile and curve of his brow. A sparkle lit her eyes, and humor tugged at her mouth. "You'll protect me from your overbearing brother?"

Pleasure widened his grin. He held up two fingers. "Scout's honor."

A giggle escaped her, and she tipped her head back, exposing her fine delicate throat. "Fine. I'll go."

He beamed, memorizing every delightful plane of her face. Even if it were all for show, he'd take it.

❦

The hammering on Ake's front door brought him out of a deep sleep. His mother's frantic voice sped him to a jog as he pulled on a shirt. He ripped open the door and there she stood, tears frozen to her face, no coat.

"Pop's out."

"Oh, dear Lord." He pulled his freezing mother into the house.

"No, Ake, I can't. I have to find him."

He ran to his room and yanked his coveralls from the closet. After jumping into his boots, he grabbed another coat. His mother met him in the hall, and he wrapped her up and tugged a stocking cap over her gray curls. There was no way she'd sit inside while he searched.

"You call Hoge?"

She shook her head.

"We'll start and if he doesn't turn up—"

A crash sounded from the garage. His mother gripped his arms and sobbed. "Oh, thank you, Jesus, thank you."

Ake parted from her and rushed to the garage door. Sure enough, Pop stood near Ake's work bench staring at the metal pieces on the floor.

He looked up at him with rheumy eyes and shook his head. "You gotta pick up your toys, Son."

Ake's throat filled with emotion as he wrapped his arms around his hunched father. "Sure, Pop. I'll get right to that."

He led him inside to join Mom on the couch. She laid her hands on her husband's cheeks and pressed her head against his.

With a thankful prayer on his lips, Ake fell into the recliner. Tomorrow he'd get in touch with Hoge. Maybe he had another idea. The lock he'd installed near the top of the door hadn't kept Pop in for very long. Dear God, Ake didn't want to dwell on the outcome had his mother not realized his father's absence. But for tonight, he'd sleep in front of one door and Mom in the recliner in front of the other. He prayed that was enough.

Yet no matter how many blankets his mother had stacked on the floor in front of the drafty door, wisps of icy air found its way in. Ake adjusted the blankets covering his body to try to block the cold against his back and went back to daydreaming. Now, how far up did that tattoo go? He knew his family would be shocked to know Stormi was inked. Judging from her strange reaction, the motif brought her no peace either, and he wondered if that meant she'd had it done before her conversion.

He regretted not discussing it further, biblically speaking. He knew that statement existed in Leviticus. They'd studied it at church. Perhaps it would have eased Stormi to know the context of the verse. It wasn't a commandment, after all.

Either way, how far did that tattoo travel? This was of intense interest to him. Strangely enough, he found himself quite obsessed by her decorated skin and wished he'd asked to see the whole design. But that would have been of bad taste, and his mother had worked too hard to make sure he didn't overstep social boundaries.

Still, the lacy pattern had piqued his interest. Such a great fortune she'd wrecked the bowl on the floor. He might have sat there stroking her soft skin, exploring the delicate black filigree. Had he seen a blue flower?

With effort he tugged his mind from exploring further and fixed his mind on her boldness. Man, that woman had no fear. Strutted right up to him and called him gorgeous. Then pulled a cocky grin, not a blush in sight. Hoge would call her brazen. Maybe even a hussy. He cringed. Ake knew in his heart she wasn't that kind of a woman. Although her mention of many men had shook him for a moment.

Did that really matter to him? Yes and no. She wasn't his and never would be, yet thinking of other men with her cut the heart from him. Whole package, she was hands down the most beautiful woman he'd ever laid eyes on. His first kiss.

Shuffling footsteps paused his line of thoughts. Pop's frail form hesitated in the doorway between the dining area and the living room. Mom's soft voice floated to him as she eased from the recliner to escort him back to the bedroom.

He sighed. Enough pulling dreams from the clouds. His parents needed his prayers. He fell asleep with the sounds of his own whispers appealing to the Lord on high.

❧ ⋯⋯ ❧

Hoge shot Stormi darts of blue death from the depths of his eyes from across the table. It was fun trying to construct poetic ways to describe the narrowed look he slung her way. She slid her hand into Ake's huge one just to see his brother simmer.

But Joni had no problem gushing over Stormi accompanying her brother-in-law to the family meal night. Baked spaghetti with pepperonis and breadsticks tasted delicious, and it was humorous to see how much food the men could absorb. And if Hoge thought his glowering hatred scared her off one bit, well, he hadn't met her mother yet.

"What? Why didn't you call me?" Hoge's voice rose in a growl.

Stormi pulled away from her thoughts to catch up with the current subject.

"Because we found him."

Ake's low voice reminded her of the Bible verse she'd read this morning. Proverbs 15:1, "A soft and gentle and thoughtful answer turns away wrath." Poor Ake probably had a lifetime to practice that with his gruff brother. She, on the other hand, needed a lot more practice.

"That's no reason not to let me know when Pop is out in the weather."

Ake's mother shook her head. "Now, Hoge."

"Ma, you should have told me."

She gave a weathered smile. "And we did. Now, we need to know if you have some thoughts about avoiding that again."

"Listen to your mother." Pop chimed in.

Hoge rolled his eyes. "Yes, Pop."

Ake's dad rose and shuffled down the hallway. Stormi felt Ake's hand tighten, and she cast a glance at him. Even though he maintained a calm exterior and a positive manner, knowing his father had been in danger had affected him. She could tell by the stiffness in his bearded cheeks, but gentleness occupied his eyes which captivated her more each day.

"We can make do, Mom," Ake offered.

"Don't be ridiculous, Ake. You and mom sleeping at the doors is simply idiotic."

Stung, a retort leaped to her mouth, but Stormi stifled it. Why did he revel in insulting his brother's intelligence? She turned to Ake, but his black eyes were guileless. Her heart squeezed. She longed to rest her head against his chest and stroke the tenseness from his face.

Whoa. She pulled herself upright. Crazy jumping in to a family disagreement. Only, her concern centered around Ake. In some strange way, she wanted to defend him, protect him. His brother showed no mercy. She bit the inside of her lip to keep a retort from flying out.

Hoge lowered his voice. "We'll get an alarm system on the windows and doors. You can arm it at night, or day for that matter, and then you'll know when he's gone out."

Mom turned her face to Ake. "Will you know how to do that?"

Hoge expelled a hiss. "It's not hard, Ma. Any idiot could do it, including Dummy."

Stormi sprang up. She could hold it no longer. "Why do you do that?"

The big man reared back and fastened a scowl on her. "What are you talking about?"

"Insinuate Ake's obtuse."

Ake tugged on her hand. "It's okay."

She huffed. "No. It's not."

Silence cloaked the occupants at the table while Hoge continued to glare at her.

"She has a point, Dear," Ake's mother agreed.

The gaze Hoge flicked in his mother's direction didn't lessen the dislike present in his eyes when he returned to frown at Stormi.

Joni stood. "How about cherry dump cake? Still warm. I think I have ice cream, too. Who's in?"

The kids appeared like magic and circumvented the table with excited cries, masking the near silence at the table. Stormi cut her eyes from Hoge, who seemed set on staring her under the table. She wanted to let out a snort. Surviving her dysfunctional upbringing and the consequences of her idiotic choices gave her a decided advantage. Stubbornness stiffened her jaw, but one half smile from Ake dissolved it. Somehow, she was going to stop Hoge, and everyone else, from calling Ake that horrible name.

Stormi glared at the blue screen. Her laptop was kaput. Death by OS, never welcome news. It meant she had to get a new system. Her podcast was due by tomorrow. She had to get online and fast. Her gaze shifted to the lone window. Snow. All the freaking time. Did it ever stop here? She had her doubts.

It's not like she hated it. It hated her. Kept her little Saturn skittering across the slippery road. She strode to the window and parked her hands on her hips. The big fluffy flakes were busy again, bringing a moving lacy look to the outside world. Gorgeous, but aggravating. She groaned and crossed her arms. Ake drove in the stuff like Santa.

She set a fist to her lips. A skidding she would go, or ask Ake. Duh. No brainer. The corner of her mouth quirked. The poor man. He'd inherited an annoying little sister. She scowled. That didn't set right. There was no way she'd think of Ake as a brother. She'd kissed him for Heaven's sake. More like a...what? Was there a title for the type of relationship she had with Ake? The thought sobered her.

No. She'd do this herself and pray for the best. Yes. Good. A sigh burst from her in a long hiss. Then why did disappointment tromp all over her insides? She growled and spun. At the door she grabbed her coat and turquoise beanie and shoved them on. She swiped her purse from the counter. Ake would know nothing about computers, so she nixed the idea of bringing him along.

The back door gave a loud protesting squeak as she shoved it closed. The snowflakes assaulted her as she twisted the key in the lock. Face reality. She didn't want Ake for his expertise in computer technology, she wanted him to drive. Her gaze swept the white landscape. Wow. That was pretty self-serving. Not to mention a lie. She adored his presence. Even if he didn't speak, she fed off his goodness. His strength.

She huffed a cloud of carbon dioxide and set off toward the car, only to grab the side of the house to keep from slipping. See? This is what happens to people who are off-kilter. She hadn't had her Bible study in three days, and her thoughts were like a heathen jungle. Ake, Ake, Ake. Lie, lie, lie. For a moment she rested her gloved hand against the siding and closed her eyes.

"Oh, God. I haven't put you first. Ake is special—Lord, I can't believe I just said that. I mean he's...he's—blather. He's special, no two ways around it. And not the negative connotation. Purely positive." Her breath's cloud intermixed with the flakes about her.

Her heart ached. She pivoted on the slippery sidewalk, glancing to the plunging gorge not five feet from the edge of her sidewalk. The snow hung on the snaggled trees down the slope. Time to start this day out right.

She unlocked the door, took off her coat and gathered her Bible. Perhaps she'd call Alan when she finished. She needed all the grounding she could get.

❧ ⋯⋯ ❧

Stormi slid the plastic card through the credit card machine and cringed at the amount. It couldn't be helped. Without a new computer, she had no way of earning a living. She pulled a tight smile as an older man rang up her purchase. She thanked him, headed through the door with her package, and plunked her fanny in the driver's seat.

She yanked the hat from her head and blew up her bangs with a blast of air. It had taken longer than she'd expected picking out a computer. Now, it was almost dark. She twisted the key in the ignition, and the little car sprang to life. A bit of stress oozed from her body. At least she wouldn't make it home because the car wouldn't start.

An older black truck drove behind her, and her head whipped around. Was it Ake? No, wrong headlights. She took a deep breath and pulled the gearshift into reverse, trying not to spin the front wheels.

With much careful driving, Stormi puttered home and pulled into the driveway.

"Thank you, God," she breathed.

The snow greeted her again as she stepped from the car. She gathered her bulky package and waddled to the back door. All was well. She'd wrap up the podcast easily by midnight. What an empowered woman she was. She snickered. That was the trend. Hashtag independent woman.

Her foot caught an icy patch, and she nearly went down. *Yes, Lord, thanks for the reminder. I know I depend on you.* She righted herself and inserted the key into the lock. Once she wangled the burden through the door, she quickly flipped her boots off before she skied across the slippery concrete.

In stocking feet she padded over to the TV tray that had become her office and deposited her burden. She glanced around the room and threw her hands up.

"I got a new computer."

The echoes of the nearly empty room bounded back to her. Empowered and independent, yes. And lonely. Double yes. Ake's face entered her mind for the millionth time. This would be a lot more fun with him here.

"I'm pathetic." With her companion, loneliness, she stooped and began the long process of unpacking the machine.

The next afternoon Stormi stared at her new computer screen. She'd been through all her files and still couldn't pull up the one she needed. This switching computers thing really sucked. If only her computer guy could isolate her files from the old laptop.

Her head thundered as she sat back in the chair. A shiver chased down her spine. It seemed chilly in here with the insulation only half done. She laid her hands on her cheeks. Did she have a fever? With labored movements she forced herself from the chair and stumbled across the room to the bathroom. After locating the thermometer, she stuck it beneath her tongue.

Ake's couch beckoned to her, and she melded into the cushions. The beeps of the thermometer indicated the bad news. A hundred and one. No wonder. She rose and shuffled to the kitchen to pull down a bottle of pain reliever. At least her week of podcasts was finished.

She returned to the couch, snatching a soft furry blanket on her way. Crazy to want to nap so early in the afternoon. No sooner had she snuggled up with her head on a soft throw pillow when knocks came at the door. She groaned and stood up, clutching the blanket about her. Through the glass she could see Ake's bearded face. She slid the door open.

"Busy?" He grinned, but his eyes flicked about.

Did he expect her to have Ray inside? She had no energy to pursue the thought any further. "No. Sick, maybe, but not busy."

Concern instantly fell over his face before he pushed his way inside and yanked the door closed. His huge hand pressed against her forehead. "You've got a fever."

"Yep. A hundred and one." She ambled toward the couch. "I hate to be unhospitable, but unless you like being sick, you better go."

She settled on the couch, swathed in the thick blanket. Still, chills ran down her body.

"I can't leave you. You don't feel well."

It took a huge amount of effort to power up a slight smile quirk at the corner of her mouth. "You're sweet, but misled. I'm a grown-up. I'll take care of myself."

"You have lunch?"

Stormi closed her eyes and drew in a long breath. "Uhhh, no. But I'm fine."

A short laugh came from the handsome man seated on the fireplace hearth. "It's nearly two o'clock. When did you eat last?"

Breathing took a few moments. Oh, how she longed to lie in her bed. Then she spoke. "Like, yesterday? It doesn't matter. You need to leave."

"Okay. But only to get some chicken noodle soup. You can't get better if you don't eat."

She swiped a hundred pound hand at him. Ugh. Her whole body felt made of heavy sandbags. "I'll be fine."

But he was already at the door. "Lie down. I'll fetch some soup. Mind if I take your keys here on the counter? That way you won't have to get up to let me in."

Her weighted head nodded. On the final downward motion she let her chin rest against her chest. "Sure. They're my extras anyway."

Her eyes burst open as the door banged shut. A throbbing sent everything in the room pulsating to the beat of her heart. Oh, migraine. She fell to a lying position as cold air sent her shivering. Brrr. Had Ake left the door open? No, she'd heard it shut. Her mind grew fuzzy as her body settled in rest. Maybe she'd feel better after a little nap.

Chapter Fourteen

At Calvert's grill, Madge went right to work packaging
up the chicken noodle soup. Ake glanced around, waved at a
few regulars, and nodded a greeting to a few others. But his
mind centered on telling Hoge he wouldn't be at tonight's
family dinner. It wouldn't go over well, but he wasn't going to
leave Stormi until she felt better.

He'd better pop in at his brother's house to let him know,
and then buzz back over to Stormi's place. She had probably
fallen asleep anyhow. He smiled as the woman handed him the
Styrofoam package.

Outside, he lowered his head against the wind. Spring was
not far behind the blast of cold air, and he couldn't wait. Once
in the truck, he thundered the engine to life and pulled from
the lot. Maybe Hoge had some work to do this afternoon, and
he could just leave a message with Joni. A groan rushed from
his lungs. Sure would be easier.

A few moments later he swung up into the slanted driveway and exited the vehicle. Hoge had the garage door open and one of the wheels off of Joni's car. He came around the corner wiping oil from his hands.

Hoge nodded his burly head. "Bro."

"What's up? Joni need a new tire?"

"Nope. Brakes."

Ake nodded and drew closer as Hoge rolled the wheel around to the front of the car. A salamander heater in the corner kept the open space tolerably warm.

No use beating the bush. "I won't be here tonight."

Hoge paused and looked him over. "You're going to be with that woman, aren't you?"

"I thought I'd hang some drywall."

"Pshaw." Hoge scoffed. "Why're you letting her pull free labor out of you, Ake? Make her pay someone to do that."

"She didn't ask me. I volunteered."

A roll of disapproving emotions solidified Hoge's face into granite. "You need to stay away from her."

"She's sick."

That froze his brother into a statue.

"She ain't got nobody, Hoge."

The big man inhaled. "Yeah, yeah. Seems like she ought to have some other friends who could nursemaid her back to health."

Ake shrugged.

"Fine. I'll tell Joni. Maybe you can stop by Mom's and get a plate of food, if you want."

His brother's words were almost congenial, and Ake gave a grin. "Sure, big brother."

"Don't call me that. Sounds like an idio—" Hoge stiffened.

With a shrug, Ake shifted his gaze. "I know. Still glad you're my brother Hoge. See ya."

As Ake reversed down the driveway, Hoge stood just outside the garage watching him. He paused when the truck did and raised his hand. Hoge's chin lifted in response. Such a ponderous look on his face. But Ake didn't meditate anymore on it. He had to get to Stormi.

A noise roused Stormi from an uncomfortable sleep. Her eyelids felt like hot cumbersome garage doors that couldn't be manually lifted. And when she did open them, the undersides scraped across her tender eyes like concrete. She stared at the high industrial ceiling for a moment. Shivers shook her body. Her cheeks had surely turned to ice. She tugged the blanket closer.

"You need more blankets?"

Ake's deep voice murmured softly from the chair by the hearth.

"When did you get here?" she mumbled over swollen tonsils.

"A while back. I've got soup. You want some?"

Her face grimaced and tears moistened her eyes. "No."

She squirmed on the couch but couldn't seem to get anywhere comfortable. "I'm just freezing."

"Let's get you to bed."

She closed her eyes and shook her head. It was too cold to stand up. But he didn't seem to take no for an answer. His arms gathered her against his chest and eased her from the couch. Her teeth chattered as he carried her to the bed in the far corner. She moaned. How would she stay warm so far from the fireplace?

The mattress was glacial when he laid her down, and she shuddered. Ake moved about the bed, but Stormi only closed her eyes in misery. Then he clutched her waist and set her against a stack of pillows. Blanket after blanket piled on top of her.

"Here, I found a heating pad. Pull it under your blankets and I'll plug it in."

She clenched her jaw to still the juddering, tugged the cold pad inside, and hugged it. After a few agonizing moments, the heating pad began to warm. She sighed with relief. The mattress lowered on her left side. She opened her eyes. Ake sat there with a tray of soup.

She shook her head.

"You need your strength, Stormi. Try a little."

Whether it was his comforting voice, his kindness, or the way her name rolled soothingly off his tongue, she didn't know. She only found herself sipping soup from a spoon he held out.

When she could stand no more, she shook her head and snuggled her head under the covers. The mattress lifted to its normal height, and she allowed unconsciousness to wrap her ailing mind into clouds of oblivion.

She awakened later to Ake standing beside her bed with a palmful of pain reliever and a glass of water. With a sniff she took them without complaint, and he tucked a box of tissues at her side. No other words were spoken, and she slipped into sleep once again.

She awoke groggy the following morning to the sound of the door opening. Ake came through with a wave, and she pulled herself upright on the pillows. She grabbed a tissue and blew her nose.

"Good morning."

"Hi," she croaked.

He approached the bed with a smile. My, he looked fab, and despite feeling like dung, a grin arced the side of her mouth. She shrugged.

"You're looking a little better. No chills?"

"I—" A lock of hair fell into her eye. My, she must look like some kind of repellant fungus, snot dripping, hair in disarray, mouth breathing out noxious fumes. She shot a one-eyed look at Ake. "I guess."

She fell back against the pillows and draped her arm over her eyes. Ick, she even smelled gross. His hand eased away her arm and felt her head.

"Well, your fever seems to have gone down. You're still pale, though."

Great. Fungus the shade of clown make-up. Her head still pounded, but with less intensity. And she'd turned off the heating pad somewhere in the middle of the night and shoved it to the floor.

"I think we're making progress."

She sneezed as he eased to the bed, and she snatched a tissue to catch the mucus explosion. "Don't look at me. I'm horrendous."

His low laughter met her ears as she went through several more tissues.

She turned blurry eyes to him. "Thanks for taking care of me, Doc."

He reached over and massaged her neck and shoulders, and she melted into the linens. She moaned as his warm hands rubbed the ache from her body. Then he massaged her head and she grew drowsy. His ministrations were better than ibuprofen. All too soon, he pulled up the blankets and stood. She didn't bother to open her eyes but pressed herself into the softness of the bed.

Noises from the kitchen indicated Ake had made himself busy cooking some kind of breakfast. She wanted to jump from the bed and take over, but the weakness pervading her body wouldn't allow her to even lift her eyelids.

She must have dozed again for when she opened her eyes, Ake was there again, with a gentle smile and a trayful of breakfast. For his benefit, she would try to eat, but she couldn't feel less like putting food in her mouth.

With his help she struggled to a seated position, and he laid the tray across her lap. She stared at the flavored oatmeal and toast.

"You want something else? I know you're not a big oatmeal fan."

Her head still weighed a ton and a half, but she managed to raise her gaze to his. "No, I'm just drained. Flu, I guess."

He nodded. "Yeah, Lucy's got it, too. Here, let me help you."

She opened her mouth to protest but was only greeted with strawberry-flavored oatmeal on her tongue. Ick, the texture made her shudder, but the warmth left a healing trail to her stomach. Spoonful after spoonful, she swallowed until she could barely hold her head up.

Choking down the last bite, she waved wearisome hands at him. "Enough."

Ake lifted the tray from her. Briefly she wondered what he was doing, but her body didn't stay curious enough to stay awake. A knock sounded from somewhere, but her body's responses ignored this little detour and slipped into blissful rest once more.

❧ ····· ❧

Ake opened the door and let his brother in.

"What are you doing?" Hoge demanded.

Ake laid a forefinger to his lips and then pointed across the room to the bed where Stormi lay asleep.

Hoge's head swung that direction only momentarily before he confronted his brother with a thunderous expression. But at least he lowered his voice. "We're fishing today. Let's go."

He shook his head. "Not me. I gotta stay here."

His brother's face grew even more stern. And Ake didn't think that was possible. "Ake, you're not her husband. Now come on."

Oh, how he wished he were. He glanced over toward the white rumpled comforter and let the implication pass over him for just a moment. Then he schooled his features and turned to Hoge. "You'll have to go without me."

Hoge's jaw worked like it always did right before he blew up. Ake lifted his hand and clutched his brother's stiff shoulder. "Come on, Hoge. It's important."

Twitches lit across Hoge's face as he decompressed. "Fine. One day. No pay."

Ake shrugged. "Sure."

His brother spun away, grasped the door handle, and swung it open. Then he turned. "One day, Ake."

The door slid shut.

Three days later, Stormi, wrapped in a soft blanket, lay against the couch cushion with a tiny smile. Black circles ringed her eyes, but a spark of health pinched her cheeks. Ake handed her a book he'd received from his mother the night before. He'd skip telling her about the tongue lashing he'd received from Hoge as he'd gripped that book in his mother's kitchen. His brother didn't appreciate him missing three days' work. But it didn't matter. Stormi was better. He'd shoulder more than Hoge's rage for just one of her smiles.

"You have to stop spoiling me." Her head lolled against the couch. "I haven't been sick like that for years."

He parked himself on the end of the couch and watched her study the back of the book's cover.

"This looks good. Did your mom like it?"

"Yeah, the church had the author come and do some kind of women's thing. She picked it out for you."

"Hmmm." She flicked the book open. "Faith or Fear. Definitely a book I need to memorize."

She gave a low, tired chuckle and then flicked her eyes to him. "I owe you big time."

Ake stretched his legs out long and crossed them. "Yep. You'll have to change the oil in my truck for the entire summer."

Her delicate forehead creased. "For real? Dream on."

He barked a laugh when she crossed her eyes. "Mom says your eyes will stick that way."

Stormi stuck out her tongue. "I'm so ugly right now it wouldn't matter."

"You're not ugly."

She leaned toward him. "Are you kidding? I haven't had a shower in four days. My hair is such a greasy mess, I could supply the oil for your truck."

"I need six and a half quarts per change," he winked.

Giggles erupted from her cracked lips. "Don't make me laugh. I don't have the energy."

"So that's a 'yes' on the shower plans for the day?"

She gave him a weak smack on the arm. "I'm thinking tomorrow morning. Behave yourself or you'll change your own oil."

He stared at the fire for a moment. "You think you can make it alone tomorrow?"

Struggling to sit up, she puffed from exertion. "Yes. Go back to work before Hoge slices you into corned-beef sandwiches."

He glanced at the clock. It was late, and he needed to check on his folks before he retired for the night. "I suppose I should go. Don't forget to drink plenty of water."

"Yes, Mom."

He rose reluctantly and stood there taking in her weary face. She was practically asleep. A pitiful smile worked its way across her pale lips, but then she grew serious. "Thanks, Ake. You were a great comfort."

He nodded, wishing he had a reason to stay and watch her drift off to sleep. But instead he made his way to his coat by the door and slipped outside.

Stormi moved slowly for the rest of the week, but bit by bit she gained back her old vitality. That had been one wicked flu bug, and she hoped Ake didn't pick it up. But he seemed healthy as a well-muscled mule, but a hundred times more handsome. The concern in his eyes when he stopped by melted her heart. What a sweetheart.

Still she couldn't depend on Ake all the time. She needed to meet some new people and expand her horizons. Alan had been pushing her to get involved at a church, and she had to admit, it was a great idea.

Still, sitting in her car eyeing the huge white-sided building made her want to turn and hightail it back to her home. She sighed and leaned back in the seat. To grow, you've got to stretch, Alan had said. Yeah. And be uncomfortable evidently. She grabbed the pink leather Bible in the passenger's seat and bounded from the car before she lost her courage.

Most of the people traffic had gone through the side door rather than the main entrance. Since it was Wednesday night, maybe they met in classrooms. She cringed as she came up on a large family making their way through the glass door. The husband, a nice-looking blond in a buttoned-up shirt, nodded to her as he held the door. Stormi scooted in, thanks whooshing from her tight lungs.

Once inside clusters of people talking and yells of children running through the gym to the right sent her searching for some sort of sanctuary. The sign with a stick woman was just the place. She scurried toward the bathroom door.

Thankfully, it was empty and she squirreled herself away in a stall. No sooner had she locked the door than a group of giggling girls entered. From their conversation, definitely teenagers. Now what? Was she going to stay sequestered in here until everyone cleared out and then sulk to her car? Toilets flushed, more giggles, and finally the gaggle moved out.

Stormi opened the door and went to stare at herself in the mirror. This was very unfamiliar. She leaned on the sink and gave herself a stern look.

"Go to class, you lily-livered coward!"

The door opened and in came none other than Joni. Hoge's Joni. What were the chances?

Chapter Fifteen

"Oh, Stormi. I didn't realize you were here. Ake never told us he was bringing you."

Stormi opened her mouth. "Uhhh. I'm not with Ake."

A pucker appeared on the brunette's brow. "Oh?"

She jumped on Joni's hesitation. "Yeah, I wanted to come to Bible study, but I'm not sure where to go."

Her face cleared. "Hold on and I'll show you."

She backed up to the wall near the hand dryer and waited for Joni to do her business.

Joni emerged from a stall and quickly washed her hands. "I'll take you to Phil's newcomers' class. You'll love it. It'll give you a chance to meet a lot of people."

Just the thing. "Lead on, Yoda."

Joni laughed. "Well, you understand that Ake won't be in there, but you can probably see him afterwards. He's in the singles' class."

Stormi nibbled her lip as Joni led her through a maze of hallways. They reached a class through the throng. Joni waved as Stormi tiptoed in and chose a chair in the back. She fumbled with her purse to cover her nervousness while people drifted in.

A couple sat beside her and the woman with a curly mop of hair leaned over and stuck out her hand. "Hi, I'm Carlie Hudson, and my husband, Sam."

Stormi pulled a tight smile. "Stormi Zobroski.

The slender woman nodded and gave a smile. Her large teeth made her mouth somewhat dominate her face. "You from Stone Harbor?"

Stormi nodded.

"We moved in about a month back. Seems like a great place. Sam manages the big electronics store over at Fulbright."

"I just moved in not too long ago, as well."

The woman with big teeth nodded, her hair bouncing. "New job?"

Meh. New life. "No, just like the area."

She nodded enthusiastically. "You married?"

Stormi sucked in a long inhale and shook her head. *Yada, yada, here's my entire life in a five minute soliloquy. Please let the bald man at the front call this thing to order.*

Like a speedy taxi zipping through the streets of New York, the man delivered her by standing and welcoming everyone. Stormi gave a sigh of relief as her biographer shut her mouth and settled into her seat. He referenced the book they were studying and questioned if anyone needed a copy. Stormi clenched her hands together, unwilling to call attention to herself by acknowledging her lack.

But dear Carlie had no qualms in waving him back with an extra copy for her, drawing the stares of about thirty people in the room. Stormi grit her teeth, but managed a thank you without unlocking her jaw.

Despite feeling like a hummingbird in an eagle's nest, once the discussion began, she grew fascinated with the material. Sure, most folks probably thought it incredibly rudimentary, but connecting the scripture references with basic Bible beliefs was what she craved. She hoped she could take the book home to pore over it at her leisure.

Her brain throbbed by the time Phil had closed the class out in prayer, and Carlie turned to her with another horse grin.

"I hope you weren't too bored going over such simple concepts. But you have to take this class before you join the church."

"Oh, no. It was fine." Stormi stifled a giggle. It was fine because it was all new. But Carlie didn't need to know that.

Her newfound friend gushed over how nice it had been to meet her and followed her husband out of the row of blue cushioned seats. Now, to get to her car. But as she brushed through the doorway, she came face to face with Ake.

Ake's face opened in pure pleasure, and a ripple of delight raced through her.

"You're here."

She grinned. "I think so."

He wrapped a large arm around her shoulders. "Are you feeling back to normal?"

"Yep." The eyes they drew kept her reply brief. Hoge's heated glance set her muscles in a clench. Soon, the whole Pearson clan had gathered in a circle around them. Nothing like being a rabbit in a fox's den.

She pulled a tight smile at Ake's mom and nodded numerous times to try to stay in the conversation. Thankfully, no questions flew her direction, and Ake's thick body guarded her from Hoge's sharp teeth snapping about.

Ake broke away and pulled her along toward the exit. She didn't complain and hurried to keep up with his quick steps. She sucked in the freezing, fresh air when she broke through the confines of the building. With a click she unlocked the car door and he opened her door. He circled the car and slid inside the passenger's seat. The church's security light illuminated the interior, and his eyes fastened on her. She held his gaze.

When he didn't speak, she bugged her eyes at him. "Yes?"

"Everything okay?"

Great. Her "I-fit-in persona" had fallen short. "I guess."

His gaze searched her face, and she panned an open expression. "What?"

He laid a hand on her arm resting on the console. "Just a big step starting a new church."

She pressed herself back into the seat as a couple passed by the front bumper. Hopefully with the darkness, they wouldn't notice the two of them cozied up in her car. "It was fine."

He nodded. "Good. 'Cause I want you to come back."

She pursed her lips. "I'll be back, Ake. I know I need this fellowship. The book you gave me was great. It's just...me trying to connect with people."

"I can come in your class, if it will help."

She grinned. "That won't draw any attention. You, following me around like a pup. I'll be fine. I promise."

"All right." His hand paused on the door latch. "I guess I better go. Maybe I'll see ya this weekend. I've got some stuff to do, but I'm sure I can drop by. I need to get started on that drywall before the next storm comes in."

Her brow puckered. "Another storm? I thought spring was nearly here."

He laughed, a deep rumbling sound that fascinated her. "You're in New England, now. Spring's a piece yet."

The passenger door opened, and he stepped from the car, but stuck his head back in with a sparkle in his dark eyes. "Goodnight, Stormi."

His expression pulled out her best smile. "Goodnight, Ake."

He shut the door and strode away. Lucky Carlie. She got to leave with her man. Her cheek twitched, claiming Ake as her own. She shrugged. It meant nothing. Just more of a general reference. Sorta.

By Saturday afternoon, Stormi paced and glanced at the clock. She'd finished several podcasts with the hope of quitting early and here she was, wondering why Ake hadn't shown his face yet. It was three o'clock. What did it matter? It was friends hanging out, not some date. She chewed her lip and made an executive decision. If he didn't come to her, she'd go to him.

When she arrived at Ake's house, his truck sat outside the garage. Strange. Was something up with his parents? Her quick glance up the slope revealed a sleeping house coated in fresh snow. All seemed well. And Hoge was nowhere in sight. Always welcome news. Just then the front door swung open and Ake, paint roller in hand strode through the door. He stopped short when he saw her.

She gave an awkward wave. "Hi."

He pulled a slow smile and walked closer. "What are you doing here?"

Not the over enthused reply she'd hoped for. Her gaze flicked to the roller in his hand. Perfect. "I came to help paint."

"I thought we'd agreed you were changing the oil?" His brow lifted and a smirk twitched his eyes.

"Nope. Painting. That's what I'm all about." She flashed a hundred watt smile and curtsied.

"Okay. I could use the help, actually. I got started late. I intended to be finished by now and be at your house to do the drywall. Hold on. I've got to fetch another gallon of paint from the truck."

She drifted toward the house but waited until he came back, swinging a fresh bucket of paint. White paint streaked his clothes, hands, and hairy arms that emerged past the folded cuffs of the flannel shirt.

"Head on in." He motioned with the paint roller.

She scurried inside and removed her coat. He led her around the counter toward a door. The fine cabinetry and wooden plank floor were a testament to Ake's knack for building. For a pole barn home, it had some nice finishes.

He swung the door open and stepped out into the cleanest garage she'd ever seen. Three of the walls were covered in white paint. One wall, still sporting mudded drywall in rectangular patchwork, awaited its turn to be covered.

"I see you went all out with the color."

He shrugged as he pried open the can with a screwdriver. "Not much on decorating. White's nice and clean."

She nodded and picked up a paint brush from a work bench. "So, I just go up and down with this?"

He chuckled and stood after pouring a glob of paint into a tray. A salamander heater at the end of the garage kept the area warm enough to take the paint. "Have you ever painted before?"

She wanted to wipe the smirk from his face by declaring yes, but that would be a lie. "Not exactly."

"Well, here then. You take the roller while I cut in. You were serious about helping, right?" Sweet uncertainty crossed his features.

Stormi reached for the roller. It was heavier than she'd expected. "Yes. Okay, up and down? That's it?"

"Pretty much."

He strode over and moved the heater across the room and then knelt to run a swipe of paint near the floor. My, he was trusting. She set the roller on the wall and pushed it up and down. Speckles of paint sponged onto the surface.

"I don't think I'm doing this right."

He rose and came back to her. "Just load the roller again."

When she stood there in uncertainty, he took her hand and dunked the cylindrical sponge into the tray and swiped down the sloped section to even out the layer.

"Oh, I could've done that."

He didn't release her hand. One brow elevated. "You sure you don't want me to show you?"

She laughed. "I've got this."

Still he resisted, his brows dancing. With a grin she yanked free of his grasp, landing the roller on her new sky blue Henley. Her mouth flew open.

A burst of laughter erupted from his lungs. "Oops."

"Ake Pearson, you're in for it now." She couldn't quite stop laughing. "What am I going to do? This is my new shirt."

He pulled the roller from her hand. "Head back to my room and grab a shirt from my closet. If you rinse it now, it might come out."

"It better." His laughter followed her into the kitchen.

"Last room on the right." He hollered between bouts of more chuckles.

Her lips twitched. What a nut. She veered to the right at the end of the hall. Hmmm. Very neat. Spartan, but tidy. Bed, dresser, side table. She headed for the closet doors on the left and pulled the double doors open.

She smiled as she flipped through his shirts, loving the smell of them, the soft feel of them, the thought that they belonged to Ake. With slow deliberation, she picked an old tan one with long sleeves. "My God is an Awesome God," splayed across the front. It already sported several stains so she tugged it from the hanger.

Once flat on the bed, she examined it, relishing the thought of wearing his shirt. With a shrug she pulled her paint-covered one over her head and smoothed the white cotton tank she wore underneath.

"Hey, I just wanted to tell you—" Ake froze in the doorway, mouth agape.

Stormi took a gasp of air and threw her hands out in shock. His eyes traced her black double-sleeved tattoos that went up both arms and created a low cut U around her neck. Crud. Why had she chosen to undress in his room? With the door wide open?

She slapped her arms across herself, as if that would keep his eyes from probing the lacy, black designs. A nervous laugh bubbled from her. "I guess I should have started this in the bathroom. Ahem, with the door closed."

A slow grin snaked across his face. "I suppose."

Strange how he didn't seem to be in any hurry. How silly, anyway. It wasn't like she was naked with pants and a tank top on. Yet, she was definitely exposed. Since becoming a Christian, she'd shown no one the horrible ink marring her skin. She dropped her arms. What was she hiding anyway? It was everywhere.

"Well, this is me."

He nodded.

"You know, freaky tattooed me."

Ake continued to stare.

"Are you planning on getting back to the painting?" She elevated her brow and gave a smirk.

"Soon."

"Gotta get your fill of the circus mutant, right? Okay." She spun slowly with her arms out. "Here's a three-sixty, in all my ugliness."

He approached when she finished her turn and brought up a finger to trace the filigree at her neck. She caught her breath and stiffened, but he took his time, following the path to her wrist.

"I think it's beautiful." Ake's jaw clenched.

She took slow intakes of oxygen. "You don't have to placate me, Ake. I know what people think of this. I mean, good people. Christian people. I've felt their glares and heard the hate in their comments. Your own family would flip if they knew. I'm sure they'd insist you stay far from me."

He brought up his other hand and traced the pattern down her other arm, sending a fresh set of goosebumps over her chilled skin. His eyes met hers when he'd finished and shrugged. "I like it."

"Then you're the only one I know who does. I loathe it."

One of his brows rose. "Why?"

A set of shivers raced down the length of her. "Because of what it represents in my life. Bad decisions, wrong choices, living only for pleasure and for what I could attain. A life completely devoid of God. If I could afford to remove these marks, trust me, I would. But they're always here to greet me. To taunt me."

Ake gripped her upper arms and rubbed to warm her skin. Waves of relaxation radiated from his touch. "But you're different now, right?"

A desire shuddered up her spine to nuzzle against him, to find some clemency in the cove of his neck. She shoved it down and clenched her teeth. Physicality right now was not the best option. She nodded. "Yes. Very different. Very saved."

Another grin tugged at the corner of his mouth as he scrutinized her eyes, dissecting the depth of her emotions. He understood. He recognized the intensity of her weakness, the worthlessness she still clutched. He saw her feebleness like no one else did. She couldn't look away.

"Then it's all washed away. Scars of what we were before only allow us to glorify God even more, because it reminds us of where we've been, of what we were."

Trembling seized her. *God, he is right. Why is it so hard for me to grasp and maintain a hold on the fact that you have made me a new creature?* Ake eased her into his arms, and her emotional brokenness bonded with the physical attraction this man held for her. She buried the spasmodic sniffles against the strong cords of his neck and the coarse beard.

In stuttering tones she muttered against his fragrant skin. "You're the wisest man I know, Ake Pearson."

"I love you."

Stormi yanked from his embrace. "What?"

Blood suffused the skin of Ake's open face, his eyes pools of honesty and vulnerability. His mouth, framed by the wiry beard, parted in surprise. Oh, Jiminy Christmas he hadn't meant to mutter those three little words that rocked her world. She brushed the tears from her face as the rough palms of his hands seared her arms. Thankfully he didn't repeat the confession.

She took a step back and grabbed the shirts from the bed. "I need to go."

With hurried steps, she abandoned him in the bedroom, ran down the hall, swiped the coat from the rack, and jerked the front door open. The winter air greeted her inked skin like a dip in the arctic, but she pushed it away to scurry to the Saturn. Its squeaky door hinges scraped across her raw nerves as she plunked her sorry rear in the seat.

She could barely register what had just occurred. Her foot gunned the front wheel drive into fishtails to mount the slope. Her only thought—*get home*. Something akin to self-hatred flogged at her psyche. The saliva flowing to her throat nearly choked her. Dear God, in heaven. What had she done? She was her old vile self again, luring men into falling for her.

Once home, she fled the car to scramble into the house to pitch the contents of her arms to the floor. Ake's shirt with the insignia, My God is An Awesome God, landed on the top of the heap. Great balls of fire, she'd stolen the man's shirt. With a groan she swiped it to her face and inhaled his scent. A shirt? She lamented taking a shirt? A piece of clothing was easily returned. But his heart? How would she restore that?

She dragged to the couch, the one Ake had carried in for her, and melted to the comforting cushions, still clutching the material of his shirt. The fireplace hearth glowed red beneath the gray ashes. She'd ignited something in that innocent man. This little façade had started out far left of true love. How could she have let it balloon into real feelings? Seeing the candor on his face pierced her soul, and she had no doubt he'd blurted the truth. Surely machine-gunning toddlers couldn't feel much worse.

She slipped Ake's shirt on and smoothed it against her skin. The long sleeved t-shirt covered every inch of inked skin. A sob rumbled up her throat. Dear God, he was still protecting her. She'd crushed his trust, and yet he loved her. She curled up into a ball and wept.

Chapter Sixteen

A ke had heard the door slam some time ago, yet he still stood frozen in the same spot in his bedroom.

He'd known it for a while, or at least he'd sensed something powerful had woven its way through his heart and soul. Maybe it had started the moment he'd laid eyes on her, or perhaps the day she'd coached him on how to kiss her. Or more likely the instant her soft yielding lips had touched his. It hadn't mattered one iota that the entire scene, the whole dating scheme had been fake. It had happened anyway.

What made him flinch was knowing he'd announced it to her, watched her cringe, saw her face pale with shock. Pure rejection. He took a breath and sank to the side of the bed. Could he have stopped it? She was soft and pliant, pouring out her most intimate secrets and fears to him. Bonding at full throttle. And the words had just exploded from his mouth.

Only now...now had been transformed to awkward. Like being shot down by his crush in the hallway outside of study hall. In front of the entire school body. At least he'd done it one on one this time. He face palmed himself. *Dummy, that didn't even count compared to this fail.*

He rose. It didn't matter. Just add it to the long list of missed desires and longings that he'd acquired over the years. He headed for the garage. It wouldn't paint itself. Perhaps over time the intensity binding his gut would lessen.

The paint had skimmed over in the pan by the time he'd leaned over to grab the handle of the roller. He removed the sticky glop and plopped it into the trash before adding more. As he rolled the white paint across the mudded drywall, his memory visited Stormi's tattoo, meandering the sexy design over her delicate arms. He relived tracing the lines clear to her wrist while she stood there.

Suddenly he realized he'd stopped the roller mid-stroke. *Put it away, man. It's all you've got of her now. Think about it later.* If memory served him correctly, she would now distance herself from him. Like a man with leprosy. He shoved all thoughts away and finished the wall in minutes.

Since the weather the following week crept up to thirty-eight, Hoge rustled all of them to the boats. Relief coursed through Ake as the plodding engine sent them out to sea. Normalcy had returned. Delusions of love receded to the back of his mind. Mostly. He hadn't heard from her. She was right on schedule. No doubt they'd bump into each other at the grocery store or at the Grill, and he'd be like, hi, and she'd be like, creeping away. He couldn't wait.

"Hand me that wrench," Hoge's' voice pulled him from his thoughts.

Ake stepped over, snatched it up and handed it to his brother in the wheel house.

"What's up your craw?"

Ake couldn't look him in the face. The whole mess was still too raw, and his brother knew his every thought just by glancing at him. He shrugged and stepped to the aft, shoving his gloved hands deep into his pockets. The last thing he needed was an "I told you so" lecture from Hoge.

Neff, Jeff and Delbert struggled with a tangle in the net and Ake jumped in, keeping his head down. He needed to concentrate. Ripping skin open today couldn't be added to the agenda. His whole focus had to be on the task at hand. No wandering thoughts. No mistakes. That would be a dead giveaway, and he wouldn't risk it today.

The knotted strings aligned, and Ake stepped away, bellied up starboard, and set his gaze on the horizon. He'd pray for Mom and Pop then tag on Stormi for good measure. But he wouldn't dwell on her. He'd do that later. Much later.

֍ ······ ֎

Stormi paced her one room apartment, letting her bare feet slap the freezing cold concrete below her while slapping her head with her hands. She'd barely slept the last week. The guilt of Ake's love squeezed the life from her heart. She'd barely managed to finish her podcasts for the week. How could her entire existence have dwindled to trying to think of ways to torture herself?

Poor Ake. Poor pitiful Ake. She could barely think of anything else. Her eyes darted to the clock. She figured Hoge had pressed them all into service today. The temperature neared forty for the first time in months. A moan crawled out of her throat. Ake had slashed his arm the day she laid those kisses on him. What would happen today?

She grabbed her coat and zipped it on her way out. Exercise might just focus her brain. The cold air bit at her cheeks, but she marched on and yanked the teal beanie on her head. Her boots crunched in the old snow still resisting the melt of the temperature. But then, two feet of snow disappeared slowly.

After several minutes she realized she strode past Hoge's house. Good grief, add cruelty to anguish and give it a swish.

Someone in a thick yellow coat worked their way to the curb. Joni. Could there be a worse moment?

"Stormi, hi."

Her eyes slid closed in dread. Keep walking or acknowledge the torment about to follow? Stormi paused. Ake deserved her best. She turned. "Hey."

Joni slid the mail from the box and shut it with a snap. Stormi eyed the large mailbox and wondered vaguely if she could fit inside.

But Hoge's wife smiled and waved her over. "Coffee?"

Yes, a cup of black plague, please, with a side of melba toast sprinkled with smallpox. Stormi forced a smile to her face. Joni's smile was far too welcoming, and it smote her further when she linked arms with her and tugged her to the front door.

"Don't worry," she laughed. "The kids are all at school. Nothing but peace and quiet within."

A shiver of self-revulsion skittered across Stormi's nerves. It may be peace and quiet inside Hoge's house, spiced with fresh coffee, but internally, nothing but murkiness, sulfur, and loathing. She plastered a semi-smile to her face.

"Park it here, girl. I've been dying to talk with you. You know, without Hoge." Joni pulled the coat from her shoulders and hung it on a chair before opening a cabinet and pulling down a couple of mugs. "I've got fresh banana bread. Up for a piece?"

Stormi forced out a laugh that sounded more like she was strangling. Maybe she was. "Uh, no. You must be the dessert queen. You had dump cake the last time I was here."

Joni chuckled and set a hand to her hip. "Have you seen the Pearson brothers? They can put away the food. Besides, Hoge's soft spot is dessert. Don't tell him I told you that."

"Trust me, your secret is safe with me." Had she ever spoken truer words?

Her companion sliced up a thick slice for herself, lathered it with butter, and popped it into the microwave. "Sorry, gotta have some. I must keep up my girlish figure."

Joni set a cup of coffee in front of Stormi, and she stared at the dark brew while her companion removed the bread from the microwave. Oh, good. The interrogation would now commence in three, two—

"All right, tell me the scoop." Joni settled into the chair opposite her.

The perfect spot to detect any and all expression changes. Stormi put on her best blasé expression. What to go with? Tell her the truth about her relationship with Ake being a hoax, or go with the lie. A strong desire to thunk her head to the hard tabletop washed over her. Instead she gave a false smile. Lie, lie, *lie*.

"What scoop do you want?"

"You know, how are things with you and Ake? You've not been over again for a couple of weeks. I was just wondering how things were going."

Stormi shored up the need to blurt. "Fine."

Joni's brow rose, a disappointed tug at her mouth. "Fine?"

"Well, you know. We've not really known each other that long." Stormi sipped the scalding hot brew. Her throat screamed. Yes, more punishment. Please, bring it on.

"Sure. I understand. But I'm excited Ake found someone. He's been alone so long. And high school was just a nightmare for the poor guy."

Ugh, swords and foils pierced Stormi's soul. The unusual companion of tears rose up her throat. Oh, no. No, *no*. Not now. No break in demeanor was allowed. She clenched her jaw and let anger rise up to take its place. How dare Joni ask such questions?

"I hardly think I need to discuss this with you."

Stormi cringed at Joni's hurt expression. One kitten drowned, now two.

Joni rose. "I'm sorry. I didn't mean to invade your privacy. Forgive me."

The tears fought harder for exposure. No. no, *no*. Oh, dear heavens, not just tears, sobs. Stormi pressed her head into Joni's tabletop, too weak to stifle another, as her shoulders shook with the depth of the emotion.

"Oh, Stormi. Shhh."

Joni embraced her from above, but she could do nothing but allow the horrible waterworks full rein. She couldn't stop it. Like the Niagara, the falls tumbled forth, regardless of any attempts to block it. After what seemed like way too long, Stormi straightened, and Joni pushed a bundle of tissues her way.

"Sorry," Stormi mumbled. Could she be a bigger idiot?

Joni sank into that blasted chair, and she could feel her companion's eyes cook her with their intensity. She glanced up. Glory, hallelujah, pity rested in Joni's pupils. Stormi closed her eyes. This couldn't be happening.

"What happened? Did you break up?"

Stormi jumped from the table and cast her gaze out the small window over the sink. "No."

Joni stood. "Then what?"

She licked her lips and fought herself for a moment. When she could hold it no longer, she let it go. "He loves me."

A slow smile stretched across Joni's plump face, but then eased to a frown. "What's wrong with that? Unless—"

Stormi blinked as realization washed over Joni. It wasn't a pretty sight, and condemnation entered her eyes.

"Oh. Oh, dear."

Go for the gusto. Stormi pulled her arms out of her coat. "I never planned for it to go this far. Really. I'm not fit for him, anyway."

"I think you're just not giving yourself a chance, Stormi. He's great. I know some might think he's a little on the slow side, but I assure you, you'll not find a more perfect gentleman. Hoge included."

She flopped the coat to the chair and grasped the bottom of her long sleeved shirt. Best to give her the goods, so she'd shut her mouth. Stormi whipped the overshirt from her body and stood shivering in a camisole, inked lines snaking the full horrid picture. Joni did not disappoint. Her mouth flew open.

They stared at one another for a moment or two. Then Joni shut her mouth. Tightness edged her mouth into a pucker. Her eyes came to rest on Stormi's once more. *Hammer it home.*

"You see, I had no right to latch onto him. Hoge was right. So very right. I'm scum. Dirty scum. Marked and used by men over and over like a cheap escort. I don't deserve any man's love, let alone Ake's."

When Joni continued to stare, Stormi snatched up her shirt and coat. "Hate to crush and run."

Stormi sped for the front door. She shoved through it and yanked the coat back on her arms. She longed to stuff her shirt into the mailbox, but decided she'd done enough damage for the day. Instead, she shoved it into a wad in her pocket.

"Stormi."

Joni's voice echoed behind her, but Stormi only broke into a run. No more. *No more. Enough abuse today, please God.* She ran until she couldn't breathe. But the deprecating self-hatred only blossomed in her oxygen-deprived body. Back in her driveway, she stopped and leaned over, hands on thighs, body throbbing, gasping for breath. She'd do anything, *anything* to fix this mess.

∾ ⋯⋯ ∾

Ake put another spoonful of Joni's chicken casserole into his mouth. It was one of his favorites, although it seemed made of dust tonight. But Joni's sympathetic eyes fed his desire to eat the same amount he always did. Yeah, and dessert rested over on the counter. Pineapple upside-down cake. Hoge's favorite.

The thought of baked tropical fruit on his tongue disgusted him. With his love of food, it would be logical he could eat like he ordinarily did. Acting relatively normal hadn't taken much effort, given he was quiet to begin with, but eating. It presented a challenge. But he'd push through.

Mom patted his hand. Joni knew something. Had she shared it with Mom? Likely not. His mother had her own sharply-tuned emotion antennas. Pop picked up his spoon to butter his rolls. Thank the good Lord for distracting Mom, even in the saddest way.

"How was the catch this week?" Mom asked once Pop's roll was finished.

Ake let Hoge answer. Ake could tell her exactly how many fish they'd pulled in and what species, but he let his brother give the approximate. Joni's eyes raked him again. Something was up with that. "Think I'll go find Lucy."

"What? No dessert?" Joni protested.

Ake's stomach clenched. "Why sure. Get it ready while I spend some time with my niece.

He rose and pulled the door open to the basement. His niece had hightailed it down there moments before to talk to herself in her little kitchen, and Ake could think of nothing more comforting than to eat her pretend cooking. He arrived at the bottom of the carpeted stairs and wasn't disappointed. She was ensconced in her play corner, setting a doll into a small high chair.

"Now you eat your vegetables, Baby. They'll make you grow," Lucy admonished the glare-eyed doll, lips pursed for a bottle.

"Got any vegetables for your old uncle?"

His pint-sized niece beamed, her curls bouncing. "Sure. You sit here."

Ake eyed the short plastic chair snugged up to the kid-sized table. Instead he went to his knees and bellied up to the plate.

"I better do this or I'll bust your chair."

She giggled, pranced over, and head-locked him in a hug. "Okay, Unca Ake."

Lucy puttered around, chattering and taking on the mom persona to a tee. Ake grinned, enjoying the distraction she set up for him.

"Eat your carrot, now." She pushed the plastic orange chunk towards his lips.

"Thanks." He took it from her only to be offered fake lettuce and a wad of corn.

His niece laid her arm across his shoulders. "When you and Stormi get married, can I come to your house?"

His stomach lurched, and he rose, sweeping the small arm from him. He gave the least argumentative answer. "Sure."

He turned, intending to stride to the loveseat nearby. Enough food. Plastic or not. And enough probing conversations. Joni stood at the bottom of the stairs. From the look on her face, she'd heard the whole interaction.

Chapter Seventeen

"Hi, Mommy," Lucy chimed.

"Hey, Pumpkin. Go upstairs and get your dessert. Eat it at the table."

Lucy set more food on the plates at her tiny table. "In a minute."

"Now."

The child glanced up. Joni's tone expressed no excuses.

"Okay." Lucy headed for the stairs.

Joni crossed her arms. Great. He was cornered. Lucy thundered up the steps behind his sister-in-law.

Her face pinched. "Marrying Stormi, are we?"

He rubbed his beard. "Not we, me."

Her eyes closed momentarily. "That the truth, Aiken Ellings Pearson?"

He straightened. Why did everyone treat him like a kid? He shrugged and crossed his arms.

Joni must have realized her gaffe and stepped forward with her hands out. "I'm sorry, Ake. But she's just not the woman for you. You've got to understand that."

"I know."

Her brows snugged together. "You know? I thought—"

She censored herself and Ake continued to stare at her.

Finally, she walked closer and laid a hand to his arm. "Ake, tell me what's going on."

"Nothing's going on."

Her eyes searched his face. "But you love her."

His jaw clenched. Had she guessed that? Was it written plainly on his face for all to see? "I never said that."

"She did."

His Adam's apple bobbed, and he was relieved to know the beard concealed it. "When did you talk to her?"

"Yesterday."

He acknowledged her remark with a tilt of his head. "She told you that?"

"Yes. And she showed me her..." Joni paused to bite her lip and look around for a moment. "Her—tattoos."

Ake's face stiffened into a mask. Something big had happened if Stormi had revealed her ink to his sister-in-law. "And?"

Joni struck an irritated pose, hand to hip. "And she's not for you, Ake."

"Because she has tattoos?"

She gave a sound of disgust. "Well, no. I mean, maybe. For golly sakes, they are all over her arms. Everywhere. Oh, Ake, she all out told me she's been used. You don't need that."

"You tell Hoge?"

"Not yet."

When he didn't speak, she continued. "Are you asking me to keep this from your brother?"

Ake made a clicking sound out the side of his mouth. "I'd never ask you to do that."

Tears sparkled in her eyes. "Ake, you're killing me."

He pulled his gaze from her. "Not sure what you want from me, Joni."

She sniffled. "I want you not to love her."

He cut around her and headed for the stairs. "Me, too."

Ake didn't care what it looked like. He needed a drive and he headed straight for the front door, avoiding the family group gathered in the kitchen. Then he paused. If he disliked the drama in the basement, his abrupt departure would bring more of that from Mom and Hoge. He pivoted and made his way back to the kitchen and worked his throat, hoping it would accept another unwanted portion of food.

Stormi combed her fingers through her dirty wad of hair. She'd taken on teaching more classes at another online university and barely had ten hours of sleep in the last two weeks. In one fell swoop she swept the papers and books from the counter, crashing them to the floor. Enough, she was near nuts looking for the one paper that hid from her. Where was it?

She gripped her head and surveyed the mess splaying on the concrete at her feet. With a scream she kicked the nearest book and sent it against the far wall. The pain in her foot sent her hopping and nearly cursing. Fine. She hobbled to the door, foregoing the coat and yanked her purse from the counter.

After slamming the door, she walked to her car and sank into the bucket seat. She gave a cry of surprise when her skin touched the cold fabric. A spaghetti strap tank top was perfect for this weather and for her mood. She should slap an "S" for sleazy to her head and walk back and forth downtown to declare her sins to the world.

With a growl she jerked the shift into gear. She just wanted to be numb. One day free of the debilitating remorse of hurting Ake. Just one day. She drove to the place she remembered could do that and pulled into the parking lot of the liquor store. Panting, she stared at the brick façade that flanked the large barred window displaying its wares in colorful bottles and boxes.

The radio blared an appropriate drinking song, and she punched the off button before sinking her hand into her purse to locate her phone. With shaking hands, she punched in Alan's number.

"Sup?"

A garbled gasp was all that met his ears.

"Stormi, that you?"

She blurted an, uh-huh, through her huffs of agony.

"Where are you?"

Good, ole' Alan. Knew right where to probe. "The liquor store."

A silence stretched which helped Stormi grab hold of sanity.

"All right. Could be worse."

"I broke an innocent man's heart," she blurted.

Another long mute moment ticked by.

"Stormi, it isn't anything God can't fix and forgive."

She cringed. What if she couldn't forgive herself? "I've failed. I did a horrible thing."

"We all do it, my friend."

"You don't," she snapped.

"Yes, I do. Yelled at my wife for dropping her phone in the toilet last night."

Stormi rolled her eyes. If only this were about cleaning off some toilet water. "You call that a real failure?"

"She cried. It broke my heart."

Her breathing slowed down. "Is she still mad?"

"Nope."

How do these people do this? "Not sure I'm cut out for this, 'do the right thing,' Alan."

"Ah, Stormi, none of us are. We're all carnal, all fighting sin constantly."

She let out a shuddering breath and shivered. "Then how can I possibly do this?"

"You need to ask God for help. Did you talk to the Lord today, Stormi?"

She pressed her head to the freezing steering wheel. No. She hadn't.

"Start the car, Stormi. You don't really want what's there. Go home, and get on your knees."

Obediently she pulled the shift into reverse. Then she eased the car forward and pulled out into traffic.

"Who's the guy, Stormi?"

"A friend."

"Then he'll understand. Get close to the Lord and He'll comfort you. You got it?"

"Uh-huh."

"Call me later, 'kay?"

"Yep."

Stormi pulled in the driveway and exited in a flurry, her skin already chilled to the bone. Once she shut and fastened the door, she set more wood on the fire. With the soft blanket, she sank into the bed, nestled in, and lay face up. And prayed like nobody's business.

After a long night of sleep, Stormi sat up on the edge of her bed, thankful for the rest. It gave a whole new perspective on her situation. So had her prayers. God hadn't sent instant healing, but He'd made the pain manageable. She had to clean the floor of the mess she'd made yesterday and get a couple more podcasts finished.

With a deep breath, she pulled herself from the bed and visited the one walled-in room, the small bathroom. Then she jumped in the shower. It would be refreshing to start the day clean with her hair done. She dried off and dressed in jeans and camisole, covered by a sweater. The tattoos mocked her, as usual, and she ignored their evil shame. Moving on.

Once her hair was dried, she glared at the pathetic mess of papers and books on the floor. Good grief. There was that paper. Right on the top. She snatched it up. Her podcast schedule she'd sketched out. With a sigh she taped it to the wall near her laptop and then flicked it for good measure.

She strode to the radio and flipped on a local station. Maybe more favorable weather would roll in, even though it was only the end of February. The obituaries came on, and she hurried over to find another station when a name caught her ear.

"Maude Pearson passed away last night, daughter of Freeman and Talia Pearson. She was born—"

But Stormi couldn't move or hear. Ake's mom. She'd passed last night. Dear holy heavens, poor Ake. What to do, what to do? Stay out of it? Undoubtedly, Joni had passed the news of her visit several times over amongst the family. Perhaps even Ake's mother had heard, and it had caused...*Oh, kill me now, if that's true, Lord.*

Or maybe Ake needed her. Such a loss. The man was linked tightly with his family and, in spite of his domineering brother, they all seemed to have each other's back. Would they toss her out on her ear if she showed up at the door?

She paced. Bleh, she could barely stand to think of Ake without running over there. And why shouldn't she? It would only be proper, wouldn't it? She knew him. She cared for him. Her jaw clenched. She was *so* going.

Stormi slid to a stop in Ake's driveway. With all the warmer weather, the pavement was nearly clear. She jumped out and clattered to the front door and pounded. Complete silence. She glanced up the slope behind her to the house at the crest of the hill. Boldness had thundered over her soul on the way over. Did she still possess enough gumption to plow through the whole depressed family and not make the situation worse?

For Ake's sake, she would. She navigated the slippery slope and approached the weathered back door. Through the glass she could see Ake and his father at the kitchen table. The coast seemed clear. The hunch of Ake's shoulders stole her breath. She tapped on the glass. He turned his head and then rose.

When he answered the door, the raw misery in his eyes clutched her throat closed. She could do nothing more than mumble an apology and hug him to her bosom. His huge bear arms wrapped around her until she could barely breathe. Then he lifted her inside the house and tugged the door closed.

"I'm glad you're here."

A small happy spiral shot through her. She gave a tremulous smile. "I'm glad you're glad."

Pop stood and shuffled into the hall. "Mom...Mom."

Stormi sought Ake's gaze. He shook his head.

"He's been calling for her all morning."

"I'm...sorry, Ake."

He shrugged. "Can't change it."

She placed her chilled hands on his furry face. "If I could, I'd give my life to change it."

A small grin yanked at the corner of his mouth, but never came to fruition. "I appreciate that. But taking care of Pop was a hard job. She deserves some paradise."

"Still, it breaks your heart, Ake."

He nodded and his jaw firmed for a moment. "It'll pass. Better check on Pop."

She let him go, and he disappeared down the hall. The house appeared too quiet. And scentless. The times she'd visited with the Pearsons there had always been food fragrancing the air. She stepped forward and peeked into the living room. Shoo. Empty. Ake reappeared from her right.

"He's lying down. Seems he sleeps more in the day than the night."

"You hungry?"

His faced scrunched up. "Not sure."

She brought her hands up to his shoulders and rubbed. Why couldn't she keep her hands off of him? But she knew the answer. She wanted to comfort him, to swipe the pain away. He blinked and straightened.

"I'll leave if you want me to. I don't want to make things worse."

He eased her into his arms and rested his cheek against hers. "I want you to stay."

She swallowed, enjoying the rasp of his wiry beard. "What about Hoge? And..."

"Joni?"

She pulled from him and fixed him with sharp eyes. "She say something?"

He studied her. "Yep."

She covered her face with her hands, but his came up to ease them away.

"Don't worry over it. Just be here."

That was something she could do. With a low moan, she wrapped her arms around him again. He snugged her closer, pressing her against the counter.

"Just let me—" His mouth found hers.

This was not a coaching lesson. This was a man hungering for his woman. A man needing physical comfort. She leaned into him, sighing with pleasant agony. She'd give herself to him if it would help. She'd surrender anything he wanted.

"Mom, Mom." Pop's voice interrupted them.

Ake pulled away and turned from her. "Sorry. Just not thinking clear."

Stormi hated that he left her. The chilly air reminded her of reality. "Maybe it would help if your father had something to eat."

He nodded glancing over the kitchen. A charming blush covered his face. "Not sure what to make."

She gave a twitch of a smile. "Leave it to me."

He went to check on his father, and Stormi made herself at home in the kitchen. She grabbed her phone, found a potato soup recipe online, and started with peeling the vegetables. Ake returned, and she relayed what he could do to help. Before long the garlic spiced potato soup bubbled on the stove. She threw some refrigerated biscuits in the oven to compliment the meal.

"So where is Hoge? I want to make sure I'm out of the way before he shows."

Ake's face spasmed. "Picking out the casket. Making arrangements."

"Without you?"

He shrugged. "Someone had to stay with Pop, and someone smart had to do the other."

She yanked on the flannel shirt he wore. "Don't do that to yourself."

His eyes raked her. He didn't seem like innocent little Ake anymore. "Do you know how beautiful you are?"

She snorted. "Being and feeling are two very distinct concepts."

He stood there clenching his hands.

"You okay?"

"Just trying not to kiss you again." He gave a grunt that resembled a laugh. "Funny. I oughta be thinking more about what to do here, but all I can think of is you."

She blinked. If she did what came naturally, he'd be all over her. But that wasn't fair. What he needed right now, she realized, was help to ground himself. "I'm nothing special, Ake. But your mom was. She raised you and Hoge right."

"Yep."

"She must have been quite old when she had you. The radio said she was seventy-six."

"I'm adopted."

Surprise raised her brows. "Oh, I didn't know."

"She had Hoge at forty. At fifty-four, she and Pop adopted me when I turned eight. Officially. 'Course she had me when I was a baby, but they sent me back to my original home."

Her brows drew together. "What do you mean—"

The back door flew open and in stepped Hoge.

Chapter Eighteen

Stormi shrank back. Hoge's tired face turned
ticked in
       five seconds.

"You."

Joni came in behind him. It was a standoff. No exit behind her. Joni gave an audible sigh.

"I better go." Stormi tried to cut around Ake's big body, but he reached out and clenched her to his side.

"Nope. You're staying."

Hoge shifted his thunderous gaze to his younger brother. "She needs to leave, Ake."

"No, she doesn't."

The elder paused as if confused, and then glanced at Joni.

Joni studied the two of them. Her hair had the lumpy, day-after look. "Let her stay, Hoge. Ake wants her to."

Message loud and clear. She was only wanted by Ake.

"Fine." He strode to the living room.

Joni gave a half-hearted smile. "Smells good in here. Do you have enough for two more?"

"Of course."

Ake's arm eased and wrapped more comfortably around her shoulders. "Where's the kids?"

Joni removed her coat and hung it on the back of the dining room chair. "At my sister's. How's Pop?"

"Resting."

She nodded and wandered toward the living room.

Ake turned and gripped her upper arms. He pressed another kiss against her lips and whispered. "Please don't leave."

She loved the blush that rose up his neck. "I'll stay all night if you need me."

He ran a finger down her face. "Probably ought to talk about something else."

She tried to smile. "Whatever you say."

Joni breezed back in, and Stormi jerked from him to locate the bowls.

"I guess you don't need help. Holler if you do." Joni exited again.

Stormi flicked a gaze at Ake. A lazy grin ghosted across his face. He did seem less stressed than when she'd arrived. She'd face a firing squad if it would only ease his mind. And Hoge was pretty much the closest thing to a line of men taking target practice on her forehead. Let him try to get her to leave.

They served up the hot soup and biscuits and laid them on the table. Hoge and Joni reappeared and seated themselves. Hoge offered an abrupt prayer and the tension was on.

Stormi blew on the scalding soup, allowing her eyes to dance around the table. Jeepers, she was a creep. No doubt Hoge knew about the tattoos, and the wild life she'd led by now.

"The funeral is Wednesday with the viewing right beforehand. We're holding everything at the church." Joni volunteered, nibbling a buttered biscuit.

Ake nodded. Pop appeared at the doorway. Ake rose to escort him to the table. He settled next to Stormi.

The old man reached over and patted her hand. "Been looking for you, Mom."

She froze.

Hoge's murderous gaze fastened on her. "That isn't—"

Joni jumped up. "Let me get you some soup, Pop."

Ake's older brother transferred his hateful glance to his wife who gave him a knowing look. She whispered, "Let him have a snatch of peace, Hoge."

"Sure, sure, let's all jump in the fruitcake."

A bout of laughter bounced out of Ake. "Mom hated fruitcake."

Hoge's lips twitched. A small chuckle flew out. Pretty soon they both were belly-laughing the strain away. Joni giggled a bit too, in between sniffs. Stormi gnawed her lip while tears threatened. She wasn't sure if she should laugh or cry.

Joni wiped the moisture from her eyes, smothering giggles as she washed her hands.

The elder brother pushed away from the table. "I'd forgotten that, Ake."

Ake grinned, but sadness lined his eyes. He turned his gaze to Stormi. "My Aunt Phoebe used to bring one every Christmas. Mom hated them, but didn't want to tell her. My aunt eventually quit the ritual about five years back."

"Yep, substituted it for toe fungus. And that dang dog." The brother snickered once more as Joni laid a bowl of soup in front of Pop. He tore into it like a hungry wolf.

Hoge sobered. "We need to call Aunt Phoebe. She'll not take it well."

Ake's face settled into mournful seriousness once more. "I know."

Pop piped up between spoonfuls, "Dang dog, dang dog."

Again the brothers stifled spurts of laughter. Ake's hand found hers on the table. "I reckon Mom would like us to remember the funny stuff."

His older brother nodded, eyeing his brother's hand on Stormi's. "You betcha."

Joni returned to her chair. "She's enjoying heaven right now. I sure never thought she'd be the first to go."

"When I came to the back door and the alarm went off, I knew it wasn't right. She always had Pop's oatmeal ready when I got here."

Stormi clutched his hand with both of hers. Emotion clogged her throat. "You found her?"

Ake turned a small sad smile on her. "Yeah."

She didn't even want to contemplate how painful that would be. Her eyes narrowed as she assessed his face. "I'm so sorry."

"I'm okay. God knows best."

She turned from him to find both Hoge and Joni staring. For once, hate didn't mar Hoge's handsome face. Stormi lowered her eyes. He may despise her, but she cared for Ake, and it didn't matter to her who saw it.

Pop rose and shuffled to the living room. Both brothers' eyes followed him.

"Is he going to understand any of this?" Ake uttered.

Hoge shook his head. "I don't know. More importantly, what are we going to do with him?"

"I'll stay with him."

"Ake, you can't be here twenty-four seven. Don't be stup—" Hoge's voice came to an abrupt halt, and he sent a flick of his gaze at Stormi.

She tilted her head and glared at him.

The elder cleared his throat. "We'll need someone to stay. Maybe you can help at night."

Ake nodded. "Maybe."

Hoge continued to throw out options, and Stormi detached from the emotions and rose. She collected the dirty bowls and saucers and started the dishes in the sink. Ake's mom had been a dedicated homemaker. No dishwasher graced the kitchen. Merely liquid dishwashing soap in a bottle, dressed in a tiny homemade knitted pink dress that had seen better days. It perched cheerfully by the black sprayer.

The concentrated liquid bubbled up into a hot froth, and Stormi dove in and started scrubbing. At the table, the Pearsons bandied about names of possible caretakers. As she rinsed the last dish, Joni stood and grabbed her coat.

"We need to get the kids, Hoge."

He cleared his throat and rose a bit more leisurely, yanking at the waistband of his khaki pants. Stormi felt the burn of his glare before she connected with his gaze. She fixed her eyes on the bubbles and reached for the drain plug.

Joni handed Hoge his coat and nudged him toward the back door. "I'll get ahold of Angus Mirrek from church. He said he'd be glad to sit with him until we get someone in here permanently. That way you can at least sleep in your own bed tonight, Ake."

Stormi dried her hands on a hand towel and drifted toward the counter, still careful to keep a healthy distance from Hoge.

"Honey, go start the car, would you? It's freezing."

Another guttural mumble came from Ake's brother before he hiked out the back door. Joni gave a small, perhaps apologetic smile and shrugged. She turned her attention to Ake and laid a hand on his arm.

"I'm really sorry, Ake. I know your brother is hurting too, even though he doesn't express it."

Ake nodded and inserted his hands into his jean pockets. After Joni gave him a quick hug, she headed for the door and disappeared through, leaving nothing but a cold draft in the room. Ake held out his hand to her, and she stepped forward to take it.

"Will you stay a while?"

She squeezed his big hand while the sadness in his huge brown eyes squeezed her heart. "Yes. For as long as you need."

A shadow of a smile rippled across his face until his dad shuffled to the door.

"Mom, Mom?"

He closed his eyes for a moment and then released her hand. Ake spun, soothing words coming softly from him as he wrapped his arms around his father. Stormi stiffened her lips into a firm line to stem the emotions thundering in her heart. Hoge might not be able to talk to Ake about the pain, but she sure could. And she would.

～ ······ ～

Angus nodded his white head as Ake showed him the code once more on the security system. It was hard to leave Pop with a man the same age. Yet, the man from his church had a sharp mind, and he seemed quite comfortable arming the alarm. It was just a matter of pushing himself out the door.

Ake fixated his stare on Stormi's charming multicolored blue/green/gray eyes and pushed his concerns of his father from his mind. But the softness of her gaze made him wonder if he, himself, would be safer here bunched up on his old twin bed.

He turned his attention to the older man. "Thanks, Angus. I'm just down the hill if you need something."

"Why don't you leave your cell number?" Stormi's practical advice contained a touch of huskiness.

Ake nodded. "Yeah, good idea."

He found a pad and scratched the digits down and then meandered toward the door. "He gets up a lot. He's been hollering for her—"

His speech halted at the gentle expression on Stormi's face. He rubbed the back of his neck. That was at least the third time he'd gone over that information. He cleared his throat and followed her to the back door. Angus lifted a hand as they slipped through the door, and Ake hesitated until he heard the lock slide into place with the faint beep of the alarm code.

Stormi leaned against him as she pulled on her mittens. The brisk night wind stirred her bangs into her eyes, and he reached up a hand to brush them away.

"Let's hurry, Ake. It's freezing."

She linked her arm through his, holding her hood with the other hand, and began to jog. He loped along in long strides, not breaking a brisk walk. As they approached the lower end of the slope, she didn't dart off toward her car as he expected, but rather tugged him to the front door. She had yanked it open before he could even touch the doorknob, pulled him through in a rush, and slammed the door.

He took a deep breath and did what he always did. Removed his heavy canvas coat and hung it on the tree near the door. His eyes flicked to the microwave over the stove. Just short of ten o'clock. Stormi shrugged out of her coat, and it joined his on the tree.

"Now, how are you? I mean really? With your father in the same room, we haven't had a chance to chat this out."

Ake shrugged and rubbed his hands together. Her hands caught his in mid motion, and then her eyes, deep with raw emotion sought his.

"Ake?"

The collar on his shirt suddenly felt very tight. "I don't know. Fine, I guess."

She shook her head. "Let's sit on the couch."

He trailed her, and she coerced him into the corner of the couch, nearly sitting on top of him, her face peering intensely into his. She placed her hands on either side of his face.

"I know this is hard on you. Your brother doesn't help much, either. But I'm here for you."

"What?" He blinked.

Stormi stroked his beard, and his thought pattern clamped on the lovely swirls of black ink on her slender arms. His eyes dropped to see if any of the lace portion peeked above her neckline. Her small fingers pressed his chin up. Their gazes met once more.

"You don't have to stuff all your grief down. I can make some hot tea and warm up a piece of pie if it will make you feel better."

When he didn't reply, she threw her arms around his neck and pressed herself against him.

"Oh, Ake. You're breaking my heart."

His arms came around her. It did feel nice to have her here even though it grew late. He inhaled the tangerine scent of her hair and pulled her on his lap. She snuggled against his neck and pressed her face against his skin. Her small body burrowed against him. Except she exuded heat. Lots of heat. He rubbed his sideburns against the rebellious lock of hair that dropped to her forehead.

Her fingers worked magic on the back of his neck, and her comfort wrapped around him like new cotton socks to icy feet. Her other hand rubbed his chest, and he cleared his throat against the rising awareness she ignited.

"It's going to be all right, Ake. We can just sit here and when you're ready, we'll talk. I don't care if it takes all night."

With a groan, he rose, Stormi filling his arms. She gave a gasp and stared at him with her mouth agape as he set her down and stepped away.

"You won't be staying all night, Stormi."

Her brows drew together. "Of course I will. You said you wanted me to stay."

He sucked fresh air into his lungs. "Not overnight."

"Why?"

Her expression cut him. But he straightened. "It's not a good idea."

Stormi rushed forward and grabbed his biceps. "I don't care what other people think, Ake. I'm here for you."

He shook his head, forcing himself to ignore her grasp on his arms. After a long moment, he clenched his jaw and set her from him. The hurt in her face made him wish he didn't have to disappoint her. My, did he wish he didn't have to disappoint her.

"We aren't married, Stormi. I won't let a woman stay with me until marriage. It's not right."

"But you need me."

In the worst way, and it shamed him to admit that to himself. Especially with his mother's body cooling a few blocks over at the funeral home. He closed his eyes for a moment and grabbed ahold of all the moral pluck he could summon.

"True. But I'll see you tomorrow."

Stormi's brows gathered thunder like her namesake. "Everyone does it, Ake. It's commonplace nowadays."

"Yep, I reckon so. But it's not God's way. It's people in a hurry. People avoiding a commitment." He couldn't resist running a finger down her delicate cheek. "Only my wife will stay the night with me."

A myriad of emotions chased their way across her features, warring with one another for dominance until finally she burst out, "Marry me, then."

Chapter Nineteen

Ake ceased breathing for a moment. Stormi seemed as shocked as he was when her mouth popped open. Only, instead of retracting the statement, a small smile flitted across her face.

His brows descended. "Now, Stormi—"

Her face cleared into a complete smile, her eyes asparkle. "That's perfect, Ake. We could hurry and apply tomorrow. We could even be married before the funeral. Then I wouldn't have to leave you at all."

She leaped into his arms and clutched the lapels of his flannel shirt. He firmly set her from him once more and gave her a stern look. "You know that wouldn't make sense."

Her fist parked on her suggestive hips, and she leaned forward with a scowl. "Why ever not? You said you loved me. You need me. It seems perfectly black and white to me."

He eyed her. She appeared a packet of fury. And suddenly it dawned on him that he was refusing to marry the woman he loved. After she proposed.

"Stormi—"

She stepped forward and pressed two soft fingers to his lips. "Hush. Let me do this for you."

His hands, weighted with resistance, fisted and unfisted while his eyes studied her expression, her fickle-colored eyes, and the beauty of her face. It was all he could do not to crush her to his chest.

"Please?"

A dimple appeared in the corner of her mouth, and the tilt of her head fell the final bit of his resolve. "Yes."

She jumped up and down and gave mini-claps under her chin. Then she dove into his waiting arms.

"You won't regret this. You won't. I'll be the best wife ever."

Ake lowered his head and reveled in her softness. Had she said something? He shrugged it off. Did it matter? She was his.

ళ ...... ఴ

The moon happened to be lined up in perfect conjunction with Stormi's only window facing the road. It filled the small apartment with a bright ethereal light. She chewed the skin from her bottom lip and glared at the red digits. Past two and she still wore a groove pacing the concrete from her bed to the fireplace.

And why? Marrying Ake felt right. It was right. She could make up for everything she'd done to him in one fell swoop. She'd enticed him to fall in love with her, and now, she would give herself to him as penance. It was perfect.

Yet something nagged at the back of her head. Maybe it was Hoge. Or Joni. Envisioning their reaction stabbed her like Goliath's spear. Sure, it wasn't a conventional marriage, but it could still be operational. He was flat-out gorgeous so there was no problem there. He constantly did kind deeds and had the purest heart she'd ever known. It would be like living with a good, good friend. With a few added bonuses. With a pause and a smile, she realized one thing was certain. She would take him on one wild ride.

The grin slipped from her face. Still, his brother would not be happy. No way to deny it. Could she face Hoge's rage? Could Ake? She took a deep cooling breath through her nostrils. Of course Ake would survive. He seemed the only one who could weather his brother's moods without coming away psychologically nicked. Or was it just her?

She stared at the walls around her and gave a sigh. She wouldn't have to live alone anymore. Ake would be there to shoulder the more physical aspects of life. The snow, the lawn. Just having someone to partner up with brightened her outlook. She could put this place up for sale or rent it out. Either way, it would help with the finances.

The schedule for her podcasts grabbed her eye. She wrinkled her nose. Why had she taken on an extra class? She didn't need it now. All would be right when she said "I do" to Ake.

She rubbed her hands down her bare skin, the spaghetti straps of her tank exposing the permanent lace, obvious even by the light of the moon. At least Ake didn't seem to mind her sin marks. She climbed in bed and flung a blanket over her to hide the tattooed transgressions. Time to relax and get a few hours of sleep. Then, she'd do her podcasts. Once that was accomplished, she'd fetch her fiancé and make good on her promise.

✤ ⋯⋯ ✥

The woman at the courthouse obviously knew Ake. When they'd asked for a marriage license, though, her shock had bled through her professional filter. The young blond seemed to know Ake quite well, and dare Stormi think she'd even flirted a bit with him?

"Hi, Avery."

Was the girl seriously batting her eyes at him? Stormi snugged up to Ake, and his arm came around her back.

"You're...getting married?"

Her face had a dewy freshness to it. Probably a former head cheerleader at her high school.

"Yep." Ake nodded glancing at the form.

"I'll never forget that day outside study hall. Remember?"

A dark flush suffused Ake's face, and he kept his eyes glued to the paper in front of him. He merely nodded.

"I'm Stormi Zobroski, by the way. Soon to be Stormi Pearson. And you are..."

The cheerleader smirked at her and shifted her thick blond hair behind her shoulders. "Avery Guttleman. Used to be Avery Coleson. Ake and I graduated together. Sort of."

"Sort of?" Despite her resolve to keep this convo centered on the certificate, a slice of cattiness entered Stormi's tone. "How can you sort of graduate?"

Miss Rah-rah shut her eyes a moment with a seductive shrug. "Well, you know. He had some Special Ed classes."

Ake cleared his throat, and the volume of it stemmed the snip that Stormi longed to let loose. "Let's fill this out on that table."

Her future husband pointed to a table against the wall while nudging her away from the window. Stormi lifted her chin and narrowed her eyes at the queen of the counter. How dare she flirt with him then pull the pegs from beneath his feet?

"She's rude." Stormi whispered furiously to Ake.

He shrugged. "Always was."

"What happened that day? The study hall day?"

The point of Ake's pen hovered above the form as he scanned the document. "Later."

She motioned to the line where he should sign before exhaling with dissatisfaction. "Ake."

With a flick of his hand, he caressed the peach fuzz at the nape of her neck, radiating sweet shivers of bliss that squelched the hair-raising ire that had clutched at her. How could he completely change her mood with one touch? Did he know how sensitive the nape of her neck was?

She lifted her eyes and perused his whiskered face. Again, it struck her how handsome he was with his jet black beard and hair, dark eyes, and dusky skin. She admired the breadth of his shoulders and the muscled chest.

He raised his eyes and then his brows in a question.

She smirked. "Just thinking how hot you are."

A quirk started in the corner of his mouth, but a twang of pain lay in his eyes.

Her brows drew together. "Was she unkind?"

What kind of question was that? Was she an ignoramus herself? How many people treated Ake with kindness and respect? Very few. She glanced over at the blond who pretended not to be openly staring at them.

"Kiss me."

His head came up. "What?"

"You heard me."

"I don't think—"

But she silenced him with her mouth. It thrilled her to feel his instant response to her lips. She leaned into him because she knew he'd bend her over. VJ kiss. He didn't disappoint. When he let her go, he hovered over her as if reluctant to move away. She stayed arched against him and returned his heated gaze. But he seemed to suddenly become aware of his surroundings and drew back. She flicked a glance at the blond. Bingo. Direct hit.

Ake stepped over to the counter. Stormi fondled the hank of bangs over her left eye and leaned into the table, maintaining her "I rule the world" stance. If the pompom girl wanted to tango, she'd stomp her beneath her boots' four-inch heels.

She threaded her arm through Ake's as he returned the form.

Avery took it with an odd smile. "Sorry to hear about your mom, Ake."

He nodded and headed Stormi toward the door. All she could do was shoot a cutting glance back to the courthouse Barbie. Once they exited the office into the sunshine, they climbed into the truck. Once the doors were closed, she pounced on him.

"Study hall?"

He stretched his neck and shrugged. "Not much to tell. I proclaimed my undying love for her in the hallway between classes. She laughed and told the whole school body."

Boy, it was a good thing they were out of that clerk's office. Death by fingernails was too good for Miss Guttlebag.

The fury that escalated into her eyeballs stymied when she locked eyes with his gentle, long-suffering gaze. He reached over and squeezed her shoulder. "It was a long time ago. Don't give it another thought. Besides," he snapped the belt over his body, "her husband's not a nice guy. I'm sure she has her own problems."

Stormi took a deep breath. He was right. But forgiveness seemed a dodging dream right now. She sent up a quick prayer that she might grab hold of it. "Right. Say. Let's go celebrate. How 'bout a burger at the grill?"

He gave that heart-stopping grin, and it was all she could do not to laze in the brilliance of it. She snapped on her own seat belt as he pulled from the parking spot. Her thoughts skittered around as he meandered through town and pulled in by the curb outside the grill. Ake hurried around the front of the truck to open the door, and she hid a smile as he played the part of gallant Sir Walter Raleigh to assist his lady.

She exited and they walked tandem to Calvert's Grill. Again, Ake opened the door for her, and she decided she could get used to being treated like a lady. They put in their order at the counter, and several patrons hailed him, offering condolences for the loss of his mother. His face grew so forlorn, that Stormi tugged him into the booth near the door and changed the subject.

"Since the funeral is tomorrow at two, we could head over to the courthouse at nine o'clock on the dot. That way we can get in and out and hurry over to the church."

Ake nodded. The door burst open behind the tall back of Ake's seat, but she pushed it from her thoughts. "Then we can—"

Hoge stutter stopped in front of their table with Joni nearly colliding into his back. He squared up. Joni, face flushed, shoved her hands into her pockets. The big, and obviously angry man, pointed a thick digit at her and thundered one word. "You."

The fellow patrons' conversations circulating around their booth came to a dead silence. Stormi was painfully aware of the stares of almost everyone in the place. Except the baby who screamed in the back section.

Ake slid from the booth and held out his big hands. "It's all right, folks. Just a misunderstanding."

A few folks nodded and most turned back to their business. Hoge, however, didn't seem to latch on to Ake's public reassurance.

"Married? You?"

Again, all talk ceased, and Joni yanked Hoge into the booth seat that Ake had just vacated, shushing him. Stormi wanted to bolt from the cushioned bench, but instead slid over, letting Ake take up the hot seat next to her.

Joni extended her arm and pressed against Hoge's chest forcing him to lean back into the padded leather. "What my husband means is Avery Guttleman called and claimed you filled out a marriage certificate?"

Hoge's face grew redder.

Ake nodded. "Yep. Tomorrow at nine."

Two huge hands slapped the table. "On the day of your mother's funeral? Are you a moron?"

The barked words caught everyone's attention once more. Joni pulled a stiff smile and spat at her husband through gritted teeth. "Hoge, cut it out."

A few quiet moments passed while the two people across the table huffed. Joni cleared her throat. "Okay. You want to get married."

"No!" Hoge growled.

"Shhh." Joni shot her husband a glare before turning an intense gaze on them. Stormi squirmed.

Joni drew a deep breath. "Don't get married on the same day you bury your mother, Ake. A marriage should be a happy union with a happy start."

"There will be no marriage," Hoge thundered.

All attention again centered on them. Joni shoved her husband. "Get out, Hoge. Come on, Ake. We need to settle this outside."

Stormi's middle spun like a cotton candy maker, and nausea unsettled her stomach. Maybe Joni didn't realize that outside there were less witnesses. As much as she hated garnering the attention of the customers of the grill, they could testify in court when Hoge ripped the limbs from her body. These reservations didn't seem to bother Ake as he slid out of the booth and then waited for her to join him. Pressing her hand to her middle she acquiesced.

Outside, the wind had picked up, and Hoge paced like a bull infected with mad cow disease. Joni paced the edge of the building and stopped at the corner near the parking lot.

Hoge lunged at Ake and jabbed him with stiff fingers. "I forbid you to marry her."

Ake shifted his weight from one foot to the other, drew Stormi close, and shot a glance at Joni.

The dark-haired woman rolled her eyes. "Hoge, really? Stop. You'll just make things intolerable."

"They already are intolerable," he snarled and spun to face her.

Quick, Ake, let's run for the get-away car.

Hoge and Joni faced one another with their own brand of glares. Ake dropped his arm and stepped between them.

"I understand what you're saying, and you're right, Joni. We'll wait. But Hoge, don't forbid this. I want your support."

Hoge stared at him. "I can't support you making the biggest mistake of your life."

"No, I'm not, Hoge. I love her."

Ake's brother seared her with blue-eyed flames.

"Yes, Hoge. It'll happen with or without you. What's your choice?" Joni murmured.

Chapter Twenty

Hoge and Ake stood toe to toe. The elder swelled with disapproval while the younger, broader one stood rigid with gentle determination. At long last, Hoge blew out a loud rasp of air.

"Fine. But mark my words, Ake. There will come trouble."

"Trouble is everywhere, big brother."

The narrowing of Hoge's eyes were the only indication he'd heard his brother's wise words. Assessing the shorter man, he rumbled, "Don't call me that."

Joni laid her hand on Ake's arm and then shot a glance at Stormi. "Maybe the week after would work for the wedding? Or the following month? Then maybe we can plan where—"

"The courthouse." Why? Why had she just blurted in an atmosphere rife with stress and tension?

The look that crossed Joni's face made Stormi want to take a couple steps backward. But she lifted her chin in defiance.

The woman reined in her disappointment with a blink of an eye.

"Remember, Stormi. Ake is very much part of a loving church who will want to be part of this celebration."

"Huh, celebration? More like a train wreck." Hoge rolled his eyes.

Joni planted her elbow in her husband's ribs and nodded slightly at Stormi. "Please keep the church family in mind. Please."

Stormi nodded, a shiver of remorse spiraling to her toes.

Hoge stepped forward and pointed at his brother. "And don't forget, you Dum—"

"I think that's enough for now." Joni sliced his sentence in half with a tight grimace of her features. Was it supposed to be a smile? "Let's go, dear. We need to get back, and let Angus have a few hours free of your father."

When Hoge didn't move, Joni tugged on his thick sleeve. Stormi crossed her arms over her shivering body. Hoge continued to glare at them as Joni pulled him along. Just before they disappeared around the corner, he pointed at her. Stormi swallowed.

Ake turned and took her in his arms. She knew he had to feel the trembling of her body. Perhaps he'd take it for the cold in the air.

He pressed his lips against her ear, his beard a rough yet pleasing sensation against her chilled cheek. She closed her eyes and drank in the balm of his body wrapped around her.

"Change your mind yet?" His voice was low and husky.

"No." She snuggled her face against his canvas coat.

After a moment he set her away from him. "I wouldn't blame you if you did."

She fastened her gaze on his dark, dark eyes, full of concern and void of guile. Was it possible to drown in a man's eyes? To be so transfixed it was impossible to draw away or even want to? His hands came up to her cheeks, and he pressed his forehead against hers. For a moment, he closed his eyes and a shaft of loss entered her soul. Hoge's rejection hurt him more than he let on.

She grabbed his collar and his eyes shot open. "It's you that should change your mind. Hoge won't give you a moment's rest if you marry me."

He stared into her eyes for just a moment and then brought his lips to hers. His gentle probing lit a rampage of fires within her in just a few seconds. When he opened those deep brown eyes, he gave a small grin. "Hoge who?"

A sigh escaped her. Perhaps it was enough between the two of them. Still, she knew the profound weight of a non-supportive family. But he released her before she could chase that rabbit far. Then he slid his cold, big hand into hers and guided her back toward the entrance of the grill.

"Think our burgers are ready?"

Her stomach squeezed. Yuck. Food? "Probably."

"Good." He paused at the entrance and caressed the lock of hair from her eye. "It's gonna be okay."

She exhaled a great deal of tension and gave a small smile. "I hope you're right."

His cheek dented with the beginning of a smile. Then his features grew somber. "God blesses us when we do what's right."

A shiver of realization entered her when Ake stroked her cheek. God. Oh, yeah. Had she dropped her God filter? But the quiet confidence on her future husband's face calmed her anxiety. Even if she veered off the right path, she was sure Ake would steer her back.

᠍ ⋯⋯ ᠍

Ake led Pop back to his bedroom for the sixth time. At this rate, neither one of them would be awake for the funeral tomorrow. He helped the tottering man back into his bed and covered him up.

"Where's Mom?"

"In heaven."

"She coming back?"

Ake rubbed his father's shoulder. "No. But she's waiting for you."

"Humph."

Despite the emptiness inside him, a smile quirked at his mouth. Perhaps Pop realized that could be a long wait. A long painful wait.

"Tell her I miss her." Pop mumbled.

The wall lit up as a distant car passed the corner down the road and drew Ake's attention. Why were there brief moments when Pop seemed almost back to normal? He stretched his neck and prayed he and his brother might be able to see more of the "old Pop."

"Now, get in bed. You boys are too big to sleep with us. Go on. Mom will come tuck you in shortly." Pop snuggled into the pillow and drifted off to sleep.

For a long while Ake just stood and breathed, wishing he were ten years old again being sent to his room. With a long inhale, he turned at last and made his way back to the very place his father had sent him. He paused at the twin bed and scratched behind his ear. How he wished Stormi were here. Just to hold her close would comfort his soul.

He eased himself to the edge of the bed. She would be his soon enough. Facing Hoge through it all wouldn't be easy. He reached up and yanked on his beard. Appeared there were several things that wouldn't be easy in the days ahead.

Burying his mother topped the list right now. Life would not be the same. The woman was probably up in heaven defending his honor even now. He grinned. She never let him feel less than what God had made him to be. How he would miss her unwavering support.

Stormi was much like that. Never had he seen her so angry than when Hoge called him Dummy. He rubbed his beard, conscious he'd need to shave in the morning, while his thought centered on Stormi as his new staunch supporter. Funny how God filled the empty spots in one's soul.

He reached over and clicked on the old cassette tape player, making sure the volume was low. His mother's voice filled the room as she read the Beatitudes in Matthew five. She'd always recorded Scripture for him. Her old school method had weathered the years. It had been his "Bible" since he was a wee kid. A thick lump lodged in his throat, and a bit of moisture wet his eyes. She'd recorded this one several weeks back, and he'd never managed to find time to listen to it. Just another example of God's care on his life.

The words his mother read latched onto his heart. He focused on the word *comfort* in verse four. His mind went over and over the verse until it became a prayer.

Then he raised his head. More moisture fought for space along his eyelids, and he squeezed his eyes shut to disperse it. He sure would miss his mother's physical presence of reassurance and love. God's love in flesh. He sighed and sank back into the mattress. How thankful he was for God's comfort, for his mother's voice, and for Stormi storming into his life at just the right moment.

Ake yanked at the coarse hairs on his chin and snipped another hank off. He assessed his face in the mirror—the bloodshot eyes, the jagged beard. A fresh sense of loss enveloped him. His mother had always liked his beard. Said it was the thickest, fullest mass of hair she'd ever encountered, even when he had been at the young age of sixteen. He shook off the thought and swished the scissors in the hairy bowlful of water in the bathroom sink.

Sure was a chore to remove it, and that was no lie. Even once he removed the stubborn hunks, he'd nearly have to scrape his skin from his face to get it down to smoothness. He rubbed a few strays away. In retrospect, maybe his mother would have been pleased for him to have left it. But 'twas spilled milk at this point.

Some thirty minutes later he splashed an alcohol-based aftershave on his jaw and sucked in air at the pain it brought. The joys of making one presentable in decent company. He quirked a grin and cleaned up the mess on the vanity. Joni had made sure he had a suit she'd borrowed from her brother. Maybe he'd get out and get one of his own by the time he and Stormi got married.

He swung into the hallway just as a knock sounded on the front door. Ahhh. Angus was right on time. He ambled down the hall, checking Pop still sorting through books at his bookcase, and continued on down to the living room.

"Morning, Ake." Angus gave a comforting slap on his shoulder. "Fresh coating of snow. Just what your mom would have ordered."

Ake let a small smile etch his face. "Yep. I think you're right. Come on in. Sure glad you could come for a little bit while I finish getting ready. I gotta pick up Stormi. I'll be back in about an hour."

The man grinned, his thick wrinkled skin gathering around his eyes. "Glad to do it. You're looking slick."

"Pop, Angus is here."

When no response came, Angus shrugged. "That's okay, Ake. You head on out. We'll be fine."

Ake nodded and headed for the back door. "'Spect I'll be back soon enough. He might not even realize I'm gone."

An uncharacteristic cynical thread crossed Ake's mind as he pulled the door shut. Pop might not even realize who he was. With a shrug, he hurried down the path to his house. Once inside, he lost no time shrugging on the white dress shirt and black suit. He stepped into the bathroom to adjust his tie. His face seemed foreign even to him without the heavy beard.

He swung through the door and pressed down the thought of the original plan of marrying Stormi this morning. As distasteful as having a wedding date coinciding with his mother's funeral would seem, he couldn't help but wish he were about to drive her to the courthouse. Carrying her through his door tonight would sure salve his despondency.

Mom's car in the drive seemed skewed, but since he had to escort both Stormi and Pop to the funeral, it appeared to be the best choice. He grunted as he dipped his head into the low enclosure. He even missed the comfort of his truck today. With an inhale, he cleared his gloomy thoughts and started the four-door Chevy.

Once he'd parked in Stormi's drive, though, his spirit took a lift. She swung from behind the building in a burgundy wool coat and black boots before he could even exit the car. Heavy contemplations laced with sadness took a back seat as he let his eyes take her in. Her hair looked freshly styled, the wedge of hair pointing straight at her left eye while the rest coifed in rebelliousness around her head in a runway sort of way. Just the way she walked, she commanded attention.

The flirty glance she threw him brought a smile to his face. Hot. Amazing that Stone Haven even had temperatures below freezing this winter with this woman living here. Yes, hot. And desirable. And dangerous. She tugged open the door, and he realized how rude he'd been just sitting there mouth agape, staring at her. He hadn't even opened her door.

"Hi, Tiger." She flashed a smile before her face turned serious. "Oh, my lands. You shaved it."

He rubbed the naked chin skin. "Yeah, I—"

But she was on him, yanking away his hand and then staring. And staring some more.

"Did I miss something?"

She shook her head. "Just when I thought you couldn't get any handsomer, Ake Pearson, you up the game. Wow."

Her hands ran over the newly exposed skin, igniting emotions in him that a man ought not have on the day of his mother's funeral. He brought his hands up to pull her from him.

"No, wait." She leaned forward and pressed her face against the smooth skin. "Ummm. Nice."

He inhaled the scent of her, heady swirling snatches of flowers and tangerines, and for a moment, he let himself relax and enjoy her body against his. Yes. This was comfort. Well, more than comfort, but it eased his sorrow, calmed the black bog of gloom in his gut.

She eased away and with a cocky grin pressed a hard kiss on his lips. Before he could respond, she flopped into her seat and fastened her seatbelt. She was the perfect storm. Never had he had such assurance how right she was for him. He could barely wait to make her his own.

Chapter Twenty–One

With the kind nature of his mother, the long line of guests arrived at two on the dot and stretched out into infinity through the church and down the stairs. Ake knew the line continued to snake around the basement of the church when he'd taken a walk earlier. Stormi stuck her head in occasionally but kept a distance most of the time, which disappointed Ake a bit. But he supposed introducing people to his future wife at the funeral wasn't exactly good timing.

Pop did his share of wandering as well, never far without one of the family trailing him. When they'd arrived, his father had approached the casket and stood some ten minutes. Just staring. He'd finally patted her hand and shuffled off.

Ake peered down at the black shiny dress shoes, glad he didn't have to wear them on a regular basis. At this rate, his smallest toe would pinch off by bedtime. His gaze caught Stormi peeking in from the back once more. He set his chin and excused himself from the family line of greeting. He needed a moment.

Outside, he caught up with her in front of the church which was relatively quiet compared to the somber parade inside. "Where are you going?"

She paused on the sidewalk when she caught sight of him and gave a small wave. "Hey. I don't know. Just here and there."

"Come inside with me."

She shook her head and tightened her arms around herself, wrapped in that close-fitting coat. "No. I just don't think that's wise."

"Why?"

Her response was a shrug.

"I need you next to me, Stormi."

Her head came up and her eyes searched his. "Okay. As long as I don't have to stay a long time."

She meandered up the sidewalk and paused beside him. He wrapped his arm around her shoulders. Her body shook with shivers. At least he could get her inside to warm up.

꩜ ⋯⋯ ꩜

Stormi steadied herself on the four-inch heels. Her footwear was a bust. Why hadn't she thrown out the old reminders of her B.C. life? Before Christ. Two hundred dollar boots that apparently had beds of nails for soles. Or perhaps the torture was magnified by the stares of everyone who entered the building. How many whispers had she witnessed while the participants' eyes flicked to her. Gee, it was not a mystery what their hushed tones were discussing.

Yet, Ake's arm draping her shoulders seemed to lessen the rawness of her heart. What a loser she was. She was supposed to be comforting him, and it seemed a little reversed. With a jaw strung tight with determination, she followed Ake as he threaded his way back through the mourners' line, her hand firmly gripped in his. She kept her eyes on the aging carpet.

He set up shop at the end of the family's line, earning a stray killing glance from Hoge. She inhaled a lungful of courage and allowed an elderly woman to embrace her, the old-lady perfume settling around her like the smell of death. She swallowed as the woman held on too long and then leaned back a bit to question who she was. Ugh. Thankfully Ake stepped in, but the flare of surprise on the woman's face at the mention of their wedding sent Stormi's sense of ease dropping to her numb feet.

That started a stream of well-wishers behind who were, of course, deeply saddened by the death of Ake's mom, but thrilled with the impromptu wedding. Intense discomfort swelled inside her into a huge blimp of pressure. She glanced to the line that still continued out the sanctuary doors. *Kill me. Kill me, now.* She manufactured another smile and shook another set of wrinkled hands.

Ake nodded to the new arrival, a kind patient smile across his face. How did he do it? The man was a saint. She forced the bile that gathered at the back of her throat down her gullet. Oh, she would *so* do this. Even if she had to crush every molar in her jaw with the effort. She could do this for Ake. Sweet, gentle Ake. She wrapped her arm around his and he looked down at her.

The sadness there made her catch her breath. Then, it dispelled a bit when he gave a small crooked smile. Yes. She could endure it for him. It was the least she could do.

Another couple stepped away, and Ake leaned down to whisper in her ear. "My shoes are killing me."

Stormi flung a fist to her mouth before any rude noise could burst forth. She turned to whisper back in the hollow of his neck. "Mine, too."

The small quirky grin he shot her cut through the morose expression on his face, and a bubble of pleasure percolated in her heart. Alan had texted her how crazy she was for committing to a man simply to assuage her conscience, but she didn't care. But then, he didn't understand how special Ake was.

Her face lost some of its brightness. Special. No. Exceptional. If Alan could only meet him, he would understand his adorable straight-forwardness, his untarnished soul. The man was the purest example of what a true Christian should be, and she wanted to bask in it, become like it, and be as unselfish as this man really was.

Her eyes left his and came to rest on none other than Miss Rah-Rah from the courthouse and a tall, handsome blond man. Yowza, extremely attractive and striking in a teal dress shirt. She pulled her attention from him and tried to plant a welcoming smile on her face as she latched onto Avery's bluebell eyes. But she cut her gaze back to Ake.

The little floozy leaned in and gave him a much too-long hug, and then shot Stormi a look as she pulled out but addressed Ake. "Sorry about your mom, Ake. She was a sweet lady."

Ake nodded. "Thanks for coming."

"This is Lance, my husband."

Had Miss Guttlebag slung her chin at her? The nerve. Stormi pushed it aside and nodded to the knock-out blond. "Nice to meet you."

He gave her the once over, flicking an interested brow. "The pleasure's all mine."

Really? Stormi pulled a tight smile, shook both of their hands, and then studied them as they walked away. Wow, he was a player. But she'd let her mind digress and was hugged off-guard by yet another blue-haired woman.

Thus the line marched through like a collection of toy soldiers. One by one, Stormi weathered each awkward acquaintance of Ake and his family. At five the funeral began, and though she hadn't known the woman well, it proved difficult to keep her tears in check.

Saints preserved, she ended up in the limo with Hoge's family. The two seats faced one another, she nestled against Ake with Lucy and Pop on one side. Hoge, Joni and the three boys sat squashed in the rear-facing seats. How cozy.

She fixed her thoughts on inventing pairs of words that described the atmosphere of the car. Oppressive, yet glacial. Abrasive but soothing. Noiseless yet deafening with resentment. Was it just her imagination? She sat stiffly against Ake, her hand in both of his in his lap.

He leaned over. "I'm glad you're here."

Stormi dared to look up. Hoge's gaze stayed firmly on the fogged glass, but Joni's rested on her with a mediocre amount of—what? Tolerance? Gratitude? Perhaps it was just apathy misinterpreted. But Lucy drew her attention by laying her head against her arm.

The sky spat snow for the vigil on the frozen ground beside the yawning earth hole. The pastor yammered some Bible verses about eternal life, added in some ashes to ashes, and meandered into a monologue.

The surrounding grief snarled her thoughts to the point that all Stormi could do was breathe the same prayer over and over. "Dear God, comfort them. Please comfort them."

It seemed a pitiful effort, her lips freezing as she murmured the words in cadence like an annoying car alarm in her head. Why couldn't she be of more help? What did one do in such instances to ease the sorrow that throbbed beneath the open tent? Lucy clutched at her sniffling mother, the three boys stoic as gargoyles, and Hoge like a face poster of misery.

And poor Pop, clueless to all, looking about one moment, still as a tree another.

Ake drew her closer beneath his thick arm, his own breath repeating the Lord's prayer. Stormi leaned her head against his chest. Life was fleeting. So intensely short. She had to make the most of it. Be there for Ake.

And she would. Lord willing, she would.

❧ ⋯⋯ ☙

"Then we'll put the flower vases here on the large white pedestals." Joni swept her arms in an arc, her face animated. "The tulle will sweep down here and be gathered at each pew. We could set a glass-encased candle encircled by the flowers of your choice on the arms. We could turn the lights low for a romantic feel."

Stormi eased herself down into an empty pew covered with a lilac padding. How lucky was that? She actually was allowed to choose her own flowers.

"Now, behind the pastor, I know we have lattice panels that we could cover with white lights and more tulle. Periwinkle bachelor buttons could be inserted in the swaths at the top.

Oh, never mind. Flowers were chosen. She worked very hard to keep her face at an impasse. Ake stood nearby, rubbing his bristled chin as if he were really trying to picture it. Then he glanced toward her. She averted her eyes.

"Pastor said he has an opening in late May."

Ake jerked up. "May? That's two months away."

Joni hesitated and then gave a little chuckle. "Well, yeah. I mean, you can't organize all this in just a week. We haven't even begun to discuss the catering and decorating the family center."

Hoge sat stiff in the front pew, silent as a prowling lion. Stormi let her eyes settle on the back of his head before allowing her gaze to travel over the huge, empty sanctuary. She could hear the kids' voices and squeals from the gym down the hall. Ake crossed his arms and struck a wide stance.

"You have to understand that a wedding is like a dream come true, Ake." Joni approached him and laid her hand on his thick forearm. "You men just don't understand how important this is to a woman.

Glory Hallelujah. Stormi clenched her teeth. This whole shebang was totally out of hand. Why had she agreed to have Joni help? A twitch started in her cheek. Because Joni had shamed her for leaving the entire church out of the festivities. And now—she was stuck.

"What do you think, Stormi?"

She caught her breath and then cleared her throat. "All good ideas. I think maybe Ake and I just need to discuss some things."

Did that sound non-committal enough? Joni smiled and clenched her hands under her chin. Ah, score. Stormi rose and meandered to the double exit doors. *Thank her, just thank her and keep walking.* Young footsteps came thundering down the hall.

"Mom, Crew stole my ball and won't give it back." Lucy wiped a tear from her reddened face.

Perfect. A distraction.

Joni strode to the door. "I don't know why you kids just can't get along for ten minutes."

Lucy scrambled behind her as she disappeared from the sanctuary.

Stormi motioned Ake over. She couldn't help but notice old hardhead's frozen stance, gaze still fixed on the front wall.

"I need to get home. I have some work I need to do."

He nodded, shooting a glance at the silent man behind them on the front pew. "Okay. Hey, Hoge we're going to take off."

The only movement to show Hoge heard his brother's words was a simple back-hand wave.

"Tell Joni, all right?"

Another wave. Unenthusiastic at that. Bleh. Stormi rolled her eyes. First Joni planned a ten thousand dollar wedding and now Hoge's consistent disapproval. What a drain. Marrying Ake on the funeral day couldn't have seemed more wonky than this. She tightened her arms across her chest as Ake guided her out the door with gentle hands. He opened the door of the truck, and she slipped in, stamping down more guilt for leaving without letting Joni know.

He revved up the engine without a pause and backed out of the space. Maybe Ake sensed the strained atmosphere as well. He pulled up into her driveway a short time later and threw the gearshift into park. They sat in the dark for several moments, staring forward at the black, silhouetted trees.

His voice came softly. "Are you mad?"

She took a deep breath. Spewing at Ake wouldn't accomplish anything. "No."

He straightened his arms against the top of the steering wheel and then dropped them. "What do you think of all that?"

Stormi grabbed the hank of bangs and twirled it. "Honestly?"

His hand came up and untangled hers from her hair. She shifted her gaze to his dark eyes, lit by the light of the moon. "Yes."

She dropped her gaze to his big hand wrapped around hers. With an inhale she collided glances with his again. "What do you think?"

He shrugged. "Seems like a lot of stuff."

Relief coursed through her. "Yes. Way too much stuff."

He tilted his head and caressed the palm of her hand. "It'd be easier to go to the courthouse."

"I agree." Hope rose in her chest. "But what about your church members? Joni said they'd be crushed if we didn't have a big wedding and reception."

He shrugged. "I think that's up to you."

She jerked her hand away and held them up. "Oh, no. No, no. I'm not going to break the hearts of all your faithful church friends."

"They'll get over it." A smile tugged at his mouth.

She bugged her eyes out at him. "Ake Pearson. Ugh. I don't even know your middle name to scold you."

"Aiken Ellings Pearson."

"Ellings? That's unusual. I like it."

He shrugged and looked away. "It was my original last name."

"Oh. That's right. You said you were adopted."

His "uh-huh" shut off the conversation. "How 'bout we just get up in the morning and get married at the courthouse?"

Her audible gasp drew Ake's attention. He elevated one thick brow.

She unfastened her seatbelt and scooted over by him and thrust her face close to his. "Are you serious?"

Chapter Twenty–Two

For some reason, Ake could not help but kiss her. His gentle peck put a curve of appreciation on her cheek. He wasn't sure if she smiled from the short kiss or from the thought of marrying him pronto, sans Joni's fancy wedding ideas.

"You sure you want to bypass all that decorating stuff? Joni seemed to think you women thought it pretty important."

An unladylike snicker burst from her. "Do you want to know my mother's wedding advice?"

"Sure."

"'Don't get married. It ruins your life.'" She sat back and tucked her arms into an angry knot. "Trust me, I didn't run around dreaming of getting married."

They sat for a few moments without a sound. Ake had no earthly clue how to follow up that little revelation, so he chose to say nothing. He could feel her body relax alongside him as the pent up stress of her childhood melted back into the nether land of lost time.

"Ake?"

"Yeah?"

"Are you sure you want to marry a sleaze like me?"

He threw an arm around her and snugged her close. With a long inhale, he pressed a long kiss to her forehead. Then he murmured, "Don't ever say that, Stormi. You're a child of God."

"It doesn't feel like it. It feels…"

"It doesn't matter what it feels like. Believe it. All those sins are gone. Gone."

She became pliant under his arm, and he decided he ought to get her inside. Stormi all soft and vulnerable often maxed out his self-control. He adjusted himself and pulled his arm free. The sound she gave let him know she wasn't pleased with the arrangement. "Where do we stand on the tomorrow thing?"

She leaned against him so he clutched the handle to pop the door open. He helped her climb down from the driver's side and then escorted her to the entry. He paused while she searched for the keys to the door.

"Stormi? Tomorrow?"

She stood under the outside light and looked up at him. "Yes. Pick me up at nine o'clock. Maybe that will give everyone time to be where they're supposed to be." She inserted the key and turned the lock, froze, and glanced back at him. "And tomorrow's Friday. We could leave town for a few days."

He twisted his lips in a side grin. "Sounds good."

One of her fingers appeared in front of his face. "And, we can avoid your brother for the first forty-eight hours. Gives us a better chance of still being alive on Monday."

A laugh bounced from him. "Don't worry over Hoge. Joni has a way."

"But you forget that we're spurning her wedding plans. She might turn against us." She sported a huge grin.

With a shrug, he gathered her in his arms. Didn't she know he'd weather a hurricane for her? Hoge and Joni were pretty low on his list of importance right now. Besides, this disagreement was just a simple tropical storm. Either way, they'd survive it together. After a good long kiss, he let her go.

"Want to come in?"

He rubbed the back of his neck. From the heat generated in that smooch, not a good idea. "Naw. How 'bout I just see ya at nine tomorrow?"

She nodded and stood on tiptoe to peck his bristled cheek. "Okay. Maybe shave before the big event? I do love me some smooth cheeks."

His lips twitched. He'd shave his whole body if she wanted, and that'd be quite a task. "Sure, Beautiful. Whatever you say."

With a coquettish swing of her hips, she slipped through the door and peeked back out. "I like the sound of that. Good night, Ake."

"Night."

He jaunted to the truck to the sound of her dead-bolt sliding home. Yep. Liable to be a good warm front going through the area with his wife permanently settled in town. Old Man Winter didn't have a chance with her red-hot looks and his passion. No, indeed.

᪾ ······ ᪾

Stormi had no sooner locked the door than her phone beeped a text message. Alan—again. This marriage thing didn't set well with her Christian friend. It bothered her a tad, but not enough to call it off. She knew this was the right thing. Marrying Ake would completely sponge away the guilt she harbored in her heart about this whole fake relationship thing. She glanced down.

What's up?

She rolled her eyes heavenward. Code for, "are you still getting married?" Fine. She'd play the around-the-mulberry-bush game. *Nothing. U?*

Reading.

Gr8.

Plans on schedule?

Bingo. There it was. *Yelp.*

Not cool.

She rolled her eyes. *Srry. Gonna happen.*

You need time.

4 what? She clunked the phone on the counter and went to pull a water bottle from the fridge. By the time she'd turned back, her phone blinked again.

Pray, read, get to know him.

She gave an impatient sigh. He ought to be happy she was marrying a Christian instead of some nutsy, abusive heathen or something. Her thumbs flew over the keyboard. *Already have.*

A yawn took over as she meandered to the couch and sat down. The phone flashed again. My, this could be a long convo.

Not enough time. U don't love him.

And that made a difference? So she didn't romantically love him. She still loved him. Alan seemed quite obtuse about the whole arrangement. It was perfect for her. She'd probably never find anyone more special—scratch—unique as Ake Pearson. She admired his wholesomeness. What better person to spend a life with?

Chill Alan.

While she glared at the phone, it lit up. Great, now he was calling. But when her eyes caught the number, she realized it was Marla. She groaned. Avoid a smart car and slam into a semi. "Hello?"

"Hey, B. It's me."

"Uh, I have caller ID."

A few obscenities shot through the receiver and then stopped abruptly. "Sorry. Old habit. I'm sixty out from you."

Stormi sat up, eyes bugged. "You're what?"

Marla swore again and then spoke excessively slow. "I'm one hour from your freaky little town."

Stormi curled her lips in and closed her eyes. What to say to that?

"You still there, Hurricane?"

"Mmm-uh"

"I'm thinking of hanging out with your sweetness. What do you think?"

Sweat dripped from her hand and ran down her wrist. "I'm not sure what you have planned, Marla."

"Don't worry about putting me up. I've got me a big papa nearby. Remember Stu?"

Stormi racked her brain to extract one face amongst a sea of faceless souls. "Not...really."

"You know, rich Stu. We called him Stu Boo. Rich guy? You know, from Miami Beach when we went three years ago. He drove a chrome Maserati?"

Her mind snagged on a snatch of memory. "Stu Boo from the slough? Oh, for Pete's sake, Marla. That guy's like a porn star."

"He's a big time producer, too. Oh, and I don't want to hear any pious judgement from little Miss Goody-goody." The Lord's name followed by a four-letter word shot from her friend's mouth.

"Marla, please—"

"All right, all right. Sheesh. You take the fun out of everything, you know that? All I'm saying is, I'll be in town. We could meet and hang out. Stu could hook you up."

A shiver of revulsion rocked through her. "No. Actually, I'm getting married."

Bleep. Bleep, bleepity-bleep. Stormi's mental censure blocked the words exploding from the phone.

"Married? Are you mad? One guy the rest of your life?"

Stormi snatched up the water bottle and downed several gulps. This night was just turning out peachy. Joni, check. Hoge, check. Alan, check. Cursing Marla, check check. Part of her wanted to flee through the door, drive to Ake's, and beg him to let her in. "Yeah. I'm getting married."

"Imprisoned, more like. Shackled, death by boredom. What are you thinking?"

"It's the right thing to do."

"That's a creepy thing to say. Who is this guy?"

"Ake Pearson."

"Aptly named. Aching. For the rest of your life."

Stormi's hand gripped the phone, wishing it were Marla's dinosaur neck. "He's a great guy."

"Whatever. Is he rich?"

"No."

"Famous?"

"No."

Marla disgorged a few more explicative phrases. "Then have him and throw him aside. Then move on to more exciting things. Like hanging at the beach bar Stu owns. Just opened. Live bands, three stories of flashing lights and moshed with people and noise. It'll be popping."

Alan's last text came through. And she pulled the phone down to glance at it at the top of her phone.

Abort this plan.

Just the thing, Alan. Time to abort any rendezvous with Marla. "Look, Marla. I know you don't approve. But I'm getting married. Tomorrow. Bright and early."

"And I'm not even in the wedding? What the—"

"It's just a simple ceremony. At the courthouse."

The sound Marla made sounded like uncourteous gas escaping. "Are you flipping kidding me?"

"No. Tomorrow at nine."

Silence stretched for a heartbeat or two before Marla spoke. "I really thought I could talk you around. I'll have to take more drastic measures."

The phone went dead. A shiver of apprehension coiled around Stormi's spine. Spurning Marla was a dangerous thing.

❧ ⋯⋯ ❧

Stormi clung to Ake's elbow. She glanced down at the revealing dress. Plunging neckline and skin tight, the sparkling gold creation barely covered her hind quarters. She knew she'd chosen wrong when Ake's eyes had flared in surprise and guarded appreciation this morning. The old bar-hopping dress had been her only choice this morning other than pants, and that hadn't seemed appropriate for her wedding. Yet from the sheer elevation of the judge's waxed brows and deeply-clefted disapproving frown that tugged her lipstickless mouth, perhaps yoga pants would have been the better choice.

The droll older woman decked in the judicial robes made a show of studying the papers through a pair of unfolded readers propped in one hand. "I see the paperwork is in order."

She looked up with her eyes only, creating a disapproving double chin as she studied them. "And both of you enter into this union with full understanding of the permanence and validity." She cleared her throat. "We're not in Vegas."

"Yes, ma'am."

Ake answered before she could counter the rise of indignation that rose from her fluttering mid-section.

"Very well." She flipped the earpieces open and perched the glasses on the end of her nose, where she could still peer at them over the tops. After a minute of full staring, she shuffled the documents in front of her. "Let's begin."

Behind them the door burst open. Stormi spun on her four inch heels, and her heart dropped to her black, stylish boots. Hoge and Joni stood just inside the glass doors huffing and puffing as if they'd run a half-marathon.

"What's the meaning of this?" the judge demanded.

Hoge held up his hands. "Stop. This isn't supposed to happen."

Stormi closed her eyes. She and Ake just couldn't get a break.

"How'd you find out, Hoge?" Ake's wounded tones tugged at her heart.

He motioned to the back of the room where Avery Guttleman scurried out of sight. Hiss. Of course.

"Uh, Madam Judge. Permission to approach." Joni muttered while her hands wrung.

"Oh, Jiminey Christmas, Joni. That's Judge Evelyn Dalton, a church member." He strode to the podium. "Listen here, Evelyn."

The judge pounded her gavel. "No."

Her stern voice froze all in the room.

"You will listen here, Mr. Hoge Pearson. You are in my court of law, and I have the authority to throw you out of said court or jail you if it's my desire."

Hoge straightened, his Adam's apple jumping.

"Do you wish to speak with your brother? Or will you continue to command me about?"

"Just a word with my brother will be fine, ma'am. Your Honor."

The elder woman leaned back in her chair, her face stiff with vested power. "Very well. We will reconvene in ten minutes."

She whirled in her chair and rose. Stormi glanced about the room as four or five people waited in the extra wooden chairs for their turns in front of the judge. Hoge shot her a withering glance before pulling Ake to the side out of earshot. Joni didn't approach from near the door and avoided eye-contact.

Hoge's furious whispers rose in the room, but still were unintelligible. Oh my. What a mess. She shifted slightly to get out of eyeshot of one of the admiring toothless men and ran a wet tongue over her parched lips. Her eyes searched the corbels and fancy woodwork trailing around the tall ceiling.

Her eyes returned to the huge judge's platform in front of her. From the corner of her eye she saw Ake pull away at one point, only to be yanked back by Hoge. Wow. Ten minutes. Who knew eternity could pass in such a short time? Ake stepped away from his brother and approached her. She searched his deep eyes but only innocence lay there.

"What happened? What did he say?"

"Nothing. We're fine."

The bailiff opened the door on the right. In stepped the judge.

"All rise."

The few seated people stood. Hoge came forward past them to pause at the judge's bench.

"I protest this marriage."

The stern woman mounted the glasses on the bulb of her nose and trained her laser eyes on Hoge. "Object. I believe you mean, object. Protestors are relegated to the sidewalk."

Ake's brother cleared his throat. "Yes, object."

"Hmmm. Let's see." She peered at the documents before her. "Are you his legal guardian?"

"No."

"Is he below the age of eighteen?"

Hoge stretched his neck. "Uh..."

The woman glared at him. "Is he or is he not?"

"No."

"Then, sir, you have no legal recourse. Aiken Ellings Pearson is of age and of sound mind. Therefore, he has the right to life, liberty, and the pursuit of happiness. With or without his brother's permission. You may be seated as one of the witnesses." She fluttered her hand toward the chairs.

Hoge hesitated only a moment before striding back towards Joni. After a quick pow-wow, they both sat in the front row, sour expressions firmly in place.

"Now, let us begin." She hammered the gavel once more.

Behind them the doors burst open once more.

"Cut me out of your life, will ya? Oh, no. That's not the way it works." Marla paraded up the aisle toward them. Behind her trailed Zora, an acquaintance of Stormi's. Now, evidently Marla's new BFF.

Oh, sweet heaven. What next?

Chapter Twenty–Three

T he gavel pounded again. "Madam, you are interrupting the proceedings of this court."

Marla flung her arm. "That's right, I am. Brought a little present, too."

She yanked a rolled-up poster from her purse and pressed it against the judge's bench in full view of the witnesses. A wave of dizziness clutched Stormi's chest. Oh, lands. There she was, in all her pre-Christian glory. On the table at Art's bar, in nothing but her underwear, tats screaming out, piercings riddling her face, her hair in a rainbow Mohawk.

She held a bottle of vodka and had her tongue out, displaying the stud buried there. Her cleavage rose to its full potential in the red lacy bra as she leaned over to mouth some raunchy country song. Or at least that's what she'd been told after the fact. The picture had circulated the campus before ending up tacked on her sorority door.

Her fingers clamped into Ake's borrowed suit. She could barely stand. And there was Hoge and Joni gawking at the photo. Jumbles of words and pounding gavels filled the air around her. If only she could focus and return to the room.

"Remove that from my bench. Now." The judge's command ripped through the courtroom.

Ake lifted his hand and tore the horrible image down. He rolled it up and inserted it on the inside of his suit jacket.

Stormi hung her head. She couldn't bear to look at any of them. When she tried to pull away, Ake only tugged her into his arms.

"Young lady, you are in contempt of this court. You will remove yourself immediately or the bailiff will arrest you and escort you from the room."

But Marla had already spun on her heel and clicked toward the door. "I was just leaving. Come on, Zora. Our work here is done."

Stormi's head pulsed. This couldn't be happening. How could Marla be so vindictive?

"Your honor, you can now plainly see this marriage is a mistake." Hoge's voice carried a note of desperation and disgust.

"Sit down, Sir."

All became quiet for a moment while Ake's hand massaged her upper back.

The judge's cultured voice filled the room once more. "Aiken Ellings Pearson. What's your request of the court?"

"I want to be married."

Stormi pulled away and searched his face. "Ake I—"

"Very well, let's begin."

Somehow, amidst the circus atmosphere, Aiken Ellings Pearson consented to be her husband in sickness and health, richer or poorer, better or worse. And this was certainly worse. She was starting this matrimonial thing off with a bang. No kiss sealed the agreement, only signatures on an official document, hers a little wobblier than usual. All the while bathed in the hatred of his brother and sister-in-law. *To death do us part.* That might be a very short time.

Somehow she managed to follow a somber Ake to the truck, Hoge sputtering behind, Joni trailing, coma-like. The sun lay on the snow, making the day seem bright. Too bright after such dark events. Ake strode to the truck and opened her door. She hopped in, yanking the dress down to hide her derriere. His brother snagged him as he passed the front of the truck on his way to the driver's side. Hoge's arms flailed. Angry whispers containing floozy, idiot, and wrong, outlined pretty clearly the direction of the discussion. As if there remained some doubt.

Ake broke away, came to the driver's side door, and yanked it open. He settled in and revved the engine. Stormi did her best to keep her eyes from the two scowling people, waist high just above the hood of the truck. They were soon on their way down the road, but not much of the tension eased. He still had the picture from Hades in his suit pocket.

He steered the truck through town and up the hill towards her house. She cast her eyes at the beautiful bay dotted with boats. Her gaze trailed out to the white caps and wondered briefly if Ake would fish today. Before she could follow that trail of thought, they were in her driveway. She let out an unsteady breath. This is where it ended. Where she thought she'd have a new start.

"I understand, Ake. It's too much. I'll be seeing you."

She went to pull the handle of the truck door and then felt a tug on her coat. With reluctance she turned to him. His face seemed a little paler than normal, which was unusual given his dark complexion. Too late, she realized he'd shaved.

"No. We came here to get your stuff."

"You can't be serious? After that fiasco?"

His face grew still. "We're married, Stormi."

"You just did that to save face."

The truck grew quiet when he closed his eyes. When he opened them, there appeared gentleness wrapped in steel. "I love you, Stormi. That's why I married you."

His hand came up to stroke her face. How did he do that? Just banish all the turmoil and replace it with calm in a matter of moments?

"That picture—"

"Means nothing."

"Ohhh." The word tumbled from her in a long stream.

She lost herself in his world of divine wisdom and gentleness while strength returned to her limp muscles.

"We'll get your stuff. Then drive till it's warm."

Her eyes widened. "Really?"

A small grin split his face. "Really."

They collected her clothes and personal items in relative silence, but the strain between them had disappeared. She'd boxed several items the night before and tossed her clothes into suitcases. Really, she owned very little. Lastly, she changed into more comfortable clothes then packaged her new laptop and schedules before shutting off the light and locking the door.

Ake loaded everything but her computer in the back. Then her perfect gentleman opened her door and made sure she was settled. Once at his house they unloaded her possessions. Then she quickly rearranged her suitcase for a trip. She didn't ask many questions, afraid the fragile marriage stupor would thaw, and he'd realize what a tramp he'd married.

Soon they were back in the truck with his and her clothes nestled together in the same bags. She slipped on her sunglasses and pretended to know where they were going. At least she knew they were leaving Hoge and Joni behind, and the specter of Marla's appearance had disappeared like a bad dream. She scooted over near him.

Ake shoved in an oldie CD of Simon and Garfunkel, and although she only recognized a few of the songs, the melancholy tones of their music seemed appropriate. Once he shifted the truck into gear, he slid his big hand into hers. Hours rolled by. As they made their way south, the snow cover disappeared, and the sun grew brighter. Finally she could hold it in no longer.

"Where are we going?"

He gave a laugh, not unpleasant, but short. "I don't know."

She turned slightly in her seat and pulled the polarized shades down her face to look at him. "You don't know?"

"Nope."

For some reason that struck her funny, and she began to giggle. It got him chuckling as well, and soon they were both laughing hysterically. All the stress, guilt, and unhappiness seeped from her body. For several minutes she could hardly contain herself.

Stormi calmed and wiped her eyes free of gleeful moisture, but couldn't quite quiet the small bursts of giggles that continued to spout out from time to time. She shot him a grin, and he returned a heart-stopping smile.

"You're the best person I know, Ake Pearson."

He shrugged. "Guess you don't know a lot of folks."

She slugged his arm playfully. "Not funny. Hey, maybe we could drive to Florida. If we go far enough, we could actually hang out at the pool. Or the beach."

"Huh. I've never been to Florida."

She squealed and slipped her hands together. "Maybe we could drive all the way to the Keys. Wow, that'd be great."

He reached over and grabbed her hand. "How 'bout we drive till it's dark, and then get out?"

She snickered. Who would have thought she'd have laughed on a day like this? "You know? That sounds perfect."

While the world went by her window, she nestled back in her seat, her hand fully engulfed in Ake's huge one. So life wasn't perfect. But when had it ever been?

Enjoy the ride. Enjoy the ride right now.

❧ ⋯⋯ ❧

Ake yanked the suitcases from the truck bed and pulled them to the glass door of the hotel. He tried to push away that old feeling of inadequacy. Why hadn't he realized he couldn't get a hotel room without a credit card? At least he'd been responsible for fetching the luggage. Anything requiring strength, he could cover. He rotated his head to rid himself of the endless driving kinks.

He supposed he should feel ashamed that Stormi had to reserve the room, but he figured that was the way it was in marriage. Each one filled in the other's missing abilities. Little did Stormi realize, she was in for a lot of filling.

All these thoughts only momentarily pushed aside the real subject on his mind. Getting Stormi alone. Talk about filling in. He supposed nature would kick in. Still, his lack of knowledge dampened his excitement of the honeymoon night. He rubbed his chin. Already stubble covered his jaw. The heavy beard was always anxious to take over his face.

The doors slid open, and there Stormi stood at the hotel counter, finishing up their reservations. Tight jeans and long-sleeved t-shirt. The tats. They kept her covered even in these warmer temperatures. When she turned to him, a coy smile decorated her face and as she approached, she gave a low whistle. He rumbled a laugh. She slipped her hand into the crook of his arm and leaned in seductively on tiptoe and whispered in his ear.

"I'm going to take you on a ride."

Ake's ears flamed. She let out a provocative laugh and pulled him into the elevator. Once the doors slid closed, she was on him like a splat ball, pressing him to the elevator wall, her hands groping beneath his jacket, her demanding mouth on his. For a moment it knocked the wind from him, but he warmed up fast, and returned her fervor right back to her.

Her hands snaked up to his neck and pulled his lips harder against hers. Then she went to his neck and licked him before alternating kissing and gently biting his skin. He kept his hands at her waist, while she slathered him in her desire, wincing in pleasure as she nipped his earlobes. And this was just preliminary elevator stuff.

The bell indicated they'd arrived, but she didn't stop her progression. Instead she backed out through the doors, still twined around him like poison ivy. A couple passed them in the hall, drawing their attention. She pulled away from him slightly, and then danced around him with giggles, touching him in places only his wife had full access. Preferably in private.

At their door, she tugged hard at his lapels and jumped on him, wrapped her legs around his waist. She threw her arms around him and stuck her tongue into his ear, and whispered. "That's right, baby. You and me—you and me all night long."

Whoa. He disentangled her from his body until she stood back on the floor. Her look of hurt confusion seared his heart. How could he tell her that while he thoroughly enjoyed her eagerness, he didn't want it to feel like something he paid for. No. This was his wife. Given his experienced wife, and he'd willingly flown in that airspace. It came with a cost, yet...

"I love you, Stormi. But I don't have to flaunt, you know, our stuff in front of others." He cleared his throat. "I'm glad you, well, want me, but this," he motioned to the closed door, "is God's gift to us. I just want it to be—"

He searched for the right word while her brow crinkled. When he found it, he couldn't believe he was going to use it. "It's special."

Her face cleared, and she sashayed forward to reach for his top button. "Oh, I'll make it special all right."

He set her from him once more. "No. Not just sex. But you and me being one. Part of each other's soul. Joined."

Suddenly the coyness fell from her face, and she nodded, looking terribly delicate and lost. The hands that had been anxious to wrench the clothes from his body just a few moments ago, grew still at her side.

"Can you open the door?" he asked when the silence had stretched too long.

She pulled the card from her purse and slid it into the metal card reader and tugged open the door handle. He stuck his foot into the door to keep it from latching locked again while she painstakingly returned the plastic card into a tight pouch in her wallet. Once she slung the small purse to her shoulder, he leaned forward and gathered her into his arms, fireman style. With their faces close, eyes to eyes, he entered the room and allowed the door to shut behind them.

He carried her to mid room and froze. She blinked at him. "Here's the part where I get stuck. Sort of."

A smile eased across her face and she laid a gentle palm on his cheek. "Oh, Ake. You're just precious."

She began unbuttoning his shirt, and he allowed her feet to slide to the ground. When she finished, she ran a finger down his bare furry chest hesitating on his belt buckle. "I don't think you'll be stuck long."

And she was right.

Chapter Twenty-Four

They drove all the following day, stopping for another glorious night, and then continued driving. Shortly past Cape Canaveral on the left, Stormi let out a long stream of air.

"I think it's warm enough."

This drew a lazy glance from her husband and a quirked brow. "Here?"

A grin eased across her mouth. My, how he'd blossomed in their shared love. She grinned. "Yep."

He chuckled. "Okay."

When highway 520 approached, he exited in the flying traffic and guided them towards the east. She inhaled with happiness. Ake at her side and the distant smell of salt. All was good in the world. After forty more minutes of Ake's golden oldies blaring from the speakers, and over several long jaw dropping bridges, they drove along the ocean's side from hotel to hotel, looking for a cheap enough place. Her fingers flew over the screen of her phone, accepting or rejecting each suggestion. Settling on a reasonable one that still had plenty of amenities, they drove into the parking garage.

Stormi stepped from the truck and stretched her legs. It felt good to leave the confines of the cab for a while. She scooted around the truck to meet Ake unloading the suitcase. She launched herself into his arms. "We're here."

His chest rumbled with laughter, and he caught her in mid jump. "I reckon we are."

She let him initiate the kiss which turned into a scorcher before he let her go. His self-conscious laugh made her smile. She linked her fingers with his as they made their way over the walking bridge. They picked up their code at the front desk and made their way to the twenty-seventh floor. Although she refrained from mugging him in the elevator, she couldn't tamp down sending him a few provocative glances his way. He merely shook his head and let out a small chuckle.

The next three days were pure heaven. Wind, surf, beach, sun, and flaming nights. When Wednesday rolled around, she knew heading home weighed on Ake's mind. Back to the snow, the cold, and the icy disapproval.

❧ ⸳⸳⸳⸳⸳ ❧

Stormi stood in the middle of her old house, hands on hips and rotated in a slow circle. Now what to do with this? Coming home to freezing cold weather had been unpleasant enough, but figuring out the details of their two houses dampened what was left of her positive spirit. Who would rent this place with a wall of open insulation stapled to wall studs? She glanced at the bed situated in the corner of the far wall. She wasn't sure there was room for it in Ake's pole barn house. He only had two bedrooms, and the second room held his treadmill and weights. Her brow wrinkled. Plus a desk with, ahem, beads organized into little color piles.

What was with that? Beads? She gave a huge sigh and crossed her arms over her chest, allowing her weight to sag to one leg. She knew very little about Ake. That had become apparent on the ride to their so-called honeymoon. The man had stacks of CDs of golden oldies from the 60's, 70's, and 80's. And even a few from the 90's. Apparently he owned none from this century. She let air rush from her mouth. Not that it was a problem, his taste in music. It just made it blaringly clear she didn't know her husband well. That sort of irked her.

She reached up and yanked on the wedge of bangs in her eyes. Time for a cut. But before that happened, she had to clear out some of the stuff she no longer needed. Or—she could just hold on to everything. Just in case. Grrrr.

She rubbed her hands down her face. What a willy nilly she had turned into. She'd pledged to repay Ake for breaking his heart, and now, when she realized how little she knew him, she wanted her own private apartment to hide in? Yeesh. Not cool.

She strode over and collapsed on the jean-covered couch and stared at the cold fireplace. It was chilly in here using the alternate baseboard heat to keep the water pipes above freezing. She tugged on the sleeve of her sweater and caught sight of the lace end of her tattooed sleeve. For once, it brought a smile. She regretted it with all her might, but Ake was very taken with it. Loved exploring it. Her cheek tightened with a suppressed smile.

Marla's face intruded her mind, ridding the secret smile from her face right quick. She plunged her teeth into her lip. How could she have done that? Brought that horrid picture and paraded it in front of not only her future husband, but her future brother and sister-in-law as well. And probably that stodgy old judge with her chin all elongated as if she smelled rotted fish.

Stormi clamped her jaw and shook her head. She knew Marla was capable of a lot of ballsy stuff, but she had no idea her best friend would turn on her like a rogue pit bull. She pushed aside the sting of betrayal.

Where had that picture gone?

⸱⸱⸱⸱⸱⸱

"Don't let him touch the net." Hoge's voice echoed off the cold morning air as the water buffeted the boat.

Delbert and the red-headed twins stepped up to grab the ropes, squeezing Ake from the winch.

He spun and stared at his brother. "Why not?"

But Hoge ignored him and strode to the wheelhouse a few feet away. Ake followed and stepped inside the close quarters and kept his eyes pinned on his stern brother.

"Get out. I'm busy." The big man growled as he tapped the gauges and checked the screen hanging from the roof for current weather.

A grunt squeezed from Ake. He may not be the keenest hook on the line, but he knew when Hoge faked busyness. "Hoge. I won't hurt myself."

The big man turned his face towards his then, temper petrifying his features. "Well, we're not gonna find out, are we?"

Ake took a swipe down his face before pulling himself up to full height, which only clipped the bottom of Hoge's earlobe. "I know you're mad. But I gotta do my job."

A humph cut off any more of Ake's softly spoken syllables.

He studied his older brother, standing there at the wheel, dodging his gaze. Then he glanced to the horizon where the misty sky kissed the silver shimmers of the water in the distance. He sent up a quick prayer for Pop, now learning to cope with a full-time health aide instead of his mom, and for Hoge, stubborn and distant as always.

"All right, Hoge. Have it your way. I know you think I can't cut it. You never have. Reckon I'll just wait."

He stepped from the dingy enclosure and meandered back to the stern, keeping his back to the activities behind him, his face to the west where Stormi waited for him. The heaviness Hoge created only lifted when she crossed his mind. He tucked his weather-roughened hands into the canvas bib at his chest. Hoge knew about love. He knew how it stole your will, changed a man forever. Ake would never be the same. He'd given his all to her, and it was never coming back.

A twitch caught in his cheek when he remembered the rolled up photo tucked in the inner pocket of his borrowed suitcoat. He had to remove it and store it somewhere secure. It was dangerous, he supposed, to love a woman like Stormi. Hoge had begged him to leave her there at the courthouse. He had to admit, that although the thought of abandoning her never entered his mind, the picture had sent a shockwave through him. To see her so wanton. Brazen. Raunchy. Wild. It had stopped his breath cold.

He could hear the thumps of their catch hitting the deck, and the smell of fish washed over him. Good cast. They would bring in a nice profit which would sweeten Hoge's disposition for a few days. He turned. Surely pitching fish into the icy hold wouldn't place him in any immediate danger. He stepped closer to grab a flopping cod from the wet deck.

Delbert kicked several that shuffled beneath his feet, but didn't say one word. That just wasn't natural either. Now, Heff and Neff, they seldom opened their mouth but to guffaw at the sharp retorts, but Delbert could never resist a good dig. Hoge. He'd told them all to shut their mouths.

Ake shrugged. It would wear off. He had nothing but time. Hoge appeared from the wheelhouse, and despite his sulky expression, Ake couldn't keep a grin from crossing his face. Even with his brother mad at him and the other three sealed in silence, he'd revel in his new married state and all that entailed. Boy, howdy would he.

~ · · · · · ~

Just another freaking happy family dinner.

Stormi stared at the broccoli cheese soup in her bowl. With all the dysfunctional family meals she'd survived, this one ought to be a snap. Obviously, Joni had done a good job with the dish. Overall the meal was delicious. And dairy. Seemed it slithered down her throat where it soured and curdled in her stomach. Why couldn't she just sip it down without her stomach tumbling? She glanced around the dining room. All was silent. Hoge at the end of the table, elbows out, Joni to his right, then Lucy who now grinned at her, cheese dripping to her chin. She shot the tot a small grin.

Then Linus, the eldest, sporting a 'tude at having to sit through family bonding time. Ake sat beside her at the other end of the table. Then the younger boys, Deacon and Crew, whom she swore were twins but were separated by a year. Then Pop was seated by Hoge on the other side, having to be reminded to put the spoon in his mouth.

She focused on one large chunk of broccoli in her bowl. Near the center. Green covered in greasy floating cheese. Squelching a desire to puke, she dipped her spoon properly in the bowl. *Just like ships go out to sea, I spoon my soup away from me.* Her first grade matronly teacher had drummed the silly rhyme into her head. Had they really eaten that much soup as young children? She shook her head to clear it.

"I take it that's a no?"

Stormi took a gasp of breath and glanced up to find most of the eyes around the table on her. Only Pop stared at the wall in front of him. What had Joni asked? "I'm sorry, what?"

Her new sister-in-law took a breath before she answered, almost as if drumming up some sort of concern. "I asked if you felt well."

A denial perched on her tongue, but she hog-tied it. She had to give some reason for not finishing the soup. "Well, I'm struggling a bit."

Not totally a lie. Of course, she didn't struggle with sickness, just the nippy atmosphere of the room.

Joni shrugged and gave a weak smile. "You don't have to eat it.

"What about me, Mommy?" Lucy chimed in. "Do I hafta?"

"Yes," she replied without a hitch.

"Eat your soup, Lucy," Hoge insisted from his throne.

"Oh, okay." The child slumped in her chair.

"And no pouting," her father admonished. "Or no treat tonight."

Lucy's eyes opened wide. "You won't tippy-toe dance with me, Daddy?"

Spoons lowered. Deacon and Crew smacked each other and snickered. Even Linus turned bored eyes to his father.

"Dad's probably got a pink tutu hidden away in Luce's closet," Deacon hooted.

Well, this was interesting. Stormi tilted her head to take in Hoge's lazy scowl at his middle son.

"No, he doesn't," Lucy thundered. "He's the Nutcracker. He's got big scary teeth. But he's nice."

"Right." Linus stood, oily hair falling in his eyes. "I'm done here, can I leave?"

Hoge nodded. Joni dabbed her mouth with a napkin and studied her eldest's departure.

"Hey Luce, does Dad prance around the room like a girl?" Crew wouldn't let the subject drop.

Lucy leaned back with a wide smile, cut her eyes to her father, and giggled. He pointed a spoon at her and lifted a brow. "Remember your promise."

The little girl covered her grinning mouth with both hands.

The playfully stern expression on Hoge's face led Stormi to believe perhaps he wasn't quite the horrible ogre he pretended to be. Then he glanced in her direction, and his gaze fissured into ice shards. Yeah. Maybe he was.

Hoge shifted his eyes to Ake and gave a side nod to Pop. "You're on parent duty this weekend."

Ake nodded.

"Watch him every minute."

"I will." Her husband continued to eat.

Stormi straightened. "I'll help."

Apparently the cold in the room dropped below zero for everyone flash-froze. She cleared her throat and spooned the liquid cheese into her mouth to cover the awkwardness. At last Joni spoke.

"I think that would be a great help, Stormi."

She glanced to her sister-in-law for a quick litmus test of authenticity. Did she really mean that? But Joni's face held real appreciation. Or just a really great false rendition. Stormi cracked a small smile.

"Can Stormi spend the night?" Lucy inserted after a long slurp on her spoon.

Joni grabbed a napkin and swiped it across the girl's mouth while the two boys roared in laughter.

"Cut it." Hoge grumped at Deacon and Crew.

"No, honey. Aunt Stormi stays with Uncle Ake." Joni replied, giving the rambunctious boys 'the look.'

Lucy studied Stormi. "Do you dance?"

The horrid picture at the courthouse flashed across her brain, but she pushed it firmly away. "I took ballet for two years."

Lucy brightened and Joni leaned forward. "Really? How interesting."

Stormi shrugged as she glanced away. "Yeah. Mom was convinced I was going to be the latest, greatest prima ballerina."

"You must have been very good." Joni again.

Most everyone stared at her. Only Pop continued to study the wall in front of him. Dear Pop.

"No, not really. It was just one of Mom's many manic phases." Crud. Why had that slipped out?

Joni looked more confused than ever, and Hoge's brooding stare didn't help.

"Can we be done?" The boys' voices merged into one.

Stormi dipped her head, thankful for the diversion.

"Of course. You can go now, too, Lucy."

The children left in a flurry and then thundered down the basement stairs. Hoge shook his head.

"At least the noise level is in the basement," Joni chuckled as she patted her husband's hand. "But let me get back to your comment, Stormi."

Chapter Twenty-Five

A whimper simmered below the blinky dairy in Stormi's stomach. *Do we have to?*

"You said manic phase. Was she unwell?"

Stormi crumpled the napkin in her lap. Dumb. *Dumb*. She knew better than to bring this up. Why couldn't she just learn to keep her big fat mouth shut? How many times had she tried to explain her mother to outsiders only to have them tell her what a wonderful person she seemed to be. Of course, that was before Mother trounced them over some insignificant disagreement and refused to ever speak to them again. Ever. Lucky victims.

"It's hard to explain. Ummm. She only noticed us when we did something that brought her attention. You know, kind of narcissistic." Okay, everyone back up. The Award for Worst Daughter was about to be given. Stormi stirred the cold soup. Ake's hand caressed her shoulder.

"Oh. That must have been difficult. Was she on medication?"

Lands, it wasn't going away. "No. She never admitted to having any problems."

"I see." Joni's voice was too gentle.

Stormi stood. "Excuse me. Bathroom this way, right?"

Her hostess nodded and she hiked a quick getaway.

Ake rose and picked up his bowl and reached for Stormi's. Hoge had disappeared into the family room, a.k.a. the "man cave."

"I'll get that, Ake," Joni protested.

"Nah. It's okay." He continued to grab the children's bowls and headed into the kitchen. Hearing the pain in Stormi's voice had left him restless. She always came off confident, bold. Reckless, even. But obviously, there was a lot he didn't know.

Joni joined him at the sink and clutched his arm. Her expression told him she'd absorbed the significance of Stormi's raw confession.

"Rinse or load?"

Ake gave a small sad smile. "Rinse."

Joni smiled. "You always fall into the position of support, Ake. And I think that's exactly what your new wife will need."

He thought over Joni's statement as he stared at his wife later that night. Stormi sure was quiet. She'd barely said a word the entire evening. He eyed her sitting on the couch with her legs drawn up, filing her nails. The dark skinny pants accented her well-shaped legs. He planted his gaze on her face. "You okay?"

"Hmmm?" She took a long breath and shrugged.

"You seem quiet."

She flashed a half smile. "I suppose."

He continued to stare at her, and she looked up to meet his steady gaze.

"I guess I'm thinking of my family. I probably should tell them I'm married."

Ake nodded, a seriousness lighting his features. "Maybe we could visit."

Stormi shook her head. "Nope. That wouldn't go well."

"How do you know?" he prodded.

She flung the nail file on the end table and stood. "Trust me, I know."

He stood and followed her down the hallway to the bedroom where she paced. Those tiny feet with red nails caught his attention, but he focused on the agitated woman.

Clearing his throat, he attempted a reply. "Maybe you could tell them, and then later, we could visit."

She paused and faced him, bringing her hands down like an angry conductor at crescendo. "You don't understand. Nobody does."

Like a dunce, he stood there, not sure how to follow that. He'd heard Hoge and other men talk about dealing with women, but he had no idea how quickly a confrontation could build. "Okay."

Stormi jumped on the bed and crossed her legs. After a slight hesitation he joined her. He lay back on the propped up pillows.

"It's not ShaVonn. That's my sister. I mean, she drives me crazy at times, but we're pretty close. Sort of. Dad split the scene long ago." She nibbled on her thumbnail, also bright red. "It's...my mother."

He nodded, sure words were not his best choice at this point.

"I don't know. It's difficult to explain. I mean, when I try, everyone just thinks I'm nuts. People are always telling me what a great person she is. Yeesh. What a joke. Then, when they least expect it, she takes their knees out and I want to say, see? That's my mom."

She reached over and rubbed his knee. He gave her a smile which just earned him a shrug.

"I know you don't understand, Ake. Your mom was great, and you're like, wonderful. I just can't explain it."

He reached over and rubbed her shoulder. "I'm sure she'll come around. You like me, don't ya?"

Stormi jumped from the bed and planted her hands on her hips. "She won't like you. She doesn't truly like anyone. But she'll find plenty of guilt to lay on me for getting married without her. It's all a game of, 'look at me, focus on me, it's all about me.'" She hung her head. "I just don't know if I can do it. I'm exhausted trying to make her happy."

Ake stood and circled the bed. He took her unyielding body into his arms. "Well, you don't have to do it today. We're in this together."

"Why can't she just love me instead of using me?" Stormi sniffed.

He rubbed her back and she melted against him. "Always remember I love you, and God loves you. No matter what."

꘎ ⋯⋯ ꘎

Stormi awoke to complete silence. And it dawned on her it wasn't the draw-yourself-up for confrontation type either. She let a small smile creep over her mouth. Except for getting her podcasts finished, she could lie here all day and no one, absolutely zero people would bother her. Or care. The grin slipped from her face. Well, Ake would. In a good way. A very good way. Her lips inched back to a smile.

But Mother—she shuddered. Why? Why did she do that to herself? Because waking to soothe the Momicane was deeply ingrained. She raised her arms over her head and the tattoos added their mockery. Both marked her soul. She shoved it away and rose. Nope. Not today.

She showered and dried her hair before she realized it was Saturday. Where was Ake? Ah, yes. Pop. He was on Pop patrol. Why hadn't this occurred to her before? Quickly she yanked on her yoga pants and a hoodie and headed to the door.

The fine hike up the slope in the chilly weather reminded Stormi how reluctant New Hampshire was to embrace spring. She could still see her breath while she crunched through the stubborn snow crust.

Sure enough. Ake was at the table. She tapped on the window pane. Smiling, he stood and walked to the door, disarmed the alarm, and greeted her with a firm hug. A deep breath of the masculine smell at his neck served as her smelling salts and brightened her outlook on the dismal day. His kiss practically made her purr.

He moved back toward the kitchen table and sat down. Mounds of messy files heaped across the surface.

"What's up? What are these?"

He shrugged and grabbed the top one in the stack. "Pop pulled them out of the filing cabinet in the office. Not sure why. He never goes in there"

Stormi took the file he handed her. "Bills for 2010." "Hmmm. Looks like trash to me. Man, you're mom sure did keep some intricate ledgers. Every single check is noted and numbered for its purpose and amount."

"Yep. That was Mom."

She flipped through several. Mostly thick folders about bills and payments. "I think you could just reorganize them back into chronological order and put them back."

"That sounds good." Relief flowed through his tones.

Right. Ake couldn't read. No wonder he seemed confused. "Okay, here. Let me just get the years back in order."

She leaned over and collected the files up to the current date. The last two, however, merely said, "Ake."

With her hands full, she couldn't inspect them, so she followed her husband instead to the extra bedroom where a desk and large filing cabinet stood. After glancing through the drawers, she relocated them to their proper spots in the bottom.

"There. See. Easy-peasy." She flashed a bright smile.

He just cocked his head. The seriousness of his face made her wonder if he was missing his mother or lamenting his inability to organize the files. She slipped her hand in his and tugged him to the door. How she hated to see him sad. The man who balmed her soul.

"Come on. There's only a couple left."

She settled into the kitchen chair next to his and pulled the files in front of her. "Did you know these had your name on them?"

"I guess I hadn't got that far." He stood to fetch some coffee.

There were several official looking papers in the front that required her brow to lower and decipher. Hmmm. Adoption papers? She glanced over at Ake. He calmly spooned in some sugar into the brown mug.

"These look like your adoption papers."

"Probably so."

She took several moments to peruse the thick packet of papers. He returned to the table and wrapped his hands about the cup.

"You said you weren't adopted until you were eight?"

He leaned back and extended his boots under the table, tipping back his head to think. "Yeah, that's right."

Her brows descended in a confused cloud. "Why were you so old?"

He shrugged. "I don't know."

She dissected her husband's face. Was he brushing the story off? Was it painful? Odd he hadn't been adopted as a baby. "What do you mean, you don't know?"

He sat up, and a cloak of pain fell across his face. "I don't really remember."

She swallowed. "Oh."

The loud "why" that hovered on her tongue was squelched by the inky darkness in his eyes.

Pop came to the door and shuffled through the room, breaking the tension in the air. He arrived at the back door, found it locked and then shuffled to the kitchen.

"What do ya need, Pop?"

"Oatmeal. Where's Mom?"

Reluctantly, Stormi set the files on the table. "I'll start some."

Ake rose and guided his father to the living room. "Andy Griffith is on, Pop. How 'bout you go see how Barney Fife's getting along, and we'll get the oatmeal started."

"Mom's late." Pop's voice wheezed out in a high thin cord.

Stormi quickly picked up her phone and searched how to prepare oatmeal. Ake's mom must have a year's supply hidden in these cabinets somewhere. Ake returned and wordlessly began to pull out the required pans. Together they had a bubbly bowl of goo in less than twenty minutes. Ake sprinkled in plenty of sugar and cinnamon and almost made it smell edible.

While he took a bowl on a tray, she made a beeline back to the files. Pop and Ake appeared at the door.

"He wants to eat at the table." Ake's calm voice contained a thread of exhaustion.

"Sure." She hugged the files to herself and wandered into the living room to deposit them on the coffee table. Paper after paper, packet after packet came to light and still she didn't have a clear idea of what had occurred to incite such a volume of judicial jibberish.

With a sigh she flicked through more documents. Incredibly official and obscure. Toward the back of the file, there appeared to be an open space. Out slid a stenographer's notebook.

From her perch in the living room, she heard the back door come open. Hoge's voice tensed her muscles instantly. She glanced toward the door. How to escape? Lunging toward the nearest exit was out she supposed. Window? Her eyes grazed the sheer curtains covering the huge front glass pane. Lots of rumbles and man syllables pulsated a warning signal in her head. *Abandon ship. Abort mission. Women and children first.*

She rose and gathered the files to her breast. No, that would never work. Hoge would demand to know what she carried.

Stormi grabbed her coat and wrapped the files within, trying to make it appear as an empty garment. Not entirely successful. Okay. Speed could be her friend here. Straight for the back door. Hi, howareya, *run.*

Pop meandered to the large doorway and stared at her. She stared back. Ake came to his side.

"Let's finish your oatmeal, Pop."

They disappeared. Hoge's huge bulk came through then, obviously heading down the hall. She stepped back behind the tall floor lamp, an echo of the eighties, but great for hide-and-seek. Once the bathroom door closed, she was off.

She walked quickly and quietly through the dining area. "I'll see you at home, Ake."

Without pausing to hear his answer, she dashed through the door to freedom. Without a jacket, the wind tugged at her clothes and sent icy fingers across her skin. Her feet wasted no time transporting her to the front doorstep through the frigid air. With a deep sigh she slid in the door, and then peeked through the curtains. Super. Satan's overgrown minion had not followed.

Stormi hurried to the couch and unwrapped her parcel. The two fat manila files beckoned to her. It would take a week to decipher exactly what was contained within. Perhaps she wasn't the only one with a rocky past.

Most of the afternoon, Stormi buried her nose in one sheaf of papers or another. Ake must have left Hoge with his Pop while he puttered around the yard, scraping the last stubborn snow-ice from the walk, raking the soil bare near the foundation, and laying out new landscape chips. The man never seemed to rest.

Yet, the longer she read, the bigger the ache in her soul. She'd catch sight of the subject of her thoughts and study him every once in a while. The words that flew from the page made her heavy. Sadness, regret, indignation.

When she finished, her legs were sprawled on the rug, her breath coming through her open mouth. The reality of Ake's beginnings were too cruel to wrap her brain matter around.

But she had no rest for her mind when Ake shoved the door open. "Smoke. From Pop's house."

Chapter Twenty-Six

She leaped from the couch and threw the pages into the air. Sure enough, from her window view, smoke filtered from the back door. With a small cry, she took a flying jump over the end table, sending the lamp crashing to the floor.

Stormi dodged through the door behind her husband's muscular form which had already made it up the slope. She'd never seen his thick football body move so fast. A prayer came from nowhere as she raced up the slippery hill to reach the back door that now stood open.

The overwhelming acrid smell of burnt coffee and popcorn assaulted her nose like a grenade. Ake fanned the air with a dishtowel, and Hoge had Pop at the wide-open front door. The smoke alarm's piercing screech was cut short when Ake reached up and yanked the battery out. Only then did Stormi's boiling blood begin to quiet.

"What happened?" She coughed and choked, leaning out the back door to spit out the horrid tasting saliva that poured into her mouth.

"There's a fan in the back." Ake hollered.

Pulling her shirt collar over her nose and mouth, she headed through the room and down the hall. Once the fan was plugged in near the back door, most of the noxious fumes exited into the afternoon air. Stormi looked around. Black streaks ran up the open front of the microwave and a completely disintegrated charred bag lay in the center.

With a pot holder, Ake grabbed a still smoking pan from the stove and headed for the door. Without ceremony, he pitched it into the yard. Charred coffee grounds flew from the singed container.

He returned with a shrug. "I guess Pop was making popcorn and coffee."

"Coffee in a saucepan?" Stormi continued to breathe through her neckline.

"Yep. And no water."

"But where was..."

"Hoge."

Ake's gaze went beyond her, and she knew the object of their thoughts stood behind her in the huge doorway.

Ake's face grew still. "You fell asleep."

Something akin to hate filtered across Hoge's face. Pop left his side and ambled down the hall and disappeared.

"Don't start, Ake."

To Stormi's surprise, her husband stepped up to the bigger man and spoke in a voice as soft as a kitten's ear. "He can't stay here anymore, Hoge. We need more help."

"We got help," Hoge barked.

"It's not enough."

Stormi stepped back, eyes mesmerized by the two hulking men.

The larger seemed to swell. "You better not be talking nursing home, Ake."

He nodded. "It's time."

"Shut up, Dummy. What right do you have to say that? What right do you have to judge? You're not even a real Pearson. You can't even remember your real name."

Stormi sucked in a breath, and the two men turned their eyes on her.

Hoge put up a meaty hand. "And you don't belong here."

"Stop it, Hoge, and listen to me."

The older brother shoved Ake from him. "I don't have to listen to you. You can't remember anything, isn't that right, little brother? Just dumb little Coe Cain who doesn't even recognize his own family."

Stormi froze. Dear heavens. No.

What was Hoge talking about? Ake wasn't sure what to say, but he need not bothered. His brother spun and lunged through the front door. It shut with a tremendous crash.

"Too much commotion." Pop ad-libbed from his bedroom.

Ake turned to look at his wife. Such a strange expression on her face. Almost fear?

"What's going on? What's he talking about?"

Stormi chewed her top lip. "Maybe you should check on your father. Then we can get this mess cleaned up. After that, we'll talk."

He nodded and wandered down the hall. Pop was fast asleep on his bed. He shook his head and rubbed his hands down his face. Grime seemed everywhere. Everywhere. And not just on the outside.

He returned to Stormi scraping the black ashes of the popcorn bag into the trash can she held. She twisted a tie-tab around the top and pitched it outside. He fetched the steel wool and cleanser and they both began the task of cleaning the microwave and stove. An uneasy silence settled between them.

Finally the last of the mess seemed cleaned the best it could be, and Stormi set a pot of chicken broth to boil and began adding ingredients for some soup.

He stood and studied her a moment. Then it dawned on him. "You read those files."

She fixed an intense gaze on his and nodded.

"And they were about me."

"Yes."

"Do I want to know?"

She came to him then and took him in her arms. Her whisper tickled his ear. "That's up to you."

For a long, long moment he just held her, absorbed her, smelled her, enjoyed the brush of her hair against his. How he loved her. She completed him. With this woman in his life, nothing was insurmountable. "Yes."

She tugged him to the kitchen table. Those crazy colorful eyes bore into his. "You were adopted, Ake."

He nodded. "I know."

But a shake of her head denied his simple answer. "Not like in a...regular way. The Pearsons had you from birth. But they didn't always have you."

Ake's eyebrows drew together. "I don't understand."

Stormi gripped his forearms and leaned forward. "You were a foster baby. And when you turned three, the court awarded custody back to your birth mother."

He lowered his head, searching for any memory of this. Futile. He had very few memories before age ten.

"If I was given back, how did I grow up here?"

"You were returned to the Pearsons when you were almost five. Only you were—"

Silence ruled the bright kitchen. He read the answer in her eyes. "Dumb."

A twitch skittered across his wife's face. "No. Not dumb. Different."

"Special."

Tears sparkled in Stormi's eyes. And that startled him. Nothing seemed to shake her.

"You'd been abused, Ake. And you couldn't remember who the Pearsons were. You had few memories of any kind."

He nodded.

"That cut on your head, the one where you had all those stitches? That's part of it. It's not your fault, Ake. It's not."

He pushed a hand up through his hair and found the knotted stripe of flesh. Something like a brand burned in his head. Old memories? Repressed pain? He jerked his head to rid his mind of such thoughts and rose. "At least the air's cleared."

"Ake." She tugged at his sleeve. "Listen. Hoge didn't take your leaving well. Your mother recorded how broken he was when you were returned to your birth mom. And then, you came back—a stranger."

He pulled from her and went to pace the living room. She stood in the doorway and stared at him. He looked everywhere but her. Suddenly he froze. "Did it have to do with cocaine? Is that what Hoge was talking about?"

Sadness throbbed from her. "No, Ake. That was your name. Your mother was a habitual drug abuser, and she christened you Coe Cain Ellings."

Ake's heartbeat seemed like a huge kettle drum echoing off the pale blue walls. "Why would she do that?"

His wife licked her lips and gave a reply that shuddered from her. "She was probably high and didn't care."

With a deep inhale of oxygen through his nose, he went back to pacing for a few moments. Then he stopped and connected his gaze to hers. "Then it's good I can't remember."

Stormi clasped her hands beneath her chin. "Oh, Ake. You sweet, sweet man."

She lunged at him and sobbed against his chest. Still a little dazed, he wrapped her into his arms. He held her there, trying to collect his thoughts. "Maybe that's why Hoge's always mad at me."

She pulled away. "I don't think Hoge is angry at you, Ake. I think he's still hurting from long ago. Have you ever talked it over?"

"Nope. Like he said, I can't remember anyway."

She laid her hand on his cheek. He grabbed it and kissed it, attempting a smile.

"I may be dumb, but I'm married to the most beautiful woman in the world."

The tremulous smile that spread across her face eased the ache in his heart. He glanced down the hall. "Well, whether Hoge is mad or not, Pop needs more help than we can give. I've got to make him see that, Stormi."

"You have to make him see a lot of things, Ake Ellings Pearson."

A quirk lit his left cheek. "Actually, I can't. But God can."

❧ ⸱⸱⸱⸱⸱⸱ ❧

So wrapped in Ake's simple acceptance of his past had her in a tizzy of admiration. Until a week later. Stormi stared at the white stick in her hand. Why hadn't she remembered this tiny detail? The wedding and honeymoon had been a chaotic whirlwind. Other than Hoge and the adoption secret, life with Ake had been peaceful. He'd enveloped her so deeply in his love and gentleness, something she'd never experienced before, that she hadn't stopped to think of this complication. Pregnant. She took a deep breath. Of all people, she should have tuned in to this possibility.

She pressed her hand to her stomach, the ripples of nausea still cramping her abdomen despite the bland crackers for breakfast. Ugh. How could she have overlooked this? She peered at herself in the mirror. Did she look like a mom? Not hardly. Would she *be* her mom? A strangled cry shimmied out her throat. Heaven spare this child from that.

With a twirl, she spun from the mirror and slapped the bathroom light off. She stalked to her bedroom and yanked the top drawer open at her dresser. With a growl she jammed the tattletale stick into the folds of her colorful panties. Now what? She tapped her foot and wrapped her arms tightly across her chest.

She and Ake were just getting used to one another. Joni and Hoge had actually started acting civil. Well, Joni anyway. They hadn't wanted her as Ake's wife, what would they say when she became the mother of Ake's children? And at ten months out. Well, it was bad timing. Completely bad timing.

Her phone buzzed on the dresser, and she grabbed it. Maybe Ake had come in from fishing early. But it was Alan, checking up on her. No doubt he thought she'd have dumped Ake already. She gritted her teeth. That wasn't fair. Alan had been a real friend. Yet his advice lately had been a little off-center.

Sup?

A little miffed, Stormi let her thumbs fly. ***Fine. BTW. Still married.***

Good. Marriage is 4 keeps.

She flopped on the bed. Yeah, keeps. Like in keeping out of her business. She took the high road. ***Need something?***

Nope. Just thinking of you.

The words on the screen strafed at her. He'd freak out if he knew she was pregnant. Oh, why not? She'd pull a chain or two and see what moved. ***I'm pregnant.***

The phone stayed quiet a long while. *There, take that, smarty pants.* His perfect Christian advice slows down when— The phone lit up.

Moving pretty fast.

She shuddered. He had no idea. She let a long breath expel, releasing her anger. It wasn't Alan's fault she was up a creek, so why did she cop such an attitude about it? It was her life, not his. Besides, why had she told him in the first place?

Her eyes dropped closed. Because she needed his counsel. As much as she churned along, dripping in confidence, apprehension dogged her every step. This new child grew within her. And this principled turn in life had more setbacks than she cared to dwell on. She pushed her pride aside and answered him. *I know. Wasn't planned.*

?

She grunted at his short answer. Yes, yes, she knew where babies came from, humdrum in monotone. But the past month had been a cyclone of events. She wiped a hand down her face. *Guess I didn't think.*

You'll be a good mom.

Her breath snagged in her throat. Where had that come from? Did he not know her at all? The man had been her classmate and a target of some of her best nastiness in high school. How could he say that? Fine. Two could play at that. She shot him what he deserved. *?*

Just know you will. You've seen it done wrong. You'll work twice as hard to do right. Congrats.

She tossed the phone on the bed. Okay. Now his real message will come through. Like, *JK, you should have been thinking.* Or, *Way to go, loser. Can't keep from getting knocked up out of the gate?* Well, all right. The last reply was more like what she would send herself, but still. The phone lay quiet. She tapped her fingers on her knee and spoke aloud to the blank screen. "Come on, Alan. Let out that righteous indignation."

Still—nothing. She picked up the device and stared at it. With a shrug she sent a quick reply. *Thanks.*

Maybe he was serious.

She flung her legs to the floor and hurried across the room to deposit the offending means of communication on her dresser once more. Let it alone. The queasiness in her belly made her stop short, but she shook it off. She pushed the conversation away as well as the information the little stick had revealed. Ake didn't need to know tonight. He had enough on his mind.

Chapter Twenty–Seven

Ake eyed her over the top of Mexican Chicken Casserole. She put her head down and stared at the food and forced herself to take another bite. It was like the man sensed something. Perhaps he'd had that heart-to-heart with Hoge, and the whole adoption mess was sorted out. Hoge had confessed his love for Ake, and they'd hugged it out in manly fashion. Yeesh. Like some 1950's sitcom. Not hardly.

He probably knew she was pregnant by just looking at her. Ake did seem chock full of wisdom. It was beyond her comprehension.

"Fishing go okay today?" She resorted to distraction.

"Yep."

"You talk to Hoge yet?"

"Nope."

She licked her lips as he continued to stare. Her molars tightened around the secret she held and she lifted her gaze. "Something wrong?"

"Nuh-uh."

Hmmm. Now if she used those answers, the truth would be, yes, something is major wrong. "How's everyone?"

He shrugged. "Fine."

His gaze continued to burn a hole through her. Unable to bear the scrutiny any longer, she dropped the fork into the plate with a clatter. "Then what's wrong?"

Ake sat up tall. His face sobered. "Nothing."

She turned a hundred-watt glare on him. "Liar."

He blinked several times, and a dimple appeared between his brows. "Just thinking how beautiful you were. And how lucky I am."

Her hands stilled in her lap beneath the table as she studied him. This wasn't a game for Ake. She'd forgotten. "Oh."

"Sorry."

His humble mutter crushed her heart, and she shut her eyes. She pressed her hands to either side of her plate and prayed for guidance. She'd managed to keep this tremendous secret to herself for a week. And for what reason? She opened her eyes, and collided with his dark, somber ones. "No. it's me who should apologize. I'm feeling...guilty."

She had to give the man credit. He continued eating to keep the atmosphere as relaxed as possible with a mean shrew sitting across from him. Nothing seemed to faze him.

"I'm pregnant." Her frank announcement froze him into a concrete bust.

His eyes took a slow rove down to her abdomen hidden by the wooden table between them and then back up. A slow smile curved up the corner of his mouth. "You are?"

She pressed her mouth together to stem the tears jabbing steak knives on the back of her eyeballs and nodded miserably. He stood so abruptly, his chair smacked to the floor. Without righting it, he circled the table, and then squatted on the floor next to her.

With a grin he took her hand. "That's great."

She wanted to flip her lungs inside out with a smart aleck answer of "is it?" but she refrained somehow. Maybe it was the genuine joyful glint in his eye. Instead she nodded.

"Wait till I tell Hoge." The grin slid from his face.

Stormi turned from him. Exactly.

He stood and rubbed the back of his neck. Without another word he returned to his seat, righted it, and sat down. She lifted her gaze to his. Plain as a twenty-foot billboard. Hope squashed. Initially, the marriage fiasco, then the adoption thing. Now this. She tossed the fork through the congealing goo of chicken and salsa.

Silence pressed in from every side. She shook her head slightly. Okay, this was their life. All their milestones and happy news would come as a funeral dirge because she'd screwed up her life, and thus snafued every bright spot in their marriage. She stuffed down the huge mass of disappointment and faked a bright answer. "Maybe you can tell him later."

Like in nine months. Surprise! *We're pregnant. Or were. Now we have a child.* Or maybe they'd have to keep that secret too. Hide him away in a basket like Moses. Ducking the poor child behind the couch when they came to visit. Shoving him in the closet and coughing over his whimpers. Despite the horrible circumstance hanging above their heads, a giggle popped out. That got Ake's attention. A brow rose.

She gave a grin. Why not laugh about it? Would it make it any less true? "You're Amram and I'm Jochebed. Just hiding a baby."

His mouth quirked. "Reckon we'll have to run to the desert?"

"How about the beach instead? There's still sand there. Does that count?" More giggles popped from her before she realized he was beside her again, pulling her from her chair.

His arms wrapped around her. "It'll be okay. Everything will be okay. Even Hoge."

She closed her eyes and leaned into her husband's strength and tranquility. Never had she felt like this, wrapped in such care and adoration. Completely treasured by a man who tolerated and transformed her mean ugliness. A prayer lit her thoughts. *God, this man is extraordinary. He's suffered so much, yet he remains ever pure and full of hope. Thank you. Thank you for a man who embraces me no matter what. And together we laugh.*

❧ ⋯⋯ ❧

Ake shut the door to his truck and meandered across the street. Spring's nose poked into the day, even at five a.m. The birds chirruped, preparing the heavens for the onslaught of light. The beginning of creation and the beginning of a new day. He inhaled a sharp breath of cool, moist air. It used to be his favorite time of day. Now, anytime with Stormi was his favorite.

He stared down at the boat docked at the pier. Hoge hustled around, the only one who'd arrived. Seemed he never beat his brother. At times he'd wondered if the man ever went home or spent the night rushing about the deck of the boat. He flicked his gaze to the *Sea Wheat 2*. Already it was rigged for sailing. Seldom did his brother not have the boats prepared.

He paused at the top of the wooden stairs, unwilling to alert Hoge of his presence. Ever since Stormi had stormed into his life, his brother's disapproval had amped up. There had always been something simmering beneath the surface, something Ake had never been able to pinpoint. A space. A separation. A disappointment? Yes, probably a mixture of all three. Perhaps Stormi had hit it square in the center. Maybe Hoge had unresolved issues with his adoption.

And try as he might, whatever it was had never resolved. Now Ake's marriage had only intensified Hoge's disapproval. A grin tugged at his mouth as he remembered offering his brother his favorite shooter. Later, he'd traded bikes. Then he'd given over his favorite BB gun. Memories snagged in a fog of forgetfulness.

But Ake learned these sacrifices only appeased Hoge momentarily. He cast his eyes to the horizon beginning to lighten with the rise of the sun and prayed for his father, asked God to hug his mother, and lifted Hoge up in his discontent. He glanced to the stars, still visible during nautical twilight, reminding him of God's ever-present direction in his life, whether he could see it or not. Then he stepped down the stairs.

Hoge caught sight of him and flung a meaty hand toward the street. "Grab the cooler from my truck."

Ake nodded and turned. Well, at least he'd spoken to him today. Perhaps he'd be back to his normal duties instead of merely sorting fish and throwing them into the well. The truck loomed before him in the parking lot, and he grabbed the large chest from the bed. Full. Good. It could get warm by noon. He strode across the lot and paused as a lone car drew near. Delbert. Soon the Double Goose twins would arrive and the other crew members for the *Sea Wheat 2* and off they'd go. His shoulders swelled in anticipation of being on the water.

Some twenty minutes later, both boats were rigged and ready for launch. Civil twilight edged in and soon the entire horizon would be bathed in the strength of solar brightness at sunrise. Hoge, the skipper in charge as always, stepped into the wheelhouse while Delbert, Heff, and Neff stepped up to untie the boat. The anchor winch cranked up the heavy weight that had stabilized the vessel through the night. Ake hunkered down on the side bench like a greenhorn and kicked a hunk of ice into the hold. It might be yet another long day.

Thankfully the waves were small this morning. Although the spring season nosed in, the wind at eleven knots had quite a bite to it. The forty-foot *Sea Wheat 1* seemed eager to go out today as it sliced through the wind. Ake picked up the scoop and sent a few chunks of ice into one of the two fish boxes. He caught the sound of blades beating the air from a distance, and he searched the sky for the state troopers. They were out early checking the boats. The many regulations weighed down the fisherman, especially on groundfish.

He glanced at Hoke. Maybe that explained his lack of appreciation for the big catches. They had to be very careful in counting the pounds of fish they hauled in. His brother always took care of the licensing details, the federal regulations. Ake stepped up to the wheelhouse to find Hoke studying a map to determine where to crank out their gill net.

"Ready to drop?"

Hoke fixed his eyes on Ake. "You don't see those other boats? We can't be within a thousand feet, Dummy. Of course it isn't time."

So he was back to Dummy. Well, at least it smacked normal.

"You don't realize how we fishermen are in dire straits. I got a crew to think of. What are those numbskulls gonna do if we go belly up because of too strict regulations?" He shook his head and then threw out his arm. "What are you thinking, Ake? You off and marry that floozy. You're just giving me more stress to juggle."

Ake shot a glance behind him to the stern where the three men waited near the winch in their bright orange rubber gear.

Hoge poked on the instrument panel to pull up the fish finder on the screen. "Now get out of here and let me do my job."

Ake shrugged and ducked out. He knew Hoge had been in constant worry over the fish regulations and count. This was definitely no time to address the adoption or to pull out the new info on Stormi being pregnant. His brother already held the welfare of the entire crew on his shoulders.

He made his way back to the winch in the stern, letting Delbert take the lead near the drum. Ever since his marriage to Stormi, he'd lost his pull master position. Hoge had put him there years ago because he'd been the strongest. Now, mouse-sized Delbert kept the ground cables winding in and out. Ah, well. Less problems with jellyfish smacking him in the face. They'd soon be changing over to lobstering when the weather warmed anyway.

The deck pitched a bit now as they moved out to deeper waters just as Hoge stuck his head out of the wheelhouse. "Now."

Delbert jerked on the lever, and the one hundred foot gillnet spun from the drum. Heff stepped to the other side, watching for snags, while Neff stepped back near Ake and shoved his ham-sized hands under his armpits. His face glowed raw and red, contrasting against his ginger hair and beard. He caught Ake's eye and gave a nod. The vessel slowed right on time.

Now they would wait and yank the whole kit and caboodle back in. The calm before the storm. He hoped they caught the right kind of fish to even out Hoge's quota. A helicopter passed over their heads.

"Troopers on the prowl today, eh?" Heff hocked a huge loogie from his throat and spit it over the edge of the boat. "Hoge'll be snapping off our heads soon if they don't let up."

"Uh-huh."

Heff jerked his head and raised his brow at him. "But then, he's been gnawing on you for weeks, hasn't he, Ake?"

Ake sent his glance to the blurry wake behind the boat. He couldn't recall any of the crew on the *Sea Wheat 1* ever calling him by his given. "Reckon."

The huge redheaded man growled a laugh. "Guess you got the last laugh with that handsome lass you netted, huh? Sure showed us, didn't you?"

"It ain't—"

Hoge yelled, "Wind her in."

The winch groaned and the men yelled directions to one another as the fish flopped to the deck. Instead of telling Heff that God had given him Stormi, he began to pray the net contained no cod. He briefly shot a glance to the sky as he chucked an eighteen inch bluefish into a basket and tossed a black sea bass to another. He instantly tossed several small haddocks over the edge, hoping he might reunite with the creatures in April when the regulations relaxed.

He shot a glance behind him. Hoge stood just beyond the puddle of twitching fish, gloved fists buried in his sides. His brother may think he didn't know squat about all the new governmental rules regarding their fishing business. But that's where Hoge was wrong. And that wasn't the only thing he was wrong about.

Soon Delbert yelled and Ake caught sight of the fuzzy ends of the cod end, marking the end of the net. Here a huge quantity of catch bulged the mesh into a bell of squiggling fish. Neff made quick work of opening the bottom, flooding Ake knee deep of fish. Getting Hoge to express his feelings and understand his marriage fled from his mind as he flung the fish to the proper containers.

❧ ⋯⋯ ❧

"Oh, Alan. I can't believe it's you." Stormi squealed and launched herself at her old schoolmate and now, mentor.

Tears fought their way through her lids and spilled down her cheeks. She squeezed tighter and tighter. Alan was why she had a fresh life. A saved life. He'd helped yank her from destination Hell.

There was no way to thank a person for such a thing. Instead she hugged his insulated form as if squeezing the threads from his coat. After a long, long, hug, she let go, laughing and wiping tears from her eyes. Thankfully the back parking lot of the chain café appeared mostly vacant. She tugged her eyes from the surroundings and focused on him.

Chapter Twenty-Eight

I'm sorry. I probably shouldn't have hugged you like that. I mean you are a married man. And hey, I'm a married woman." A hiccup giggle cascaded out. "But I just can't ever express to you...my gratefulness for, you know..."

Her throat throbbed from trying to push out her emotions. and tears continued to tighten her esophagus until she had to stop. And pathetically she continued to flap her arms as if that kicked in to translate when her voice couldn't.

He laughed. "Hey, it wasn't me. It was the Holy Spirit that made you aware of your need for Christ's forgiveness. I can't take credit for any of that. I'm just a messenger."

She clasped her hands at her lips, trying to stem the insanely stubborn tears. "True. But if you hadn't taken the time to reconnect with me online, I'd probably be dead, right now, lying in a grave and spending eternity in torture."

Alan gave another half laugh and bumped his glasses up on his nose. Such a humble guy, nerdy, even. At least that's what she'd pegged him as in school. Gracious, how many teenagers seriously read their Bible in study hall? And when the devil costume appeared, decorating his locker in derision by the jocks, he simply removed it and went on his way, quietly leading by his example. She'd lost a good horned mask in that prank.

He shrugged. "I was just glad I had a revival close by."

"Two hours is not close by, Alan."

"Still. Close enough." His eyes dropped to her belly. "Are you feeling okay?"

She took a deep breath. How to not dump all her anxiety about the baby, Hoge, and everything?

"I'll take that as a no?"

"Actually, I have felt just strange. My stomach feels...hard sometimes." She paused to gaze at him at the precipice of full blurt.

"You've been to the doctor?"

"Of course. I may be a hot mess, but I'm not stupid." She sniffed as she jammed her hands into her white parka. "I haven't heard the heartbeat yet, but the doctor says it's not quite time yet."

"Well, it could just be anxiety."

He didn't know the half of it.

"You want to grab a sandwich really quick?" He pressed a hand to her back, and she stepped towards the restaurant. Mid-afternoon lulled the place to just a few customers.

With a deep sigh she let him escort her to the door, while she found a tissue in her pocket to blot away the stray mascara on her face.

They found a table near the large wall of windows. She still couldn't suppress the smile. "I owe you like fourteen hundred apologies, you know that, right?"

He grinned as he took the menu from the table. "Shoot, that's just from freshman year."

A laugh burst out, but she shook her head, feeling emotion rise again—not from gratefulness this time. From regret.

Biting her lips she raised her head. "I'm serious, Alan."

He peeked over the menu. "I know. Forgiven."

She yanked the cardboard partition down. "How do you do that?"

"What? You're tearing up the menu." He raised his eyes, humor resting there. "They'll throw you out."

She reared back and gave a snort. "I'll drag you along with me as an accomplice."

"Hostage, you mean."

They shared a laugh till moisture seeped from their eyes. The waitress arrived and they put in an order. But when she left with her tri-folded menus, Stormi doggedly went back to her question.

"But how do you forgive so easily? I'm being honest here now. Sometimes when Hoge starts and says the most insanely unpleasant dig or just looks at me with those bushy, bossy exploding brows throbbing, I want to thunk him in the chest. And that man is just huge. He'd kill me in a millisecond. Dumb big oaf."

"I never said it was easy."

Stormi's mouth fell open. "But you just said..."

A sad grin lifted his cheek. "You think I didn't know whose Devil's mask was plastered to my locker our senior year? Sure I did. It hurt. You get over it and move on."

She sucked in a mouthful of air. "You knew?"

He nodded.

A couple walked by their table with a pair of chattering kids, drawing her attention for a moment. "Your mother must have hated me."

"My mother was a praying warrior. I think you topped her list for several years. She still asks about you."

"Oh, Alan. You're killing me right now." King Kong must be throttling her neck. She could barely breathe.

He reached over, the sunlight catching his plain brown hair, his brown eyes softer than a tulip petal. "It's what we do, Stormi. We pray for lost sinners. We persevere when life tugs us down. 'We are pressured in every way, but not crushed; perplexed, but not driven to despair; hunted down and persecuted, but not deserted, struck down, but never destroyed.'"

Stormi pressed a fist to her mouth and contemplated the solemn face before her. He was right. First it had been Mother. Then her life choices. Now Hoge. She'd been pressed, struck down, emotionally, psychologically, even physically, but she was still not destroyed.

◈ ⚬

Ake clenched his hands on the grips of the steering wheel in the mostly empty lot. He'd followed his wife, hoping to catch a late lunch with her. It was a rare day indeed when Hoge hauled the big net in and gave them all a few hours off. But today, the catch had been monumental. Maxed their quota out. He'd contemplated sitting with Hoge and airing their differences. But he chose instead to chase down Stormi. Big mistake.

He tried to focus on his brother's smug face from earlier. It was much easier than thinking about his wife with her arms draped around another man, hugging him for all her worth, wiping her eyes in obvious pleasure at seeing him. His steamrolled heart stuttered to force life-sustaining blood through his constricted veins.

Hadn't he wondered secretly in his heart? That little whisper that told him she couldn't be trusted with a background like hers? But he'd never fed that ugly flicker, never let it flare up. Now it roared and consumed him as he leaned back and shoved the truck into the gear.

He quickly got out of traffic and headed towards his hometown, no destination in mind. Without much thought, he'd pulled into the meandering cemetery where he'd buried his mother. The single-lane curving road doubled up on itself and wound to the back section where the twin-hearted gravestone, fresh and shiny, shone in the late afternoon sun.

He stopped mid-lane and exited. His boots sank into the wet spring soil. The pile of soft new sod mounded upon his mother's fresh grave forced him to drive his fists into his pockets. He came abreast and stood at the foot of the rectangular patch of tumbled clods. Maude Anne Pearson. Gone but not forgotten.

"Mom, you kept a lot of secrets." He harrumphed and his body seemed to deflate. "Stormi's got them too, apparently. And Hoge."

He kicked a clod of dirt and fought the unrest that threatened to steal the air from his lungs. "Pop's not doing good, Mom."

Much better subject. Handy he'd learned to push away that heavy feeling of pain. Store it. Duct tape it up and shove it away. Right helpful.

He crossed his arms and glared at the mound of dirt. "We have to put him in a home, Mom. I know you disapprove, but..."

A catch caught in his throat. "I know what you're thinking. I won't divorce her, don't you worry. She's having my baby."

He nodded as if she'd answered. "Yeah, I know she doesn't love me. It's okay. I think only really the Lord does. Maybe you and Pop, too. At least back when he could remember. But then, forgetting isn't all bad."

Coe Cain

The vision of Stormi with that man in the parking lot pulsated through his brain.

"Yep. Maybe Pop is better off the way he is." He spun and strode back to the truck.

❧ ⸺ ❧

"What are you doing?"

Hoge's voice came right unwelcome as the back of Ake's hand plowed against the truck's engine. He grunted. Maybe if he ignored him, he'd go away.

"Dummy. It's too durn cold to be out here under that piece of junk you call a truck. Why aren't you in the garage?"

Ake slid out from underneath and stalked to Hoge and shoved him hard. "Go home."

Hoge stepped back in surprise. "Boy, you in the mood to sign your death sentence?"

He threw the wrench down, and it clanged against the asphalt. Then Ake stormed to the house and slammed the door. A drink of water and a deep breath might calm his choppy insides.

Unfortunately, Hoge opened the door and came through. The lock. What a time to forget that. Hoge stood staring at him, a puzzled look on his face.

"Ake. What's going on?"

"I could ask you the same thing. You practically let Pop burn the house down."

"Now you listen—"

Ake had had enough. He threw the glass against the far wall, and it shattered against the drywall, sending shards tumbling onto the T.V., water flying. "Get out of my house."

Hoge held up his hands and backed away, a strange expression flittering on his face. Without a word he turned and exited through the door, shutting it quietly.

Waves of anger came to rest one by one on the shore of sanity. He hung his head. He hadn't had an angry outburst in years. It disgusted him. His mother would be terribly disappointed. She'd worked hard to calm him.

He grabbed a towel and wiped the water from the wall and hunted for the shards. He had to get a handle. Stormi would be home soon. He couldn't let her know he'd seen her in the parking lot with another man. He couldn't. The truth straight from her lips might kill him.

Once he'd pitched the glass pieces into the trash, he jumped in the shower. Somehow he had to erase that image from his mind. And carry on.

Stormi waved goodbye to Alan. Unbelievable. She'd been able to thank her mentor in person. There wouldn't be much she'd trade for that. She couldn't stop grinning as she drove across the city. Things were just beginning to smooth out. Make sense. She could see the light at the end of the tunnel.

Despite Alan's advice, her marriage was working out. This pregnancy would just glue it all together. It would only be a matter of time before Hoge came around. Yeah. Sure it would sting when the whole adoption/pregnancy mess came out, but she was just certain everything would settle into blessedness. She sniffed. Oh, good grief. The hormones were sure making her weepy.

She detoured to her favorite specialty grocery store. Ake deserved a special meal. And he'd be out for hours yet, so she had plenty of time. Maybe she could even stop off at the baby store. A shiver of anticipation rippled up her frame. Yes. Life suddenly made sense.

Her impromptu stops turned into a longer visit than she'd thought, but then, Ake hardly got in before six. She still had plenty of time. Her headlights pointed the way up the hill beside Pop's house, and she gratefully drove up to the garage and pressed the opener. Just as she thought. He wasn't even home yet.

But to her surprise his truck was in the garage, and he was stooped beside the rear left tire. The truck was jacked up at a precarious level. What was he doing? He shot a glare at her headlights. She turned the engine off which powered down the bright lights.

"You startled me. I didn't expect you to be in the garage. What are you doing?"

For a moment, he didn't answer. Then a mutter. "Brakes."

"Oh. Shoot. I just shopped and shopped thinking you'd still be out."

He lifted the unwieldy tire and settled it on the lugs. The ratchet clicked a fast pace as he cranked on the bolts. But he said nothing. Probably a little peeved she'd gotten home late.

"I'll hurry in and get dinner started."

She returned to the car and dangled all the bags on her arms. But he was there by her side, taking them from her with a grim face.

"I'm sorry, Ake. I really am. I can get these."

But he was halfway to the house, so she followed him. What a dork she'd been. Why hadn't she called? Because that stupid boat rarely got a phone signal, that's why. He laid the parcels on the counter and returned to the door.

"That's all..." she completed the sentence to an empty room, "there is."

Cold air rushed to her ankles. She pondered his quick exit, but when he didn't return, she assumed he'd gone back to finish the brakes. No matter. Dinner awaited. Jamaica Jerk chicken with sautéed onions and a rainbow of peppers. She couldn't wait to get started.

She puttered about the kitchen, checking the recipe on her phone as she stirred, fried, and cooked. Meal preparation was something Stormi rather enjoyed. That was unexpected. Definitely a step up from Mother's fried bologna sandwiches. On Thanksgiving. Ugh. Not a thought she wanted to entertain now. She hummed as she filled the bowls and set the table.

When all was ready, she called Ake, and he came in to wash. She soaked the pans and threw the rest of the dirty dishes into the dishwasher as she waited for his return.

They sat and he blessed the food. She sliced the chicken open. Perfecto. That's right. The next big reality TV chef. Oh, yeah. She stifled a giggle. More hormones, no doubt. She cut a glance at her somber husband. He, on the other hand, seemed to have grazed on downers.

"What time did you get home?"

He shrugged.

She lowered her fork. "Was it late or early?"

"Early."

He peered at the chicken as if he expected a hundred dollar bill to come racing out. It was awesome chicken, but seriously.

"Ake?"

After a long pause, he looked up.

"What time?"

With a wave of his fork he mumbled, "Elevenish."

Her mouth dropped open. "You've been home since eleven? Why didn't you call me?"

He stilled. "I wish I had."

"Well, me too. I—" Her phone buzzed on the counter. She scowled at it. "I've had two calls from Marla today. There's no way I'm answering."

Again with the shrug. He stood with his plate wiped clean and strode to the sink. Then he made a beeline for the garage door.

"Where are you going? You can't be done already?"

"Yep."

The door shut off her next question.

Chapter Twenty–Nine

Well, that was a disappointment. So much for this special meal. Meant nothing. She stuck her tongue out and blew a raspberry as she rose to clear the table. Hoge must be riding Ake hard. Then her motions came to a stop. Why had he come in early? Perhaps he'd ironed out everything with Hoge. Judging by his demeanor, maybe not.

She mentally pushed it away for now. With dishes, her podcast to plan for, and the new baby clothes she'd purchased today, she had enough on her plate. They could discuss it when he came back in.

It neared ten o'clock when she smoothed the little onesies into neat little piles. Just generic little underthings, but oh, how tiny. They wrenched her with the thought of such a small person being in her care. Frightening even.

She glanced at the clock, exhaustion reminding her of the late hour. What was Ake doing out there? He had to be freezing.

With a tiny garment wrapped in her hands, she made her way to the garage door. But when she opened it, only her car rested there in the dark. She flipped on the switch. Everything in its place. Weird.

She shut the door firmly and made her way to the front of the house. But once she poked her head out into the cool night, she knew he was nowhere to be seen. Her glance rose to the hill. At Pops? He hadn't mentioned it being his night to stay.

A deep breath pulled the refreshing air into her lungs as she stepped out into the moonlight. Only one way to find out. The clouds drifted across the dark spring sky with a wisp, threading their way across the moon. Then a larger one trailed in and blocked the bright orb completely. Stormi shivered and hurried to the back door.

Her taps on the window pane of the door echoed through the eerie night. She was afraid to grab the doorknob in case she set off the alarm. The lights were out, too. Why hadn't she brought a flashlight? The porch light to her left flicked on, and the door opened. There stood Ake, sleepy-eyed.

"Yeah?"

She stared at him. Was he serious? "Are you staying here tonight?"

He nodded.

"Oh. Okay."

The door slid shut and the locks clicked into place. Her breath froze in cloudy puffs that enveloped her. Something wasn't right in Denmark.

She retraced her steps to the house and let herself in. Everything would be cleared up in the morning. It wasn't like he hadn't spent nights with his dad before, it's just he usually told her. She shrugged. Perhaps he was still miffed she hadn't returned earlier.

Once snuggled into her pajamas, she climbed into bed and set her phone on the end table. At least she'd have the whole bed to herself. She tossed. Then rolled over. Numerous body adjustments later, she sat up. Having the whole mattress wasn't as comforting as it used to be.

Time became a monster that mocked her in red digits. 10:46. 10:47. 10:48. *Okay, count. One, two, three, four...one thousand and thirty-seven, one thousand thirty-eight, one thous*—stop. Obviously it wasn't working. 11:23. 11:24. *Stare at a light spot in the room and don't allow your eyes to close.* Her eyes began to water and ache. Oh, for pity's sake. It wasn't a juvenile staring contest. *Fine. Just listen to the sounds, don't think.*

11:59. Blink, blink. Thoughts boomeranged around her head until her heart beat rapidly. *Get a drink. Pee.* Ahhh. Better. Any second now, sleep would come. Like at this very moment. Or...now. No, really, NOW.

12:23.

She flipped the blankets from her legs and swung them to the floor. Ake. She missed Ake. Something was not right. A deep breath did nothing to calm her. She rose and walked through the house, peeking out the window toward the hill, but the house was shrouded in blackness.

Fine. She'd get up and do something useful. She meandered to the extra bedroom across the hall. Podcasts. She could finish up a few and have a little extra time during the day. The frumpy bun wobbled, reminding her of her unkempt appearance. No worries. A comb through the hair and a shirt thrown on would give the appearance of a perfectly manicured professor.

She hurried to her bedroom and completed her task and returned. After settling into the chair in front of her laptop, she organized her materials around her on the desk. Such a nice area to complete her courses. Better than her old "apartment-slash-old garage." Her eyes went to the velvet covered table with an assortment of beads. Ake. She inhaled.

Alan would quote something about here. Something about sleeping and unresolved conflict, or some other stinking wise mush. She shrugged. Which clash should she address first? A barrage of people pounded her brain for attention. Hoge, Marla, Mother, the baby, Pop, Alan, Ake? She groaned. Ake. Precisely why she couldn't sleep.

With a shake both mental and physical, she stared at the screen. "Beginning on page forty-one of your syllabus, you will see the topic of discussion."

Once in professional mode, she completed three more podcasts and logged off. Dandy. That opened up all kinds of time. She glanced around the room for a clock, and then realized this was the one place in the house that didn't have one. Hmmm. Something very profound tugged a sleep smile to her face. A place without time. She stretched and yawned and made her way to the master.

Reality thumped like a pitchfork handle to the head. 2:47. Her phone buzzed. Maybe Ake. Perhaps he couldn't sleep either. Thank goodness. She hurried to the bedside table and settled on the side of the bed.

Nope. Marla. Why hadn't she deleted her number from her phone? This was the third call today. Well, no time like the present, in the corridor of darkness. She thumbed through the selection until she'd pulled up Marla's number. The digits glared from the screen. Her hand hesitated. Hussy. Vindictive witch. Traitor, turncoat, Napoléon, Jezebel. The mental thesaurus wouldn't shut down. She snickered when Torie came to her head. At least Mr. Dart from History 101 would be proud.

Her lips compressed into a scowl. *Just erase it. Delete her from your life.* With a deep breath she...froze. A call lit up her phone again. Marla.

The phone buzzed in her hand. Why? Why was she calling over and over? Stormi groused out a few imaginary replacements for naughty words and stood, pressing the green answer button.

'What?" The word left her lungs in a shout.

"Oh, Stormi, Stormi."

Stormi could barely recognize her old friend's, or rather, fiend's voice through the sobs. She clenched her molars and narrowed her eyes in the dark room. Why had she answered? "What do you want, Marla?"

"Please help me. I'm trapped."

She and Marla had played a lot of tricks. A ton. Prey on the weak; devour the poor. Probably another stunt. Marla screamed and pounding became evident in the background.

"Please, Stormi. There's like twenty of them."

"Twenty who?"

"Johns." A wail wavered over the line.

Was Marla shooting straight? Or luring her into a trap? "Where are you?"

"Giovanni's party house."

A sharp breath made Stormi pause. "In Boston?"

"Yes. Please. I think I can crawl out the back window. Hurry."

Stormi stuttered. "But that's more than an hour away—."

Pounding interrupted her and Marla gave a whimper. "I beg you, Stormi. Please help me."

Thoughts raced through Stormi's brain while she hurried to the laptop in the guest room. Walking into that type of area of the city was dangerous. Not that she and Marla hadn't done it before. But this sounded a step more dangerous than college partying. Was Marla really in trouble?

Ake. She could take Ake. Marla whispered the address as Stormi pounded it into the search line. Boston was totally foreign. But her online map would guide her there nice and neat. She backed away from the computer with thoughts of Marla swirling in her head. No. Ake couldn't go. He had his dad to care for. Hoge? The cringe that contorted her face told her she would never stoop so low.

Okay. Just her. Fab. Well, on the positive side, Ake wouldn't know until tomorrow. She stood with her ex-best friend begging in her ear. The misdeeds of Giovanni coming to life in Stormi's head.

She laid the phone down with the tearful voice still sobbing her predicament. Jeans, sweatshirt. Baggy. Layered. Hat. Heavy coat. Too bad she'd ditched her Old woman Halloween wig a few years back. That would be very handy about now.

She stepped out into the dark with her car keys in her hand. "Please God, let this be for real. Keep us safe."

With an uneasy shiver, she slid into the car.

∽ ⋯⋯ ∾

Ake's eyes cracked open. Stormi's car. He sucked in a sharp breath and rolled over to check the clock. She was leaving in the middle of the night. Why would she be—he swung his legs to the floor of the single bed of his childhood. Never in his life would he have pictured himself trying to survive infidelity. Shoot, he never envisioned finding someone to marry. Perhaps he could just fix his mind on that.

He laid his hand on his Bible on the nearby end table. Suddenly the stories of Hosea his mother used to read hit a little too close to home.

He rose. No sleeping now. Best check to see if Pop had managed to step over the empty soda cans he'd strewn in front of his bedroom door. Then pray. Pray that Stormi could choose the right way, embrace her marriage, and actually love him. Pray that he could endure the saga from his front row seat.

∽ ⋯⋯ ∾

Stormi glanced toward her phone for the five-hundredth time. The tangle of Boston streets resembled a dizzying bird's nest. She wiped the film of unease from her lips with the back of her hand. Definitely not her best move leaving behind one of two hulking men in her life. But then, when you brought the big guns, did they get out more ammo? Perhaps it was best she'd come alone. Small and stupid might just creep in and retreat without being noticed. Maybe.

Her car shuddered as a huge truck passed her on the Tobin Bridge. The myriad of lights pulsated like a terrible migraine. Somehow she never imagined grubbing for Marla's location during her first trip to such a historic city. She shivered as she cleared the Mystic River. Signs flew past. Paul Revere Park, something, something Bunker Hill Bridge. How much farther?

The beauty of downtown ruled the dark sky with the broken patterns of light bathed in a golden light, making her gasp in appreciation. Too bad it couldn't be enjoyed with a little less adrenaline. She continued to follow traffic, a full fifteen miles above the speed limit just to stay in the flow.

The area turned more commercial, and she turned at the computer generated voice. Public alley? Had they run out of names for streets? The higher the apartment buildings the lower the needle edged on degenerate neighborhood scale. People lined the dirty sidewalks, distorted psychedelic gang names strewn down the buckling brick walls.

Her eyes went up. Shouldn't there be like a wad of tennis shoes hanging from a wire or something? Her phone friend announced her destination. Stormi pulled into an empty spot between a dumpster and an old white van. She glanced up the brick building.

Wire cages surrounded some sort of metal patios. Several contained cheap plastic furniture. She counted up. Third floor, Marla said. The window with the purple curtain. Access to the fire escape. But how could she utilize the fire escape with the bottom ladder pulled up?

She pinched her lip and prayed. This had better be legit. She yanked the Saturn into reverse. Perhaps she could reach it from the car's roof. Once she pulled under it, she grabbed her phone. No one knew where she was. Probably not wise. Yet, Ake would be asleep. Waking him would just throw him into protective mode. No. She'd tell him later. The phone tumbled to the passenger seat.

She climbed from the small car and glanced up through the darkness. *This is dumb, dumb.* Stormi ducked back in and snatched the phone. At least she could call 911. She dialed Marla's number. It rang and rang while dogs and humans shouted from some distant location.

When the line flipped to voice mail, she slipped the phone in her pocket. With a deep breath, she scaled the hood and slid over the car to the roof. Her fear came in puffed clouds of carbon dioxide. She stood slowly, straining to reach the ladder. Ugh. She would have to jump. Marla had better be about to die.

With a deep breath, an audible prayer hissing past her lips, she leaped. She landed with a groan, the metal rung greeting her neck with a stab of pain. Her sweaty hands clenched the wrought iron sides, while she huffed her breathing to a slower speed. She pressed the bridge of her nose to the black bar and closed her eyes for a second. This was nuts.

But she paused only a moment before climbing higher. It didn't take long to gain the first platform. She stepped to the stairway that led to the next level. Once there, the purple curtain lay before her, but fear strangled her lungs. The window was wedged up just an inch. Her signal. No turning back now.

She pried her fingers into the opening and yanked up. It gave with relative ease. About here would be where black gloved hands reached through and grabbed her. But nothing happened. She swiped aside the purple curtain. The sight of Marla sprawled on the floor, half clothed, catapulted Stormi through the open window without caution.

Her ex-friend whimpered, and her eyes cracked open as Stormi knelt beside her.

"You came."

The darkened room, lit with a desk lamp covered with a red scarf, contained only a rumpled bed and a cluttered desk and chair. A strange overwhelming smell permeated the air. Like burnt plastic. "Yeah, not my smartest move. You okay?"

"Am now."

Stormi grabbed a throw from the bed and covered Marla. "Let's get you out of here."

"No. Wait." Marla begged, her smokey eye makeup and contoured face a smeared mess. "You were right."

Laughter and thumping music pulsed through the thin door. A loud smack made the door shake. *Get her out.* Stormi snugged the blanket up around Marla's bare shoulders. "No time for this. We gotta go. Can you sit up?"

Bony fingers clenched hers, making Stormi pause. She surveyed her childhood friend. Bleached hair in disarray, face contorted in a mask of misery. Marla shook her head with vehemence.

"I can't move," she huffed.

Another loud pop sounded against the door. How long before a mob forced their way through the entry? It sounded like a huge frat party on meth laced with steroids. The walls pulsed with the bass line of the music that was loud enough to be a live rock concert. Front row. Stormi scanned her friend. Could she physically climb through the window? "Where does it hurt?"

Her long lashes fell to her cheeks as a grimace shuddered over Marla's face. "Everywhere. But mostly inside."

Fear spiraled through Stormi while her thought splintered into possibilities. *Think straight.* "We've got to get you to a hospital."

"No. It's not that. It's me. I can't live like this anymore." Raw sobs tumbled from her as she clutched Stormi's arm.

Sounds faded into the background. Stormi peered deep into Marla's eyes. Was she too toasted to understand? "You're right. Welcome to rock bottom, Marla. And the only one who can save you is Jesus Christ."

Although puzzlement wrinkled across Marla's forehead, she nodded.

Desperation boiled Stormi's thoughts to one bare-boned basic. "You're on your way to hell."

Chapter Thirty

Tears filled Marla's widened eyes and spilled down the outside corners. A moan snaked from her in a haunting wail. "I'm already there."

"No. You aren't. You think this is bad? This is just a scuff on the gym floor of real hell."

Marla began to tremble.

Stormi shook her. "But you can change it. You can change it all right now."

"Don't lie to me," she rasped.

"It's not a lie."

A sliver of hope threaded through the agony of Marla's gaze. "How?"

"Ask God to forgive your sins. Acknowledge Jesus Christ as His only Son. Ask Him to be your Savior."

Marla shook her head, crying louder. "He can't. You know what I've done. You, more than anyone, know what I've done."

Stormi released her and sat back on her heels, never letting her gaze leave hers. "Exactly. Because I *was* you, Marla."

Her friend's lip quivered. "Tell me how, Stormi. If it's possible, tell me what to do."

With heads pressed together, Stormi led Marla through a simple sinner's prayer. The woman, stained with every sin, begged the Creator of the universe to pardon her. Jesus Christ's name passed her lips in new awe.

An unexpected calm cloaked the room. Stormi yanked Marla from the floor, clamped an iron arm around her friend's waist, and staggered toward the window. Someone shoved against the door with a solid shoulder.

"Dear God, keep them out." At the sound of splintering wood, the warning sirens in Stormi's skull nearly blared audibly. She shoved Marla's limp body through the opening, and they clanged to the metal platform outside the building.

The quiet night muffled the disturbing party sounds from inside, and the joy within Stormi blocked the pain of landing on the metal roof of her car. Bear hugging Marla, they slid to the broken concrete.

"Thank you, God. Now speed us away," she rasped aloud.

Strength surged in Stormi, flinging the door open and tossing her friend to the back seat. Marla groaned, head and shoulder slumping to the floor. A calm message floated into Stormi's head. *No time. Hurry.*

Exactly. Nix repositioning or a seat belt. She slammed the door and sank into the driver's seat. A thick male torso leaned out the window above her, and she shoved the gearshift into reverse.

"Nice timing, Lord." She floored the gas pedal, and the gangly little car squealed away from the filthy brick buildings. The Boston streets masked them as she sped away.

❧ ⸱⸱⸱⸱⸱⸱ ❧

Ake took a deep breath watching the early rays of morning light up the living room and spread across the popcorn ceiling. He had a perfect view from his reclining position on the faithful couch. He'd given up on getting to sleep after Stormi's car motor had faded into the distance. But Pop was safe, and soon the caregiver would arrive. Footsteps echoed down the hallway.

"Where's Mom?"

He drew a sharp breath through his nostrils. Correct or jump in? He chose to jump in. He whipped a leg up and swiftly down to raise himself from his lying position. "She'll be back soon. Let's get you to the bathroom."

Thankfully his father appeared satisfied and allowed Ake to escort him down the hall. Once his pop was engaged, he strode toward the kitchen. Oatmeal. Always oatmeal.

The lumpy liquid congealed into a clear goo. He sucked in a sharp breath. Stormi's exact description. Never was that woman far from his thoughts. He grunted as Pop sat at the table. He was fooling himself. Not one second had gone by when that gorgeous pixie hadn't occupied his brain. If only— nope. Door closed.

He grabbed a soup bowl from the cabinet and filled it with the hot cereal. He carried it to the table with a spoon and set it before his father. A knock sounded at the back door. Super. Cindy had arrived.

"Good morning. Hello, Ake. How are you today, Mr. Pearson?"

Pop rose and shuffled from the room still chewing the last spoonful of oatmeal. Not much of a greeting.

"Sorry, Cindy. He seems fine." He pulled the bowl from the table and dumped it into the sink.

She flopped her coat on the chair and waved a hand. "Nah. This is how it is with Alzheimer's patients. No biggie. Fishing today?"

Definitely. "Yep."

"Anything I need to know today?"

"The usual."

"Okay, well, I'll get your father dressed and ready for the day. Perhaps we'll go for a drive."

He nodded but stared at his house down the slope. He couldn't face her. He couldn't even listen to her voicemail. In his frustration, he'd deleted it. Why listen to her excuses? His heart barely functioned now.

Cindy disappeared down the hall, humming. Ake paused a moment and then followed her, cutting into his old bedroom. The door slid shut soundlessly. Mom had never totally cleaned out his closet. Surely he could find something suitable for work today.

The smell of mothballs itched at his nose as he rummaged through the old clothing. Most of these were remnants from high school. Too many bowls of Mom's clam chowder would insure he'd never be able to use any of these again. He grabbed yesterday's clothes from the bed. Dirty was better than looking Stormi eye to eye.

He dressed in double time and headed out the door. At the dock, loading ice onto the boats and prepping the motor and nets helped pull his mind from the tragedy that had become his life. Hoge dumped the last shovelful of ice into the hold and clenched him in a stare.

"What are you wearing?"

Ake shrugged.

But he didn't stop. "Isn't that your regular coat? Where's your canvas?"

Silence seemed the best choice. He stepped to the deck and headed to where they kept the extra raingear. At least he'd be dry. He shrugged on the thick oily jacket that smelled like rotten mackerel. No matter.

Hoge stepped into the close space. "Answer me."

"I forgot it." Lies came tough to Ake's tongue.

His brother's rugged hand gripped his collar. They locked eyes. "What's going on?"

Ake locked his jaw against the truth. Years of being burnt by his blurts had finally paid off.

Hoge's blue eyes narrowed. "It's her, isn't it?"

He managed to control everything but the twitch under his left eye.

His brother growled and the thick mitt clamped to his collar shook him. "I told you, Dummy. She's worthless."

"Stop."

"Dagnabbit, Ake. I told you she was trouble—"

Ake shoved his brother away. Clarity froze Hoge's face. *He knew.* Ake shoved his hands into the borrowed slicker and spun.

*

"Good morning, sleepyhead." Stormi greeted.

Marla staggered into the living room wearing borrowed pj's. Stormi sat flicking through a magazine. Thankfully her friend's arrival had broken her train of thoughts of where Ake could possibly be.

"Morning." Marla's voice sounded much like the tires against gravel.

Her friend balled up in an armchair against the wall and rubbed the blond hair from her face. "So, where's the hubs? Shouldn't he be pummeling me by now?"

Stormi let out a low hum. She wished she did know where Ake was. She'd left a voice mail on his phone after several attempts to reach him. But that was none of Marla's business. Better to avoid. "Do you remember anything from last night?"

A somber mood rippled over her face. Today, in the mid-morning light, her face looked young, fresh. Except for her eyes. "Every detail."

Doubtful. "Like?"

Marla's face tightened. "I owe you a huge thanks, Stormi. I treated you like pus, and you were there when I needed you most."

Not the detail she was most concerned with. Stormi shrugged. "And?"

"I'm trying to say sorry, okay?"

She nodded.

Marla jerked up and grabbed a comfy throw from the couch. "I'm freezing."

Stormi dropped her gaze and flicked a page. Not sure why. She hadn't looked at the previous one.

"Okay, we'll talk about the huge gray elephant in the room. I'm a Christian now." Marla pulled the blanket up under her chin. "Whatever that entails, I've no idea."

"Marla...that's not exactly—"

"Don't worry, Stormi. I'm aware." She took a deep breath. "My sister's been trying to get to me for years. Used to drag me to church as a kid, remember?"

A smile tugged at Stormi's mouth. "Yeah."

Marla gave a deep sigh. "I understand now why you changed. Before, I thought you were faking, trying to squeeze me out, trying to ruin our fun."

A tear dripped from Marla's eye.

Sadness welled in Stormi's gut. "Only it wasn't really that fun."

Marla's hand closed around her throat. "No."

They sat for a long time without speaking. Unpleasant memories washed over Stormi. How easily they could take over. She spoke to stifle their power. "What are you thinking?"

"I need to retrieve my car from Boston. The earlier the better. Then I need to go to my sister's."

Stormi nodded. Excellent. Tasks to occupy her mind. And Marla remembered. And understood. And was saved. Praise Jesus.

⧸ ······ ⧹

Cramps started just as Stormi tugged on the gearshift of her old Saturn. She pushed it from her mind. Marla needed her. It was just stress. The baby, Hoge, Ake, everything. Only, the last week the pains had seemed to double. Once she worked everything out with Ake, they would ease.

Marla chugged milk and dug out her every misdeed since she'd turned six. It was as if she had to get it all out of her system before she could truly embrace a new way of living. Stormi didn't care except for the queasiness that seemed to clench her belly.

By the time they'd reached Marla's car at a hotel parking lot, she felt positively ill. But she tightened her jaw, determined to see this through.

Marla hugged her and cried on her shoulder. "Thank you. I wish I could do more than that, Stormi."

"Don't be silly. We'll always be friends. More so now. More than ever."

Marla gave her a watery smile and hopped into the car. Thank goodness Marla had ridden with someone else to the horrible apartment last night. Pain spiraled through her, and she pressed a hand to her stomach. Marla waved as she drove away.

Nausea rolled up her throat. She shut her door and stumbled toward the front of the hotel. The pain in her lower back had become unbearable. She'd reached the foyer when she realized the unwanted warmth. She hiked towards the counter. She needed a restroom. Yet when she arrived at the granite countertop, she could only breathe a quick command. "Call an ambulance."

Everything spiked to a surreal level as she slid down the front of the check-in counter. Lots of panicked voices floated above her. Then sirens. She should get up. If only she could reach her car, she was sure she could drive home.

A man appeared and blocked the hotel ceiling. He was dressed in a uniform. My, what a fuss she was creating. She tried to concentrate on the words the man spoke. "I'm Curt. We're preparing to transport you to the hospital. Can you tell me where it hurts?"

"My stomach and my back. I'm so...lightheaded."

"Uh huh. Let's get her on the gurney."

He faded from view as a cramp choked her uterus. "The baby."

The EMT reappeared. "Are you pregnant?"

"Yes." A sob wrestled up her esophagus.

He continued to barrage her with questions as she glided out into the sunlight and into the ambulance.

The crash of the vehicle doors closing made her jerk. She reached out and yanked on the man's blue shirt as he sat beside her.

"It's okay. We'll get you checked out."

"Ake."

His dark brows descended. "More pain?"

She shook her head. "No, my husband."

He took the phone number she chanted through the pain. Blackness threatened to take her from consciousness. *God, no.* She couldn't lose this baby. She just couldn't.

The wail of the siren and the crushing pain took all her concentration, and she shut her eyes. How would they ever contact Ake? Pain escalated and she cried out. Then lights careening, needles, smells, and more contractions. Then blood. Everywhere.

"God, oh, God," was all she could mutter as the pain meds kicked in, and the doors of her consciousness slammed closed.

❦ ······ ❧

She awoke with a cry. The baby was gone. She knew it before she knew reality. The chrome safety rail reflected her warped eyes back to her. Very fitting. She wondered vaguely if she could raid the morphine cabinet and knock herself out until the deadness eased in her soul.

A blue uniformed being appeared in the corner of her eye and paused at the machine that repeated the same beep over and over. Undoubtedly, it was broken. Her heart no longer beat.

"There you are. Hello, Mrs. Pearson. You're at Portsmith Regional Hospital. How are you feeling?"

"Is my baby dead?"

The long pause was as good as an answer. Stormi closed her eyes.

"Ma'am. I'm sure the doctor will be in to talk to you soon. Your husband's on the way.

"Ake?"

"Mr. Pearson, yes ma'am."

The woman reached and adjusted the IV loop that lay plastered against her skin, tugging every hair. Stormi grabbed the nurse's hand. "Tell me."

The thick dark-skinned nurse pursed her full lips. "I'm sorry ma'am. Yes."

She nodded against the pillow. Why had she needed confirmation? The emptiness in her belly had been like a storm horn blaring. Moisture filled her eyes.

The nurse patted her arm. "Is there anything I can do for you?"

"Put me out."

The woman's cheeks tightened. "I'll check your chart."

She disappeared through a soundless door that closed on sloth feet. The white curtain hung lifeless after a slight ripple in the nurse's trail. Stormi closed her eyes.

She must have dozed off into a dark world for she came to consciousness when the curtain moved again. Ake sat in the puke green hospital recliner near the bed. His black eyes held a universe of sorrow. She pressed her lids closed. His warm hand landed on her arm. But she couldn't look at him.

"I lost the baby."

"I know."

She lay for a long time, eyes closed. Her throat's muscles twitched convulsively, and she gnawed her lips raw. Each breath proved a huge hurdle. Wouldn't healing come with each passing second? Every moment? Surely. God—

No prayer came.

Chapter Thirty-One

A ke took great care to help Stormi into the truck. The woman appeared a mere shadow of the person she had been. Dark circles rimmed her eyes. She barely spoke. Her head hung as he tucked a blanket around her in the truck seat. As devastating as this had been for him, it seemed to have nearly killed her.

Silence rode with them the whole way. Knowing what to do proved a great challenge to Ake. Talking seemed trite, touching was repelled. That left stillness which sucked the oxygen from the interior.

Once home he helped her from the truck, but she pulled away and staggered to the front door. Stormi toddled straight to the bed, leaving Ake to trail her, her hospital paraphernalia and purse in his arms. Before he could reach the bedroom door, it shut in his face. He sighed and stored the articles in the extra room.

He wandered back to the living room to collapse on the couch. Hoge didn't even know what had happened. How could he tell him when the man didn't even know they'd been expecting. He rubbed the back of his aching neck. His brother would be at the top of the hill caring for Pop. He oughta go and explain he supposed.

Instead, early shadows obscured the room and closed out the day while he sat motionless.

Ake awoke to the sound of an interior door. He moaned as he sat up on the couch. In his exhaustion, he'd spent the entire night in the living room. It was still dark, yet he sensed it was his usual time to head to the wharf. Not today. Stormi needed him. Somehow he'd weather Hoge's anger for not coming in. He rose and headed for the hallway, only to nearly collide with his wife. "Good morning. Sorry."

"Why are you here?"

Not the response he'd hoped for. "I'm staying home."

"Why?"

The gloom of the room made it impossible to see her expression. Her voice seemed robotic. He ran his fingers down her arm. She stepped away.

"Stormi, you need someone—"

"No. I don't" Her shadowy form continued to the kitchen. "I'm tossing back more drugs and returning to bed."

He stood for a long moment, watching her open the fridge door for a nightlight and then fill a glass with water. She shook the pill bottle before sticking it into the appliance to check the label. She threw her head back, shut the door, and shuffled toward him. He didn't dare touch her.

"Go to work, Ake."

Sadness gully washed his gut when the bedroom door clicked closed. It would be real helpful about now to talk to Mom. He headed for the laundry room for the clean clothes folded on the dryer. In two shakes he was dressed. He scraped a hand through his hair and headed for his truck in the garage.

He drove slowly while he prayed. Things sure seemed to go downhill right quick. With some hesitation, he pulled into the parking lot across from the dock. Was there any point in staying home? Better to throw himself into normalcy and seal his eyes on the horizon to pray the day away.

Too late to stop by and ask Joni to check on her or make arrangements to pick up Stormi's car. His wife would probably sleep all day any way. What they needed to do was talk. He heard guys discuss the old marriage communication card, but he'd never realized how important it really was. Talking wasn't a thing that came naturally to Ake by any case. And most of the time, that worked well for him.

He shoved it from his mind. Better to focus on keeping Hoge out of his face.

❧ ⋯⋯ ❧

"I said, go now."

Ake narrowed his eyes at his brother. Never once in his life had he gone to collect a marine battery they didn't need until later. If it were really necessary, why hadn't Lester delivered it like he always did? He shrugged. At least it was fewer hours to sit in the living room alone while Stormi barricaded herself in the bedroom like she had for the last week.

"Fine." He pivoted and strode toward the truck. The tight feeling in his chest bordered on anger. Not his usual companion. He yanked the door shut with a little too much force. Two hours of driving listening to his own thoughts didn't sound good. He pushed the Simon and Garfunkel CD into the drive. Their bittersweet tones of unfulfilled dreams and romance fit right in to his mindset.

He grabbed the phone, remorse filling him as he thought of her message he'd deleted. She might not answer, but at least he needed to let her know of his detour.

⁖ ⁖⁖⁖⁖ ⁖

Yep. Exactly. Fury heated her face. Stormi snatched her cell phone from the black puddle. As was life. Like an expensive electronic device dropped in water. This is what she got for coming to her old apartment as soon as her car had been delivered home. Something about Ake's place seemed to suffocate her. Already too many bad memories. Or maybe just one big one.

She shook the droplets from the case and hopped back into the vehicle. By the time she'd arrived at Ake's, the screen was dead. Just too much symbolism. She let a curse slide through pursed lips and regretted it instantly. Even though, she was mad at God.

Once inside, she dumped the phone in a bag of rice. Nothing to do but wait. She made a bee line for the drugs. Last pill. As much as she craved to be asleep twenty-four/seven, she knew it was time to survive without meds. But not yet.

The pill descended down her throat like a bale of rusted barbed wire. No matter. In twenty minutes, it'd be, adios. Poor Ake. Alone again tonight. Somehow she would make it up to him, but not tonight.

The hammering continued. Grogginess clawed at Stormi's struggle to come to consciousness. Again the jackhammer. She groaned and pulled to a sitting position on the side of the bed. Someone pounded on the front door again. It must be Ake. Had he lost his key? She glanced over at the clock. Six thirty-seven. She'd been out for four hours. More or less.

She rose with a wobble and rubbed her face down. The thumping started again as she gained the living room.

"I'm coming." She yanked the door open.

Hoge in all his hugeness stood there. And he didn't look happy. Big hairy deal.

"What?" she demanded, pretzeling her arms across her chest.

But Hoge wasn't looking at her. He glanced around the shadowed room. "Who's here?"

She growled. The man had picked the wrong day. "No one, you oaf."

His huge mitt pushed the door open. She stepped aside as he marched in. Her mouth dropped when he continued down the hallway. Echoes of both doors opening down the hall met her ears. What nerve.

He arrived back at the end of the hall and shot blue bazookas at her. "It's time for you to go."

With a snort she spun to find the pill bottle. Too late she realized she'd taken her last one. She jammed the pill bottle on the counter and anchored her hands against the edge. "What do you want, Hoge?"

"It's not about what I want. It's about what Ake wants."

She turned from her hunkered position and froze behind the counter. Dizziness assailed her. "You're not making sense."

"I'm making perfect sense." His voice dropped to a dead calm. "Ake wants you gone."

Dread shakes set up camp in her chest. "Where's Ake? I want to talk to him."

"He's not coming. That's why I'm here."

The shakes graduated into trembles. "What are you talking about?"

"He can't do it. Ake's too soft. But I'm telling you, it's time for you to leave."

Stormi fastened her hands on her shaking forearms. "I'm not going anywhere."

"Neither am I."

She swallowed a lump. "Ake—"

"Isn't gonna show. It's just you and me. Get packing."

Something within Stormi crumbled. It was over. Hoge was just the final ax swing. Feeling more dead than alive, she tottered to her room on legs no stronger than toothpicks.

Blindly she jammed most of her things into her three suitcases. Then sealed herself in the bathroom for one last moment of her ill-born marriage.

When she emerged, Hoge had stowed her possessions in her car. Her mind closed in, squeezing out rational thought. Who was she kidding? There were no thoughts.

She drove as long as she could before pulling into a large parking lot. The travel center had little business past two a.m. She climbed in the back seat and pulled a throw over her. Just a nap. A freaking nap. Oh, how she wished for those pills.

Sleep came after much time. Not a restful kind. The sleep that barely shuts out the environs. Undoubtedly, she heard every truck enter and leave the lot. Every click of the gasoline nozzles had prodded her semi-consciousness. She roused around five, returned to the driver's seat, and headed back out to the interstate.

Destination: Narcissimville. She'd discovered something she'd never wanted to know. Dying without death was possible.

Mother stood blocking the doorway to the house, a half smirk-half scowl scrunching her features. "I knew you'd be back. This is what you always do. You're never there for me, but I have to accommodate you."

"Mother, my marriage is over. I lost a baby. Okay? Are you happy? I'm as miserable as you."

Stormi dragged her luggage behind her and to her unheated room. Mother would not come back there. And she needed a simple rubber room.

"I knew it. I tell you, you take the cake. You never listen. I told you not to move that far away. But, nooooo. You never think of anyone but yourself."

Stormi let the slam of the door punctuate her mother's last jab. Please let her have some card game to go to, or some stranger to pretend to help, while hating her own family. She slid the lock into place. Either way, she wasn't coming in here.

She grabbed the pilled blanket off the bed and huddled in the floor between the two twin beds. Her mother's continued tirade faded into the background. Roiling anger collided with pure misery. Tears trickled down her face while she ground her jaw.

How. Had. This. Happened?

Ake kept his vigil by the back door. The house had been empty last night. Clothes were missing, Stormi's phone lay in rice by the bedside. Had she left for good?

Pop shuffled in, looking for lunch. The oatmeal was long gone. But Ake couldn't focus on anything but the absence of his wife.

"Where's Mom?" The wheezy voice tugged him from his thoughts.

Stress jabbed him. "She's dead, Pop. Gone."

A look of surprise danced across Pop's usual emotionless features. He headed for the hall with a plaintive cry. "Mom. Mom!"

Ake palmed his forehead. Now why'd he do that? Getting Pop into a panic wouldn't change a thing about Stormi.

He stepped into the kitchen and tugged a frying pan from the draining tray. A quick grilled cheese sandwich would satisfy Pop. His father shuffled into the room and stared at him, face blank. One of the few perks of Alzheimer's, he guessed. He quickly forgot wrongs. Ake couldn't help but feel a little envious.

Once he'd assembled the sandwich, added a few cooked apples and some chips, he herded his dad to the table. Then he pulled his flip phone from his coat pocket. He dialed a rarely used number.

"Ake? What's wrong?" Joni's voice made him yearn for his mother's voice.

"Pop's fine. It's Stormi."

"What's going on?"

He took a deep breath. Could he dump it all on her over the phone? "Can you come to Pop's? Without Hoge knowing?"

A pause lit the line. "I'll be right over."

Ake managed to get Pop to lie down for a nap before Joni arrived. Unfortunately, Joni brought a large shadow. Hoge.

Joni shrugged when she met his eyes at the back door. "I tried, Ake. Really."

"What about the kids?"

Joni trailed in, followed by his brother. She removed her scarf and coat and laid them across the chrome chairs. "Well, that's the hitch. Linus is in charge. And since your brother had to come with me, we have limited time before the throw downs begin."

"They'll be fine," Hoge muttered as he lowered his bulk into a chair.

Joni continued to stand and parked her hands on her hips. "Yes, well, we'll see. Now, what's up?"

"You better sit."

Uncertainty lit her soft brown eyes. "Okay."

"Stormi was pregnant."

A gasp came from his sister-in-law. "Was?"

Ake flexed his neck and chose to stand. "She lost the baby last week. The day I missed work."

Hoge's eyes dropped.

"Oh, Ake. I'm so sorry." She brought a fist to her mouth. "Is she all right?"

He shrugged. "I don't know."

Joni's brow knotted. "What do you mean?"

"She's disappeared." Ake changed his mind and flopped into a chair.

The room went silent.

Joni's mouth froze into an open cavern. "Like in gone?"

He gave a short nod.

"Oh, my."

Ake toyed with the idea of coming completely clean. Did they need to know he'd caught her in the arms of another man? He cleared his throat.

Hoge growled. "Can't say I'm surprised."

Joni jerked her head to her husband. "Really? This is what you're going to do? You can't find a shred of compassion for your only brother?"

"He's better off without her."

Ake stood. "I need to go look for her."

"Of course. Hoge will stay with your dad."

"What?" Hoge spread his hands wide. "Not my turn."

Joni rose. "Tough. When you're mean and unsupportive, you pull Pop duty."

Hoge harrumphed. "You're just as unhappy about this marriage as I am."

Ake grabbed his coat and paused by the door. "Does it matter you both disapprove? She's my wife, under God. I'm not giving up on her."

He tugged the door closed and marched down the hill. He would find her. One way or another, he would find her.

Chapter Thirty-Two

Ake's resolve never wavered as he searched town. First, he started at her old apartment, then every downtown business. He scanned the parking lots and streets while asking random folks along the way. He had no shame in begging for information. Perhaps his many embarrassments as a kid had prepared him for this very moment.

Next he drove to her college. This proved more difficult. He checked the building he'd brought her to in early winter, but no one even seemed to know her. The other buildings were much the same. He ended up at the administration building where he tried to pry information from the robotic receptionist. But all he could get was that wherever she was, she was still entering updated classes.

He settled back in his old truck and pounded the steering wheel. Where could she be? He took a deep breath and sent a prayer heavenward, then pulled the shift into gear. New plan. He needed a map and a phone. Start in this county and gradually work his way outward. Eventually something had to turn up.

He drove back to the house, went in, and tossed his keys on the counter. Time to get the map. He would find her. And bring her home.

❧ ⋯⋯ ❧

The question was, how long could she stay in this room without food and water? So far Stormi was on her second day, and her stomach clenched with hunger. But mostly thirst. Stormi clenched her teeth at her own weakness. A bathroom wouldn't hurt either.

She gazed out the window. The room wasn't freezing, but chilled enough to make her shake. Fourteen cars had driven past since her arrival. Three dogs had meandered by, and one squirrel. She glanced at her computer on the floor. Just as well do another podcast and wait for Mother to leave the house. She laid a hand on her flat stomach and a wave of intense grief took her breath. Of all the things in the world, she couldn't bear her mother's self-righteous sneer this morning.

Midway through her third podcast, the door slammed. She glanced through the blue satin curtains. Mother shouldered her big purse and swung into the car. Praise the Lord the old bomb started, and she drove off.

She rose and stretched. Her body ached, her soul bled. At least she could move around. Stormi opened the door and entered the back porch. A gloomy day greeted her through the windows along the wall. She went through the closed door to the kitchen.

The place was trashed like always. Table covered with dirty dishes, papers, napkins. More filthy dishes and pans crammed the sink and counters. Well, Mother was the same. With a deep sigh, she treaded to the tiny bathroom. Much the same in there. Floor filthy, hair-encrusted toilet, dingy scum circled the bathtub. Ugh.

After washing her hands in the chipped sink, she made her way back to the kitchen. The least she could do was clean for her room and board. Then maybe she could find a bit of food not covered in roaches.

She found some fairly fresh lunchmeat in the fridge and quickly stuffed it into her mouth. Then she tore into the dishes. Nothing like mindless chores to occupy one's mind. She wondered vaguely how Marla was doing. Perhaps she'd dig out her number and use Mom's landline phone.

It took several hours to return the kitchen and bathroom back to an acceptable manner. And just about the time she gathered the last of the towels and inserted them into the washer, a car parked out front. Mother—perfect timing as always. She headed for her cold sanctuary at the back of the house.

◈ ⸱⸱⸱⸱⸱ ◈

"You're going to work today."

Hoge's face was purplish-red and swollen. Why he'd bothered to come over proved a mystery. Ake wasn't sure when he'd seen him this angry. He went back to his map spread across the coffee table and enclosed yet another area with a colored pencil. "No, I'm not."

"Blame it, Ake. Stop being an idiot. You're not going to find her. She's gone."

Ake chose to ignore him as he studied the map. The last week had been unfruitful, but that couldn't last forever.

"You're just going to search the entire United States?"

"Yep." Ake expected an explosion, but Hoge merely strolled to the opposite side of the table and stood. At last, Ake looked up.

"She left you, man. Get it through your head."

Sadness welled in Ake's chest. His brother may have a point. Already he'd gone through how many tanks of gas. He'd have to slow the search. Besides, if he went to work, he'd calm

Hoge and have more resources to search with. He folded the map. "All right. Let's go to work."

Go to work, care for Pop, search for Stormi. Lifetime assignments.

Fishing proved productive that spring. Summer continued to supply the *Sea Wheats* with plenty of catch. Relief washed over Ake as he threw the fish into the separate buckets. Good catch kept Hoge happy and off his tail. But a moment didn't go by that he didn't think of Stormi and pray for her.

He supposed he should just go to the police station and declare her a missing person. But in his heart he knew she wasn't. Missing, that is. She'd left. Pure and simple. He sucked the salty ocean air into his lungs as the deck lurched. But the why is what stuck in his craw. He couldn't let her go, knowing the pain she'd suffered when they'd lost the baby. Her eyes had been so empty, so hopeless.

Sure, his heart was still bruised after seeing her with another man. But he was sure if he could locate her, they could work through it. After all, he still loved her. Loved her with his whole being. Imagining life without her, well, he just couldn't.

Privately he scanned the local areas and drove from town to town to check. Best to keep Hoge out of the know. He stood to stretch his back and caught a sunrise beam of sunlight rippling across the shimmering waves. Yeah. Stormi was like that. Like a flash of light. Full of sunshine and energy. How he longed for her.

He slumped over and grabbed a handful of fish. Letting the others see his mournful face only invited insults. Best to carry on. The deck leaped with hundreds of fish. Tomorrow would be the same. Meanwhile, he'd guard his heart and wait. The Lord was faithful.

❧ ⋯⋯ ❧

Stormi walked faster. The routine. Always follow the new routine. It kept her sane somehow. Moving out of Mother's house had been the best thing since she'd married Ake. She sucked in a shuddering breath. Why? Why did she let his name in her head? It threw a perfect routine out the door.

Get up. Walk. Drink orange juice. Podcast. Clean house. Shower. Read the paper. Drink a health shake. Wash clothes. Watch the news. Volunteer at the animal shelter. Fall exhausted into bed. Blink at ceiling for four hours. Rinse and repeat. Nowhere in that list was think about Ake. Nope.

Sweat poured from her forehead. Too stinking hot to walk this long and this hard. A sob managed to trip up her throat, and she swallowed it. Everything was fine. All would come out in the wash. She neared her junky trailer, and depression washed over her like a tsunami. Who was she kidding? Trailer trash. That's all she was.

Anger clenched her jaw and moisture threatened. Oh, no. No, no. Not at this stage. She shoved the key into the weathered lock and thrust the door open. She slammed the door closed. Now, orange juice.

Yet she stood, just inside the door surveying the dump of her furnished trailer. She wanted to be in a certain pole barn house with a certain hulk of a man. With innocent eyes and a hug that healed.

She stomped the shaky floor over and over. "But you can't have that. He deserves more that you."

A whimper snaked out. She hugged herself tightly and spit out every almost-curse word she could come up with. When she finished, she huffed with exertion, fury, and agony—a sorry ball of emotion that made her want to puke.

Finally tears worked out her eyes.

"I'm not a crier. I won't cry." Her hand slid over her flat stomach. An ache so deep, a spasmodic sniff made her lip quiver. She shook her head as the tears leaked down her face. Impossible. She'd survived worse than this. Why was this so freaking hard? As she tried to force the breakdown to stop, it only increased.

"Why?" she tilted her head and yelled at the ceiling. "It's time to move on. Time to forget. It's done. Suck it up and start over."

She stabbed the heels of her hands into her eyes. But nothing eased. The ceiling answered not a word and the blasted silence slithered around her soul. She pointed a finger up. "You promised. You said you'd be with me, no matter what. So why? Why can't I get over this? Why can't I forget Ake?"

Because you love him.

With a gasp, the tears froze on her face, her body stilled. She loved him. Her marriage wasn't an apology or retribution. It was love. Simple adoration. She loved Ake with all her heart, like she'd loved no other.

She collapsed on the grungy carpet in the middle of the room. "I love you, Ake. Oh, crap. I love you!"

The ceiling tiles seemed unimpressed. What was she going to do?

◈ ⸱⸱⸱⸱⸱⸱ ◈

Despite the good summer of fishing, Hoge had grown touchier and touchier as the days had passed. But now he was just plum nuts. Fishing on a Sunday? Ake protested. "We can't go out with just you and me, Hoge. We need the crew."

"No we don't."

His brother continued to check the instruments on the panel in the wheelhouse. Ake stepped into his brother's domain. "Don't be crazy, Hoge. We can't fish alone."

Hoge's thunderous face snapped to his. He shoved him out of the enclosure. "Telling me what to do now, Ake? Dad and I used to fish all the time before you showed up."

Ake threw his hands out in surrender. "That was a much smaller boat."

Hoge spun and returned to his monitors. "You don't know squat."

"There could be a squall coming in, too."

In response, Hoge thrust the throttle forward and the *Sea Wheat 1* pulled away from the dock. Ake shook his head. He hadn't even finished checking the weather monitor. And they had no ice. Had Hoge lost his mind? Never in his born days had his brother insisted they fish on Sunday. Nothing made sense.

He meandered across the deck to his usual spot, his feet knowing the uneven tilt of each wave by instinct, and turned his face toward the wind. A chill now filled the air. Summer waved goodbye at twelve knots. He set his gaze on the horizon, praying for Pop, Stormi, and Hoge.

The boat went out farther where the waves were choppier. Soon the coast and the buildings faded into a mist on the far western horizon. Not one boat could be seen. Ahead the sky appeared gray. Anytime now, Hoge would holler to let out the net.

Instead, he cut the engine.

Ake rose. The waves slapped the sides of the boat. The wind lifted his hair. The smell of dead fish and fresh ocean salt intermingled as he waited for Hoge to step from the wheelhouse. But he didn't. In the distance, Ake could see the bigger waves moving in. Why had they stopped here? What was the reasoning for being so far out with the storm front in their face?

He strode to midship and stared at Hoge. His brother's gaze was fixed on the horizon. After several minutes, the big man shouldered out and set his hands on his thick waist.

"I made her leave."

"What?" Ake shook his head. "Who are you..."

Then like an anvil to the skull, he knew.

Hoge shrugged. "It was for your own good."

Shock and then fury rooted Ake to the deck.

His brother ran a hand through his hair. "I didn't know about the baby."

The deck pitched, but Ake barely acknowledged it. He stormed forward and shoved his brother against the wheelhouse. Hoge's eyes widened in a flash, and he came back with a swipe. Ake dodged it and chucked his mitt to his chunky brother's midsection. The grunt Hoge breathed assured him the punch had struck home.

Again, Hoge's sad attempt to clock him went airborne.

"You had no right to do that." Ake kept his peripherals on Hoge's fists. His trunk always twinged when he got ready to fire. Dead giveaway.

"She's no good."

"Stop saying that." Ake grabbed his collar and tossed him to the wet deck and pounced on him. He snugged Hoge's arms up tight against his body with his knees and jammed his forearm under his jaw.

Hoge growled while tossing side to side, trying to unclamp Ake's legs. He squeezed harder, and blood rushed to his face at the effort.

"Let me go, Dummy."

Dummy. Dummy. *Dummy*. Forever the idiot. Sanity briefly left, and he pummeled Hoge's face. Enough. No more. He saw red until the same hue covered his hands in the form of warm moisture. He stopped, heaving, staring at his fists. Then at Hoge's bloody face. His brother had grown still.

Ake shoved away and paced to put a distance between them. The boat tossed, catching his focus before Hoge appeared on his heels, yanking him back to the deck. They smacked together and rolled across the wet wood until their bound bodies struck the port side. Hoge thunked his ear, and Ake reached out to squeeze his brother's windpipe. He'd end this right quick.

The floor fell, and they landed at an angle and slid across the slick wood. Suddenly starboard greeted them with a splash, Ake landing on the bottom. His attention switched to behind his brother's big stupid head, and the wheelhouse rose above him. That's when he knew.

Storm.

"Stop. Stop!" Ake shoved Hoge's head against the side and slithered out from below him. He popped up and took a few scarecrow steps to gather a little balance on the rocking deck.

Hoge rolled over and pushed up on his arm. Then, he too, looked around. He staggered to stand and stared at his brother. He pointed and bellowed, "This is your fault."

The wind buffeted him, and the sky had frothed a dark gray. Thunder rumbled in the distance. The *Sea Wheat 1* churned on the foaming waves, the dips ever growing.

But Hoge pointed again. "You left."

"What are you talking about? I'm still here."

"Before. When we were kids. You left and when you came back, you didn't even know me."

Anger drained from Ake's body. This wasn't the time to toss about the events of his childhood. The storm would be upon them in minutes. Then there would be more to fear than their own anger. He tottered to the wheelhouse. Hoge beat him there and grabbed his shirt anchoring them to the wheelhouse with his other arm.

"And everything was gone."

Ake wrenched from him. "What are you talking about? Can't you see the storm?"

But Hoge's face loomed closer. "Your drughead mom and her methed-up boyfriend cracked your head open. Don't you get it?"

The rain began to fall, peppering their frozen faces. Acid burned up Ake's throat. "It's why I'm a Dummy, isn't it?"

Chapter Thirty–Three

The look on Hoge's face said it all. "The social worker shouldn't have taken you from our family. You should have never gone back to that abuse. When you came back, I promised myself that no one would ever hurt you again. I had to protect you from her, Ake. That's why I sent her away."

Protection. That was it. That explained a lifetime of Hoge's anger. Anger that masked pain. How Ake's peace offerings had always been rejected. Even from as far back as Ake could remember. All the appeasing never worked because Hoge feared losing him. Afraid something else would happen to his little adopted brother. And now, his protective brother had run off the best thing that had ever happened to him.

The storm around them caught Ake's attention once more. Things were really messed up. And now, life-threatening. Hoge's mistake with Stormi would have to wait.

Lightning flashed overhead, and the *Sea Wheat 1* tipped up to ride the swell. Hoge's feet slipped out from under him, and he slid down toward the stern. Ake looped his arm around the wheelhouse wall as Hoge struck the stern and then grasped the side. *Rope.* They would need to tie themselves to the boat.

When the boat fell to the bottom of the swell, Ake hurried into the wheelhouse and groped for the loops of hemp in the lower shelf. As the boat continued to pitch, he anchored the rope around the bars behind the wheelhouse. He glanced toward Hoge, who struggled on his knees to gain the bow of the boat.

He flung the rope towards his brother and then dipped into the wheelhouse. Time to alert the Coast Guard and get the engine roaring.

⋙ ⋯⋯ ⋘

Stormi picked up the paper. Right on time. Calm Sunday morning. Just keep doing what makes the time tick by. So this was Ake's revenge. Or maybe God's. Her, trying to get over Ake. Oops. She transgressed. No thoughts of Ake. Just the headlines, the classifieds, and maybe a glance at the gossip column.

She took a deep breath. The musty smell of the old couch made her throat hurt. She pressed the sports page to the cushion, careful not to waft the dust up.

Mid-column a car drove up. It only gave her momentary pause. Forty trailers brought in all kinds of traffic. Especially the one on the back corner. But the pounding on the door brought the inked paged down. Only ShaVonn knew she was here.

She rose and went to the door. ShaVonn's distorted mug eyed her door through the peek hole. She zipped the chain from the lock and tugged it open.

"What?"

ShaVonn slid past her and paused in the middle of the room. "Alan contacted me. Something about a 'Joni?' Who's that?"

"Joni?" Her mind spun. "What else did he say?"

"That you need to call her. I think you really freaked out Alan. Did you lose your phone? I guess he called every church in Stone Haven to try to find you and hooked up with this Joni. Who is this chick anyway?"

Stormi grabbed her sister's purse.

"What are you doing?"

"Phone, ShaVonn. Now."

She tsked her but gave up the phone. "Here's the number."

With a swipe, Stormi snatched it from her sister and quickly dialed. On the third buzz an uncertain voice answered. "Joni?"

"Stormi? Oh, thank God. You've got to come back. Like right this minute."

She stepped down the hallway, away from ShaVonn's prying ears. "You know that's not wise. Hoge—"

"Hoge caved. Early this morning he told me that he forced you to leave. I sent him to level with Ake and apparently they took out the boat. Just the two of them."

"I'm in Georgia, Joni."

"Get here fast. The Coast Guard is out looking for them."

Something clenched Stormi's heart. "Why? What's happening?"

"A huge storm. And they're caught in it. Please, Stormi. You've got to come home."

Home. She took a deep breath and pressed her back against the paneling in the narrow hall. *Ake.* In danger. "Oh, God," she muttered. "I'll be there as soon as I can."

She tossed the phone on the bed, praying while pulling her suitcase from the closet. ShaVonn appeared at the door. Stormi ignored her and jammed her belongings into the bag.

"Well?"

Stormi swept past her and raked the toiletries from the vanity. "It's Ake. He's out on the boat during a storm."

"What can I do to help?"

"Get on that phone and get me a ticket to Boston."

"You're not driving?"

"No. Be reasonable. It's an eighteen hour drive straight through. I needed to be there five minutes ago."

"Gotcha, okay."

With a zip, Stormi shut the bulging case and dropped it to the ground. She snatched her purse and checked for money and her ID. ShaVonn's voice echoed to her from the living room. *Please let her find a flight. Please, God.*

She grabbed her laptop and made for the door.

"You've got a flight in ninety minutes."

She jogged to the front door with her sister close behind. "Super, ShaVonn. What would I do without you?"

"Just be safe, going off all half-cocked. And call me. Got it?"

Stormi shoved the large suitcase into the back seat and flung her purse to the front. "Got it. Oh, and ShaVonn? Pray. Just pray hard."

❧ ⋯⋯ ❧

Stormi didn't realize until she'd sat down in the airport shuttle that she had no phone. No way to get in contact with anyone. She shoved away this minor detail and raced through the huge airport to find her gate. Nothing mattered now but getting back to Ake.

Security checks were agonizingly slow. And then she left her driver's license and had to jog back to get it. The flight was delayed twenty minutes, and the passengers boarded like caged sloths. Oh, Lord, if she didn't kill someone before she arrived, truly there was a Santa Claus.

At long last, Stormi leaned back in her seat and the plane took to flight. And since she basically stared God face to face through steel and rivets, she whispered a fervent prayer for Ake.

"Please, God, don't ever let me be this stupid again. Never let me take advantage of the best blessings you've ever given me. And please, oh, please let Ake and Hoge be safe."

The plane leveled, and Stormi rode the clouds with earbuds jammed in her ear, praying for time to pass. By the time they'd landed, Boston neared dusk. Rumbles of thunder could be heard through the plane's hull. Great time to blast outa the huge city in a rental car. *Get off the plane, get off the plane.*

She scurried through the airport, wishing she hadn't checked her bag. Oh, the dance of the slowest carousel on earth began. Some thirty minutes later, her bag birthed through the rubber strips, and she sped off toward the car rental booth.

Once at the lot, she raced for the nearest car, loaded the luggage with a fling, and jumped in. She tried to find a news station in hopes she'd get some information, but nothing turned up. In frustration, she flipped it off. Driving through Boston would take all her concentration anyway through the spattering rain. She racked her brain to remember the highway she needed to get on to make it to Stone Haven. Fear snaked down her vertebrae. Had they found them yet?

"Coast Guard. This is *Sea Wheat 1.* A forty-foot fishing boat. We've been caught in the storm. Two passengers on board. Need assistance. I repeat, need assistance. We are approximately twenty-five miles out from shore due east, over."

Ake let up the receiver button on the VHF radio bolted to the ceiling. So far no replies from channel sixteen. And complete darkness now edged in. Not good. He checked the marine GPS screen. He should give the coordinates again. A battered Hoge stepped in the shelter as the boat rode a huge swell. Both of them gripped the side of the doorway to keep from losing their feet.

"Tie that rope around you." Ake barked as he squeezed the trigger to deliver the distress signal once more. Tricky while trying to steer the boat through the thirty foot swells. But the foamy white water doused the deck, and equipment slid from side to side. The craft was much like a speck of Styrofoam in a wave pool. Unless the sea continued to come in. Then they'd be mere pennies at the bottom.

"Shut up."

Ake barely had time to process Hoge's rude reply. A wave yawned above them, and Hoge shoved him over to get to the controls. Ake wasn't about to wrestle him for it. Hoge knew this boat and what the hull could weather. He brought the speed down and rode the waves, just short of facing full in. The white cascades of angry water engulfed the entire deck as they came down into a water hole. Buried in a sea of boiling ghosts. The wiper blade beat furiously. Ake checked the bilge pumps as he prayed they'd live to see another wave. The radio blared, deafened by the cacophony of wild water around them.

"Copter up and heading your way, *Sea Wheat 1*. Identify your position, over."

Through his shivers, Ake felt the warmth of relief cocoon him. They'd heard. Now, if they could only survive Satan's sea.

"Shoot. The winch!"

Hoge's shout could be heard above the waves. He shouldered out of the wheelhouse.

"No, Hoge." Ake yelled. His head swiveled to see Hoge stumble then slide toward the stern. There the winch wobbled back and forth. One good twist would unseat it completely.

"Dear God." Ake sputtered. What was his brother thinking? Had panic clouded his mind? He couldn't begin to lift that piece of equipment, let alone drag it across the deck to safety in this squall. Terror squeezed him when his eyes trailed the rope, snaking down the soaked deck to the end, curling and snapping in freedom.

Hoge was untethered.

Chapter Thirty-Four

The winch thunked back to its support as they floundered about in another hole of writhing, sucking water. Ake gripped the walls, feeling the *Sea Wheat's* nose tip up. He cut his gaze forward. A wall of water greeted him. Dear heavens.

"Hoge!"

His brother went airborne like a slo-mo reel of a skydiver, arms sprawled, twisting. The boat skewed under the pressure of the sea, and Hoge disappeared into the foaming froth. Dreaded words branded Ake's thoughts like a smelting fire.

Man overboard.

He burst from the wheelhouse, his hand gripping at the rope, checking its security. Hoge appeared in a wave not far off, his arms up, face warped in panic. God, what to do?

Lengthen your rope. He quickly obeyed the mental command. A yellow flash of the inflatable rescue boat in the wheelhouse lit his brain. He maneuvered back to grab it, his attention on the wave to ride the swells. He returned to the port side to catch a flash of Hoge resurfacing in the oscillating waves. He was too far to reach him with the painter line. Not wise to be untethered from the boat. Now what?

Jump.

Ake didn't question the directions that flowed through his brain, but clamped the boat's line to the rope around his waist and rolled over the side into the chilling waves.

"God...God...God," was all Ake's brain could repeat.

Ake surfaced in the wildness and took off in a sidestroke. A wave ballooned before him and Hoge's one arm rose above the waters.

I'm near. He let his body submerge to use both hands, blindly yanking the emergency line. Immediately the rescue boat puffed out into shape. Ake sank to keep the boat from injuring him. He sputtered to the surface and swam around the yellow device. Lightning zapped from sky to water. There he was. *God help me.*

The wave pitched his brother very close. He struck out to grab him, but he missed and his brother's blue shirt disappeared into the deluge. A miracle. Connecting with Hoge in the swell of water fireworks would take nothing less. He dove, a prayer filling the inner crevices of his soul.

He banged into something solid. A fish? No. Fish did not wear garments. Ake grabbed and pulled the heavy body against him, his lungs near to bursting. Hoge seemed limp.

Get to the rescue boat.

A surge of water buoyed him to the surface. Ake sucked air into his lungs. He wrapped his arm about Hoge's neck and sidestroked to the yellow flash rising and dropping in front of him. Amidst the surging of the waves around him, he wrestled Hoge's still body over the side of the air-filled sanctuary.

Ake clutched the rope along the side and pounded his back. After several thumps, his brother sputtered and vomited. He pushed himself up on his elbow, Hoge's eyes registering the situation.

"Ake!"

A shadow darkened the water. Ake turned. The letters he'd memorized as *Sea Wheat 1* met his face.

Gurgling. Then blackout.

❦ ······ ❧

Stormi didn't bother to head to a house. She went straight to the dock. Men in slickers stood about in the rain. A few broke away and ran to the grill across the street. She yanked the small car to the curb and leaped from the vehicle.

"Where's Ake? Have they found him? What's going on?

The group of men turned as she screamed at full run towards them.

"Whoa, there, little lady. Who ya looking for?" A man with thick brows caught her as she collided into the group.

"Ake, my husband."

Odd mutterings and stares flashed around the roughnecks until Brows spoke again.

"Best get you over to the Grill. Joni's there. They're set up around the short wave—"

Stormi spun and raced across the road, heedless of traffic. The man's last word, radio, hung over her head. Rain plastered her hair to her head and obscured her vision. But she managed to keep the neon sign in view.

Like a sewage rat, she thundered into the hushed environment, sputtering. "Joni?"

From the bar Joni turned, surveyed her quickly before scurrying over to hug her. "Oh, my lands, you're soaked. Mitty, get my coat. Have ya got a blanket, Madge?"

People gathered about her in sympathetic murmurs. God, what did it mean?

She brushed away their help. "Where is he?"

Joni took her shoulders. "We don't know yet. Last we heard they were both in the water."

Alarm hollowed her stomach. Stormi searched her eyes. "What does that mean?"

Joni shook her head. "Not good."

A cry ripped from her throat, and the people around her disappeared. She stared at the worn floor tiles. She was too late. Ake might never return again. She spent the last months of their marriage miles away, cut off from him, and now...

"Get her to the booth."

She sat in the stiff seat while coats and blankets encircled her. Joni appeared across from her, and grasped her limp hands.

"Stormi. Listen to me. This is the way it is. Being a fisherman's wife. It's dangerous work. You've got to be strong."

Stormi focused on her intense green eyes. She took a pant breath. "I am strong."

Joni nodded, understanding dawning. "Yes, you are. We have to wait. And pray."

"Ake will make it."

Joni nodded, eyes rimmed with tears.

"Hoge will too."

A little sad laugh escaped Joni. "May it be so."

She clenched her teeth. Stormi willed it with a frantic prayer.

Then a sad smile stretched Joni's face. "But God may have other plans. And we must be prepared for that."

Stormi fought the anger and denial that gushed within. Joni was right. As much as she wanted to believe it would all be okay, sometimes God said no. Tragedy was reality. And she would have to make her peace with that. Stormi laid her forehead on the table and closed her eyes. But she didn't have to cave to the negative. Digging her fingernails into hope, she bit her lip and whispered into the Formica. "Save them, Lord. Save them."

Stormi spent over an hour with her face pressed to the worn table at Calvert's Grill, her fingers firmly gripped in her hair, praying her heart out. The shortwave radio squawked out a comment or two from the copter circling the area for signs of the boat or the men believed to be overboard. No return signals had been intercepted since the first distress call. The black box at the counter sputtered again.

"We have located object. Appears to be a rescue craft, over."

Stormi's head came up.

"Roger."

"One man is in the craft, the other in the water. Approaching, over."

"Roger that."

"What's happening?" Stormi tore from the booth and stood in the middle of the room.

Everyone grew still.

"Man in craft is waving. We're deploying basket. Trooper going down, over."

Short phrases continued to hiss from the radio as the copter and rescuers continued to position the craft and basket for pick-up.

"Steady. Ease forward, hold position to take the load, over."

Breath became foreign. Would they never announce who it was? Were they injured? Were they alive?

"*Sea Wheat 1* floundering. I believe we have our men, over."

How could time drag to a halt? Hypothetically impossible. Yet in this room, time ceased.

"We have recovered Hoge and Ake Pearson. There are injuries, over."

"Roger that. Ambulance will be deployed to the dock, over."

Stormi tore towards the door and burst through it into the pouring rain. She sprinted across the road to the spattering of men along the crest of the rocky edge. But now darkness had descended, and the cursed storm only deepened the blackness. Nothing appeared on the horizon.

"Stormi."

She didn't bother to turn. They had to be out there. Somewhere.

Joni appeared, wrapped in a slicker. She said nothing but wrapped another yellow raincoat about her and then clenched her forearm. A siren let out a piercing wail behind them. Stormi shook the droplets off her eyelashes. How was this real?

Her eyes pried through the darkness, and at first, she imagined a pinpoint of light. Then, it became a moving point, growing and growing as time, once again, became tangible. Soon the thumping sounds of beaters cutting through air reached her ears. The copter circled and landed in the empty lot next to the grill.

A throng of soaked people hurried across the street and Stormi fought her way to the front. Two troopers emerged trailed by Hoge, looking worse for wear. With agonizing slowness a stretcher came forth, and the ambulance pulled close, light flashing red against the building. Stormi gasped and stepped forward but was restrained.

Ake lay sprawled across the white board and Stormi clawed her way through the arms and bodies and darted. Red oozed from his plastered hair, his skin corpse white. She clutched at his shirt and moaned. He was so cold. So cold and still.

Conversation shimmied about her, but she wouldn't release her grip. Soon she and Ake were loaded aboard the ambulance, and they went screaming into the night. She laid her head on his chest and bawled.

❧ ······ ❧

Oxygen flowed at a crisp clip through his flared nostrils in a huge breath. His lids were reluctant, but he forced them open. Ake almost wished he hadn't. They burned, like they'd swelled too big for his skull. And speaking of skull, it throbbed and resonated with the sounds around him. Beeping and murmurs. And maybe a horse galloped in there, somewhere.

The white ceiling greeted Ake's aching eyes, and just about the time he decided it wasn't worth it to open his lids, Stormi appeared.

"Oh, Ake. You're awake."

Her whispery voice awakened that old protectiveness, and he attempted to rise.

"No, lie back."

Oh, right. The white ceiling. The beeps. The storm. *Stormi.* "You're here."

A soft laugh made one side of his mouth quirk.

"Yes."

"Took a storm to bring you back, huh?" He attempted to pull his mouth into a full smile, not sure he'd nailed it.

A whimper greeted him, and then her cheek pressed his, warm and sweet-smelling. He closed his eyes to soak it in. Even through the pain, he savored the contact. After a moment, she pulled away, and he wanted to snatch her and snug her up close to his body. But his arms appeared as sandbags, so he only fastened his gaze on her. Thankfully, she didn't disappear.

Instead she stroked his garment, some thin, cottony whatnot, and tugged the blankets up higher. "Be still. You need to heal."

His vision quivered. Meds, ready to knock him out. "I reckon. The *Sea Wheat 1* didn't play fair."

Her face crumpled again, and tears lit the corners of her eyes. Ock, he shouldn't have said that. With much effort, he brought up his arm and snagged the material of her sleeve. "Don't leave me, Stormi."

She shook her head. "I wouldn't dare leave you."

He gave a nod, or at least he thought he did. Mister pain-management drug tugged at the blinds of his eyes. He pushed out his last word. "Good."

Sleep claimed him as he reveled in her touch.

❧ ······ ❧

She tapped her new phone and ended the call. Marla's voice had charmed her into an even better mood. Her eyes shifted to the recliner where her husband lay sprawled, still asleep. Praise the Lord he was home where he belonged. Stormi tiptoed around the counter to get a better view of his gorgeous face, covered in stubble. The hank of dark hair covered his new stitches, now completely healed.

How her heart broke when he'd shared how hurt he'd been when he's seen her with Alan. Ake had thought the worst, deleted her message, and yet, he'd still searched for her. Still wanted her. Still loved her. What an amazing, understanding, forgiving man.

She pored over his dear strong face. How could she have ever left him? She'd married him to redeem her deed, and ended up madly adoring the big hunk. His eyes flickered open.

"Whatcha staring at?"

"You."

"Why?"

"Because I'm insanely in love with you."

His eyes flickered wide and he kicked the footstool in. He rose and circled the couch to embrace her into a toasty hug. "I'll never grow tired of you saying that."

A knock sounded on the front door. Stormi let go of her husband, and he turned the doorknob. There stood Hoge in all his glory, Joni at his side.

"Can I talk with you?" Hoge's voice was quiet.

Ake shrugged and stepped back.

They entered and Stormi moved toward the hallway. "I'll be in the back."

"No," Hoge's answer came back. "I'd like you to stay. Please. What I have to say involves you both."

With a swallow, Stormi drifted toward the recliner.

Hoge and Joni removed their coats and sat on the couch. Ake grabbed a stool from the counter and perched on it. "What's up? Pop okay?"

His brother nodded and cleared his throat. He leaned forward and rubbed his hands between his knees. "Yes, he's fine. And I think you're right, Ake. We need to find a nursing center that can care for him, for his own safety."

Ake nodded.

Again Hoge rumbled his throat to clear it. "But that's not what I came here for." He stood and stuck his hands into his back pockets. "I came to apologize."

"For what?"

His brother's hands flew out. "For everything. I've never treated you right, Ake. And the truth is, I hurt like heck when you came back. You were this little brother I'd looked forward to having. You became part of our family. We tried to adopt you, but adopting a foster kid is a tricky business. A long agonizing process. And then the courts thought it would be a great idea to return you to your birth parents. And that's when everything went wrong."

Hoge paced, rubbing the back of his neck. "They hurt you, Ake. That scar on the back of your head is from their abuse. And it took everything from you. When the social worker brought you back to us, you knew nothing. You had to learn everything all over again. You didn't even remember me."

Ake nodded. "I'm sorry."

"No, it's not you who should be sorry. It's me. I was mad at you. And I was mad at the world for what it had done to you. I

didn't want to get attached to you again, even after the parents' rights had been severed, and we legally adopted you. I couldn't let it go. I was afraid to...love you again."

Chapter Thirty-Five

Tears gushed to Stormi's eyes.

Ake stood. "I'm sorry you were hurt, Hoge. I love you. But, I'm fine. I'm better than fine. I don't want to remember. Don't you see? God took those bad memories from me. And maybe you think I'm this ruined, big dummy, but I don't. I consider God erasing that time as a blessing. He gave me much more than I ever dreamed. A loving family, you, Stormi, and most of all, he made me realize my need for a Savior. I won't ever wish that away, Hoge. It's a blessing."

Hoge catapulted forward and flopped his big arms around his brother. They both stood there, wrapped in each other's embrace, sniffing.

"I love you, man," Hoge huffed. "Please forgive me."

"Always."

Hoge drew back and held his brother at arm's length. "I'll never call you a dummy again. You're smarter than I am. And that's no lie."

A grin snaked across Ake's mouth, and his eyes dropped to the floor. "You're the best brother I could ever have."

Suddenly Joni was up. "I need a tissue."

She hurried down the hallway towards the bathroom. When she returned, she leaned over the recliner and hugged Stormi. "I'm sorry I ever caused you any pain."

Stormi rose to return the hug. "Me, too."

Hoge turned and Stormi stepped back. "I've been an idiot to you. Please accept my apologies."

She nodded.

Joni rushed over to hug Ake tight.

"Well, we need to go. We're off to visit a few nursing facilities for Alzheimer's patients. I'll let you know how it goes, and then we can discuss the best place for Pop." Hoge slapped a big paw on his brother's back.

Ake nodded. Their visitors grabbed their coats and made their way to the door.

Once they were gone, Stormi stared at her husband. "Can you believe this? Everything seems to be working out."

She threw herself into his arms and giggled against his neck.

He pulled away. "Maybe not everything."

Stormi's mouth dropped open. "What?"

Ake jerked his head. "Come back here. I've got something for you. I was going to show this to you before Hoge and Joni showed up."

Holding his thick forefinger in her hand, she trailed him. Touching him seemed as necessary as air. But he led her into the extra bedroom, a trail she hadn't guessed, and pulled her toward the small table. He selected a small box from the stacks against the wall.

"Take off your jacket."

She blinked. "But I'm cold."

"No, you're covering. Take it off."

Why did the man know every thought? She gave a sigh. He was right. She should be over this by now.

The tattoos greeted her as always, and she looked away. But his hand beneath her chin brought her gaze to his dark one. Wow. He smoldered.

"Look at yourself." He spun her toward the full-length mirror.

"Ake." She tugged away from the reflection.

But the man's grip was feather coated steel, and he held her firm. "I mean it, Stormi."

A heavy emotion rose in her chest as she extended her arms. She peered at them, covered in swirling patterns she wished she could rip away. Her entire arms and chest were tattooed black lace. Oh, why. Why had she done it? The black marks were like a trail of burning shame.

"God doesn't care how many holes or marks you put on yourself. You're beautiful, with every scar and mark. You lived, you've learned. You're a work of art."

Her face froze into a blank mask. "No. It's not. I was drunk, drugged, and morally bankrupt when all of this became mine. And it will always be here. I'll never be able to afford the removal of this much ink."

"No, Stormi. It was nothing but a storm in your life. You lost your way for a while. But God threw you a lifeboat. One that will never let you down."

She lifted her moist eyes to his. The man was a saint. Thickness strangled her throat. "People won't understand. Good people. Christian people. I'll always be judged because of it."

"You've kept this secret for so long, but it's there telling everyone that you've not only survived, but live anew. It's not something to be ashamed of, it's something to reveal. It's your witness to God's glory and his power to change people."

Dropping her eyes, she realized he was right. It had been like a horrible storm she couldn't stop, much like the one her husband had survived. And it became something she hid at all cost. But it was really her witness. A testament to God's redemptive work on the cross. Proof that no matter what her sins, no matter the depth of her trespasses, God had forgiven and had made her new. Even Marla had embraced that grace in her own life. No manmade mark or horrible scar could ever hide the value that God had placed on her soul. The tears she'd held for so long began to fall.

"You are precious in the Lord's sight, Stormi. And you're precious to me." He pulled a tumble of black wiring and turquoise beads from the box. "I made this before I knew about your tattoos. Look, it matches."

She rubbed away the tears. The jewelry looked like black lace with its intricate swirls and carefully placed blue beads, perfectly reflecting the same pattern that covered her skin. How had he known?

He reached gently and fastened it about her neck. Then he turned her toward the mirror. In the simple black racerback tank, the jewelry lay against her skin like an ensemble. The patterns of ink continued down her arms to her wrists, her hair in a chic crop, her eyes peeking from under the long bangs. From behind, Ake wrapped his arms around her and laid a soft kiss against her skin.

"You're beautiful, Stormi Pearson."

And she was. And in God's sight, she always had been.

"Don't ever leave me, Ake. I might forget."

A laugh rumbled from his chest. "No worries."

She gripped his thick forearms. "I mean it."

He turned her in his arms and laid his hands on each side of her face. "Never lean on your own understanding, Stormi. God's got this. And he's got you. And Lord willing, I'm not going anywhere."

"I'm a mess, you know."

"I'm counting on it." His head descended and the kiss robbed her breath.

Yes, God had stilled the storm. And the Stormi. All while turning her one-eighty. From the bad to the good. From flamboyant and angry, to loved and precious. Yeah, she might not ever be good at it, but it didn't matter. God *did* have this. And having Ake, well, that didn't hurt any either.

Peggy Trotter loves to hear from her readers. You can find her at:

peggytrotter.com

peggytrotter.blogspot.com

diamondsinfiction.blogspot.com

Twitter: https://twitter.com/Peggy_Trotter

Facebook: https://www.facebook.com/PeggyTrotterAuthor

Goodreads:
https://www.goodreads.com/book/show/25294770-year-of-jubilee

Amazon Author's Profile Page:
http://www.amazon.com/Peggy-Trotter/e/B00V15P2LU/ref=ntt_dp_epwbk_0

Don't miss the third installment from the **Unchained Souls Series** by Peggy Trotter, coming soon! From *Unchained Souls Book 3~**The Secret Mirage***

Chapter One

Mirage ran her fingernail along the choppy top of the marble tombstone. Blossom and Charlie Freet. Now vegetable-drawer chilled three days. Enclosed in urns in red cherry boxes, settling in the deep subsoil. Their parts dematerializing into particles.

No. Not true. Which would have disappointed her hippy-throwback parents.

"Blown to smithereens," one of the drivers had announced before realizing her presence, clearing her few possessions from beneath the counter at Vylona Environmental Services.

VES Renewing, Revamping, Recycling.

Trash. Make it simple. Make it true. And junk drivers rarely had manners.

But perhaps her parents had a closer brush with an environmental-nourishing burial than she could have planned.

Either way. Sunglasses on. Backpack snugged. She was tripping. Just a normal walkabout. Her parents had always supported her need to roam.

Two gravediggers a section over caught her eyes. Their shovels chucked a beat into the grainy October ground. One, an old high school acquaintance. Their relationship was obscure enough to ignore, familiar enough for pointed questions.

With one last caress across the marble, she set her foot in the opposite direction. Audience unneeded, unnecessary, and unwanted. Near on twenty feet from the bricked columns bordering the exit by flying crow, heavy running footsteps sounded behind her.

Shutters drawn. Door dead-bolted. She dug her nails into the nylon straps at her chest.

"Wait."

Still too faded to acknowledge. Her chin weathervaned with the wind, the perfectly distracted angle. Her slouch beanie, hiding her red sandstorm hair completed the cut-off. Hurry feet.

A hand latched onto her elbow.

"Hey there, Freeaac..."

Freak. Never Freet. Yeah, she knew the final consonant well. Dead parents gave a respect she long desired. Only now, she didn't care.

Leif Kollin Bowmaunt. Voted most likely to party.

Reality? Drug head. Once one of her greatest tormentors. Now, pock-marked, and thin as a stalk of celery. Meth supplier to the region's high schoolers. Convicted, sent up, out and shoveling dirt for the city's cemetery.

And digging for dirt on her.

She stared at him, but didn't dare remove her sunglasses.

"Sorry about—you know." He shrugged in the vague direction of the fresh graves behind her.

She gave a short nod. Her signature. Then she turned. The hand clamped her again.

"I mean, tough sentence. Huh? Both of them." He swore. "Man. We were all talking down at Tino's. Your dad was a hoot."

A hoot? Her fingers snatched his thick pinky finger, and yanked.

"What the—?"

Hands clench. Feet go. Walk. Walk faster. Each step kept her mind in neutral.

"Listen, Freak," Leif Kollin Bowmaunt called, vice-president of the Senior class. "Just paying my respects. Screw you and your family."

Duly noted. Status unchanged.

More muffled curses followed her as she continued her trek. The brick arch cast a shadow over her as she passed under. Once through, she paused. It seemed brighter here somehow. Her only regret was not being able to take Mama and Papa along. But the urns had been too unwieldy.

Besides, they never demanded to accompany her on her walkabouts. Papa Charlie's bad knees and Mama Blossom's electric wheelchair had them comfortably stabilized in that small farm house.

She looped the edge of town. The post office peeked at her from Main, the dime store, and the pool hall. She dodged the church. A few people waved from their yards. Just out of respect. She ignored them.

She reached the far edge of town and chose a country rock road over the main highway. A no-duh choice. Quiet, less traffic, better scenery. More selection in camping facilities.

Goal: warmer weather, calmer seas. Therefore south.

Bohemian lifestyle had always suited. Even when choked with grief.

The wind reminded her of the tenth month, but the sun encouraged. She glanced down at her black yoga pants to her favorite rain boots, clumping along, covered in giant sunflowers. The one thing she would miss was her collection of rain boots. But she had her goat ones in her pack. No more room for more. Besides, these were the only two pair that had survived. Each step clunked comfort up her spine.

She patted the bills in her brown hoody's pocket. Greyhound money for bad weather. Or whatever. The smell of smoke now filtered to her nose. The black ruins on the right side of the road clawed at her insides. The old homestead. Gone. Everything was gone. Possession meant nothing. Never had. But Blossom and Charlie?

She took a sharp breath and set her gaze ahead. The wooded area before her would soon envelope her and she would camouflage right in. Blend in. Disappear. Right sun flowered rain boot stepped out. Time to fade away.

References

All Bible Verses used in *The Secret Storm* are from the Amplified Bible (AMP) Copyright © 2015 by the Lockman Foundation. Used by permission. www.Lockman.org.

"He hushed the storm to a gentle whisper, so that the waves of the sea were still." Psalm 107:29

"Therefore if anyone is in Christ, he is a new creature; the old things passed away; behold, new things have come." 2 Corinthians 5:17
<u>Full version of the passage</u>: "Therefore if anyone is in Christ [that is, grafted in, joined to Him by faith in Him as Savior], he is a new creature [reborn and renewed by the Holy Spirit]; the old things [the previous moral and spiritual condition] have passed away."

"Flee the evil desires of youth and pursue righteousness, faith, love and peace, along with those who call on the Lord out of a pure heart." 2 Timothy 2:22
<u>Full version of the passage</u>: "Flee the evil desires of youth and pursue righteousness, faith, love and peace, along with those [believers] who call on the Lord out of a pure heart."

"A soft and gentle and thoughtful answer turns away wrath." Proverbs 15:1a

"We are pressured in every way, but not crushed; perplexed, but not driven to despair; hunted down and persecuted, but not deserted, struck down, but never destroyed." 2 Corinthians 4:8, 9
<u>Full version of the passage</u>: "We are pressured in every way [hedged in], but not crushed; perplexed [unsure of finding a way out], but not driven to despair, hunted down and

persecuted, but not deserted [to stand alone]; struck down, but never destroyed"